HARD RAIN

MANFRED PICHLER

ISBN: 0987149806
ISBN-13: 9780987149800

The moral right of the author has been asserted.

A Michael Crow Novel.

A Techno-thriller.

Printed by CreateSpace, an Amazon.com Company

Mindshock Publishing.

www.mindshockpublishing.com

DEDICATION

To Helen for her endurance, patience and superior command of the English language. And, to all the megalomaniacs out there - look up and smile.

CHAPTER 1

The train to the city is late and usually any delay in my daily routine would have me climbing the walls. However as I ease into my new-found 'don't care' state, I see it as a kind of test. I peruse the biography of a well-known businessman at the platform news stand, preferring non-fiction these days—finding it stranger and less predictable than the pulp fiction churned out like so much fast food.

I sit at the platform coffee shop and read about how to re-market every-day stuff. It seems there's no need to worry about creating anything new—just come up with catchy ways of marketing the same old thing and hey presto, 'an empire'. Make a toothpick new and exciting by bringing them out in cool new colors, then watch the cash roll in.

Finally, the train winds its way through the station, pushing wind and debris into the air. I sneeze, my eyes irritate, and I wonder why I'm here.

I enter the train and quickly find a seat before the school kids take them all. It's been ten years since I last travelled by train and I'd always hated the blank stares, finding myself inanely transfixed by glimpses of the industrial world as it rattles by. I preferred to rush headlong into the city, with the roof of the Saab open, the noise, the jostling for position, the second by second calculations of which lane would give me the one-second boost I really needed. The tending to phone calls and text messages like a seasoned maestro, as the radio hammered with voices and music.

But today, I'm too tired for all that and content just to immerse my-self in the sea of blank faces. I rest my head against the train window that now vibrates annoyingly and try to continue my daydream. With eyes half closed, I notice a man talking to an infant in a stroller. He holds up a storybook with familiar illustrations of dwarfs and castles and reads from it. It's a tender scene with the infant reaching out and gently touching the man's hand. He is well-dressed, distinguished, grey, late forties or early fifties. He could be the father or grandfather of the child—it was hard to be sure in these days of late parenthood. To the right of him sits a much older man, his eyes closed and dozing. Opposite them, a young boy and girl, a couple barely in their teens, sit close together chatting intimately, quietly.

The train stops at a station and a gang of youths enter, quickly transforming the far end of the carriage into a private club. They huddle around a ghetto blaster that is suddenly too loud. Every now and then manic shouts erupt. The main offender, a large tattooed youth with a shaved head lets out a stream of profanities, bringing embarrassed looks from the handful of commuters. If I needed another reason to avoid public transport, then this was it.

We're half way through the journey, stopping at stations every few minutes, when I notice the last station rushing past. Had I caught the express? A moment of elation quickly turns sour as another angry shout bursts through the carriage.

"Look at me bitch!" A tattooed youth is standing over a young girl, who avoids eye contact with the menace now towering over her. "This is what you want, isn't it?" he forces a laugh, pulls down his pants and exposes himself.

Her boyfriend beside her strains to find some inner strength, but fails to move or even speak. More youths from the group come over to besiege the young couple as madness takes hold with surprising speed. The man with the child steadies the pram, stands up and approaches the group. He portrays authority with ease, but the youths disagree. One of them strikes him from behind with a firm fist across the back of the head. He drops to his knees, but grabs one youth by the leg, pulling him to the floor. A series of punches and kicks follow before the man lies still on the floor.

Another member of the gang has his hand on the throat of the boyfriend, pinning him to his seat, while the largest youth stands up, walks to the stroller and pulls the infant out. The infant is in fact a little girl, perhaps two years old. She looks stunned, bewildered, an angelic child with large eyes and blond hair—a living doll. She starts to cry and clutches a furry toy rabbit close to her chest. While recklessly balancing the infant in one hand, the youth takes hold of the carriage door with the other. After a grinding split second, I realize his intent, but the wide-eyed innocent child does not. And how could she? For her, the truth of this world is still a few merciful years away.

With her legs and arms flailing, she looks to her father, who desperately struggles to get up. The old man, now wide-awake, lunges toward the youth holding the child in a surprising bound of physical effort. Another youth quickly intercepts him and strikes him down, hard. A loud crack resonates above the tumult as a boot pushes into the back of the old man's neck. He lies on the floor, motionless.

Fear paralyses me. All I can manage to do is stare into the eyes of the youth holding the child. In one motion, and with a grotesque grin forming on his face, he pulls open the train door and thrusts the child outside at arm's length. She stops crying as the rush of cool air fills her lungs, her toy rabbit falling from her hand and gone.

In that split second, the child's eyes lock to mine and I'm sure I saw a final realization, a final desperate searching for a reason. Perhaps she spoke to me, I don't know. And in another instant she too is gone, tossed out of the open train door like the toy rabbit before her.

I remain frozen, the life drained from me. I close my eyes, but it's too late, the evil has invaded me. It burrows deep into my brain, invades my soul and with mind numbing dread, I know it will always be there. What was *me*, my life, my understanding, everything I'd seen, heard and felt, all of it leaves me in that instant. I shut down, only vaguely aware of screaming, crying, and laughing. I try to move, but feel only a warm, wet sensation trickling down my leg.

The train slows into the station. The doors slide open and the gang lunges out, high on adrenalin and whatever else is running through their veins. I see a blur of movement as the girl's father struggles out of the carriage and limps back along the platform to retrieve his broken child. I hope she's not too badly disfigured in death. I hope she died quickly and without too much pain.

I hear the young boy on his cell phone trying desperately to describe the horror to police, but he manages just to whimper. The girlfriend is still screaming, her body convulsing with each breath and the old man lies on the floor, with his head at an unnatural angle. In the reflection of the window, I see myself, motionless too, but for no physical reason.

Is this what happens in war, when self-preservation kicks in? Some people shut down while others thrive. Does it engage senses and responses we never knew we had? Instincts programmed long ago in some forgotten chromosome, rarely called upon now but once essential for our distant ancestors surviving a harsher world.

I never paid much attention to religion, always thought of it as another story, another club, another agenda. Other people's reality, not mine. I imagined countless generations saw much evil, evil of the human spirit—the worst kind. Conscious and premeditated. Unable or too frightened to accept this aberration, we gave it a name, an inhuman form, to detach it from ourselves—the Devil, we called it. Yes, the evil deed was the work of the Devil, that's what made him do it.

I thought I'd glimpsed this evil from time to time, but from a thousand miles away and through the safety of a camera lens. But today, I experienced it up close and personal and it was far worse than I could have imagined.

A crowd of commuters gathered outside the carriage, aware something had happened, their mouths asking questions and their eyes searching for answers. But did they really want to know? Weren't the tortured cries of 'Oh, my God!' enough to warn them?

I see someone entering the carriage, seemingly oblivious to the turmoil and enclosed in his own reality. A young man with long straggly dark hair, an incarnation from the 1960's and holding a small radio to his ear. I hear it clearly, as he walks past, and I recognize the song drifting from his radio, on this afternoon, on this railway station and in this carriage.

The words belong to Bob Dylan and like a prophet of the ages, his voice cries out, to me...

I met a young girl, she gave me a rainbow,
I met one man, who was wounded in love,
I met another man, who was wounded with hatred,
And it's a hard, it's a hard, it's a hard, it's a hard,
It's a hard rain's a-gonna fall.

CHAPTER 2

I was glad to leave the police station, with the accusing looks starting to get to me. Obviously, I was no hero and slunk out to take a taxi home.

I heard a news report on the car radio. A loud, angry voice bursting through the ambivalence, "Some piece of shit killed my father for a bag of money. They shot him in the back for the hell of it. He did what they asked him to do and he died anyway." A brave voice, but one filled with overwhelming loss and sorrow.

"Scum like that have no right to live," the taxi driver snarled from the front seat, while eyeing me suspiciously through the rear-view mirror.

The senseless nature of the latest crime spree echoes through the city and gathers the wrath of its entire four million residents, as though the collective conscious has finally had enough. But are these crimes so unusual? Surely, it goes on every day and in every corner of the world. And hasn't it always? So this time it's a security guard shot dead by thieves whilst delivering money. It's sad, but hardly an earth-shattering event. So why all the attention? Why the outrage? And why now? The world has always balanced on the edge of anarchy, hasn't it? Differences in race, religion and wealth have always been the prime movers of death and destruction. So aren't we getting ahead of ourselves, maybe just a little? We can't, after all, escape the confines of our DNA.

The live cross on the radio finishes with more pleading and anger from the son of the guard. My cell phone rings, the caller ID reads *Lewis*, my lawyer.

"Michael, the meeting is about to start, where the hell are you?"

"I've been delayed. Give me ten minutes."

"Are you OK? You know you don't have to sell this shareholding, you can claim minority oppression," he is hard to hear on his hands-free.

"No, I'm comfortable with it. And to be honest, I've been done with it for a while now."

"OK, I'll see you there." I pictured his cell phone surgically implanted in his ear.

I remember my previous life and the press release framed on my office wall. *"After graduating with a degree in electrical engineering, Michael Crow invented a new software technique to analyze sound vibrations. Crow's software provides a soundwave fingerprint of sorts. The breakthrough technology provides advance warning of a developing fault in almost any piece of machinery, the exact position of any faulty part, and an accurate prediction of how much life it has left."*

This captured the attention of several investors a few years ago, when I needed it. Having recently graduated with a degree in electrical engineering, I was high on ideas and low on money. And, for small underfunded companies, financial assistance usually came in the form of business angels, otherwise known as business piranhas. I was at the mercy of the back-street market where people in dark suits lined the shadows, and pounced on anyone who dared stumble.

So, with a couple of piranhas on my back, the product development was completed and today is sell-out day. The other three shareholders required several meetings to decide the value of my remaining shareholding in Vibrolert. It was a sad indictment of how quickly a nimble and innovative company of engineers morphed into a beast of burden, and stripped its founder of all rights.

In any case, now I'll be free to start the rest of my life. Perhaps I should have held on for the public float, but more years or even months with these fools would have been insufferable.

In two days time it'll be my thirty-fifth birthday. Perhaps I should take it easy for a while, maybe buy a boat and drift around the South Pacific. I haven't been free-and-easy since my university days, and even then it wasn't that free or easy, but I still managed to relax. Over the past five years Vibrolert sucked my energy like a cancer, and in the midst of that, I married, had a daughter, divorced and recently started a new relationship.

I could have become lost in self-importance, like so many do, but I think I resisted the temptation well enough. By developing the bulk of my software at home, I avoided the office as much as possible, with its time wasting politics and pitiful soap operas.

I discussed my sell-out with only a handful of people, thinking some might see me as a quitter. With the new shareholders and their influx of money over the last couple of years, I've noticed *them* becoming more and more hands-on. Before that, my majority control allowed me to do as I pleased, but now I'm just another cog in a wheel, and that's not particularly inspiring, not for me.

With the growth of the company came more and more meetings, meetings about meetings, accountants and lawyers. New managers appeared like weeds, as did their agendas. In the end, the company was no longer mine and it no longer needed me. A bitter pill I guess, but one that that needed swallowing. I just hoped it wouldn't end up stuck in my throat.

With today marking the end of a chapter in my life, I'm probably down on my emotional cycles. They say it happens now and then, but I suspect it's more to do with my recent brush with public transport, and the lingering question of 'what the hell am I going to do with the rest of my life' I've been avoiding. In any case, the 3.9 million dollars will buy some time and perhaps a few distractions, at least until I recharge.

The taxi driver mumbles something and I realize we've arrived. I step out and hand him a twenty-dollar bill. He immediately speeds off, confident in his assumption that the five-dollar difference was a tip.

I walk past the city buildings and notice the signs of dullness and ageing. In fact, everyone walking by appears tired and dull. The meeting is at an office tower a block away and I start to feel the heat of the day. I soon break out in a sweat and hope to find the building lobby cool.

Sweating tends to come easily to me, and on business in South East Asia, the beads of sweat forming on my forehead and running down my face, distracted and annoyed me. It came not from nerves but from lugging a heavy demonstration case across the city, in extreme heat and humidity. After arriving at my destination, I often searched out air-conditioning vents, even asking people to change seats with me. I guess they thought I studied power seating, which immediately raised their suspicion and made it that much harder to gain their trust.

I enter the coolness of the tower lobby and then the elevator. I read the info screen, *2.10 pm Friday*, and ascend to the twentieth floor. I watch through the glass façade as Sydney Harbor sparkles like a blue diamond, its arching bridge joining the two halves of the city. I lose myself in the reflections as they dance along the steel structure of the bridge, bringing it to life. The lift stops abruptly and a sudden burst of apprehension slaps me back to the here and now.

I step into the reception area and see the others through the glass wall of the meeting room, seated. Dressed in generic dark suits they look content, a happy clan of successful businessman, without an original thought among them.

I enter to a round of handshaking and comments. At the head of the table, Geoff Felding the current CEO of Vibrolert, remarks loudly, "Michael, good to see you!"

"Geoff, always a pleasure!" I lie, but with a smile.

Robert Webb, the principle investor and his business partner Neil are there, like peas in a pod. Old money private school friends who played on the same football team in college and now played on the same company boards. Not even Geoff was really in 'their' team. He was new money, not yet fully ripened or quietly sophisticated as they were. He would never get there in his lifetime, but perhaps his children or his children's children might one day find reluctant acceptance.

The investors contributed several million dollars to keep Vibrolert funded during the last year, whereas Geoff had put in no money, his only contribution being his 'expertise'. In replacing me with Geoff, both Robert and Neil agreed it allowed me more time to concentrate on the technical tasks of product development, without the distraction of running the business. Losing the CEO position was one frustration; the other was the thirty percent of Vibrolert shares Geoff managed to accrue—in lieu of his usually higher fee, Robert told me. Apparently, we were lucky to retain his services at all.

I notice Geoff's shinny gold cufflink and his demeanor even more plastic than usual. Obviously, this was just as much a payday for him. Also present were the mandatory accessories of the modern age—the lawyers. The company lawyer, who'd I met on a several occasions, but could not now recall his name. He was one of those who blended into his surroundings, taking it all in only to sting his victims in his own time by stealth and meticulous planning—the most dangerous variant of the species. The louder ones were fully absorbed in their own self-importance and always telegraphed their punches to anyone who would listen. They inevitably shot themselves in the foot.

Then there was my lawyer, Lewis. A nice enough guy who romped with the wolves but somehow managed to remain unscathed. He was a train wreck in so many ways, disorganized but quick on his feet to compensate. He worked long hours, seemed genuinely interested in the endless paper shuffling and position jostling that was the modern practice of law. Unfortunately, he killed off one relationship after another through lack of interest in anything else.

"You'll be able to buy a few rounds of drinks with this check," Geoff shouts again, more pleased than a pig in shit.

Several copies of the severance contract appeared on the table in front of me, in anticipation of the signing ceremony.

"You'll take some time off?" Robert probed.

"Yes, maybe do a bit of travelling," I said, giving him less than he wanted.

An awkward silence followed, with only the sounds of scratching pens and shuffling papers. I glance at Geoff who smiled his plastic smile and remembered our many discussions over the past year. He was the fifty-six-year old professional manager of businesses usually much larger than this, and I was the 'young pup', as he called me. It was obvious from the day we met that a tug of war would ensue. He may have been well organized. He may even have had a reasonable business plan, but he was just too fake and his speeches too pretentious. However he did impress Robert, and with millions of dollars at stake, the investors wanted 'a proven and steady hand at the wheel'.

"Well, that's about all there is to it," Geoff smiles again and hands me a check. I pocket it without looking "Gentlemen, thank you," I smile back. "I wish you all the best and hope you'll do great things with the technology." I resisted the urge to wish them all a nice life.

"I hope this investment meets your expectations Robert, and that perhaps you will find some time to relax," I add with sincerity.

I think we had a mutual respect. Robert was approaching his sixty-seventh year. He was an intelligent and honest businesses man, with all the right connections. Even as a 'boutique' investor, he still racked up over eighty hours a week on his various projects. With that sort of money, and at that age, it's hardly something I would be bothered with.

And so, with the documents signed the deal is done, including a non-competitive clause locking me out of the industry for five years. At least they thought that much of me.

After a final round of hand shaking, I left the building less than an hour later, with no fan fare, no gifts and no celebratory drinks. In fact, I've never left any place of work without receiving a wad of legal documents and a few veiled threats.

Walking to the taxi rank, I pondered what that said about me.

CHAPTER 3

Arriving back home in the early evening, I remember my cell phone had been off for most of the day. I had two missed calls, both from Helen, my girlfriend. A few weeks ago, I would have had twenty messages in that time, but I kept reminding myself that was another life.

I returned her call.

"Where have you been? Did you hear the news? Was that the same train you were on?" she asked in quick succession, having missed her real vocation as a criminal prosecutor to become a nurse. Do I tell her? It means having to open the wound.

"Yes," I said. "But I didn't see much, and it was all over quickly."

However, she was too smart and I too unconvincing. She probed further, about the little girl, how she died, and how could someone do such a thing? I agreed it was terrible, but could we talk about something else?

"I'll come over and cook a meal," she suggested.

"Sure, that would be nice."

The doorbell sounded at 8.10 pm and I was glad to see Helen standing there. She was tall, attractive, intelligent and looked younger than her thirty-four years—the consummate nurse and friend.

We ate and discussed my departure from Vibrolert and the future. In the short term, we agreed, I should simply lay low and recharge. Maybe we could holiday together in Europe or some idyllic South Pacific island. It sounded enticing. We hadn't yet discussed living together in any serious way. She worked near where she lived, west of the city in a large public hospital, and I lived in the southern suburbs. The distance between us was an hour by car and since I was now unemployed, I suspect she might be thinking we should set up home in her part of the woods.

We'd been together for six months, but almost from the day we met we had a mutual bond and understanding. Helen had had a stressful day working the emergency ward and I too felt drained and ready to collapse. I told her I needed some time to myself, she understood and left just before midnight.

My home was my castle. Perhaps not the castle I could now afford, but a large modern home in a picturesque lakeside suburb twenty miles south of Sydney and complete with almost every electronic gadget I could find. The minimalist furnishings were modestly salubrious in a practical way that suited my lifestyle. The view, which came with a private jetty and my specialized home workshop were all that I needed.

I sat in my lounge chair, alone in the dark. It seemed like only minutes whereas it was several hours later when the cold hues of dawn snuck through the window blinds. Was it a dream or was I fully awake, I can't remember. Thoughts raced in all directions and at some point, I think I either lost my mind or found it.

At first, I tried to resist the strange, rampant machinations, but then decided to just sit back and enjoy the show. After all, wasn't I in control of my mind? I'd never questioned my sanity before, yet the images that danced before me now were pure fantasy. As they evolved, they started to become real, maybe even attainable. By the time the sun slapped me across the face I had an idea, but one vastly different from any I'd had before.

Suddenly hungry, I launched into breakfast with a sense of purpose and turned on the three-metre widescreen TV mounted into the wall above the fireplace. I chose an international cable news channel rather than one of locals, and the screen quickly filled with the image of a young woman sprawled out on the road. The camera panned back and forth to reveal several more bodies lying contorted on black asphalt. Some of the bodies were small, children, and a street shopping mall as the backdrop. But in this scene no one was shopping. Here, people were staggering about, screaming, crying and bloodied. The vision jumped from one body to another as a female reporter described the incident, the result of which we could all too clearly see anyway.

"*A vehicle, police believe a light blue Ford sedan, intentionally sped through this crowded shopping mall this afternoon. Six people have been pronounced dead at the scene, four women and two children. No names have yet been released,*" the caption read Phoenix, Arizona and the reporter spoke with a voice too shaky to be a seasoned pro.

I studied her—a young, smartly dressed woman, with smeared makeup around sad eyes. She steeled herself, looked directly into the camera and continued, "*The ambulance officer told me he saw a four year old boy and his younger sister applying bandaids to their mother …*" she paused, her words falling almost silent, "*… but their mother was already dead.*"

My senses, only barely recovered, were under siege again. Had it always been like this or was a new wave of madness? Did it signal the belated onslaught of the new millennium, or had I been so transfixed on my work that I hadn't noticed before?

I kept watching while I ate, but quickly lost my appetite. I left the kitchen and entered my workshop. Standing there, looking at all the high tech gear I'd accumulated over the years.

I wasn't quite sure where to start, but knew the pieces of my new life started here somewhere.

CHAPTER 4

Two days and two nights in the workshop passed quickly before the phone rang on Monday morning.

"Mr Crow, we would like you to come to the station please," said Senior Detective John Trobe.

"Sure...why?"

"To view a line up," he sounded serious in his monotone.

"OK, when?"

"As soon as you can, thank you."

I drove to the police station and meet Trobe at reception. He motioned me to follow him along a corridor and into a darkened room, where through a window, I saw several men filing into the brightly lit room on the other side.

"They can't see you. Take your time and identify anyone you might remember," Trobe instructed.

We stood in silence as each man held a numbered card and turned left, right and then straight at me, or so it seemed.

"Number three, he was in the train. He held the radio," I stammered. "And number five, he held the young man around the neck."

"Are you sure?"

"Yes."

"You'll sign a statement to that effect?"

"Yes."

"We also need you to look at some other mug shots."

"Sure."

I sat alone in a small room, the buzzing of fluorescent lighting giving me a headache. After several minutes of paging through the cream of the criminal world, I heard raised voices outside, one of which was Trobe's.

"We have two suspects in custody. We believe we know who the perpetrators are, and we will find them. It's just a matter of time," Trobe said.

"Detective, I have considerable resources and would like to assist you," said another voice, courteous yet just as firm.

"Mr Cooper, thank you, but I suggest you concentrate on your family and let us do our job" Trobe insisted.

I couldn't resist peering through the door opening to see Trobe speaking with the father of the murdered child. The name and the face now triggered my memory. He was Brendan Cooper, founder and CEO of SatCOMM Corporation, a global communications empire. The guy was worth billions and he travels a commuter train with his child?

Voices trailed off as Trobe walked Cooper out.

I refocused on the photographs and a few minutes later found myself staring at a ghastly face, already permanently etched into my brain. A tag identified him with just a number. Trobe entered the room.

"Found anyone?" he asked flatly.

"Yes. This is the guy who threw the child from the train," my voice barely audible.

"You're sure?"

"Yes." I felt nauseated.

"OK, that's it for now. We'll call on you soon."

I signed a statement with a shaking hand and drove home.

On the way, I picked up a few items from a hardware store and returned to my workshop. I felt safe in my workshop, like a rabbit in a burrow, content to extract myself from the world for prolonged periods.

I wound twenty meters of insulated copper wire around a one-meter length of steel pipe with a hollow centre large enough to fit a metal dart. I connected a power supply to generate an electrical current through the wire, which in turn would cause a magnetic field to propel the dart out of the tube end at a staggeringly high velocity—or so the accepted theory foretold.

With the power supply plugged in, the pipe firmly secured in a vice and the end pointed at three sand bags, I flicked the switch on. The pipe shuddered and a high-pitched hiss emanated from the end. I had programmed the power supply to shut down after three seconds, which was all the time the power supply or the copper wire could take before melting.

I watched in fascination as the equipment recorded a 200-ampere surge through the wire. Heat radiated from the pipe. I unplugged the power supply, just in case it sprang to life on its own and peered into the end of the pipe. I noticed the dart had gone. I searched the sandbags and found it stuck halfway through the second bag. Not a bad result, but I needed even more energy.

I set the dial higher, perhaps beyond the limit of the power supply, but I needed to know. The limits had always to be tested—a particular obsession of mine. Without waiting for the pipe to cool, I inserted another dart and plugged in the power supply. I flicked the switch again and heard an even louder hiss from the pipe end that was suddenly painful to my ears. The vice that held the pipe and the pipe itself shuddered in unison. Lights around me flickered and the acrid smell of burnt electrical insulation filled my nostrils.

I waved my hand over the pipe feeling a more intense heat this time, much too hot to touch. I unplugged the power supply and searched the sand bags. I found nothing. Thinking the dart may have fallen out near the vice, I checked the bench top and floor. Had it vaporized? I looked behind the final sandbag and found a hole the size of the dart clean through the workshop wall. Peering in, I saw the dart had penetrated the entire six inches of solid concrete.

I felt somewhat excited by the silent power I'd wielded, and just a little more empowered now. It was after midnight when I finally lay on top of my bed and slept.

I woke in the morning to the sound of the phone. It was Trobe again.

"Mr Crow, we need you back at the station for another line up." He hung up without waiting for a reply.

Have they caught him? Do I have to face the killer again? Will he stare into my soul and impart more evil? I felt my recent empowerment quickly vanish as I stepped into the shower.

I wasn't in the observation room long, before the line up parade entered on the other side of the mirrored glass. I felt myself jump backwards when I saw him, my heart taking off like a freight train. Trobe saw my reaction and the blood of embarrassment flushed across my face.

"Number one, that's him. He stood on the old man's neck!" I froze, incapable of moving even if I wanted to.

"The old man died of a broken neck. Mr Crow. You need to be completely certain."

"Yes," I said, my eyes fixed on the creature behind the glass. "Er ... what about the others?"

"We found another youth we believe was part of the gang, but he is deceased."

Now the blood drained from my face and I imagined myself as some ridiculous chameleon.

"Is the child killer disposing of witnesses?" My voice an involuntarily shriek.

"We have no evidence of that Mr Crow."

I left the station wondering whose side the police were on. As the main witness, I certainly didn't intend to entrust my life to them.

On the drive home, Helen rang and I immediately felt guilty for not calling her earlier.

"How are you?" she asked brightly.

"Good," I adjusted my headset. "I've caught up on some sleep. What about you?" I tried hard to match her mood.

"I'm good, but it's been busy here."

"Are you free for dinner tonight?" I asked. "Maybe the Chinese place near you?"

"Sounds great, but I don't think I can get home before seven."

"That's fine. I'll meet you there at eight?"

"OK."

I didn't want her coming to my home in case I had a crazed killer stalking me. I thought about the absurd succession of events over the last twenty-four hours and was almost tempted to laugh. Almost.

I stopped at an electronics supply store on the way home and picked up more parts for the new power supply. Back in the workshop, I stared at the contraption and wondered how I was going to put this ridiculous thing into use. A one-meter long steel pipe wrapped with wire and weighing several pounds is one thing, but that it gets red hot after a single shot and needs a massive power supply, well, that's a little hard to hide, not to mention somewhat restrictive. I felt deflated and frustrated, but suddenly hungry.

I threw a hot dog into the microwave and stared at the dog in the roll, moving around and around on the glass dish. Why does it need to rotate like that? Are the microwaves directional? And why does the dog heat up so much quicker than the roll? Is it the fat content? The water? I read somewhere that microwaves vibrated water particles at high frequency and this caused the heating effect. The oven bell sounded, I opened the door, grabbed the dog, unplugged the microwave and took both back to the workshop.

It took a few hours to pull the oven apart and inspect its inner workings. The components, particularly the transmitters intrigued me. I had spent years working with sound waves where components were larger and more power hungry, but in this higher frequency range, the parts were smaller and required less power.

I searched the internet for information and read that microwave power densities for mobile phones and communication links operated at around five microwatts per square centimeter. The sticker on the side of the oven stated a power output of six hundred watts. I measured the physical volume of the oven and calculated an equivalent power density of five watts per square centimeter, a million times more than a mobile phone. I surmised that if I could direct the entire five hundred watts of energy into a tight beam, of no more than a centimeter in diameter, I could fry bacon from a kilometer away. It sounded intriguing, but the problem was to produce a parallel, coherent beam—a microwave laser. Not an overnight task, I suspected.

CHAPTER 5

Helen looked radiant across the table and I considered myself lucky that she was still interested in me, particularly of late. She quickly bored of men and six months was a long-term relationship for her.

"You look a little distracted tonight?" she probed.

"Sorry, I don't mean to be. Just stuff inside my head I can't seem to shake."

"You still haven't told me much about the train incident. What did you see?"

The waiter filled our glasses with water and handed me a wine list. I read while considering an answer.

"Well, I saw a piece of human trash end the lives of two innocent people. But it seems that's the way of the world now, and perhaps it's always been. Perhaps I've been an ignorant self absorbed fool for the last thirty-five years and hadn't noticed." I was suddenly concerned at how this comment had bypassed my brain and ended up in her ears.

She looked saddened.

"I'm sorry, but I'd be lying if I said this hasn't affected me," my mouth continued without control. "You spend your day looking for ways to help people and I've been trying to work out how to erase them from the planet."

"Michael, I've never seen you like this before—"

"Hey, there's probably a whole book of psychological post-trauma mumbo jumbo that can explain it, but for now let's pretend I'm completely sane and eat. I'm starving."

"Maybe you should see someone..."

"Hey, I'm fine, really," I smiled and crossed my eyes to ease the tension. Not a chance would I tell her I'd been acting on these thoughts. I didn't want to admit that to myself. Nor did I want to tell her about the child-killing maniac on the loose, who was probably searching for me right now.

The waiter filled our wine glasses and to my relief, the discussion meandered to topics more domestic.

"How's your brother doing," she asked

I hadn't thought about anyone for a while and almost forgot I had family. "Come to think of it, it's been a couple of weeks since I last heard from him."

"Wasn't he in the middle of some legal battle?" she showed concern, perhaps because I showed none.

"You're right, I should call him. Last time I checked, his property deal had come off the rails, and he and his partners couldn't agree on anything. But it's a common theme for him."

"I'd say the common theme is the Crow family gene." At last, a smile came my way.

"Maybe, but I'm a little annoyed he hasn't rung to ask me how I'm going." Apart from Helen, Tom was the only other person I'd really spoken to about my Vibrolert sell-out.

"He gets so wrapped up in his own stuff, he only surfaces every couple of weeks, and that's just to make sure no one has died." I added.

"That's a bit rough, but it does sound vaguely familiar..." Another smile.

After dinner, we drove back to her place and spent the night together. She'd left for work by the time I woke and I had only a vague recollection of kissing her good-bye in the pre-dawn darkness.

I didn't waste much time getting dressed and drove to the electronics supply store for the third time in as many days. I probed and searched for the parts I needed and was pleased when the store attendant offered to deliver the special items, not currently in stock, directly to my home.

On the drive back, Trobe rang and I cringed at the unwanted familiarity of his voice.

"Mr Crow, we have had an incident with a witness," he said in monotone that had to be taught at the academy.

I pulled the car to the side of the road and stopped.

"What's happened?"

"Mr Cooper has been assaulted."

"By who? How is he?"

"He's in critical care at the moment, but we have no reason to believe the matter is related to the train incident."

"Not related!"

"However just in case, I suggest you avoid public places for the time being."

"OK," was all I could manage and he was gone.

I swung my car into the parking lot of a large shopping mall and within minutes returned with six microwave ovens in a trolley. Further along the road, at another store, I bought another six ovens. Would buying twelve at the same store have been any less suspicious?

Returning to my workshop, I began dissecting the ovens and discovered that the microwave emitters could be located remotely from the control circuitry. This meant they would fit snugly into a standard ceiling down light, with the rest of the circuitry hidden in an electrical switchboard and connected by a length of cable.

The field trial would take place in my house entry terrace, which was ideal. Not too big, close to the workshop and front door monitor, yet separate enough to be safe if things went wrong. With a roof and wrought iron sides, fixed panels at both sides, a gate at front and a hedge to the street side, it was private enough.

I cut several round holes in the plaster ceiling and installed the microwave emitters into new light holders. I had just built the world's largest microwave oven and luckily, I'd recently upgraded the house power supply, so supplying the required ten thousand watts shouldn't be a problem. I felt a burst of apprehension, the time had come, yet what should I test it on?

I drove to the local pet shop, where the kind woman at the counter told me he was very friendly and popular with the kids, and they often came to feed him after school. I thanked her, handed over fifty-five dollars and returned home with a large white rabbit in a cardboard box.

I placed the rabbit on the floor of the terrace and gingerly closed the house door behind me, trapping him within the wrought iron enclosure. I stood staring at the power switch for several minutes, the monitor displaying the entry terrace where he was now standing on hind legs and sniffing about. I wondered whether he would make a noise when I zapped him and would I hear his death squeal through the solid timber door.

He explored my terrace for a while, as I watched, unable to move my finger frozen on the switch. A minute later and I knew I couldn't go through with it. Hell, if I can't do this to a rabbit I should quit this crazy shit now.

I opened the front door, rescued the ball of fur and placed him in the rear garden, where he immediately started grazing on my plants. As I watched him hop about, the vision of the little girl in the train, clinging to her toy rabbit, invaded me.

I checked my freezer, pulled out a frozen chicken and placed it on the floor of the terrace. In the workshop, I set the microwave timer to one minute and turned on the power. I heard a slight hum from the switchboard and watched the frozen bird through the monitor.

Surprised to see no effect on the naked torso after a full minute, I ran to check the bird. It felt cold, having only just started to defrost. The terrace ceiling was over two metres high, which was the distance from the microwave emitters to the 'target'. Perhaps it was too far.

I found some rope and strung the chicken up closer to the emitters, tying off each end on the wrought iron panels, and then turned the power on again. This time the effect of ten thousand watts was immediate and the bird performed a macabre dance in the air, its skin popping and sizzling.

After a minute, I checked and found it hot and starting to cook. The pungent smell of seared microwave chicken filled the air, leaving me nauseated. As I untied the bird, I heard a car pull up in the driveway behind the hedge. I hurried to put the bird and rope in a plastic bag, as Detective Trobe strolled onto the terrace.

"Hello, Detective," I said, surprised my voice functioned at all.

"Mr Crow, I hope you don't mind. I was in the area and thought I'd see how you were doing."

"Nice of you, but it's all fine here as you can see."

I wondered if detectives had a special knack of reading minds, and was conscious of the new ceiling lights the terrace had acquired. And would he notice the yellowish chicken fluids on the floor?

"How is Mr Cooper?" I asked, walking to intercept him before he came too close.

"He is stable and should recover quickly. He was hit hard on the back of the head, but unfortunately he didn't see his assailant."

"But we assume it's one of the youths from the train incident?"

"In my business Mr Crow, we don't assume."

Just when I think he might be human, he reverts to robot. He checks his watch and glances at the bag I'm carrying.

"Something smells a little odd there," he pointed at the bag.

"I tried to cook this damn chicken," I said, half opening the bag, "but didn't much care for the smell of it. I was just off to buy one from a professional."

"Good for you Mr Crow."

I watched him squeeze himself back into his car and perhaps he even smiled a little. I waved him off and dumped the foul-smelling chicken in the rubbish bin.

I drove to the nearest KFC, just in case he was tailing me, but lacked the desire to eat the dinner-pack I bought. Driving the final block to my house, I saw a car I didn't recognize parked opposite my driveway. I wondered if I were showing signs of paranoid behavior when I instinctively stopped several houses back from mine.

I got out and walked slowly toward the dark, silent vehicle. The frantic pounding inside my chest ensured I could only hear my heart and nothing else. Having checked to see the car was empty; I took my shoes off and tiptoed through my front yard, keeping to the bushes and shadows.

I stood still, feeling the cold night dew soaking through my socks. As I squelched around the side of the house and into the back yard, I heard something move in front of me. I jumped backwards and knelt down, straining to see through the darkness with beads of salty sweat stinging my eyes.

I found myself staring in the red gleaming eyes of a large white rabbit. He looked at me and winked, perhaps as a thank-you for not frying him earlier.

I crept back to the front yard and hid under a bush. I pulled out a remote control from my pocket, the electronic key for all the house locks and external lighting, and pressed a button to bath the entire property in bright white light. I continued to watch and listen from the safety of my bush.

After several minutes, I decided I'd had enough of hiding. I stood up, walked toward the house and reached to open the terrace gate. I let out a silent scream when standing before me was an enormous creature with a shaved head. The killer of Cooper's child loomed large in the doorway, aiming his crazed stare directly at me like a weapon. I moved backwards and slammed shut the iron gate between us.

I continued to step backwards as we stared at each other.

"You're going to lock me *in* your house?" he laughed.

"No, you're free to go. Just close the door behind you," I said, hoping feeble humor might save my life.

Still glaring at me, he moved back and obligingly closed the front door.

"You're right," he said with a smirk. "We don't want to leave the place looking suspicious, when they investigate your disappearance."

As soon as he shut the door I pressed the remote in my pocket and prayed I'd hit the right button. A loud metallic click sounded as the locking system engaged. This caught his attention. He tested the door and the gate, which were both locked tight.

"Look, I'm just fucking with you man. You don't finger me and I don't bother you. You're a business man, right? Call it a business deal," he said.

His smirk lessened only slightly as he casually leaned against the wall of the house.

My anger grew as the balance of power shifted. The guy even sounded half intelligent, which made his crime that much worse, if that were possible. I should call the authorities and have him dragged away, and then live in fear for the rest of my life waiting for his release. Or I could—

"I've set off the silent alarm and need to go inside to deactivate it. Otherwise, a security guard will turn up. Just give me a minute." I said.

"Whatever man, just don't fuck with me. I can break through this door in one minute and be pounding on your head the next."

I didn't doubt that as I ran around house, fumbled with the key to the side door and burst inside to turn on the microwave switch. I watched him through the monitor as he stood leaning against the wall, just outside the throw of the beam.

"Hey fucker, come on," he shouted.

"OK, just give me a second."

I needed to move him to the centre of the terrace. I was frantic, so close yet—

"Can I pass you some cash, you know, to seal the deal?" I asked.

"Sure, right, whatever man, let's seal the damn deal."

I searched my wallet and pushed two hundred dollars under the front door, hoping this would move him to where he would receive the full sum of the microwave beams from each emitter.

Without blinking, I stared at the monitor and saw him bend forward. Surely his head was now within the beam? But he stood up again and casually counted the money. Nothing was happening! With sudden dread I realized the microwave timer was set for only one minute, and had already switched itself off. I quickly reset it for two minutes, turned it on and scrambled for more cash.

"Hey man, let's get this over with," he demanded with a loud crash to the iron gate from his jackboot.

"I've got some more cash for you." I offered.

"If you've called the cops man, I'll take you on a little train ride," his words trailed off.

I glanced at the monitor and saw him staring into the camera, straight at me, and slid the extra notes under the front door and waited. He's going to lose it soon and kick the place apart. I clenched my teeth and waited for the full onslaught, but heard nothing. A full minute went by, then two, then three, and still nothing.

I returned to the front yard, watching the man intently as I approached the terrace gate. He was leaning against the wall, but this time his eyes offered only a lifeless gaze from a blotchy red face. He blinked rapidly and breathed in a slow, regular rhythm. Was it an act? Would he spring to life and snap my neck as he would a limp chicken? I prodded him with a stick through the iron panel, but got no response.

I ran to the workshop and rummaged around, returning with a fire lighter, the type with a long nozzle. I pushed the lighted nozzle through the iron panel and applied it to the palm of his hand. I smelt his burning flesh, but still he didn't respond.

I looked behind me, expecting Trobe to mysteriously reappear, but saw only a floodlit, silent, empty night. I fumbled with the remote and turned the lights off.

Had I really fried his brain? This was another surreal moment in a rabid succession of them. I sat on the cold steps of the terrace for several minutes and stared in awe at the zombie I'd just created.

Tentatively, I reached in his pockets for car keys and walked to his car, started the engine and parked in the driveway. Summoning extra courage, I unlocked the iron gate, still half expecting him to leap out at me. He remained motionless as I inspected the blistered skin on his scalp and forehead. I peered directly into his eyes and decided it was true—I'd really exorcised this demon.

Unsure if he could walk or whether I'd have to carry him, I tugged on his arm. To my relief, he took my lead and shuffled along with me. Perhaps some brain cells had survived.

I leaned him against his car, opened a back door and slid him into the rear seat. He managed to remain upright as I drove to the same railway station the train had stopped at after the death of Cooper's child. I left him there, obediently seated in the rear of his car.

With my mind now reeling, I slowly walked the four blocks to a taxi rank. I arrived home with the dawn light, and thankful the taxi driver had not been a talker.

CHAPTER 6

The incessant ringing of the phone pulled me from a deep sleep. I picked it up, taking some time to recognize the deep voice at the other end.

"Mr Crow, we need you back at the police station." Detective Trobe announced.

"Have you found more of them?"

"Just as soon as you can please." Click.

With only a few hours of sleep, this particular interview was going to test me.

I ate, showered and drove to the station.

"We have another line-up for you, Mr Crow."

I followed Trobe along a now familiar corridor. Several men were already lined-up and I was surprised to see the child killer, slouched in a wheel chair to the left of the group. I'd almost started to believe last night was a dream, but there he was, in full but perhaps not quite living, color.

I felt Trobe's eyes boring into the back of my head.

"Recognize anyone, Mr Crow?"

"The guy in the wheel chair, he threw the child from the train," I said. "But he wasn't in a wheelchair at the time." I turned and searched Trobe's face, still not convinced he couldn't read minds.

"No, I suspect not Mr Crow. We have a doctor on the way to check on him, but it's most likely a drug overdose of some kind."

"Too bad," I said. "Is that it?"

"Yes, but don't go too far."

"Why?" my voice suddenly an octave higher.

"The trial, Mr Crow. We will need you to testify."

"Yes, of course." I needed to get out of there before my defenses deserted me completely.

"Detective, can I ask what hospital Mr Cooper has been admitted to?"

"The Mercy General."

Helen worked there. I rang her as I drove, explaining who Cooper was, that I needed to see him and could she help. She found the request a little strange, but she would see what she could do.

Standing at Cooper's bedside, I saw a man who was down, but I guessed not out. He was reading the Financial Review and had three cell phones by his bedside. Obviously, the rule of no cell phones in hospitals didn't apply to him.

His hair was immaculate and his fingernails glowed from a recent manicure. He looked up and removed his reading glasses and his expression was one of surprise at my presence, particularly when I explained who I was.

"Mr Cooper, I'm sorry I didn't do more to help," I stuttered, summoning the courage to put words to banished thoughts. "But the men who did this have been found and... well, they won't be harming anyone anymore," I offered, almost apologetically.

I was aware of Helen watching me and wondered what she was thinking.

"Good, because it saves me the trouble of having to rip their heads off." Cooper said with a seriousness that startled me.

"I understand."

"Do you? Do you really *understand*?"

He locked me in a stare, under which I squirmed.

"What's your name again?"

"Michael Crow"

"Mr Crow, it's hardly your fault the world is full of murderous pigs."

"I just wish—"

"What's that saying? All it takes for evil to flourish is for good men to do nothing."

I stood transfixed, a rabbit caught in headlights and this man was about to run me over.

He looked me up and down before continuing, "Perhaps you are a good man Mr Crow, not overly brave, but at least you got involved."

I turned a darker shade of red, "I guess so. I'm very sorry for your loss."
What did he mean *involved*?

I got up to leave and heard him say, "Thank you."

I nodded and walked out of the room. A few steps along the hallway and Helen caught up with me.

"That was a little intense, are you OK Michael?"

"Yeah, I'm fine."

"You know you shouldn't take that macho stuff to heart."

"Some would say better to die with pride, than to live in shame."

"That's just plain stupid. You should get some rest. I'll come over later to cheer you up."

"I think I need to sleep for twenty-four hours. Can we catch up tomorrow instead?"

She nodded. I kissed her and left.

On the way home, my paranoia escalated another notch. Had I left my fingerprints or DNA on the killer or in his car? The television crime shows would have you believe the police could get a positive match from body odor alone. I wondered what Trobe knew or suspected. Would he connect the killer's morose state to me? And what did Cooper mean by *involved*?

I arrived home, showered vigorously and vegetated in front of some inane TV game show before falling asleep on the sofa.

CHAPTER 7

My brother Tom and I crossed an undulating sea, climbing up the back of ocean swells that surged beneath our jet skis. The further we went, the more distant the last few days seemed. We found some nice wave action on the windward side of the bay and I reveled in the cleansing effect of the salt-water spray in my face.

After an hour of vigorous wave bashing, we skimmed along the shallows before landing on a small sand spit in the south of Botany Bay—a holiday resort only to thousands of sea birds.

Lying on the beach, even the pungent smell of eons of bird excreta failed to bother me. I felt relaxed for the first time in what seemed like a lifetime, yet my new life was only several days old.

I watched a large freighter steaming up the main channel only a short distance away, mesmerized by the wake that followed behind it in a slow motion fade.

"Hey we should ski behind those things, the wave action looks huge," Tom suggested.

"Yeah, and so do the sharks that follow them."

I picked up a handful of sand and considered the life force that began and ended with the sea.

"So what's the deal with you and your partners?' I asked, knowing he would rather talk about himself.

"I don't know, it's all fucked. One day everyone's friendly, downing vodka and counting money, and the next it's lawyers at ten paces."

"Why?"

"The usual stuff, ego, greed, take your pick."

"Partners are not your thing, I warned you years ago." I said.

"Yeah, but some things you can't do on your own."

"Maybe those things aren't worth doing."

Anyway, the sun was too warm and the water too clear to bother with all that.

"My week went well," I prodded.

"Oh that's right, the final solution. How did it go?"

"Signed a few documents, received a check and the deal was done."

"You'll want to come on board one of my projects then, with all that spare cash?"

"Not right now, but thanks anyway."

"So what are you going to do?"

"I don't know, maybe save the world." I taunted.

"There's money in that?"

"No, there's life in that."

"Really, what do you think you'll do?" he insisted.

"I don't know, maybe nothing. Can you imagine weeks, maybe months, without doing a deal?"

"No."

"Have you ever wanted to do something more with your life, other than just make money?"

"No," he said as if the question itself were sheer heresy.

"Come on."

"Anyway, what else is there? Everything else gets boring and besides it means I can buy lots of really big toys."

"You're a sad case."

"Didn't you have a mid-life crisis when you divorced Alison? Are you allowed two?"

"This is more like a mid-life awakening."

"You should take a holiday, and then get back in the driver's seat."

Discussions with Tom were like a friendly table tennis match—until the urge to win overwhelmed him and he wanted to whack the ball down your throat.

We jumped back on the jet skis and crashed through more waves, westward across the bay and along Georges River, which led into the lake system where we lived. Our houses faced each other across fifty meters of water, and he peeled off to his place and I to mine.

With the jet ski docked on the pontoon, I went inside, showered and made a sandwich. As I took the first bite, the doorbell rang. I checked the security monitor and saw Detective Trobe's stoic glare staring back at me.

With some hesitation, I opened the door.

"Mr Crow, I need to ask you a few more questions."

"Sure. Come in Detective."

"Can you account for your whereabouts last night?" he asked bluntly.

For the first time he appeared a little fazed, even unsure. Was it me he was unsure of?

"Why?" I asked, wondering if I already looked guilty.

"The remaining youths from the train incident," he said, studying my face, "we've found them both deceased."

"And, you think I had something to do with that?"

"For the record Mr Crow, could you tell me where you were last night?"

"I visited Cooper in hospital, then came home and went to bed."

"What time did you arrive here?"

"Around 6 pm.

"Alone."

"Yes."

"I see."

He seemed to be considering me seriously for the first time, and I noticed faint beads of sweat forming on his brow.

"Do you mind if I have a quick look around, I don't have a warrant?" he asked.

"Sure, be my guest."

I ate the rest of my sandwich while tracking his movements on the kitchen monitor. He returned several minutes later.

"What's your line of business Mr Crow?"

"Research and development. I founded a technology company several years ago and sold out recently. So I guess you could say I'm currently unemployed."

"And in no rush to make ends meet from the look of this place."

"I've done alright, a few rough patches along the way."

"Aren't there always," he said as he walked to the front door.

"Detective, can I ask you a question?" he nodded while gauging me. "You don't really bust a gut over scum like that, do you?"

I held my breath, waiting for him to either jump down my throat or confide in me.

He took his time responding.

"We treat all crime seriously, Mr Crow."

I followed him to his car.

"How did these two die?" I asked.

"They were both decapitated."

As he drove off, I thought about Cooper's comment to rip heads off. Perhaps his prayer to the decapitation fairy had paid off.

Standing alone in my entry terrace, I peered at the numerous down-lights that now adorned the ceiling. I hoped I had unplugged the emitters from the power supply, and tried to imagine the feeling of my brain heating up from within.

I noticed a box on the floor with a label identifying it from the electronics parts store. My special items had arrived and I whisked them inside to the workshop. I thought about Helen and my daughter Nicole, who would both be staying over this weekend. I calculated I had twenty-six hours to work and sleep. I worked.

I removed the lens from a large telescope I'd bought and mounted the microwave emitters in one end. I hoped the mirrored interior would focus the beam into a parallel, coherent state and then out through the opposite end. I had some idea of what to expect, but there were so many variables it was hard to be certain. I was sure some of the microwave energy would be absorbed into the sidewalls of the telescope. In fact, the whole thing might well melt down or even explode.

I painted an entire wall of the workshop with a heat absorbent paint and used a thermal imaging camera to record the distribution of microwave energy on the wall. This way I could fire the beam into the wall and see exactly how tight the beam spread would be, as well as the overall energy efficiency of the thing.

Seventeen hours later, I had an energy beam capable of cooking an egg from ten meters away. Encouraging, but the downside was the need for an inordinate amount of power. Judging by how the telescope heated up after just a few seconds, there was a high degree of inefficiency in the process. This was most likely in the mirror wall and I needed to find a material that would better reflect the microwaves and therefore minimize the absorption. And I couldn't rely on what worked in the visual wavelength to be effective in this higher frequency range.

I researched possible materials on the internet, and learned about microwaves, x-rays and gamma rays. The only thing differentiating these waveforms was wavelength. The higher the frequency, the shorter the wavelength and the less energy needed to travel the same distance. Blue light can push through thirty meters of water, but not the longer wavelength red light. Maybe the solution was to increase the frequency, as well as improve the reflective material inside the telescope.

One article in particular caught my attention and it described the materials used to coat gamma ray telescopes. It even detailed a design for a waveguide to funnel and collect tiny particles of energy from outer space. Some of the materials were foreign to me, but I remembered meeting an astrologist a few years ago. He worked for a government research agency and was interested in using Vibrolert to predict and counteract the natural vibrations in the earth, in order to assist in deciphering the delicate low energy images from deep space. It was Friday night but I imagined these guys lived like bats anyway, with staring at the heavens all night long. I found his number and dialed.

After a few minutes of friendly banter, he seemed knowledgeable enough and offered to provide some sample materials like those used in the massive dish arrays that collected extremely short wavelength energy. Without sounding too desperate, I suggested I might drop in on Monday morning, as I would be in the area anyway—the telescope facility was 360 kilometers away.

I set the alarm for 7 am and waited for sleep to engulf me. But that didn't happen and I tossed and struggled with my thoughts all night long.

Despite getting out of bed at 5 am, I still managed to arrive an hour late to pick up my daughter from my ex-wife's apartment.

Nicole answered the door and jumped into my arms. She was excited to see me and always full of energy. I held her and grappled with images of Cooper's daughter, being thrown from a moving train.

Alison and I exchanged quick hellos and goodbyes, the quicker the better these days. She seemed to be deteriorating, both physically and emotionally. I suspected depression, a drug problem or both, and worried about Nicole.

The weekend went smoothly and by Sunday night, I'd almost forgotten my recent strange quests. I even considered cancelling my trip to meet with the astrologist, but perhaps a long drive in the country might be therapeutic. What else did I have to do anyway? I wondered about the strange ideas I was obsessing over, and knew this wasn't a healthy state of mind, but for the time being, it was the only obsession coming my way.

I spent several hours at the telescope facility with Professor Nagy, a generic stargazer type with long grey hair and beard who looked remarkably like the poster of da Vince that hung on the wall of his office. In addition to being an astrologist, he also had a PHD in chemical engineering.

I extracted information from him with ease whilst feeding him the donuts I'd brought with me—an old sales trick I'd used on occasion. I explained my thinking about applying vibration analysis techniques to more exotic types of waveforms. He handed me a bunch of high tech materials and wished me luck.

I couldn't wait to get home and worked through the entire week, stopping sporadically for food and sleep. Few phone calls interrupted me and Helen seemed satisfied I was on the mend, giving me as much time to myself as I needed. In any case, the hospital was understaffed and she was busy herself with extra shifts.

By the end of the week, I had grown a beard, felt a few pounds lighter and could confidently boil a cup of water from fifty meters away, and in under three seconds.

CHAPTER 8

The phone rang but I lacked the desire to deal with it. I heard Helen's voice on the answering machine and decided to push through the fog to pick it up. A grunt was all I could manage.

"Michael, are you OK?" she asked with hesitation.

"Yeah, but tired. How are you?"

"Good. Hey, you'll never guess who I saw."

"You're right..."

"Mr Cooper's wife was just admitted."

The excitement in her voice woke me further, "What's happened?"

"I'm not sure, but it's a serious injury of some kind. She's in intensive care."

"And Mr Cooper?"

"He's at her bedside"

"Maybe we should have lunch at the hospital café. It'll be my treat."

"Well, that's an offer too good to refuse..."

I drove to the hospital under a perfect cloudless sky. Perhaps the last few days were just an aberration and life would return to its usual, civilized routine.

I drove into the car park and the thought quickly vanished upon seeing several skinhead youths, like those I saw on the train. They were shouting abuse at hospital staff and anyone within earshot. One youth had a grotesque face tattooed on the back of his baldhead that screamed, 'Look at me, I'm bad!'

I parked at the closest point I could find to the hospital entry and slid inside. I waited for Helen and ran through the possible scenarios in my head. I gave her a hug and realized I'd forgotten to buy flowers, again.

I missed her, the feel of her, her smell, the way she stood tall and proud, her graceful yet sensual manner. People smiled at her instinctively, even after she chastised them. As we walked to the hospital café, I looked around for any signs of Cooper, Trobe or anyone else I'd met in a recent nightmare.

We ordered toasted sandwiches and sat at a table.

"What's happening with the Coopers, and where are they?" I blurted.

"Actually, I'm fine thank you, and it's been very busy here of late..."

"Sorry, and you are looking great..." I stumbled. "I've missed you."

"Good, perhaps there is hope for you. Cooper's wife was assaulted last night and it could have something to do with riff raff outside. Are they still there?"

"Yes, nice bunch. Why haven't the police hauled them off?"

"I don't know, maybe they haven't done anything illegal yet."

"What are they doing here?" I asked, still confused.

"Other than just shouting Cooper's name a lot, I don't know."

"Is Cooper here?"

"He's in intensive care, talking with the doctors."

"Can you get me in to see him?"

"Why?"

"I don't know. To ask if I can help?" I mumbled.

She wasn't buying it and searched my face for the real reason.

"I have some things to do in intensive care anyway. If I think the timing is appropriate, I'll let him know you're here. That's all I can do," she looked annoyed.

"Great, that's fine. Thanks."

"Michael, you really need to let go of this guilt trip."

"I know. I am. Can we catch up later in the week?"

"I've got my midwifery exams in two weeks and need to study all next week," she quickly exchanged annoyance with a tease. "But I could squeeze you in this weekend."

"I can hire a cottage by the sea?"

"Sounds great," she said, with a hint of dubious that I would follow through.

A commotion erupted, with people running towards the hospital entrance. I saw Detective Trobe's large form among them. Helen and I ran with the others and once outside we heard angry shouts from the car park.

I saw Cooper on the ground with a medic by his side. Police were restraining three of the tattooed youths as another lay on the ground, a stream of blood oozing from the side of his head.

Cooper struggled to half standing and shouted, "I'll send you all straight back to hell," his eyes showing a wildness that made the threat entirely believable.

"You're dead and your family are dead," snarled the tattooed head in response. Neither Cooper nor the youth seemed to care who might be listening.

Trobe approached a deranged Cooper and whispered something in his ear. Cooper calmed down, but continued to stare down the youth. Perhaps this was not a good time to chat with Cooper. I decided to leave and told Helen I'd call her later.

My legs felt weak and walking to the car without stumbling proved an effort.

On my way home, I decided my new venture needed a large utility van and stopped at a car-yard. The van I chose was four meters long and had two meters of headroom. I used my credit card and mused at the sudden accumulation of frequent flyer points that would accrue. The salesman assured me the van would be delivered later that day, which gave me time to gather some parts for the grand fit out.

By late evening the following day, I'd mounted the microwave laser, as well as a rack of car batteries in the back of the van. The batteries would charge in parallel and deliver a higher voltage in series to an alternating current inverter—a serious mobile powerhouse.

I stood back admiring the silent peacekeeper I'd created and the phone rang.

"So when are we heading off?" Helen asked.

A sinking feeling engulfed me.

"Dinner has been arranged for tomorrow night and we leave the next morning, to a secret romantic destination." I lied, but well.

"Really?" she sounded excited and suspicious. "And you didn't feel the need to let me know this sooner?"

"I was just about to... what time can you get here?"

"I'm on an early shift that day, so is 4.30 good?"

"OK."

"What do I need to pack?"

"A bikini and a fur coat."

"Yeah right. Are we flying?"

"No, driving. It's a local escape."

"OK."

Having scraped through that, I needed to make a few calls.

After a sexually charged night and ravenous breakfast, Helen and I motored along the southern coast road. I'd rented a small cottage on a cliff edge overlooking the Pacific Ocean where the proprietor assured me I would taste the salt spray from the waves below.

Along the road, I noticed a large dome structure on a hillside. It looked similar to the building that housed the telescope I'd visited recently, but this one had an unfinished, weathered look about it. I found it intriguing and noticed a for-sale board out front.

We arrived at our cottage just after noon and decided to lunch at a small fishing village a few minutes up the road. We came across a quaint restaurant on a pier, perched on stilts over the water. I mentioned the domed building to our waiter, a local. He told me it was to be a private observatory, but the eccentric owner had died before finishing it. That was almost a year ago now and it had been listed for sale ever since. Observatories, it seemed, were not hot property right now, even those with a sea view.

We enjoyed lunch before taking a leisurely stroll along the beach. The rest of the weekend was spent enjoying each other's company, and before long Sunday afternoon was upon us, and a relaxing weekend had come to an end.

CHAPTER 9

Helen left for work in the early hours of Monday morning, leaving me in a floating half sleep. The enticement of the observatory soon drew me out of bed and to a phonebook. Perhaps I could transform the place into a huge workshop, well away from prying eyes and other distractions. On the other hand, I could restore it as an observatory and spend some time staring at the heavens. Either way, it would allow me to enjoy the tranquility of seaside living, away from the madness here.

I found a phone number for the local real estate agent. The smooth voice at the other end suggested a price of 2.4 million dollars would see it bought. I told him I would be passing by in a couple of hours and might stop for a quick look.

Driving back along the same road without Helen seemed a little underhanded, but that was pleasure and this was business. The agent mumbled something about the premature death of the retired astrology professor, that he spared no expense on the building, and that soon the market would appreciate 'hobservatories', so snap this one up before the secret was out. The building was physically huge and in reasonable condition, considering it had been deserted for the better part of a year. After some verbal dancing, we agreed on a figure of 2.2 million and I signed the contract.

I returned home and spent the next few days fine-tuning the van-mounted laser and its various ancillary systems. I preferred the idea of firing pulses through the van window, rather than having to open it, but calculated the absorption of energy by the glass could crack it. The van had long narrow windows high up and all round, so opening the most suitable one at the required time shouldn't be too much of an inconvenience.

The next morning Helen rang, "Did you hear what happened?" she asked, excited.

"No..."

"Cooper's wife died last night and the police have taken Cooper into custody."

"His wife *died*? They arrested *him*? *Why*?"

"You remember the youth who Cooper attacked in the car park?"

"Yes."

"Well, he was in hospital recovering from head wounds and Cooper attacked him again, here in the hospital, this morning, with a hammer! The kid is in a coma and they don't expect him to survive."

"Shit, this is out of control. Are the gang still at the hospital?"

"No, they're gone and I heard they belong to a cult. They call themselves *The Slived*. The police are all over the hospital and they fear a revenge attack by the gang."

"You should take a few days off while this all blows over."

"No, I'll be fine."

"Slived?" I repeated. "That hardly sounds scary."

"Spell it backwards."

"Devils?" I said slowly. "I see, how clever. Do they have a hole somewhere they call home?"

"Apparently it's a commune of sorts just outside the town of Wentworth Falls, in the Blue Mountains."

"You're the little detective today."

"It's the only topic of conversation around here at the moment, what can I say..."

By Friday, I couldn't restrain myself any longer and drove to Wentworth Falls, a small country town some 150 kilometers inland, west of Sydney. It lay at the southern foothills, a gateway to the Blue Mountains wilderness area and a popular destination for hikers and kayakers.

I asked the owner of the local general store about the sect and quickly got the feeling *The Slived* were bad news.

"Property values shot to hell when they came to town," the shopkeeper grumbled. "They have a place over the ridge and down in the next valley, along that dirt track," he pointed on a map to a sketchy trail that snaked its way through the back hills. "But they don't take kindly to visitors."

With this advice running through my head, I drove up the track, physically willing myself forward with every click of the odometer. After an hour or so of slow pot holed progress, I emerged over a ridge to find a cluster of small huts surrounding a larger brick building nestling down in the distance on the valley floor. The steep sides of the valley were thick with scrub and towering trees, turning to overgrown grassy slopes and finally to flat mowed lawns where the compound grounds began.

The entry gates were elaborate with a boom gate that blocked all through traffic and the barbed wire fences around the perimeter ensured no access, other than from the main road. I marked the position on the GPS, performed a hair-raising multipoint turn on a track no wider than the length of the van, and drove home.

I found an internet site dedicated to satellite image photography and paid the twenty-dollar membership. I downloaded photos of Wentworth Falls and its surrounds, which showed only a single building at the location of the cluster I saw, but the images were a year old.

I noticed a fire break encircling the hills to each side of the valley. One of the tracks, wide and more gently sloping followed a high voltage transmission line across the ridge. The top of the hill looked to have a clear line of sight to the valley floor, three kilometers away. Somewhat of a concern as I had only tested the laser to a hundred meters. I had some work ahead of me and a few field trials as well.

I also made a note to buy a dozen frozen chickens from the supermarket.

CHAPTER 10

The next morning, I drove an hour south-west to where dirt tracks criss-crossed open grasslands and the occasional elevated outcrops with trees made for a perfect target range. I drove over a ridge away from the main road to be sure I would be out of sight of passersby.

I hung frozen chickens from various trees, the interval between each bird roughly half a kilometer. I parked on a hilltop and observed the macabre scene of naked hanging birds before me. The telescopic lens I'd fitted to the laser provided a clear view of the targets, and the infrared lens gave an accurate indication of the heat that would be experienced by the birds once the microwave pulses were sent to them.

Making sure the van's battery racks were fully charged, I checked the screen and locked-in the image of the first bird. The software routine I wrote last night would help with tracking a moving target by characterizing its unique heat signature. Since the birds were already dead and stationary, I wouldn't need it unless the wind picked up and they started to sway excessively.

I was reasonably pleased with my efforts over the past two weeks—revenge it seemed, worked wonders as a motivator.

I brought the power supply online, confirmed the first target and noted its distance and temperature. Two degrees, it was only just starting to defrost. All that remained was to set the duration of the pulse and fire.

After a one-second pulse, the infrared monitor indicated the temperature of the bird had risen only five degrees. I fired off a four-second pulse and the monitor showed another five-degree rise. It should be heating up quicker, something was wrong.

I checked the power supply in case it had malfunctioned and looked back to the screen to see that the bird's temperature had risen another *ten* degrees. How was that possible? Was the beam still on? I disconnected the power supply to make sure the beam was not 'leaking'. When I looked back again, the bird's temperature had continued to rise—by yet another *ten* degrees!

I secured the instruments in the van and drove over rocks and clumps of dirt to where the bird hung from a branch. I smelt the pungent but now familiar odor of micro-waved chicken and gagged.

With a thermometer, I checked the bird's surface temperature—seventy degrees. What was going on? I felt heat radiating from the bird and noticed it appeared physically larger, swollen. I plunged the metal tip of the thermometer deep into the carcass and a hot yellow liquid spurted out, barely missing my head and covering my right hand. I quickly wiped off the foul muck as a searing heat took hold.

The thermometer indicating a staggering one hundred and ten degrees as yellow liquid continued to ooze from the bird's various orifices like lava. I stood in awe as I watched the bird cook from the inside out.

I prodded further with the thermometer to release any remaining liquid. Using a knife, I cut the bird open and felt nauseous as blobs of yellow clumps and fluid fell to the ground. It seems I'd purchased the birds stuffed.

But why had the interior heated up so much quicker than the exterior? Was it the higher frequency microwaves making for a deeper penetration?

I returned to the hill and fired a pulse into the second bird that hung patiently, a kilometer away. The monitor showed a surface temperature rise of only five degrees, but when I arrived minutes later to examine the bird, its skin had risen to thirty-five degrees and its internal temperature measured seventy-five degrees.

I continued the same process with the other birds, and then, at the last one, almost three kilometers away, I measured an internal rise of only thirty degrees. Externally the skin showed no sign of blistering and was cool to touch.

I felt satisfied driving home as the evening light faded. The battery rack had fully depleted its charge for a total of fifty seconds of microwave laser bursts. It was certainly power hungry, but all I needed were a few short shots—after all I wasn't planning to wage war on the entire chicken population.

I would charge the batteries over night and head out again tomorrow, but this time without my chickens, and to a different spot with a different, more deserving, target.

I sat in the kitchen contemplating my evening meal while listening to the news. I heard a familiar name and turned to the screen. The reporter described how Brendan Cooper, the CEO and founder of SatCOMM Corporation, one of the richest men in the world, was taken into custody today on assault charges, which were expected to be upgraded to murder. The reporter went on to speculate about the future of his global communications empire. How it might be savaged by the stock market. I felt sad for Cooper. His life had been turned upside down by a series of mindless acts inflicted upon him and his family by mindless individuals. I hoped the justice system would be lenient.

I despised the impotent, helpless feelings that seemed to have plagued me recently, the loss of control, the cowering, and the fear. After dinner, I visited the railway track and placed flowers on the spot where Cooper's daughter had died.

I woke as the sun rose and forced down breakfast while imagining contract killers wolfing down a plate of lamb brains without much effort and then kissing their wives goodbye and heading out for another day of murder. I couldn't imagine such a state of mind, and in any case, what I was planning to do wasn't really murder. It was more like deactivating the criminal element—a kind of social lobotomy. I didn't want or need them to be dead. Those I intended to seek out represented an unacceptable risk to society, and since good people were persecuted every day, it was time, in my infinitely small way, to redress the balance.

Some attributed random acts of destruction to a supreme, mystical and enlightened 'being'. They ignored the fact that somehow this 'being' continued to trip up and destroy good and decent people every day. I hated randomness, distrusted coincidence and spent my entire working life creating order from disorder, and this urge was still as strong as ever.

The light of science progressively illuminated the so-called 'mysteries' for what they were—just stories told to help pass the cold, dark nights of centuries past. And now, science saw fit to provide me with my very own 'new age' spotlight. Having psyched myself to the point of screaming, I checked the van and the battery charge one last time before driving off for a day in the valley.

The dirt roads winding up the hillsides were a little steeper in reality than they appeared on the satellite images of Wentworth Falls and its surrounds. Nevertheless, the van was up to it and I reached the top of the designated hill just before midday, parking beneath ominous high voltage transmission lines.

True to the satellite information, I was three kilometers from the valley floor. Peering into the sect camp, I observed only a handful of people milling about. I set up the scope, tuned in the images and scanned any heat radiating objects—people, animals and cars.

The system functioned well, but I noticed as people walked past each other, the software occasionally becoming confused and switching targets. I played around with it a little more, trying to define a more specific visual signature for each target.

An hour later, I had a more reliable tracking tool, but still failed to find any suspect activity going on. I tracked a goat for an hour and noticed the system locking efficiently to its meander around the camp.

It was late evening when the angle of the sun started to reflect into the targeting system, causing it to lose its locking. I was interested to see how the system coped at night and decided to stay until morning. Driving back at night with the headlights on would only raise suspicion anyway.

I had only half a sandwich and some cold coffee to sustain me. I thought about using the laser to reheat the coffee, but that might be pushing my luck. I used the time to continue refining the software and watched as the sun set over the valley—a wonderfully natural display, but one tainted largely because of my presence.

It was pitch black when I ventured from the van to relieve myself against a tree. Looking down into the valley, I saw a campfire and heard raised voices. I turned on the targeting system and used the night lens to decipher the activity deep within the black void.

There appeared to be twenty or more figures gathered around a campfire, all watching a large central figure speaking. The long robes they wore reminding me of a medieval scene. I could hear sounds but not individual words and aimed the infrared lens on the talker among the group. He displayed an agitated, angry manner and I needed a listening device—one of those miniature dishes that gathered and amplified sound. I'd seen them in a spy shop recently and made a note to buy one.

The infrared images became progressively clearer as the night cooled the surroundings. I aimed the sights on the centre of a man's forehead, watching as the system automatically tracked his head movements with millimeter accuracy.

At 2.30 am, the group dispersed and I managed to catch a few uncomfortable hours sleep in the back of the van before sunrise. I drove home, thankful I could finally defrost with the van's heater turned on high.

I woke after only two hours' sleep to the phone ringing, surprised to be fully dressed and laying on top of my bed.

"Mr Crow, my name is Mal Abela. I'm a lawyer representing Brendan Cooper. We would like to confirm your availability to testify at Mr Cooper's trial—about the events leading to the death of his daughter."

"Of course," I stammered, still foggy. "How is he doing?"

"Not too well I'm afraid. His eight-year old son has been missing for almost twenty-four hours."

"Who?" I asked, sounding like an owl.

"I can't really discuss it. The police are involved and we, they, suspect it's the same group."

"This *Slived* sect?"

"Yes, but the police don't seem to have enough evidence to take any action," he paused. "You should be careful yourself Mr Crow."

I thought about my trip to Wentworth Falls yesterday, when the sect would surely have been under surveillance by the police, as would my van, exposed high up on the hilltop. I needed to find another location and further away next time, not too far and with a good line of sight.

I scanned the Wentworth Falls satellite images again and found another flat hilltop. This time it was higher up and further along the ridge and just on five kilometers from the sect camp as the crow flies. Apart from the extra distance, it looked to be an ideal location.

It occurred to me that the van I had was the same model as those used by the local power company, which presumably maintained the high voltage transmission lines that ran along the ridges. I found a local artist and paid him an exorbitant amount of money to replicate the power company logo on both sides of my van.

Whilst the artist performed his work, I scoured the internet for real-time digital video-enhancing software. I grafted one of these into my targeting routines and hoped it would help with the extra distance. In theory, I should be able to acquire and hold a target at up to twenty kilometers away or more. I expected some rigorous trial and error on the next road trip.

After the van makeover, I still had a couple hours to find a long-range listening device, but this wasn't proving easy. There were numerous forms to fill out, including a mandatory user registration for the more sophisticated 'ex-military' models. I threw some cash at the store owner and he miraculously produced the latest model from under the counter—in fact one that required no paperwork whatsoever.

I found a few other interesting bits and pieces, including a microwave detector that would help me quantify transmission losses through glass, rain, dust, cross winds and humidity. This would help to better understand the characteristics of the laser.

I rang Helen on the drive home. She was still busy with her studies, which was fine by me. I could spend the next few days completely immersed in my new obsession, without feeling guilt for neglecting all others.

I continued working on the targeting systems well into the night and through the following day, stopping only to draw up a few sketches and draft specifications for the planned observatory renovations. I brought forward the settlement date for quicker access to the property.

In the morning, I was ready to try out my new vantage point. As I drove through the town of Wentworth Falls, I noticed several police cars parked along the street. I stopped at a store, bought a paper and asked the clerk about the activity in town. He wasn't sure but suspected it had something to do with the sect.

I drove along a track for several kilometers before veering off onto another, smaller track, toward the ridge I'd identified from the satellite photos. The track seemed passable at first, but then started to rut badly, causing the van to bounce and slip violently. I found myself watching the equipment in the back as much as the trail in front.

Finding a wider spot to turn the van around proved difficult and it was easier just to keep moving forward. I finally emerged over a crest and onto a flat hilltop. Below me, a long way in the distance, sprawled out on the valley floor where the sect buildings, much like yesterday but smaller, a lot smaller. This would be challenging.

I positioned the van so that only the side window needed opening for the laser barrel. I started the computer, checked the power supply and scanned the valley from the computer screen.

The images I saw astonished me. With the digital zoom and visual enhancement software, it seemed just as clear as it had before, when I was almost half the distance away. I switched to the infrared lens and found I could easily track individuals moving about, although the heat of the day hadn't taken full hold yet. I panned and zoomed around the entire valley with speed and precision.

I noticed several 'hot' images scattered through the grass on the slopes surrounding the camp. I switched to visual mode and zoomed in, but couldn't discern much through the thick grass that stood a meter high and swayed gently with the breeze.

I switched back to infrared and was able to make out the form of a man lying down. I scanned other, similar hot spots, now that I knew what to look for and saw more men lying on the ground amongst the tall grass. They seemed to be in a poised position, with several facing the main track that led to the closed metal gates, while some looked up at the sky.

I searched the sky with binoculars and saw the tiny spec of a helicopter circling high overhead. Looking down on the dirt track, I saw two police cars speeding along toward the camp gates. Inside the camp compound, shaved heads and bare torsos were filing out of the huts, carrying an assortment of rifles.

The police cars pulled up at the camp gates and two officers burst out assuming battle stances behind open car doors. One produced a megaphone and I aimed the listening radar mounted on the top of my van in his direction. But even with the wind blowing toward me and the filtering techniques I'd employed, all I managed to hear were a few scattered, muffled words.

Within the compound, I saw three youths approaching the police. They came within spitting distance and stopped. Both parties seemed to be talking, but the body language looked tense to say the least. I assumed the document the police were waving at them was a search warrant, yet the youths didn't appear overly interested in its jurisdiction.

I focused on the first police car and saw an officer with a radio handset. I turned on the police scanner and performed an auto-search for the strongest signal in the band. A few seconds later, the voice coming from the scanner matched the movements of the officer's mouth.

"It looks like we have a standoff Captain. What do want us to do?" the voice said.

"Hold your ground. We have requested tactical response. ETA, ten minutes," another replied.

It all seemed to be proceeding along a well-worn path—a gunfight, people on both sides dead, and if Cooper's son was in there somewhere, he'd be in trouble.

I panned back to the figures lying in the grass. One of them was no longer prostrate but squatting half upright, pointing something in front of him towards the sky. I switched to infrared and the vision became clearer—the man had a rifle pointing at the police helicopter.

I locked the targeting system onto the crouched figure, rechecked the power supply, programmed a one-second pulse and fired. The rifle dropped to the ground and the figure slumped forward. After a few body jerks, the man remained motionless.

I locked onto two other people lying in the grass and gave them the same treatment, then turned my attention to the youths standing defiantly at the main gate. Several more had gathered behind the front line of youths as back up, while others stood guard in front of the huts, arms folded and guns at the ready.

An impressive looking black van powered along the dirt track, leaving a dust storm in its wake. The tactical response team broadsided to a halt beside the police cars and I could almost hear the cavalry trumpets.

I anguished over whether I should fire pulses at the front-line skinheads, fearing that should one suddenly drop to the ground, the others might assume an attack and engage the police in an all-out battle. I couldn't pulse them all simultaneously, but if I reduced the pulse duration, I could attend to them one at a time, leaving them standing but otherwise inert.

I fired off a tenth of a second pulse at the biggest and meanest looking frontline skinhead. The infrared scan registered no increase in heat from the point on his head where the pulse had entered. But I noticed he was blinking quickly, unnaturally so. And his expression, which had been angry and defiant seconds before, was now blank and benign. He seemed frozen in time, but continued to clutch the gun and stare at the police.

I was running out of time and decided to just double the pulse duration. I fired at the other skinheads, choosing the pulse entry point carefully, remembering enough about brain anatomy to stay clear of the lower back of the head, the brain stem—where a loss of vital functions, such as heartbeat and breathing would result in an instant drop to the ground.

I neutralized those at the front gate and several others around the camp for good measure. The police, unaware of the unusual event happening before them, continued to address their skinhead opponents through the megaphone. I played around with the listening radar some more and finally started to hear words.

"Put your weapons down and move back with your hands on your heads," boomed the voice of authority.

There was no response from any of the youths as the officer repeated the request, which sounded now like an ultimatum. Then, as if in slow motion, the mayhem commenced. One of the youths stumbled forward, the red laser spots dancing over him like insects. I saw a dark liquid seeping from his back where I guessed the silent bullets had just punched through. Another youth swayed left to right, releasing his weapon and dropping to the ground in a sitting position.

The largest youth, who had received the shortest pulse, was now the only one looking directly at the police. He must have had enough brain cells remaining to continue the quest and slowly raised his gun. His arm had moved only a few inches when his whole body jerked backwards. This time, I heard the offending gunshots. The other youths didn't pursue revenge, with several looking only haphazardly in the general direction of their fallen comrades.

The police severed the gate chains and closed in, weapons drawn. The youths who remained standing, swayed with the breeze that now pushed through the valley. I'd seen enough, and with the helicopter still overhead, there would soon be hordes of police scouring these hills. I closed the van window and rattled back down the hill. Rather than go home, I would leave the van in the observatory basement, until whatever blew my way had blown over.

Once at the observatory, I rang a taxi to take me back home to the suburbs. I thought about the power I'd wielded. Only one tenth of a second from five kilometers away and human brains had clicked into neutral, and permanently as far as I could tell. I felt intoxicated, relieved and remorseful all at the same time and tried to think of myself as just a gardener removing society's unwanted weeds. Just a charity worker, no more and no less.

CHAPTER 11

The siege near Wentworth Falls was the lead story in all the news broadcasts and it ended with the death of only two sect members, which I found intriguing. A spokesman for the tactical response team referred to it as a reasonably 'clean' result, considering the blood bath that could have ensued.

"Our highly trained people minimized casualties with surgical precision," he announced with the smoothness of a recruitment officer. That was fine by me, we needed more law enforcement, and they needed my laser technology. I wondered what the glossy sales brochure might look like.

However, there was no mention of Cooper's son, which concerned me. I'm not sure why, but I suddenly felt the need to visit Cooper again, now that I had something more to offer than just words.

A security guard greeted me at the front gate of Cooper's estate. Thinking this might not be such a good idea after all, I tried to hide my disappointment when the guard instructed me to drive on to the main house.

I walked up the stairs and through the double solid timber doors that stood three meters high and were open. I entered to an enormous granite and marble lobby where two spiral staircases twisted upward to my left and right. Between the staircases, a statuesque palm tree stood several meters high, commanding a central position under the three-storey glass canopy. If the intent was to impress, perhaps even intimidate, then it worked.

A well-dressed elderly butler escorted me to a colorful garden, where Cooper sat in a chair under the shade of an elegantly sprawling willow tree. A water fountain cascading nearby, together with the scent of the rose garden, brought a sense of peace and tranquility to the place. One could almost forget the state of siege this man was under and scenes from 'The Godfather' came to mind as I approached Cooper, seated comfortably in a large cane chair amongst the fallen rose petals.

"Mr Cooper, thank you for your time," I said, trying to gauge whether the territory was hostile.

"Please, call me Brendan, and thank-you for coming. I haven't had many visitors lately. It seems my associates are keeping a safe distance." He smiled.

The slow, almost slurred speech suggested tranquilizers, alcohol or both.

"Brendan, I must be honest. I'm not sure what compelled me to come here today."

"Michael, walk with me," Cooper stood up uneasily. "I have no doubt there are listening devices around here. Perhaps even the roses are bugged," he smiled at the play on words.

"Michael, we are *all* involved," he continued while I braced. "But some of us have the capacity to do more, to *control*. Perhaps there is something you can do."

He eyed me carefully. "I've found out a little about you, I hope you don't mind. You know, *individuals* are the difference between success and failure, in business as in life."

The guy had just lost his entire family, was facing years in prison, and still had the desire to personally offer me a job.

"Brendan, with all due respect, I'm flattered but—"

"Hear me out," he instructed with a dismissive wave. "The world we live in is changing, evolving…"

Hoping this monologue would reach a conclusion sometime soon, my frustration raised another notch when his phone rang. Apparently, Detective Trobe had arrived at the house and we walked back to the lobby in silence.

"Mr Crow!" Trobe seemed surprised to see me.

"I was just leaving—"

"Before you go," he insisted. "You've heard about the incident at Wentworth Falls yesterday?"

I nodded and Cooper grunted.

"The medical reports suggest many of the youths there suffered severe brain lesions, and are in fact in a permanent catatonic state." Trobe stated.

When neither Cooper nor I responded, he continued, "Four of the youths died at the scene—two from a particularly bizarre cause of death I'm told."

Was it two or four? I could barely contain my excitement, and fear. How should I react to this? I decided to stick with what I was doing—look blank and concentrate on breathing.

"Let's hope they suffered immensely," Cooper snarled and turned to wish me a good day.

I couldn't get out of there fast enough, consciously restraining myself from running the last few steps to my car. I assumed however, that it was Cooper under suspicion and not me. But I felt he didn't care, and that somehow he wouldn't spend a day in prison. Money is power and power is freedom. However now, I too was firmly planted into this strange world, whether I liked it or not.

I switched my phone on and called Helen. I needed to get out of this dark reality and she was my conduit to all things normal and decent. As I dialed, my phone alerted me to a text message just received. '*I will have a particular caller diverted to your cell phone. He is the man who has my son. I have deposited money into your account. Use it as necessary to bring my son back. BC.*'

I reread the message several times. Was this guy for real? Who did he think I was? Batman?

It was after midnight when I finished with the additional software routines to improve the targeting system, and then fell asleep for several hours before waking to a headache that pulsed in rhythm to my heartbeat. I shook my head in disbelief as the memory of the last few days flooded back and wondered if anyone would believe me, even if I wanted to tell them.

CHAPTER 12

With the purchase of the observatory now complete, I checked my bank balance. The figure flashed on the screen and I immediately refreshed the image, thinking some crazy pixels were playing games. But it came back the same—12.6 million dollars.

I checked the credit column and found a transfer of ten million dollars from SatCOMM Corp. Was it payment for Cooper's son's ransom? I reread his text about the phone call to be diverted to me from some deranged skinhead, and was relieved to find no calls had registered on my phone.

I stared at the phone, daring it to ring but feeling nervous that it might. I wondered what I would say if it did ring. What would he say? I guess he might ask if I had the money, and let me know that if I involved the police then the kid would die—the usual routine. Then there would be the stupid midnight rendezvous for the exchange, where I'd probably get shot and bleed to death in some sleazy gutter, And there my story would end.

The phone rang just as I took a bite of toast. I quickly spat the mush into the sink when I heard a deep male voice I didn't recognize ask, 'Mr Cooper?"

"Hello?" I said.

"Who is this?"

"Excuse me?"

"Is that Mr Cooper?"

"Um no... I'm Mr Cooper's assistant."

"Well assistant, I suggest you get your boss on the line, now."

"He can't come to the phone at the moment. The police are all over him, but I have the money," I said, sounding like a complete fool.

A silent pause as I held my breath waiting for a barrage of abuse.

"How much have you got?" he asked.

"The agreed sum," I said, trying to keep the tremble from my voice. "But I need to know the boy is still alive."

I heard a child's voice in the background, but didn't know if it was Cooper's son, having never heard him before. I felt fear tightening its grip on me.

"There's a café on the main street—" I started.

"Shut up."

"It has to be in a public place, otherwise forget it," I said, sounding slightly Bogart now.

"The Plaza shopping centre, central Parramatta, do you know it?"

"I think so."

"Stand at the fountain in the centre of the mall and wait for my call." The voice was strong and determined.

That was not good—I needed a direct line of sight to him from my van.

"No," I said simply.

"No?"

"No, none of this run from here to there shit."

I heard him laugh, "This is your first time?"

"You'll have to call me back—"

"What? Are you stupid?"

"I just have to think about this, it's all a bit quick," I hung up before he had the chance to jump through the phone line and bite my head off, or worse still, laugh some more.

His caller ID had read 'private', probably a prepaid service with a bogus name. But wasn't Cooper the owner of one of the world's largest phone companies?

"Brendan, its Michael Crow. Can you talk?"

"Not at the moment."

"I need to locate the exact position of a cell phone."

"You'll need to talk with Mr Lee, our Technical Support manager." Click, he was gone.

I rang SatCOMM and asked to speak to Mr Lee. After listening to the on-hold promotion, *SatCOMM Corporation, the first to offer true high def global video communication services*...a voice said, "Hello."

"Mr Lee?"

"Yes, and you are?"

"Michael Crow. Mr Cooper asked me to call you. I need to track a cell phone…"

"Mr Crow, do you know where our offices are?"

An hour later, I arrived at the global headquarters of SatCOMM, where the firm occupied the entire forty-five floors of an impressive black monolith in the city centre. When Mr Lee, who was in fact Cooper's personal assistant, greeted me, I explained what I required. As the officious Chinese PA led me down a series of corridors to a secure electronics laboratory, I felt a little more at home and quickly discovered some interesting facts about the future of wireless communications.

"Mr Crow, as you might know, all cell phones have for some time now had an embedded GPS chip," Lee explained. "Therefore, the exact physical location of the phone can be determined at any time."

I nodded as a layperson might.

"All that is required is for the phone to be switched on," he smiled.

Mr Lee provided me with a portable cell phone locating transceiver. The device was not much bigger than an ordinary cell phone and its operation seemed simple enough. It just needed to remain on-line with SatCOMM in order to locate the target cell phone, making sure to avoid tunnels, basements and bad weather.

I drove to the observatory to collect my van with the transceiver facing me in its cradle on the dashboard. On the way, my phone rang with 'target' now identified as the caller, rather than 'private'. I looked across at the locating unit and was pleased to see it was already tracking the call.

I held my breath and answered.

"This is your last chance shit-for-brains. Say nothing and do exactly as I tell you."

"Just tell me how you want this to go and I'll do it," I acquiesced with real sincerity.

"Wise move."

While I listened to his instructions, the transceiver flashed up a confirmed location. When he finished I told him I understood and read the address from the transceiver display, *10 Clipper Street, West Parramatta*.

I felt another long and hellish night coming on.

I drove the van out along the coast road. The kidnapper was to call at 5 pm, the time I was due to arrive at Parramatta Plaza. Fortunately, he had his cell phone switched on and the transceiver confirmed his stationary location in West Parramatta for the entire journey there.

It wasn't long before I'd parked a few meters from an old house, in an old part of town, where dilapidated shacks straddled each other on both sides of the street. To get a clear line of sight, I had to park directly opposite the house and debated the wisdom of this. Whoever was inside would surely be suspicious of a van not usually parked in the street.

I decided to remain where I was and kept the engine running. Climbing over the seat and into the back of the van, I fired up the computer systems and started with a low power sweep of the house from one end to the other, a meter above floor level. Any bodies of differential heat should be visible through the thin timber walls and windows.

A few minutes later, I still had nothing resembling a body and increased the power. This time a hazy human-like image appeared amongst the hash. I watched the monitor while loading the Vibrolert software, which should help filter the image further and eliminate the interference problem. I checked the battery charge and found I'd already used up twenty percent.

I scanned the house again and my breathing paused. The front door had opened to reveal a person, standing in the doorway and looking directly at me. I switched to visual mode and zoomed in on a tattooed youth with a shaved head, who now unleashed his most menacing stare directly at me. I identified him as a target to the firing system just as he commenced his stride toward me, with one arm behind his back.

My hands shook as I concentrated on typing the number 0.1 for the pulse duration. I pressed 'Delete' instead of 'Enter' and hurriedly retyped the number and pressed 'Enter' this time. Thankfully, the target lock held and the pulse hit him square between the eyes. He immediately slowed his advance and stumbled. I watched, daring not to blink and sent him another pulse for good measure. I only wanted him dazed and not falling over. Who knows how many more skinheads where in there and ready to turn my van, and me, into Swiss cheese.

The youth, now seated on the gutter at the edge of the road, had a handgun clearly visible by his side. I scanned through the front door of the house again, but the dark interior made it difficult to discern anything. I switched to infrared and saw the faint outline of someone standing directly behind the open door. I increased the scan power and identified the form of an adult. I fired a pulse through the door, and watched as the form behind slumped down and sat still.

I waited a few minutes and watched. The battery indicator displayed only thirty percent of charge remaining. I considered running inside to rescue the child, but only had so much courage in reserve, and I'd run dry. Instead, I drove to a public phone box and made a quick call to the local church. I told the kind sounding woman about a child in distress at a particular address, and that a rescue might be in order.

On the way back to the observatory, while passing through a small seaside town, I decided to stop for food. I pulled over in a vacant parking area and saw a group of youths huddled around a lone car some fifty meters from me. The evening light was fading and a thick sea mist already blanketed the town, making it difficult to see and hear. They looked suspicious, and gangs were on my alert list these days.

I started up the computer and directed the camera and microphone in their direction. I heard grunting sounds and a woman's plea, "Please, no..." then suddenly a male voice, loud and clear cutting through the fog, "Come on man, give me a turn," followed by more grunting and whimpering.

I resisted the urge to change into a superhero suit, deciding instead to lock the targeting system onto the ape-like figure in the centre of the group. I checked the battery charge indicator, pleased to see it had recharged to fifty percent, and gave him a short pulse to the back of the head. He immediately fell to the ground, a reaction a little more sudden than I'd expected, or wanted. I rechecked the pulse duration and saw I'd set a 3.0 second pulse instead of 0.3. At such a short distance, I pictured his brain turning to hot liquefied chicken stuffing, melting from the inside out.

The huddle dispersed in confusion to reveal three men standing over a partially naked woman. She was spread eagle across the bonnet of a car as the men searched their incapacitated friend for wounds. One looked around the car park, and paused on my van.

I decided this was as good a time as any to test the multiple target locking software. Using the computer mouse, I drew a circle around the group and the system quickly identified and confirmed a lock on each person. I excluded the woman, now curled up on the bonnet, by clicking on her image.

Their actions indicated they suspected someone in the car park was to blame for their friends' incapacitated state. One of them pulled a gun from his pocket and started waving it around. I was stunned when he aimed and fired at my van. A few seconds later, he fired another shot at me. I hit the floor as a sharp metallic twang echoed through the van. A searing pain tore through my left shoulder and I felt a warm liquid oozing down my right arm. I heard another shot and clenched my teeth in anticipation of more pain, waiting in a frozen state for a full minute before gathering the nerve to crouch up and check the screen.

What I saw left me cold. The woman on the car bonnet lay motionless, abandoned, her blood streaming over the front of the car and onto the asphalt in a thick, steady flow. The three men were twenty meters away, dragging their disabled friend along with them.

Realizing the sweet taste in my mouth was blood I withdrew my teeth from a lacerated tongue. I locked them all as targets and clicked on the multiple fire icon. They all dropped to the ground, and wouldn't be getting up any time soon.

I ran over to the woman and tentatively touched her arm. She was warm, completely still and not breathing. I placed her arms beside her and tidied her clothing, giving her back at least some dignity in death.

I walked over to where the four men lay and rolled one over on his back to get a better look. A creamy liquid oozed from his mouth, nose and ears and with it, a haze of steam swirled into the night air, appearing like a departing soul. My stomach convulsed and I suddenly found myself vomiting over their corpses. With rubbery legs, I managed to fall across to the gutter where I sat and reflected on yet another surreal moment in my life. Perhaps this time I did set the power level a little high... And worse still, I'd left my DNA all over them.

Feeling stupid as well as sick, I picked myself up and staggered back to the van.

I arrived at the observatory well after midnight, the only comfort being that I received no further calls from the kidnapper. I touched the hole in my shoulder where the bullet had gone clean through, almost succumbing to the waves of nausea that washed over me every few minutes.

I bandaged the wound and lay on the sofa. I found two phone messages on my cell phone, one from Helen, asking if I was OK and wishing me good night, and the other, a simple *Thank-you*, from Brendan Cooper.

CHAPTER 13

After several hours of broken sleep, the dawn light provided me with an excuse to stop trying. I dressed, showered and drove to the observatory. On the way, I rang Helen.

"Hi, how did your finals go?" I asked, hoping I'd remembered the dates right.

"Good, so far. My last exam is tomorrow."

"I've been thinking about a holiday. How quickly can you drop everything and come to Europe with me?"

"Europe?"

"Sure, why not?"

"I don't know if I can get the time off work. How long would we be gone?"

"Maybe a couple of months?"

"I don't know... it's a bit sudden."

"Have a think about it and talk with your manager. Tell her your boyfriend is losing his mind and it's his only hope."

"When would we leave?"

"In a couple of days..."

"Michael, what's happened? Have you done something stupid?"

"No, like what? I'm just taking your advice, and it feels like the right time. I'll make it worth your while—first class and all expenses paid..."

"Mmm..." I could tell she was warming to the idea, but suspicious of my reasons.

We agreed to discuss it over dinner tomorrow evening, when we celebrated her final exam.

I called my mother for a quick chat and to let her know I'd be taking an overseas holiday with Helen, for maybe a few months. She was pleased. She liked Helen and saw in her a similar strength of character to her own.

The phone rang as soon as I had hung up.

"If you're serious about this trip, I have ten weeks of leave owing and my manager's encouraged me to take them all," Helen said, excited.

"When can you leave?"

"Next week?"

Is she calling my bluff? Is this what I wanted to do?

"I'll make the arrangements," the words fell from my mouth.

"You're sure? Are you OK? You sound a little strange."

"I'm just tired."

"When I start with the paperwork, I'll be seriously annoyed if this doesn't happen—"

"Nothing short of prison or death will stop me," I insisted, with real sincerity.

"I'll drop in on my parents tonight and catch up with you tomorrow evening?"

"OK, I'll cook us a dinner and let you know the details."

"It's a deal," she said, excitedly.

I rang my travel agent and booked a couple of first class tickets to Athens. From there we would head to the Greek Islands, hire a car and tour Greece, Italy and Austria. I'd always wanted to kick back in the mountains for a few weeks of skiing, schnitzel and lager. After that, who knows? Who cares? Assuming, of course, I can get out of this country first.

I felt drained of energy and struggled to clean and lock down the observatory in preparation for an extended absence. I connected several internet cameras to a computer and brought the whole thing up on an internet site. I tested it more than a few times to make sure it was reliable and protected against hackers.

The cameras covered specific areas of the observatory, the front, the rear and various internal views. They seemed to be work well, with a pan and zoom control that I could operate from anywhere in the world, and any movement triggering the cameras to record to hard disk.

I looked around one more time before driving back home.

Sleep came intermittently as my head and shoulder throbbed relentlessly through the night. The travel agent rang in the morning and despite several pills over the last twenty-four hours, the pain still made it difficult to concentrate. She confirmed the Athens flight would depart at noon tomorrow, and that she had booked a two-week cruise of the Maldive Islands as a starter.

I started to feel the river of relaxation flowing through me—perhaps the next few weeks would push this insanity back to the dream world, where it belonged.

I made breakfast but succeeded only in picking at it. I searched out my passport and attempted some packing whilst checking the observatory cameras a few more times. I cleaned the house and fitted real lamps to the extra light fittings the terrace ceiling had acquired recently. Now I did have the brightest entry in the street.

Over the past week, I'd relocated most of my workshop to the observatory, so even if someone entered the house, there would be no evidence of any suspect activity here.

I drove to my daughter's school in the afternoon to pick her up and take her to McDonalds for dinner. I was hesitant to tell her I wouldn't be seeing her for the next several weeks, and reassured her the time would go by quickly. But still the word 'deserter' hung over me. I'd already given her that feeling once in her short life and swore I wouldn't do it again.

I toyed with the idea of flying Nicole over to meet up with us somewhere in Europe, but that might be expecting too much of Alison—she didn't owe me any favors.

I dropped Nicole off at her mother's place and arrived home to find Helen parked in the driveway. I gave her a hug and told her I planned to cook a roast for dinner, lamb rather than chicken, having recently developed an aversion to chicken.

"Is this the start of the, *I-only-have-eyes-for-you* routine?" Helen asked.

"Could be."

"Sounds a little scary, the last time I saw that guy was…first date?"

"Well, he's back."

The smell of dinner reminded me it had been a while since I'd last experienced hunger. I rolled out the vintage red wine, silver cutlery and even lit some candles.

"You're looking a little withdrawn Michael, are you OK?" "I'm fine, but always better when you're around, darling."

"Michael, there's romantic and then there's just plain corny."

"You're right, I need this break."

"And what have you been up to over the past week?"

"Just talking with some people about some projects."

She gave me a look that said, 'I can read your mind' and I believed it. By looking away, I'd hoped to shut off this invisible conduit, but succeeded only in feeling guiltier.

"Are you still stalking Brendan Cooper?"

"Stalking? No of course not, but I did visit him the other day at his house."

"Is that a good idea?"

"Probably not..."

"Michael, you need to let this whole mess go. The trip away will help you recharge and hopefully you'll find more *positive* projects when you return."

"You're right," I held up my glass and tried to change the subject. "Music?"

"Sure, something relaxing."

"Light and romantic? Jethro Tull?"

"At least you still have some humor, for what it's worth, but I'd prefer Norah Jones thanks."

"Hardly a compromise. You'll need to take some books for the plane trip, because I'll be in a vegetative state."

"Yeah, I know, I've flown with you before—it's a real blast."

We finished the meal, lounged by the fire, made love, went to bed and made love some more.

I woke to the sound of Helen saying goodbyes to what seemed like a cast of thousands over the phone. Fortunately, I had more than one phone line and did the same, but covered fewer people in less time. My brother insisted he would come over and drive us to the airport, which was a nice gesture, if somewhat out of character.

I checked my phone frequently, surprised to find no messages from law enforcement. I wondered if Trobe thought of me as a fiendishly clever type, who could wave a magic wand and send street thugs dribbling to the nearest nursing home. But more likely, he considered me the scared nerdy type with undeserved dot com riches.

"Any reason you're smiling to yourself?" Helen asked.

"Just a flash back to last night darling..."

"Well don't get yourself too excited, your brother is at the door."

CHAPTER 14

hated flying, even more so than train travel, and found long-haul flights particularly excruciating. But at least this time it'll be cut in half with a stopover.

We were seated in economy class, a last minute hiccup where first-class had been overbooked for the first leg of the flight. Apologies were conveyed and the difference refunded.

Even in spite of this I felt relaxed, with no business that needed doing, no second guessing motives, no late nights in seedy restaurants with a bunch of suits and no postulating about how to close the sale. This time I could get as hot and sweaty as I liked, in just a T-shirt and pair of shorts. Better still, it would take me far away from microwave ovens, dead chickens and oozing brains.

Even with an engineer's training, it still seemed absurd that tonnes of metal could launch itself into the sky. Nevertheless, that's just what happened at noon on a brilliant sun drenched Sydney day. I looked over at Helen as she watched the light blue of the sky meet the dark blue of the Pacific, in a perfect line across the horizon. I think I really love this woman, but somehow that scared as much as excited me.

After the meal service and a movie, Helen slept. I put on the headphones, listened to music and reflected on my life, particularly my recent life. I shook my head as I recalled the insane events over the past few weeks. It didn't escape my attention that I had actually *killed* people, *many* people in fact. Whether they were actually dead or seated in a wheel chair, drooling, it was the same thing. I didn't believe in God and heaven, yet always thought of myself as a good and decent person, worthy of such a place if there was one. I wondered about that now. If Helen knew what I'd done would she walk away? Is the killing of killers a legitimate exemption? I'm sure I'd saved lives, but was my moral account still in the black? I doubted it.

I drifted back in time and pictured Cooper's daughter and the look in her eyes. I know I can live with what I've done, but I'm not sure I could do it again. I wished I could shut out the voices and sleep, but had no such luck as I pondered and justified to the meandering tones of Tull's rock flute.

I woke with a sinking feeling, a stiff neck and a dry mouth. At six feet three inches tall, the slightest recline of the seat in front usually implants the meal tray into my chest, and renders any leg movement impossible. Only the sudden explosion of fluorescent lights tops this as we start to descend. So far, the flight was living up to expectation.

We landed in Colombo just before midnight, suffering sleep deprivation whilst lining up in the arrival hall, where more stark fluorescent lights flickered incessantly. Standing was an effort, the humidity palatable and the foreign smells thick and nauseating. There was too much eye contact from the locals and the luggage became heavier by the minute. The only thing that saved the day was the air-conditioned limousine ride to the hotel.

Several hours later, after a reasonable night's sleep and the midnight airport trauma just a memory, a tropical sun crept through the bamboo blinds. I stumbled into the bathroom and sat on the toilet. Looking around, I wondered why 'five-star' had so many interpretations around the world. Was this a five-star gecko, with its googly eyes circling, stuck to the wall above me?

We spent a leisurely day in Colombo before boarding a short flight to an exclusive resort on one of the outer Maldive islands. We did all the usual things one does on a secluded island getaway and shared a real connection, body and soul. We discussed our future on a beach beneath a bright moonlit night, while an army of crabs toiled to beat the rising tide.

A few days later, we boarded the flight to Athens, my mind in a pleasant state of free float. I was alert to my surroundings, but not governed nor overwhelmed by them. In fact, I was completely happy and content—

a wonderful feeling that unfortunately never lasts much longer than the blink of an eye.

The first class seats near the front of the main level on the airbus were luxurious, and the possibility of actually sleeping on a long haul flight occurred to me for the first time. I took the window seat and Helen the aisle—she always drank lots of water and needed frequent access to the toilet. Through the window, I watched the sunset over Colombo as the lengthy boarding procedures played out.

Finally, the aircraft doors closed and we were waiting to taxi out to the runway.

Suddenly a commotion sounded behind us. Someone, a man, was shouting loudly with a guttural Middle Eastern accent. I looked behind, as did others, to search the cabin and saw a dark-skinned bearded man stepping out of his seat several rows behind. He was looking intently in our direction, and to the cockpit. Another man, similar in appearance and several rows behind the first also stood up. The two men walked together to the rear of the cabin. Three rows behind us, two more men sprang from their seats and walked quickly to the front galley. As they passed us, Helen's hand tightened on mine.

"It's OK, they're probably air marshals." I whispered to Helen, but knew these men didn't have a legitimate look about them, their eyes darted about like those of a fox in a hen house.

Seconds later, the sound of two gunshots resounded from the galley. Helen ducked her head into my chest. I saw one of the men pushing through the fragmented door to the cockpit, while the other stood guard over the flight attendants now crouched on the floor. Muffled, agitated sounds came from the cockpit, and then silence.

I saw a flight attendant listening fearfully to a large man standing over her, her eyes fixed on the rifle he pointed at her chest. She rose unsteady from her seat and spoke in a tremulous voice over the PA.

"We wish to advise this aircraft has been sequestered. Please cooperate by holding your passport in one hand and putting your hands on your head."

Sequestered? Was this the new low-impact word for hijacked? Whimpers and muted cries of despair filled the cabin, while people rummaged for documents. Helen searched my face for strength and hope, but I suspect she found neither.

Again, here I was staring into the face of evil. Worse still, this time Helen was in the bowels of hell with me. I saw tears forming in her eyes and wanted nothing less than to rip the heads off these people. I tasted blood as my teeth scissored my tongue, again.

A loud crack resounded through the cabin from the front. Shouts and screams multiplied throughout the cabin. Desperate eyes searched desperate eyes. I looked through the window and felt a sinking sick feeling as I saw the body of a man dropping to the tarmac like a crumpled doll, thrown from a hatch somewhere behind us. I closed the window blind, but not before noticing the absence of people outside—there were no police, no medics, not even a security guard.

I heard footsteps approaching from behind and turned my head as another Middle Easterner with a rifle slung over his shoulder walked through the cabin gathering passports. I avoided eye contact with him. Not so much out of fear, but more to conceal the anger that gripped me like a vice and blazed red hot from my eyes.

Should I lunge for the rifle, put him down and pick off the others with sniper-like precision? Maybe not. Hollywood does a great job fostering inadequacy amongst us mere mortals. Besides, I had no idea how to use such a weapon and had a greater chance of injuring myself. Who were they after? Americans? All westerners?

Another announcement from the flight attendant jolted the cabin.

"Would Mr Samuel Edwards please raise his hand?"

I noted the English sounding name as dozens of pairs of eyes searched the cabin for Sam's lone hand. The call was repeated twice more and the name sounded vaguely familiar to me, but I wasn't sure why. I peaked under my window blind every now and then to search the tarmac for another fallen body.

Helen leaned across to look out of the window. "What's happening out there?" she whispered in my ear.

"Nothing," I closed the blind. "We just have to try and stay calm." I held her hand.

People were muttering and whimpering—the sounds of escalating fear. The cabin air quickly became stale, hot and oppressive. I heard some of the younger men talking in hushed voices across seats and aisles. The whispers became louder—they were saying something about the gunmen wanting the world to pay more attention to human rights. It didn't sound like the usual self absorbed reasons for a hijack. Maybe they would have a conscience. Maybe they would set us free to show the world the humanity it lacked. And maybe one day pigs would fly.

Now that the shock had subsided, the adrenalin would fuel a rash form of bravery, a danger period the gunmen would have prepared for. No sooner had this thought crossed my mind than I saw a young man stand from his seat directly behind me. He entered the aisle and walked toward the rear of the plane.

A short, sharp shot sounded through the cabin as an invisible force snapped him backward. Blood sprayed the cabin ceiling in a startling concentric line of red. He lay on his back less than a meter from me and I could hear his gurgling, fading cries for help. A new silence now gripped the cabin—one that recognized death was possible, perhaps inevitable.

A gunman came from the rear and stood over the gurgling man. "See," the gunman growled to no one in particular, "you move and you die. Now the world will take notice. People are dying in our countries, and for you," he waved his gun around the cabin. "You rich westerners, who think you can buy anything you want. Well maybe now, you'll think again." Another gunman came from the rear of the cabin, and they both dragged the dying man to the front galley.

Helen drew closer to me and I felt her trembling. The silence was broken only by sobbing adults and crying babies. Time seemed to stand still and in the space of a few minutes, this violation had become the centre of our universe, with all else just a distant memory, a previous life we would never see again.

"Please keep your cell phones turned off and your window blinds down," the flight attendant announced in post shock monotone.

I wondered what the outside world knew of our situation, if anything. We were in the third world, hijacked by third-world bandits for some third-world agenda. Would anyone really care? There would be no negotiation, and soon enough these animals would turn feral and that would be the end. It was that simple. I thought of Nicole and her broken world, in which her father never came home. Would she forgive me? And who would be there protect her against the evil of this world—her mother?

The verse of a song flashed through my mind, *I knew if I had the chance, I could make these people dance.* I would make sure they danced in the air with a noose around their necks. If I could I would put an end to their miserable lives without blinking, that much I'd learned about myself over the past few weeks. Then again, is what I've done just coming back on me? Does karma work that quickly? Or is this just a case of random evil in a random world?

The cabin lights extinguished and a faint smell of fresh air drifted past. I saw the fading daylight filtering into the cabin from the rear somewhere. Had another hatch opened? The new air, though still humid and dank, led some to believe the ordeal was over. Passengers started to rise from their seats, talking and looking about. Suddenly, an almighty barrage of gunfire erupted through the cabin, ripping through people, walls, ceilings and seats. Bodies and bits of the aircraft cabin exploded all around me as the aisles filled with debris. I gripped Helen's hand tighter, pulling her closer, and trying to squeeze us both against the sidewall of the aircraft, into the impossibly small gap between the seat and wall. A blinding light assaulted my eyes, followed by a shock wave that wrenched the air from my lungs, turning my hearing off as if by a switch. A cascade of sparks and shrapnel bounced around the inside of the cabin like a meteorite shower. The pungent smell of firecrackers filled my nostrils and a stabbing pain in my chest cut short each breath.

I felt Helen shaking violently and saw her reaching behind her, to her back, frantically groping in the intermittent dark and light. The emergency lighting struggling to maintain its purpose, leaving me with only glimpses of the ongoing destruction. It reminds me of strobe lighting at a nightclub, but here the walls and ceilings are dark red with blood and flesh, clothing and luggage seemingly suspended in mid air, floating about in slow motion.

Helen moved her mouth, but I heard nothing. The ringing in my ears becoming so intense that all I could do was to try to read her lips. She pointed behind her, to her lower body. I ran my hand down to her buttock, right and then left. Without understanding, I felt her right side again, the side exposed to the aisle. It felt cratered, fleshy, wet and hard on my fingertips. A sudden realisation made my stomach convulse. Her right buttock was gone. I closed my mouth to keep my stomach contents from hurtling outwards.

I wanted to hold her even tighter, to stop the shaking, both hers and mine. I searched the caverns of hell that was Flight 372 and saw only rows of shredded seats, with just a handful in their original position. Crumpled, dismembered bodies lay haphazardly intertwined with the seats, like life-sized dolls tossed among the garbage. The smell of blood mixed with gunpowder was overpowering, and one I would never forget.

I saw a bright light and sensed fresh air, this time from the front of the cabin. Had the hijackers vacated the plane? I pulled up the window blind and saw passengers, injured but alive, tumbling down the inflated slide from an exit near the centre of the cabin. The tarmac was still dark and deserted, as though this event hadn't been worthy of an audience. I saw an inflatable slide deploying from the exit just in front of us and turned to Helen. There were tears spilling from her eyes and a look of complete despair.

"You're OK Helen, you'll be fine, let's get you out of here," I shouted but heard my words only as a distant drone.

Blood flowed from her wound, but I couldn't bring myself to look too closely. We needed to get to a hospital and I wondered what we would find there. I summoned non-existent energy to move out of the seat and searched briefly for my own gaping wounds, but was surprised to find none.

I helped Helen stand and was surprised she could support herself, at least on her left side. We stumbled together to the front exit, a short distance but littered inches deep with debris, hard and soft, bone and flesh.

At the cabin door, there was no one to wish us a nice day, the crew had gone and the cockpit door, riddled with bullet holes, was thankfully closed.

I cradled Helen in my arms and we rode the slide down to the tarmac. She moaned in pain as her brain started to register the full extent of the injury. Then her eyes rolled back in her head and she lost consciousness.

On the tarmac people wandered about in silent stupor. Some tended to the injured, some screamed in pain, and others just screamed. I looked for someone in authority while struggling to carry Helen. I pushed into a crowd gathered around several people in white and red uniforms—medics tending to wounded on the ground. I tried to explain the seriousness of Helen's injury to anyone who would listen, and eventually one did. Without speaking, he looked her over and immediately ordered a stretcher.

Minutes later, we are inside an ambulance with Helen on a drip and under a heat blanket. The medics seemed to care and performed their duties competently, efficiently. I felt embarrassed for thinking it might be otherwise. I held her hand, spoke to her, and reassured her as much as I could in my own helpless state. I felt my legs trembling as I watched her unconscious, bloodied form. I hope she knew I was here, and couldn't help wondering if she would be scarred or even crippled for life. Maybe she would die here.

Our hopes and dreams, our lives were completely shattered in an instant. I wished I were lying there instead of her. I'd heard people say that before, but always doubted its veracity. But right now, right here, I felt it to the core. Helen had dedicated her life to caring for others and this was just not fair. But weren't the innocent and the good always the victims? There was no reason and no answer, and there never would be, as disturbing as that was for those espousing divine meaning. The only certainty was that evil would always exist and that was it. I tried to stop from thinking altogether.

The medics didn't say much. They looked remorseful, sad. Perhaps they even felt guilt, unfounded as it was, that this had happened in their country. Ten minutes felt like an eternity before we pulled up at a small, shabby-looking hospital that was no different from the buildings around it. Helen was cold to touch and her breathing labored through the oxygen mask. I hoped we wouldn't have too long to wait, doubting my ability to remain calm much longer, now that the shock was subsiding.

A nurse with a trolley emerged through the double doors of the emergency entrance and quickly sucked Helen into the bowel of the building. Inside, the place looked much like a hospital back home, but less cluttered and sparse on high tech equipment. I felt a hand on my shoulder and turned around.

"Hello, I'm Dr James Roberts," a man said with an Australian accent. He was tall and well dressed in a spotless white coat, and offered a smile that reassured.

"I'm Michael Crow and this is my girlfriend, Helen. Our plane has been hijacked, there was an explosion..."

"Yes, I know. Mr Crow, please wait in my office, the nurse will take you. I'll examine Helen and be with you shortly."

"Thank you."

I didn't want to be separated from Helen and reluctantly followed the nurse. I wiped my eyes and read the diplomas and awards that adorned the walls of his office. James Roberts appeared to be a well-qualified man who had studied medicine in England and Australia.

I checked my cell phone in case, miraculously, it had a signal. I found an intermittent network and tried to call Tom, but without success. I decided to send a text message hoping it would eventually navigate its way through the electronic backwater. The message simply read, *Come to Colombo immediately. Bring money. Helen is injured.* He would stew on this for a while, but he would come.

The doctor entered the room.

"How is Helen?" I asked, barely managing to form the words.

"Stable, however she's lost a lot of blood. She's a lucky young lady. Most of her gluteal muscle is gone, yet the hip and pelvic bones seem intact, and thankfully there is no damage to the spinal cord."

I started to breathe again.

"She's strong and there's every reason to be confidant," he concluded.

"She'll be OK?"

"Yes, I think so. We've cleaned the wound and stopped the bleeding."

"Will she walk again?" the words lunged from a raw throat.

"Yes, I believe so, but perhaps not unassisted. She'll need extensive reconstruction surgery and therapy. We need to get her back to Sydney as soon as possible, as infection is always a problem here."

"How long before she can travel?"

"A few days."

More *days* in this hellhole?

"Mr Crow, we need to check you over too, you have blood coming from your right ear."

"Sure, but I need to see Helen first."

In spite of the tubes running in and out of her nose and mouth, she looked peaceful. I sat in a chair, held her hand and whispered to her. The nurse bandaged my head and chest, finding two cracked ribs and a pierced eardrum.

After downing several painkillers, I sent Tom another text, *Hire a jet and a nurse. Call my lawyer Lewis to arrange the money. We're at Kowbula Hospital, Colombo.* What's the use of money if you can't buy life?

Three hours later, I woke feeling cramped, sore and exhausted. The pain in my ears and chest made for a fitful sleep. I tried to imagine the white-hot shot of pain should the rickety cane chair I had perched in all night suddenly collapse. The nurse informed me I had a phone call. I kissed Helen's head—thankful she was sleeping and finally at peace.

"You were on that hijacked plane in Colombo?" Tom asked.

"Yes, it made the news?"

"I saw it on a cable channel, but nothing much on the major networks. They didn't say anyone was killed or injured…"

"One of the hijackers set off a bomb in the plane after they tore up the whole cabin with machine guns. There must be a hundred or more dead. Helen was injured by the blast and she lost part of her right buttock. I need to get her back home for surgery."

"Fuck!"

"How's the plane hire going?"

"It'll cost 200k or thereabouts."

"Fine, did you talk to Lewis about the money?"

"Yes, are you're sure about this?"

"Yes."

"When do you want me there?" he asked.

"We'll be ready to leave in few days."

"I'll let you know our flight schedule. Are you OK?"

"I'll live."

"I'll ring Mum and Alison, and tell them I've spoken with you."

"Thanks."

"Hang in there, I'll see you soon."

The nausea washing over me I suspected was due to too little food and too much adrenaline, but still I couldn't bring myself to eat.

I entered Helen's room and was surprised to see her eyes open. I cursed myself for not being there when she woke. She saw me and the tears flowed, both hers and mine, but the tubes in her mouth made even that difficult.

"Don't try and talk, you're going to be fine," I reassured her. "There's a good team here looking after you. We're in a Colombo hospital and your doctor is Australian. He seems very good." I spoke slowly, wondering how much she remembered or even understood.

"We're flying back to Sydney in a few days. We'll make you better soon enough, I promise."

She gave me a look that told me she knew better. I bit my tongue to stop from wailing like a baby.

"I'll go and get Dr Roberts and be back a minute." I said, as she squeezed my hand. "I'll be back soon, I promise."

I barely made it out the door before I started to cry for real. I sat down on the floor of the corridor with my face in my hands. When the sobbing subsided, I looked around and saw other people, alone and in clusters, in similar states of distress. The corridors of hell were full to the brim.

I saw James walking towards me and stood up.

"She's awake. Can you take a look at her?" I almost pleaded.

"I'm on my way to do just that. Are you OK?"

"Yeah, I'm fine."

We walked into Helen's room with positive attitudes at the ready, but mine quickly vanished when I saw the pain in her eyes, her face blotchy and swollen. The doctor pulled a tissue from the box at her bedside and wiped her face. I thought about the relative value of life. Was this doctor's life worth that of a hundred Wall Street tarts, a thousand mindless criminals and a million misguided terrorists. Yes. Was it fair to judge the value of life? Absolutely.

As James performed his various checks on Helen, a nurse arrived with more drugs to add to her drip. It had an immediate effect and she drifted off to sleep with a look of peace returning to her face. James suggested I eat before I passed out and asked me join him for a meal in the hospital canteen.

"You're from Australia?" I asked, while toying with a pungent smelling chicken curry.

"Yes, Sydney."

"What brought you here?"

"Well, it's not the money," he smiled. "I come from a long line of doctors. My father is a plastic surgeon in Sydney. He was a little disappointed I didn't follow him in that field."

"So why didn't you?" I ate a few mouthfuls of the curry and hoped I could keep it down, at least until I found a toilet.

"Well, I was going to, but then…it's a long story, and perhaps you've had enough tragedy for the moment."

"I'm sorry, I didn't mean to pry."

"No, it's OK," he insisted, then continued. "My wife and I were in New York on our honeymoon two years ago. We were walking down Fifth Avenue when she was hit by a stray bullet. She died in hospital a few hours later. She never regained consciousness and I never found out who or why."

"I'm sorry," I managed, ashamed at merely belonging to the human race.

"So I decided there were more important endeavors than making a living from vanity. Not to judge those who do, it just wasn't for me."

I liked him. He seemed comfortable with his role in the world, and exhibited none of the aloofness that often taints people of profession. He was only in his mid-thirties, but exuded a calm maturity that comes from life experience, and unfortunately too often from tragedy.

I asked him what he knew about the hijack.

"Not much. They, the hijackers, have kidnapped a British diplomat, and wish to exchange him for the release of several imprisoned comrades."

"Samuel Edwards..." I remembered now, but was surprised at the request for a prisoner exchange.

"Yes, he's the assistant to the British High Commissioner in India."

"I remember on the plane, one of the hijackers talked about rich westerners being able to buy whatever they wanted. He seemed to refer to something specific, but it was all a little strange. I didn't get the feeling they were after an exchange of people or money."

"It's hard to say, there are always so many agendas in play in these situations."

"The lack of coverage in the western media is also strange. Perhaps we're just desensitized now."

"Yes and the press operate differently depending on the place and time, especially the Western media. Unfortunately the degree of interest depends on what's happening in their backyard at the time."

"Do you have any idea why this happened? Why here and why now?"

"I don't know for sure. Security in places like this is poor and access to Westerners is relatively easy."

"What about the government and the military? Surely they don't want this kind of anarchy?"

"Someone's anarchy is someone else's way of life. It's a fine line and the government doesn't want to upset any particular group too much, because their own hold on power is fragile at best."

"What about the impact on trade with the West?"

"That's not going to happen. The West needs it just as much. We still want the cheapest clothing, the cheapest electronic gadgets and its places like this where all that comes from."

"Do you expect more of these atrocities?"

"Unfortunately, I think it's inevitable." He looked as though he was stating the obvious, and perhaps he was.

"I would like to get Helen back to Sydney as soon as possible. My brother is arriving by charter jet in a few days,"

"We'll see how it goes. She's stabilizing well and we'll prepare her as best we can. I'll let you know when she can be moved, but there will be risks."

It seemed like no one offered any guarantees anymore.

"I know a good doctor in Sydney who can continue her care. I'll phone him today," he added.

"How much and to whom should I pay for Helen's care?"

"The hospital here relies mainly on donations. There are no set fees."

I nodded.

"So what about you?" he asked.

I told him a little about myself, but it seemed somewhat lesser in comparison to his life.

"My future will be about Helen's recovery," I said.

"That will be a tough road...but you will both get through it."

My bottom lip started to quiver and I clenched down on an already heavily lacerated tongue.

"We have a research facility here at the hospital, for investigating gene technologies and stem cell harvesting." James said, helping to divert me from a full blown melt down.

"Why here?"

"We do the field trials here because Western governments are not prepared to deal with the moral questions."

"Could this research eventually help people like Helen?"

"Yes. It may sound farfetched, but teaching old cells forgotten tricks could result in re-growth and regeneration on a macro level—in fact, we hope to eventually reproduce entire organ and limb structures."

"That sounds incredible."

"Several facilities around the world are well advanced, but I believe we are leading the pack."

"What about funding?"

"There are individuals and organizations that have more money than some small countries. And nowadays almost everyone, including the very rich, has been touched by some form of cellular deterioration or malfunction. Cancer is the now the number one killer in the western world."

"What about the big drug companies? Wouldn't they be steaming ahead with this? There must be mountains of money in it."

"In general, the corporate world is fixated on short term goals with minimal investment. Our research started ten years ago and we've ploughed through tens of millions with little return. We do have one or two significant corporate sponsors, but in the main it's just a too long and uncertain a path for profit centers and investors."

"How advanced is this technology? I mean, could it be used to help Helen now?"

"No, not yet. We're only just progressing from cell cultures to mice. It's possible we could be in a position to trial some procedures on human patients within a few years."

Years!

"I'm sure Helen and I would like to take part, or at least contribute in some way."

"The doctor I've referred you to is my associate. He practices at The Royal Prince Alfred in Sydney, and he also runs our research facility at St Georges."

"So you still have an Australian connection?"

"Yes, we develop our theoretical technologies at St Georges. You may have heard of us a couple of years ago, in relation to embryonic stem cell harvesting?"

"I can't remember…"

"Well, anyway there was some negative publicity, and that's the reason we now do the applied research here. In addition to being an excellent researcher, Dr Mark Woodcock is also a highly experienced surgeon."

James handed me his card and flipped it over. On the back were details of the foundation's bank account. I showed no surprise, after all this was the new world, where money buys futures of all sorts.

"How long will Helen be asleep?" I asked.

"Several hours. We are monitoring her continuously. In the meantime would you like to have a quick look upstairs, where we do our research?"

"Sure."

CHAPTER 15

After a quick tour of a rather sparse laboratory where we avoided several rooms marked 'no access', I returned to Helen's room and sat in the cane chair next to her bed. I watched her breathing, labored and deep, an effort as her body sought vital oxygen to help repair damaged muscle and tissue. My tears flowed freely and I no longer cared who saw.

Against the window, a torrential rain beat down, washing the city clean, or so I hoped. I sent a text to Lewis asking him to transfer two hundred thousand dollars to a numbered Swiss bank account. I included the agreed code to authenticate and wondered what he might be thinking.

I needed fresh air and stepped out of the hospital entry and onto the sidewalk. I let the sound and smell of the third world envelope me as people hustled in all directions, oblivious to the downpour that drenched them daily. Cars horns sounded continuously and every minute the sky illuminated with an electric burst, followed quickly by a deep growling, more felt than heard.

I walked along Lotus Road, past government buildings to a large open roundabout where a hundred identical small cars ploughed in from all directions. Some hadn't bothered to turn their windscreen wipers on, and some drove through the dark rain without headlights. Did they trust each other this much? Was life so much cheaper here? Or were spare auto parts that hard to come by.

I continued past the Ministry buildings and across a bridge toward a clock tower. Behind the tower, I crossed overgrown lawns and a low rickety brick fence, into a sea of dilapidated headstones. A banner over the old wooden church doors read, 'Kerkoff – Old Dutch Cemetery'.

I passed by the crumpled headstones and leafy palms, pausing to read the out-of-place European sounding names. Here lay the defeated colonialists, forgotten as the weeds of the eastern anarchy flourished freely over them.

I walked deeper within a canopy of palms, through thick brush that shut out the city sounds, leaving just an eerie silence. A little further along I heard noises—whispers and grunts. They came from behind the ruins of an old stone building now directly in front of me. It was almost too dark to see as I stumbled over dead leaves and branches, making too much noise.

Suddenly a dark form leapt toward me, striking my chest with its full weight. I fell backward through the air and crashed hard into a tangle of pin-sharp branches. I sensed some creature still nearby, the foul stench unmistakable, but I couldn't see it. I managed to gulp air and summoned the energy to run, in no particular direction.

I saw a light glowing faintly in the distance and ran toward that, hearing nothing but my heart pounding and the scraping of branches across my body. I felt the weightlessness of freefall and hoped for a soft landing. It came soon enough and with a head jarring thud. I lay flat on my back and waited to feel my limbs again. I felt no pain, but knew it would come. I braced myself and squinted, the dull moonlight barely penetrating the thick tropical canopy on top of me.

I listened for the creature and wondered how long it would be before it found me. I managed to raise my head and search out my legs. I saw that one leg lay straight whilst the other pointed to the sky at a right angle. This unnatural rotation of the knee sent a wave of nausea rippling through me, and I groaned.

Sitting up, I tentatively touched the leg that pointed skyward. I felt nothing and looked closer to see bare skin, skin too dark in color to be mine. I pulled at it, stunned at my sudden strength.

I shuffled up, managed to stand and pulled at the leg some more. I dug at the ground with my hands and felt other limbs just beneath the surface—boney and with a thin pasty flesh that come off in lumps with surprising ease. The overpowering smell of rotting flesh so thick that even breathing through my mouth made me gag.

I no longer cared if the creature found me and wanted this nightmare to end once and for all. The sky brightened as the moon emerged from behind the dark monsoonal clouds. I looked around and saw a ghostly garden of limbs growing from the soil for at least a hundred meters in front of me. Some pointed straight up while others jagged at various angles. I walked slowly through the uneven loosely clumped soil, noting how strange it was that there were no heads or torsos anywhere to be seen. It appeared to be a human garbage tip, not quite covered over or washed out by the constant rain.

In the distance, the light still glowed from a structure I couldn't quite make out. I walked toward it, avoiding as many limbs as I could, and feeling flesh and bone buckling under my feet. I felt a deep vibration through the ground, which became more intense as I closed in on what looked like a large concrete tunnel, and the light glowing from within.

Entering the tunnel, the wet slush caused me to stumble before falling head first into a meter deep muddy pool. I stood upright, wiping the sludge from my mouth, nose and eyes. The smell was vile, yet somehow familiar. I realized what it was and vomited horizontally into the dark void. I was knee deep in a river of blood.

Every cell in my body wanted to run away from this place, yet the light and the low drone beckoned me forward. I felt strangely resigned and without control as I lunged forward through the dark bio-sludge.

I was chest deep in it when I felt solid steps under foot. This out-of-body experience was now quite vivid as I watched myself emerging as a dripping bloodied corpse up the stone steps. I surveyed the surroundings and saw a concrete platform leading to a large steel door. The doorframe appeared uneven, as though the structure had been somehow deformed. I pulled on the door handle and was surprised it opened with ease.

Inside, the low relentless drone rattled my teeth and bones. I felt nauseated and disorientated. The occasional fluorescent light flickered in the distance at just the right timing to keep me from falling into the deep channels dug out of each side of the concrete walkway. Abruptly, the vibrating drone ceased and the ensuing silence became even more unnerving, leaving me feeling strangely exposed.

I looked around for a place to hide and found only a large forty-four gallon drum off to one side. My ears still buzzed and I could barely make out the sound of voices in the distance, from deeper in the tunnel. Here the path widened revealing a large underground cavern with several smaller tunnels breaking off into the darkness in different directions. Voices and light came from the right side where a wider tunnel extended outward from the common centre.

I moved slowly under the dim light, close to the wall but away from the ever-present pits and channels carved into the solid rock at great expense to someone. This new tunnel was smaller with tiled walls, floor and ceiling. A tray of electrical cables replaced the channels to each side of the path and the lights were now brighter and more frequent.

I came to large heavy door and peered through its glass window. Sprawled out in front of me for at least twenty metres in each direction was a white tiled room. There were several large machines standing two meters high and connected to pipes a meter in diameter.

Several people with dark skin and blue uniforms worked on a machine off to the right of the room, its internal contents splayed out neatly on the white tiled floor. The insignia on their uniform read, 'Moctas'. I'd never heard of it and made a mental note to search the web when, and if, I got back home.

A bell sounded from within the room and I ducked down under the window. When I dared to look again, the room was empty. I opened the door and walked inside.

It smelled like a hospital but looked more like a laboratory. A red liquid dripped from an open pipe that had connected to the machine, which I saw now was an enormous pump, as were the other five in the room. The pipes came down from the ceiling to the pumps and then back up again. I touched the red liquid with my finger and smelt it, it was blood, but much thicker than normal.

Behind the pump was another door and beyond that, a staircase leading upward. I took one step at a time, pausing to listen and watching as drops of blood dripped from my clothes, marking my presence for all to see.

At the next floor level, I opened the door slightly and peered through. I struggled to focus on the white room with its occupants dressed in white vinyl uniforms, white gloves and boots, and their faces covered with a clear plastic visor. They stood around stainless steel tables and worked on limbless, headless human torsos with large knives and small electric circular saws that buzzed in the air like free-floating prehistoric mosquitoes. They cut various organs from the torsos quickly and efficiently, placing them on conveyors that ran alongside the tables. The hearts, lungs and kidneys I could identify, some other organs I could not. When they finished, the empty torsos disappeared through trap doors that opened up to swallow them. As soon as the top closed, a roaming assistant with a gurney slapped another torso down on the blood soaked table.

This was seriously fucked. I considered blasting through the door to put a stop to it. However, it was more realistic to quietly retreat down the stair.

On the floor below, I was pleased to see the technicians had not returned and I ran across the pump room and back through the tunnel. I felt the low drone of the pumps starting up again and hid myself within its cloak of sound.

I moved down the concrete stair and plunged without hesitation into the chest deep pool of blood and guts. I ploughed through the tunnel to the field of limbs, and then lunged through the prongs of palms, not caring about the prickly undergrowth scratching my face and hands red raw. I was exhausted before I dared to slow down.

Resting in the darkness, I realized the labored, rasping breathing I was hearing was in fact not mine. I crouched low and moved slowly in the direction of the breathing, with every branch I stood upon sounding like a firecracker.

Hearing footsteps, I fell to the ground and hid under a canopy of dead palm leaves. Like animals foraging, the faint outline of several figures come into view less than five meters away and directly in front of me. With heads hung low they pulled up roots and other vegetation from the ground and ate them eagerly. They were human, yet somehow not. Even the long rags they wore failed to hide their deformed appearance, with arms that were too long and legs too short.

One looked in my direction and I held my breath. It had wild eyes, one lower than the other and a wide jawed mouth. The ears were large and pointed outward like a bat. One of them came closer and sniffed at me. Then, back from the direction of tunnel, a horn sounded loudly and the creatures scurried away.

I waited a full minute before making my way back through the church grounds and to the street. I crossed the bridge and past the government buildings amidst a strange silence, the city seemed completely deserted now, and I had the feeling that someone or something was following me.

I entered the hospital through the main street front door and lunged up the stairs to Helen's floor, managing to evade hospital staff. Finding a shower room, I locked the door and stood fully clothed under the lukewarm water for ten minutes before I was satisfied I'd completely washed away the blood.

I found Helen sleeping peacefully in her room. I sat in a chair next to her bed and felt the raw sting of the scratches on my face and the aching of muscles.

After an hour of trying, I gave up on sleep and spent the rest of the night watching the street life of Colombo through Helen's window, and pondering about all manner of strange things.

In the morning, the nurse brought me breakfast and a facsimile from Tom. She treated my scratches, which were now open wounds and seeping a clear fluid. The reddish anti-inflammatory cream she used reminding me of the blood I'd waded through last night.

Tom's fax was a flight schedule that showed an arrival time of 6.00 am Friday, four days from now. James entered Helen's room and asked about my new injuries. I told him I fell while walking around town last night. He suggested I be more careful next time. I let him know there wouldn't be a next time.

We spoke about the logistics and risks of moving Helen. I was concerned about the move, but more concerned about not moving her. The sooner she was in a country that didn't slaughter their citizens and in a hospital with full facilities, the better would be her chances for recovery.

He told me he had business in Sydney and asked if he could join our flight. I quickly agreed. I wanted to tell him what I saw last night. To ask him what he knew, and what the hell was going on here, but I suppressed the urge. I didn't know him well enough and didn't want him to think I was a loony. The thought also crossed my mind that he could be involved. That somehow the body parts factory and the deformed humans were related to his research here.

Over the next few days, Helen slept, while waking only occasionally. She received fluids and medication though a drip with the pain requiring increasing doses of morphine. I also slept for an hour or two, but spent more time in the shower. It seemed no matter how much I washed, I couldn't get rid of the stench of blood.

In VIP lounge of Colombo International, such as it was, I broke out in a cold sweat from constantly looking around, startled by the slightest sound and nervous of anyone appearing suspicious—and here, that was almost everyone.

I watched Tom's Learjet landing while Helen lay on a trolley provided by the hospital. She drifted in and out of consciousness as a nurse tended to her. James arrived only minutes before our scheduled 7.15 am departure and we all crossed the tarmac together to the refueling Learjet.

Tom emerged from the smaller than expected aircraft and leaped down the stairs toward us. We hugged, probably for the first time in our lives, and his words, "You look like shit," made me smile. We all squeezed into the cramped interior of the Learjet and with Helen's trolley secured, the door was finally closed on Colombo.

During the ten-hour flight to Sydney Tom, James and I spoke about politics, religion and science, particularly medical science, while Helen slept. I still couldn't bring myself to talk about last night. Perhaps part of that was because I wanted to forget, and the other part was that I no longer trusted anyone.

When the familiar sight of Sydney Harbor came into view, I shed tears of joy. After we cleared customs, Helen, James and the nurse boarded the ambulance, while the rest of us collected the luggage and travelled to the hospital in the minibus Tom had hired.

Once at Prince Alfred we were warmly greeted by Dr Mark Woodcock, who had a friendly manner and looked much like James' twin. Mid thirties, slim—the generic medical professional of the kindly type. He immediately took charge of Helen's care and we followed him like an entourage to her private room on the fourth floor.

So far I couldn't complain about the service.

CHAPTER 16

The bed I slept in was that comfortable I felt like I'd been floating on a cloud for the last fourteen hours. I checked out of the hotel and hobbled across the road to the hospital, feeling like a combat veteran with every muscle and joint aching. It wasn't the most luxurious hotel I'd ever stayed at, but it was conveniently located close to the hospital.

I cautiously entered Helen's room and found Mark examining the readouts from the various machines connected to her. She was awake and the tubes in her mouth and nose had been removed.

"Good morning," I whispered and kissed her.

"What happened to your face?" her voice sounded hoarse and sore.

"I fell in Colombo. I went for a walk around the city while you were asleep…I'm fine."

She looked at me with concern, and suspicion. I needed to improve my lying technique.

"You've met your doctor?" I asked. She nodded.

"Yes, she's been quite brave. We've cleaned the wound and taken swabs," Mark said. "We need to make sure there's no infection before we prepare the wound for healing."

I stroked her forehead and winced at the thought of that much pain. I sat with her, holding her hand, words too difficult for either of us, and soon she fell asleep again.

On my way out, I caught up with Mark to discuss Helen's treatment. I asked how they could hope to fill the void where the muscle and flesh had been blown away. Apparently, fatty tissue implants and skin grafts were the state of the art, but they would do little to hide the injury. She would also need muscle re-growth to have any chance of walking properly again, and apparently that technology was still a few years off.

I wanted to know more about this bio-engineering stuff, and both James and Mark indicated they were happy to involve me somehow. Whether they were searching for more donations or they felt I could contribute, I wasn't sure. Anyway engineering is engineering, and I could always work into the *bio* part.

I drove home with the bellowing sounds of the morning shock-jock even louder than usual on the radio. "Detectives today arrested a man for the murder of his wife and three-year-old child. After two days of searching through the local rubbish tip, the bodies of mother and child were found this morning by police," he almost shouted before clearing his throat.

"Here is a man who lied to police, to family and friends. He told them his wife had left him, and then he shots her in cold blood, with a spear gun of all things. And, it gets worse! This monster has the callous tenacity to take his three-year-old daughter shopping, to buy another spear gun. Then, he uses this to kill *her*, shooting a spear right through her tiny heart. Allegedly, I am required to say." He paused.

"In my forty years as a journalist, I thought I'd seen it all. I was in Vietnam. I was in Rwanda. I've witnessed some foul, vile acts of man against man. But this, this is just plain *evil*," Another pause, perhaps too long for radio, but he was the station's flagship jock and he could pause for as long as he wanted, and he knew it.

"Let's take a break," he said and a bouncy jingle for laundry detergent filled the airwaves.

I tried not to visualize the young girl holding her father's hand, antici-pating with delight the choice of which long silvery spear to buy, but I did. And I let myself imagine her young heart, trying to hold onto life, beating in defiance of the metallic intruder rammed into her by her own father. I felt sick and angry, again.

The jock returned. "There is more I could say about this case, but I can't because it's before the courts. What I will say is that I'd always opposed capital punishment, sometimes vehemently, but from now on, not any-more. No longer can I defend what I once considered a sacred right—the right to life. Now I say bring it on, let's embrace capital punishment for heinous crimes like this, crimes of unspeakable evil. The lines are now open and I'll take your calls."

Several callers agreed with his advocacy of capital punishment, adding that perhaps a prolonged execution involving real suffering might be in order. Some added that the execution should be televised, and some just cried without saying a word.

Then a man came on, sounding educated and calm, "Steve, I've led a reasonably good life and I've done all right. But you know, these privileges we enjoy, the privilege to live in a free society, which we now take for granted, and which was won through hard work and sacrifice. It seems we are not worthy of such a privilege, at least not right now. Maybe in the future, after we've matured a little more and understand what freedom really means, when we understand the social responsibility it requires of us all. But for now, we need to get serious and let private enterprise take care of it."

"What? You're suggesting corporatized policing? Corporatized vigilantism?"

"Call it what you like, but it's just simple supply and demand. If people demand a more ordered society, then the best way is for corporations to be founded to provide such a service."

"That's a dangerous path—"

"So was the path to defeating Hitler."

"But that was approved by the heads of several governments—"

"You're suggesting that politicians and public servants make better decisions?"

"No, of course not. In fact, if you listen to my show regularly you'll know I think the majority of them are fools, but the price of failure would be anarchy."

"And the price of doing nothing?"

"I'm uncomfortable with the concept, but appreciate your call."

A few callers considered the man's comments intriguing. Some even suggested they'd buy shares in such a company when it listed. The discussion inevitably turned to big brother societies and restricted personal freedoms. Perhaps that would be the price to pay to get beyond these problems, but was it too high? I suspect it would have been five or ten years ago, but maybe not now. I suspect now the collective conscious had started to turn, to focus on the next stage of societal evolution. Better still would be to predict evil before it manifests, and weed it out in advance. But was *evil* something that could be predicted? Or was this evil, this uncertainty in human behavior, the very thing that allows us to invent, imagine and progress? Could good and evil ever be separated? Does one need the other to survive, evolve? I suspect not, and it certainly didn't help Dr Jekyll.

I remembered 9/11, Bali and the numerous embassy and subway bombings around the World. But like most people, I filed away the horror and went on with life. What else could I do? But now, the violence, the evil, was in my face and repeatedly taunting me.

I arrived home, my head pounding and the pain in my chest making breathing difficult. I reapplied the bandages, tightening them good and proper, so that when the pain peaked, I passed out on the bathroom floor.

I woke a few hours later when it was dark and cold. My eyes and wounds pulsed with every beat of my heart, and the stranger staring back at me from the bathroom mirror was unrecognizable.

There were no messages, no calls from police, no newspaper reporters, in fact not a call from anyone—all somehow strangely disappointing.

I was struggling with breakfast when the phone rang. It was James Roberts inviting me to meet with him and Mark at St Georges.

James showed me around the facility, describing the progress they'd made with active stem cell cultures. The place was impressive and showed no lack of funding, with state-of the-art laboratories on the lower level and the upper level setup as a boutique ward, accommodating several patients in luxury. Although I noticed, the ward was currently empty.

We talked about possible procedures and treatments for Helen, which succeeded only in depressing me further as they all involved long periods of time. As the topic moved to a more technical level, I pushed James to describe the current state of the research, and quickly got the feeling they'd hit a roadblock of sorts. I offered my assistance, for what it was worth.

"Sure, perhaps a fresh pair of eyes may help. Let's have a talk with Mark," James suggested.

He led me to the elevator and we descended back down to the secure laboratory level. A dome-shaped retina identifier next to a large steel security door scanned James as he peered into the camera. The door hissed open and we entered a labyrinth. It reminded me of the human butchering station I'd seen in Colombo and a chill shot through me.

A tall man, late twenties and dressed in a crisp white coat, appeared from behind a bench and introduced himself as Warren, the lab technician. We followed him through a maze of stainless steel benches, instruments and computers to where I recognized Mark Woodcock hunched over a large stereo microscope.

To our left stood a two-by-two meter whiteboard, full of strange hieroglyphics, some of which were vaguely familiar to me from high school chemistry. The white coat handed to me, together with the ritual hand washing, made me look and feel 'medical'.

"Michael would like to offer a fresh mind, rather than one tainted with the baggage we bring," James said to Mark.

They smiled while I blushed.

"My knowledge of medical science and biology are really limited—" I insisted.

"That's OK. We've investigated your background a little, I hope you don't mind? It's standard procedure when someone makes a sizable donation." James said.

I felt inadequate, and apprehensive about where all this was heading.

"It seems you have a gift for thinking outside the box," James continued, while I imagined the scratches on my face glowing like a beacon. "And we would like to use you as a kind of springboard, if you don't mind."

I nodded.

"Are you familiar with the unique properties of stem cells?" Mark asked.

"No, not really."

"It's what's known as a biological clean slate, an undifferentiated cell found among differentiated cells within a tissue or organ. It can renew itself and change into any one of several specialized cell types, either tissue or organ. We're trying to determine the specific triggers which might promote cell plasticity, that is, the ability of adult stem cells from one tissue group to regenerate into cell types of another tissue group."

"And we've been stuck on that for quite some time," James added.

"I've heard the term, *embryonic stem cell* before, but I'm not sure exactly what that means."

"Mark, why don't you fill him in. I'll be back later."

"Sure. An embryonic stem cell is a stem cell derived from an embryo. It differs from an adult stem cell as far as it is *pluripotent*—that is, it can differentiate into any cell type, whereas adult stem cells are generally limited to differentiating into their tissue of origin, or so we thought. But we have seen adult stem cells regenerating into different cell types, after applying a trigger."

"And the problem?"

"Well, we haven't been able to apply this trigger consistently, or with any confidence. In fact we've been stuck on the question of what the trigger actually is for several months now."

"Do you have any idea of the *form* such a trigger might take?"

"Well, it could be an internal or external trigger, or a combination of both. Cell genes control the internal signals, specifically the DNA, which carries a multitude of codes, some of which we know but many we don't. However, we do feel the trigger is most likely external, from chemicals secreted by other cells, or by contact with neighboring cells and molecules. We don't quite know which, or it could be environmental."

In other words, almost everything was up for grabs.

"What have you observed so far?" I asked.

"Well, it's hard to say if it means anything or not, but we had a batch of cells in a culture medium, and the next day they had regenerated into different types of cells, but we have no idea why. It's never happened before and we haven't been able to reproduce it since."

Software routines started to execute in my head, branching off into familiar if-then-else statements. For me, problem solving was like a drug and once hooked, I was up for the whole ride.

"OK, let's start with the environment, since anything else is beyond me anyway. Show me the exact location, the complete setup as it was, any heat sources, temperature fluctuations, nearby electrical equipment, sources of contamination, vibration sources, everything."

Mark looked at me as if I'd suddenly grown another head, "But, we've been through a lot of that already—"

"That's fine, but can we do it again anyway? There's a reason for everything and I have a suspicion the answer lies in this room somewhere."

After an exciting start, the session at St Georges was long and unfruitful. I drove to the observatory annoyed and deflated. The sun was rising and the morning felt crisp. I decided to take a stroll around the grounds to clear my head.

The renovations were taking shape before I left for Colombo and it was clear the place would make a fine engineering lab and offer the seclusion I craved. Once inside, I sought out my loft room and turned on the computer. I scanned the internet for new and interesting pieces of equipment and a few hours later, I had ordered several items for a grand total of 1.2 million dollars. With the rest of the planned renovations, another two million would be drained from a rapidly depleting account and I'd be down to my last million.

I checked the account balance in case I never saw such numbers again and stared blankly at the screen. It read just over 18 million dollars, with the credit column including several more deposits from SatCOMM.

Should I call Cooper? Part of me wanted to distance myself, but I was inexplicably drawn to him.

"Brendan, it's Michael Crow. How are you?"

"Michael, good to hear from you. I'm doing all right, considering," he sounded flat.

"Your son is OK?"

"Yes, he's fine, thank you for your assistance. I'm very sorry to hear about Helen."

I wondered how much he knew about my life.

"Michael, you should come by tomorrow, there are a few things I would like to discuss with you. Would noon suit you?"

"Sure..." I answered with some trepidation.

I caught a few hours of sleep before driving to Prince Alfred hospital in the afternoon. I found Helen awake but not particularly bright, and kissed her on the cheek, noticing her eyes heavily swollen.

"Hi," she mouthed,

"How are you feeling?"

"Crippled..."

"Hey, you'll be OK. There's a great team of doctors here looking after you."

"Sure, but who's going to donate their ass to me?" Her voice strained.

"Look, Mark and James have been working on stem cell technology for years. They have facilities all over the world and the main one is right here in Sydney, and they've asked me to assist..."

"Michael, you know shit about medicine," Helen said, with renewed energy.

"It's bio-engineering, and I'll get the hang of the *bio* part."

She looked at me with complete hopelessness.

"Trust me," I pleaded. "Mark and I slaved away for hours yesterday on a huge whiteboard. We even fired up some hi-tech gear."

"Well, I feel better already."

"Are you hungry?" I stroked her hair.

"I am, for the first time in a while. Where are we going for dinner?" Her faint smile turned quickly downwards and the tears started again. I leaned into the bed and held her.

"What if I bring in some Italian food for you, and we can have a romantic dinner here?" I suggested.

"I don't think I'm supposed to."

"I'll ask Mark and surprise you. Maybe tomorrow, but now I need to head off to meet with Mark at St Georges."

I felt guilty for not staying with her, and it showed.

"Sure, you might as well go do some *bio*-engineering. I need to sleep anyway," she said and turned her head away from me.

At St Georges, I was surprised when the retina scan opened the lab door for me. I wondered if I might even get my name on a white coat. I found Mark and James seated, staring at the whiteboard, the contents of which had altered only slightly since my departure in the early hours of this morning.

I felt suddenly hungry and flipped open my cell phone to dial the local pizza place.

"Anyone else hungry?" I asked.

"Sure."

"Not for me, I'm heading off," from James. "And you shouldn't have that on in here." he pointed to the phone in my hand. "It won't work anyway, we're fully screened."

I put the cell phone in my pocket and dialed the restaurant from the lab's landline.

"Where to now?" I asked Mark, who was deep in thought.

"I'm not sure. We've been tossing around the possibility of using time-lapse microscope photography on the stem cell cultures, in the hope of capturing the actual process of regeneration. If we get lucky there, then we can work backward to find specific triggers."

"I've been thinking. Do you know what the process of regeneration actually looks like? I mean, have you *seen* it. How long does it take and how do know when the process has started, in case you miss it?"

"No, we don't know. But we do know roughly what it *should* look like. We have several samples of stem cells in differing states of change."

"Can I see them?"

He led me through another environmentally sealed door to the back lab, where he picked out a culture dish from the conditioning chamber. He placed the dish under the microscope and the image of cells appeared in magnified form on the large plasma screen overhead. Mark looked a little confused as he studied the image.

"These should be HSCs, but some are not..." he paused and re-checked the descriptor on the side of the dish, before checking several other dishes.

"HSCs?"

"Yes, hematopoietic stem cells."

"Hematopoietic?" I sounded like a parrot mimicking his words.

"They're found in all types of blood cells and organs within the body. The most common type of stem cell in fact," he said, but still distracted about something.

"What about the others?"

"Well, several seem to be nerve stem cells, but they must have been regenerated from the base HSC cells."

"Did you apply any triggers?"

"Well no, that's the mystery."

"When did you last check this dish?"

"They were marked by Warren, after he'd performed some tests yesterday. But there's something else..."

"What?"

"The cell division rate is several times higher than it should be."

Over the phone, Warren confirmed the culture should indeed be HSCs and that he was on his way in.

"How do you know they have regenerated? Is there a test to show that these started as HSCs?" I asked.

"If there were only HSC cells in the dish, then the nerve cells had to have regenerated from them."

Mark turned up the magnification on the scope until only a few individual cells covered the entire two-meter screen.

"Look," he pointed to the central structures of the cell and turned on the hard disc recorder. "The HSCs are dividing into HSCs, and the nerve cells are dividing into nerve cells. The regenerative process itself has either been suspended or is no longer active."

After a few moments of intense observation, Mark suddenly shouted, "There!"

I squinted, as he pointed to a particular cell dividing. Other cells were dividing as well, but he seemed particularly excited by this one cell.

"It looks the same as all the others to me..."

"No," he said, magnifying the image even further. "This one is regenerating from a HSC to a nerve cell," he pointed to the diagnostic on the computer screen.

I watched as the cell completed its microscopic change. A change that appeared negligible to me, but to Mark it was as though a completely new universe had opened up before him. He even failed to notice Warren rushing into the lab.

"When did this process start?" Warren observed the screen intently.

"I'm not sure. I'll need to count division rates, observe the change process a little more, and work back a time line. I'd say we're in for a long night." Mark sounded excited and cautious at the same time.

Warren brought out several more cultures of HSCs as we tried to figure out possible trigger mechanisms. We tested, discussed and eliminated possibilities while eating pizza, but still managed to shed little light on the actual trigger mechanism.

In the early hours of the morning, we all agreed sleep was the best option.

I felt in my pockets for my car keys and phone, the two essential items of modern life. My cell phone had several messages logged and was on silent mode, rather than switched off.

"Hey, guys," I held the cell phone up. "It's been on the whole time, right next to the cell cultures."

Mark and Warren stopped cleaning and looked up. Slowly the possibility dawned on their faces.

"What's the nature of the radiation from those things?" Mark asked.

"Microwave frequency, at one milliwatt per square centimeter," I replied, perhaps a little too succinctly. "Let's put another culture under the scope and test it with the phone."

"Shouldn't we consider a more structured approach?" Mark suggested.

"You've got plenty of stem cells, right?"

"Well, yes—"

"Then how would structure help us? Why not try to recreate the process right now."

Warren brought out a new dish of HSCs and placed it under the scope. I put the cell phone in the same relative position as before, and we watched and waited.

An hour passed without any change to the cells and the battery charge on the phone had drained to one quarter.

"Is there anything different about these cells?" I asked.

"No," Mark reassured.

"Then let's wait another hour." They seemed to have given me the lead, so I continued to take it. "Are you recording this?"

"Yes," Warren answered, but rechecked the record status anyway.

We stared at the plasma screen and watched the movement of the individual cells as they divided.

"Incredible," Mark whispered.

I looked to the other two for understanding, as to me, the cells seemed to be doing much the same thing as they had been for the last two hours. "I don't understand..."

"Look closer, these HSC cells are dividing into *nerve* cells." Mark checked the cells with the computer diagnostic and confirmed the regeneration.

"I've never seen the actual process in real time before." Warren said, excited too, and neither of them daring to blink.

"There are three separate effects here," Mark explained. "The rate of HSC cell division, the regeneration and the rate of nerve cell division."

"And all that from a single trigger?" I asked.

"Perhaps, but there could be other triggers hidden behind the phone's radiation."

"I think I know of a piece of equipment that might help us. Can I have it delivered here? I'll need some lab space and a bunch of stem cells to experiment with." I asked, with growing elation.

"Sure," Mark said, without taking his eyes off the screen and not asking what I had in mind, which was just as well as I wasn't too sure anyway.

The lobby of the SatCOMM building housed a neck straining five-storey atrium—certainly an impressive waste of space if nothing else. I took the high-rise elevator to the fortieth floor and noticed the four higher levels all required key access. As the doors opened, a pleasant looking well dressed woman greeted me.

"Mr Crow, we're expecting you. Please come this way."

We entered a large room with a panoramic view of the city on one side and a huge video screen on the other. The woman ushered me to one of several plush chairs in front of the screen.

"Mr Cooper has asked that you take a few moments to view a presentation. Can I offer you some tea, coffee, water?"

"Strong black coffee would be great, thanks."

I was pleased when the lights dimmed and the blinds rolled down, so I could take off my sunglasses without squinting in pain. With no sleep last night, this meeting would be particularly challenging.

What followed on screen was a comprehensive summary of the worldwide activities of SatCOMM Corporation, and twenty minutes later, I was convinced the firm would take over the world. But why had this privilege been bestowed upon me?

Cooper entered, the blinds rolled up and a barrage of sunlight poured in. I was tempted to put on the sunglasses again, but decided to put up with the pain.

"Michael, it's good to see you," Cooper's smile appeared genuine enough. "I'm very sorry about the incident in Colombo and your girlfriend...It's dreadful, these animals are taking over the world. How is she?"

"She's regaining her strength in preparation for a series of surgeries. We're fortunate to have some talented people caring for her."

"Where there's life there's hope, right?"

"Right," I said, as the memory of his recent tragedies slapped me. "And how have you been?"

"It's been difficult. You know Michael the world is changing, evolving. And I fear the transition to the new world may be painful for many."

"The new world?"

"Well, yes a world that is truly *civilized*. Anarchy is hardly conducive to progress, and I, like others, feel it may be time for those who have something to contribute to this process of change, to step up."

I hoped he might continue and that this might all make some sense.

"Michael, you seem to have an energy, a focus, a...talent that's unique."

I wanted to laugh, but stopped myself before any sound escaped. I felt my headache getting worse as Cooper's face showed an intensity I'd seen before. I braced myself for what was sure to come.

"I have many rich, powerful and influential, friends. Many have suffered loss, personal loss, as you and I have. And what we all have in common is not just a desire for revenge, but for a more permanent shift in the status quo," he watched for my reaction, but a blank expression came easily to me.

"Michael, we want to rid society of criminals, completely and finally. I believe you can contribute to that, and I can provide you with whatever resources you may need."

It took me a couple of seconds to realize that I had no response to what he was saying.

"You need not say anything right away. Just think about it, and think about what you may *need*."

"Brendan, I think the pain killers are getting the better of you. I'm just an engineer."

"Exactly, just do what you do best."

"I am, and right now that's working with the doctors to put Helen back together."

"I understand, and I would do the same for my family if I could."

Another slap. Was it intentional?

"Brendan, about the money."

"Don't give it another thought, it's yours. I have plenty. Use it wisely."

An uneasy silence followed, and I considered leaving.

"Michael, have you been following the news?"

"Yes, now and then..."

"The man who killed his wife and daughter in the vilest manner..."

"Yes," my throat became dry and any possibility of standing quickly evaporated.

"Apparently this animal is currently residing at Longbay Prison," he prodded as I waited for the crunch line. "This animal has caused a good friend of mine to suffer more than any man should. In fact he may never recover from the loss of his daughter and granddaughter."

We locked stares for several seconds before I searched the floor for a way out.

"My friend has made a generous contribution toward our quest," he added, pointedly.

Sure, hell, and why not take out the rest of the riff raff at Longbay for good measure. Was this guy for real? Was there any point in continuing this? Was there any way out? I made an attempt.

"Brendan, I should be getting back to other things, Helen—"

"Do you believe in chance, Michael? That things will somehow *work themselves out*?"

"No, not really."

"Nor do I. I believe in clarity of thought, in planning, in action rather than reaction, and in leaving as little as possible to chance by bringing order to disorder."

"Then perhaps a military career might still be an option for you..." I braced.

"Michael, for good to win over evil, good needs to be smarter."

A catchy phrase and I wondered if he'd read my mind recently. I summoned every ounce of energy just to stand up.

"You and I are the same in many ways," he shook my hand vigorously, holding me captive.

I finally exited through the lobby feeling a clammy wetness under my shirt. What chilled me most about the interaction was that his words echoed my own thoughts. But verbalized like that, they sounded more like the ranting of a lunatic.

As I drove, I replayed the conversation in my mind and laughed, nervously.

I arrived home and examined the progress of the observatory works through the internet cameras. I rang the contractor to discuss the additions, careful not to let on I was watching the whole time—there'd most likely be some union rule forbidding that. I rang several suppliers to discuss the specialized waveform generator I had in mind for St Georges.

"It would need to be custom made," one engineer told me, "and may take several weeks to assemble, with a price tag upwards of four hundred thousand dollars."

"I'll email you a detailed specification today, tell me you can deliver it within five days and I'll add twenty percent."

"Er...sure, I think we can work with that."

They say money talks, but a lot of money shouts and screams, and I started to like the sound. Should I return Cooper's money? Perhaps not today.

As I started work on the analyzer specification, I noticed a few emails I hadn't read highlighted in bold text. Most were from friends and family letting us know they were thinking of Helen, but one was from an unfamiliar source.

Even with the most sophisticated virus shields, I still had an aversion to unsolicited mail, but it scanned clean, so I opened it. A series of automated slideshows scrolled across the screen, with police captions and codes. There were several images of a man holding the hand of a young girl in a sporting goods store. The young girl is watching him, smiling. I punched the escape key to terminate what I knew would come next, but it was too late. There she lay amidst the garbage, a metal spear through her chest, bruised and grey in death. A pink doll lay next to her, with blond hair just like the child. And the doll was lifeless, just like the child. I thought of Nicole as I stared into her sad, open eyes. Had she realized before she died that her father was a monster, and that she had come from evil?

I ran to the bathroom and slumped next to the toilet bowl into which I deposited the meager contents of an empty stomach. For someone who didn't believe in divine destiny this was sounding more and more like a prophecy from hell. What should I do now, crank up the death bus and hit the streets again with microwaves blazing? The risk was too great and I wasn't really a street fightin' kind of guy—that much I'd learned about myself.

I dragged myself up off the floor, filled a glass with water and returned to the computer. The screen displayed a final image—a beady-eyed nobody, a mousy little man with oily, stringy hair with soulless eyes. His only reason for existing was to unleash the evil he harbored. I tried to comprehend, but couldn't even get close. I picked up the phone and dialed.

"Brendan, does SatCOMM have a cell phone tower within a kilometer or so of Longbay Prison, and with a clear line of sight?"

"It's not something I memorize Michael, we have several hundred towers around the country."

"If not, then perhaps you should. Even prisoners deserve good coverage. And it may provide an opportunity to do some field testing, of new technologies..."

He deciphered the meaning.

"I'll look into it and let you know." He replied.

CHAPTER 17

I rang Lou Miles, who had been my chief electronics engineer at Vibrolert for several years. Lou was a short balding man in his late thirties. We spent many hours pondering over technical problems and saw the sunrise through bloodshot eyes on many occasions. Lou enjoyed researching and inventing, more so than he enjoyed people and the world outside. For those like us, the lab was a cocoon, a safe haven of infinite possibilities, hypnotic in its promise of unraveling the unknown. And once hooked, nothing else could compete, at least not for long.

For Lou, his talent and dedication gave rise to success more times than not, and I knew I could trust him. But developing these technologies was a tall order, and one I needed to be guarded about, even with those I trusted.

"Lou, how's Vibrolert doing?"

"It's doing OK, but less than enjoyable of late. You know how it is—timesheets, justifications, proposals, meetings..."

"Have I been missed?"

"Certainly not by Geoff, he's changed the place already."

"You think you're ready for some new action?"

"I didn't think it would take you long, but this is quick even for you."

"I have some development work for you if you're interested. It's in the communications field—long range microwave stuff."

"Sounds nice, but what about the non-competitive clause I signed?"

"I don't see a conflict. When can you extract yourself from Vibrolert?"

"I guess I'll need to give a month's notice..."

"They'll pump you for information then pay you out on the same day. Geoff will be expecting some kind of exodus after me."

"Michael, is this a long term thing?"

"What about 400k for the next six months and then, well, who knows—"

"OK, that's long term enough."

"There's a downside though. My facility is on the south coast. In fact, it's a renovated observatory perched high up on a cliff face overlooking the Pacific Ocean. You could stay in one of the lofts there or rent a beach shack nearby."

"That's a downside?"

"I also need you to source some good technicians and engineers, guys you can really trust—no egos, no solo artists, discrete, trustworthy, you know the type. And by the way, there's a hell of a pizza shop in the local village."

"Now you're talking."

Helen was watching TV, her eyes blazed red and angry.

"Hey, what's wrong?" I asked.

"It's the news. The murderous pig who killed his wife and daughter," she pointed to news footage of a mousy middle-aged man, trying to cover his mousy face with a newspaper, while being led from the courthouse steps.

"I know," I turned it off.

"How can anyone—"

"Try not to think about it. Have you had anything to eat? Are you hungry?"

"I'm fasting. I have a surgical procedure tomorrow morning with Dr Woodcock."

"That soon? When did he talk to you about that?"

"Earlier today, he said it was just a simple biopsy."

"Did he say how long it would take?"

"An hour or so. Michael you look worn-out, and more so every time I see you. Are you eating properly, sleeping?"

"I've pretty much given up on sleep, but I think I ate earlier today."

We talked while I picked at a hospital dinner. She wasn't surprised when I left a half hour later to return to St Georges. I assured her I would be back soon.

When I entered the lab, I overhead James and Mark discussing Colombo and it sounded like James was going to return there next week. They saw me and stopped. James left and I asked Mark about Helen's procedure.

"Couldn't she be treated here, rather than at Prince Alfred?"

"This is a research centre, Michael. We're hardly equipped for general care, much less intensive care," Mark answered quickly.

"Sure, but she seems much better to me, and hardly requiring intensive care I would have thought."

"Michael, don't let that white coat get to your head."

"But you do need patients to help test your research?"

"Yes, from time to time." he seemed hesitant.

"But I don't see any patients here?"

"No, not so much here."

"Where, Colombo?"

He glared at me, "Yes, occasionally."

"The government there is OK with that? Experimentation?"

"It's not *experimentation*." His face turned red.

"I'd be happy to make another donation..." I said, backing off.

"We'll discuss it later. How's the instrument procurement going?" Mark asked, changing the subject.

"I hope to have it delivered here next week."

"Off the shelf?"

"Not exactly. But with the mods I have in mind, it should help find the exact fingerprint of that illusive trigger."

"Just like that?" Mark raised an eyebrow.

"Well, it might take the better part of the day..." I taunted.

We postulated theories for cell trigger mechanisms for an hour before a wave of exhaustion swept over me. It was close to midnight and I needed to be with Helen as she prepared for her procedure in the morning.

I made my way to the hospital, parked in the basement and caught a few hours of sleep in the car.

I watched Helen wake. She looked peaceful for the first time in a long while and I held her hand as the nurse went through the pre-op's.

The afternoon was warm and sunny as I drove to the observatory. I thought about the various people I'd come across recently, and neutralized. Surely, someone somewhere must be investigating the mysterious

afflictions that had sprung up around town. The lack of news or any obvious police investigation made me nervous, implying perhaps a secret task
force of some magnitude. Were they watching me now? Were they monitoring my communications?

I pulled over to the side of the road and pressed a button for the roof
of the Saab to slide back. I scanned the sky for helicopters and peered into
the bush at the side of the road for black surveillance vans. I thought about
how paranoia could easy get out of hand and would not Cooper with all his
resources know whether someone was watching me, us? After all, he was
just as involved.

I called him.

"Brendan can you tell me if this cell phone is secure?"

"Yes Michael, we taken the liberty of shifting you onto one of our
more secure frequencies—the benefits of being a SatCOMM blue-chip
subscriber."

Did that mean he could also listen to my calls whenever he liked? I
needed a backup cell phone, just in case.

"I've been thinking about Detective Trobe—I haven't heard from him
lately..."

"Well, Mr Trobe now runs global security for us, here at SatCOMM."

I was stunned. "And the investigations he'd been conducting?"

"I think they caught all the real criminals in that case...didn't they?"

More intrigue from the corporate man of mystery. Did I trust him?
Did I trust anyone? Was hiring Trobe symbolic of Cooper 'buying' law and
order? Was he making a statement? Who knows? Was it possible for law
enforcement to ignore vigilantism? Perhaps it was.

I continued along the coast road, paying less attention to the skies,
when Lou rang. "I've just resigned and Geoff is on the phone with Robert
now."

"Good. Do you know of any hotshot internet guys, the type who can
break into anything and are trustworthy?"

"They call that an oxymoron don't they? I do know one or two who
dabble, but you know these guys tend to do well enough on their own—
dedicated career soloists."

"Yeah I know, anyway see if you can find someone suitable. There's no
need for a long-term commitment, just a couple of months accessing information stored in various databases around the world."

"I'll see what I can do..."

I drove up the observatory driveway and parked on the gravel next to the dome entrance. I spent the rest of the day working on specifications and software, as well as searching through reams of technical data and information on the net.

I scanned the internet webcasts and found reports from Colombo. Apparently, two of the hijackers had been caught, but their fate and any progress on finding the others was all a bit ambiguous. Samuel Edwards was still in the terrorist's lair, minus an ear. I got the feeling not much was going to happen with any of these men and soon they would be free to plot more acts of terror. I searched the 'Moctas' name I remembered from the cesspit in Colombo, but found no hits.

In the evening, I rang the hospital and spoke with the nurse. She told me Helen's procedure went well and she was now sleeping. I continued working before falling asleep on a pullout bed in my loft.

I woke the next day to the sound of construction vehicles arriving, lots of shouting and banging. The place was crawling with contractors, like worker ants tending a bloated queen. Throughout the day, the ants kept me busy answering their various questions and I couldn't blame them since I kept changing the layout and finishing details.

I sent a text to Lou asking him to come straight to the observatory for our meeting. I was intentionally unclear about the task I had for him and he didn't insist on knowing too much. He knew me well enough to just trust.

After a quick tour of the place, Lou and I started work in the afternoon and continued through night and into the early morning. Neither of us liked to waste time. We were the all-nighters, the junk-food-on-the-keyboard type. We operated on absurdly short timeframes, in contrast to the competition—the multinationals, who were over-burdened with too many chiefs, too many planners and not enough doers. Some of these monolithic giants would inevitably trip over and disappear from the corporate landscape, too egocentric to see the threats coming. This was the capitalist jungle, where I loved to steal beneath the foliage and bite at the heels of giants.

I looked at the time—3.20 am.

"Lou, there are several lofts upstairs, with pull-out beds—just pick one."

"A productive session you think?"

"Yes, but I need to get back home tonight. I have a few things to attend to tomorrow. You're OK to continue here on your own?"

"Sure."

The Saab roof was still open and a mind-numbing wind blasted me, just cold enough to subdue the thought of what I might be doing a year from now. I arrived home just before sunrise and slept for two fitful hours, feeling even worse when I awoke.

For the next few days, my routine was pretty much the same, alternating between Prince Alfred, St Georges and the observatory. Lou was making a valuable contribution to the research and enjoying it. It was slow progress, a frustrating but familiar grind.

The contractors' at the observatory were working double shifts and the place quickly started to resemble the NASA facility I had in mind. Several supercomputers, each with sixteen cores, linked to form a processing powerhouse. Within the dome complex, I designated areas for electronic design, mechanical engineering and software services. The terrace level above the dome ran along the entire circumference, and was fitted with five private lofts and three glass walled meeting rooms. People could work and sleep here, day and night.

The residential wing would join to the main dome by a large glass canopy, which also housed a tropical garden and pool. This would help get rid of another million or so dollars, which was just as well, as I was finding large bank balances made me nervous.

I caught up with Lou and his rapidly expanding team of technicians working on the miniaturization of the waveguide and the variable frequency transmitters. If successful, it would mean less power drain, smaller hardware and the ability to experiment with different wavelengths of microwave energy, and in real time. The guys were excited to be at the forefront of communications technology—and other frontiers they didn't quite understand yet.

The work of our new cyber snoop, Alan Rae, was a little more esoteric. Alan, a tall, lean, thirty-one year old, who didn't notice grunge was last century, still broke out in pimples from too much junk food and was completely absorbed in his own cyber world. This new breed of virtual human had just enough personality to function in the real world, although I suspect he only ventured there when he absolutely had to. Lou had known Alan for several years, having met at a sci-fi convention, and they still got together for the ritual Trekkie nights. He was 'safe', Lou said, and he knew the internet as if he'd invented it.

"Alan, how's progress?" I asked.

"I've managed to sneak into several law enforcement databases and downloaded around twenty thousand records before coming across some serious encryption. I'm changing tack and prodding at the edges of the government network now."

"OK, but be careful not to leave your cyber-prints behind, especially when you're sniffing around the federal system."

"I'm a ghost."

"I believe it."

I didn't tell him why I wanted this information, because I couldn't think of any plausible lie. Nevertheless, the 200k fee should be payment enough for his discretion.

My cell phone rang.

"Michael, your equipment has been delivered," Mark stated abruptly.

"The supplier's technicians will install and pre-test. I'll be there in an hour or so. How's Helen?"

"She's doing well. She says she'd like to see you some time..."

"It would be easier if you could treat her at St Georges."

"It's against my better judgment, but she seems to be healing well. I'll have a room made ready for her."

Perhaps my latest donation helped after all.

On the drive to St Georges, Alison rang. She said Nicole should spend more time with me, which was a nice change as she often put obstacles in the way of my access. The way she said it however, made me wonder about her relationship with Nicole.

Alison had had a string of failed affairs after we split up, all short-term and all morons as far as I could tell. She was reasonably attractive and only slightly unstable—most likely from the drug habit she acquired in the final year of our relationship. I didn't see it coming, but then again I wasn't really looking. I'd been totally absorbed in keeping Vibrolert afloat and spent less than an hour a day with her. Perhaps she was lonely and drifted into drugs. Perhaps it was my fault. In any case, I should meet this latest installment, since my daughter would be spending more time with him than with me.

I joined the supplier's technicians who were busy commissioning the waveform analyzer and ordered enough pizzas to keep us all focused for the next few hours. I found from experience that this rich form of carbohydrates was excellent brain food.

Mark was unsure about all this hardware, where it would live and how it would work, but he shared in the excitement of the technology. Especially as it smelt so new and looked so sleek.

"Have you heard from James?" I asked, thinking he would be in Colombo by now. Just the thought of the place left me cold.

"No, not yet, but he would have arrived there a few hours ago."

I splashed water on my face to freshen up for the drive to Prince Alfred. All this time wasting commuting was getting to me.

The silent hum of instruments and subdued lighting in Helen's room provided an enticing calm and isolation from the rest of the world.

She turned her head in my direction. "Hi, stranger," she whispered and smiled.

"Has it been that long?"

"Yes, it has. What have you been up to?"

"Just working my butt off," I cringed at the word that escaped all too quickly, but she didn't seem to care. Was her good mood due to painkillers?

"Working at what exactly?" She asked.

"Um...I'm developing some new technologies..."

"What new technologies?"

"Just an idea I had. You know they come to me from time to time."

"You're working from home?"

"More or less."

"Alone?"

"Mostly. How did your procedure go?" I said, hoping to change the subject.

"Dr Woodcock seemed pleased with the biopsy results, and the healing of the wound," a depressed look crossed her face. "He suggested we start with simple exercises."

"But that's good, isn't it?"

"Michael, this is going to take forever..."

I leaned over the bed and held her. "It seems you're being transferred to St Georges?" I smiled.

"Yes, but as nice as I'm sure it is...it's still a hospital."

She paused and looked unsure about something, "Michael, we need to discuss a few things."

"Sure…"

"You really are clueless at times, aren't you?"

I gave my best clueless look.

"When I go home, and I hope to one day, am I going to my place or—"

"Yes *my* place. I'll set up for you there. Everything you need, even a live-in nurse if you want."

"Sorry to interrupt you both. Michael, can I see you for a minute?" Mark looked more serious than usual and he retreated to the hallway before I could answer.

"Mark, hold on. What's up?" I had to run to catch up with his stride along the corridor.

"You need to see this…"

I entered his office and saw him pointing at the computer screen, the Stem Corp website—the organization James and Michael operated. A message posted on the bulletin board read, *'We are an operative arm of the Al Assirat and James Roberts is to be tried for crimes against our people.'*

An image showed James holding what looked like an Indian newspaper, with yesterday's date.

CHAPTER 18

I was hoping to regain my appetite in time to enjoy the breakfast I'd prepared, but had no such luck, and just picked and prodded at the edges of a fried egg.

I decided to call Cooper.

"What assets do you have in places like India, Sri Lanka, and Pakistan?" I asked, too abruptly.

"None at the moment, but we plan to offer our new generation of satellite phone services throughout the Middle East, Africa and India. Why do you ask?"

"I have a colleague in Colombo, who may have been kidnapped by terrorists."

"When did this happen?"

"In the last twenty-four hours."

"What's his name?"

"James Roberts."

A long pause.

"Then you should contact Interpol." He suggested.

"His people have alerted the authorities, but it seems with extremism like this there's not much they can do."

"Yes, extremism seems to be a global epidemic."

"What do you mean?"

"Well, it's not public knowledge yet, in fact little more than isolated reports and speculation, but several countries are supporting each other in an effort to rationalize large chunks of the Middle East, Asia and Africa. Superstates are rising out of the third world dust to replace the web of failed authoritarian regimes."

I gripped the phone. *"Rationalize?"*

"Yes. Egypt is annexing Libya, Niger will take over Chad. Saudi will control eastern Africa and South Africa will acquire Namibia, Botswana, Zimbabwe, Angola, Zambia and Mozambique. There are even rumors that several West African countries have invited France to 're-colonize' them."

"Just like that?"

"More or less? It's a brokered deal courtesy of the NWO."

"NWO?"

"The New World Order."

"Right...And what's the American and British position on all this?"

"Well they are part of the process, a silent partner, you could say. The deal is simply that the new super-states would be democratic, that they would be humanitarian, and they would strive to eradicate extremism and terrorism in all its forms. Stable government means better management of natural resources, including oil, methane and uranium. This puts downward pressure on energy prices and improves the economic outlook for all. It's much like a corporate takeover—if it isn't performing, buy it, reorganize, re-manage, jettison the liabilities and turn a profit."

"Buy entire countries?

"Sure, and why not? Through decades of mismanagement, many continue to accumulate more debt than assets. They don't have any real revenue streams and most will never be able to pay their interest bills. In other words, they're ripe for a takeover."

"And who have you got your eye on?" I asked, throwing caution to the wind.

"No, it's not for me. I think the whole concept is doomed to failure. Countries belong to the people who have inhabited them for generations. They'll be a lot of discontent and violence. It's not a sound investment by my measure. I'm happy just to trade with them and let them fight amongst themselves."

My mind flashed to the independence wars in Croatia, Bosnia and Herzegovina, where men turned into killing machines almost overnight in a frenzy of ethnic cleansing. Then, just as quickly, the same men returned to their roles as loving, caring husbands and sons, attending church as though nothing had happened. Like some incongruous switch of evil had flicked on, and then just as quickly off again.

"Do you have any ideas, Michael?"

"Prayer?" I suggested.

"Nothing more tangible?"

Where was he heading with all this?

"I'm not sure what you think I can offer...but I would appreciate any advice on how to extract James Roberts..." I tried to change the subject.

My cell phone beeped with a call waiting. Cooper said he would look into Robert's case. I thanked him and switched to the incoming call.

"Dad, can you come and take me to school today?" Nicole's fragile voice replaced Cooper's drone.

"Is everything all right?"

"Yep. Pleeease..."

"OK."

I wondered what could be wrong, but needed to make some phone calls before picking up Nicole.

"Lou, how far away is a finished prototype laser?"

"About a week."

"We need to demonstrate it in three days, and there are a few features I'd like to add."

Lou was silent while I ran through a list of items.

"I'll need another three techs to help with the workload," he concluded.

"Sure, hire as many as you need."

I rang Cooper again.

"You mentioned a new generation of satellite phones..."

"Yes, the SatFone. Small, compact, hi-def visual and broadband comms direct to orbiting satellites. No drop outs through bad weather and completely secure. We have several satellites in construction right now."

"How do you plan to launch these satellites and when?"

"The Chinese are offering attractive rates for delivery. We expect to send the first to China within the next few weeks for launching."

"I've got some bits I'd like to add to it. Can you have one delivered to my facility, along with an engineer, someone who knows the thing inside out?"

He considered the request before replying. "To where, Michael? These things are large and heavy, not to mention expensive. What if you drop it? What facility do you have?"

"It's a large workshop—"

"I'd like to see it first."

It was against my better judgment, but I invited him to visit the observatory.

I arrived at Alison's house and found Nicole sitting on the brick fence out front. She appeared upset.

"Hey Nic, what's up?"

"Nothing. I just wanted to see you."

Something was wrong, but it could be anything from not getting her favorite toast spread to—

"Wait in the car. I'll let your mother know I'm taking you to school."

"She's not home, only Bill is there."

I knocked on Alison's door and waited. I heard slow heavy footsteps, and then the door opened to reveal a large disheveled man with snake-like tattoos down the length of both arms.

"Can I help you?" he mumbled.

"I'm Nicole's father."

"Alison's not here."

"Where is she?"

"Out."

"Nicole called me to take her to school."

"OK," he looked to Nicole seated in my car, then back at me, displeased.

"She was sitting in the street, upset." I said.

He simply starred at me as if I were a bug in his face.

"I'll take her to school." I said and turned to leave. The door slammed shut behind me.

Seated in the car, I gripped the steering wheel until my knuckles turned white.

"Nic, is this Bill guy treating you well?"

"I don't like him."

"Has he said or done anything to make you not like him?"

"No."

"Then what makes you say that?"

"He doesn't like me."

"He might be shy," or just plain stupid.

"He shouts at Mum."

"Does he shout at you?"

"Sometimes, but Mum shouts at me too."

"Look, don't worry about it. I'll talk to your mother later."

I parked in the school grounds and walked her to the classroom, before ringing Alison on her cell.

"I just took Nicole to school." I blurted.

"Why?"

"Because she rang and asked me to."

"Why would she do that?"

"She was upset, and I'm her father."

"Well that's interesting, and how many times have you taken her to school before?"

"If she lived with me, then perhaps I would more often. And who is the Neanderthal living at your house?" She had a knack of turning me tactless in quick time.

"Neanderthal?"

"That's a large hairy ape-like creature with limited brain function. Why do you let him shout at Nicole?"

"It's no wonder you can't get along with anyone, your communication skills suck."

"I do just fine. Is he living with you?"

"That's your business?"

"Nicole is my business."

"All of a sudden?"

"No, all of the time."

"I don't want to do this now."

"How long have you known this guy? And how do you know she is safe with him?"

"Do I ask that about your friend?"

"No, but she's not a guy."

"I see, so guys are more dangerous and untrustworthy?"

"You know what I mean."

"I'll talk to Nicole about it," she terminated the call.

What now? Should I take Nicole home and start a protracted custody battle? Alison wasn't really unfit to be a mother and the best I could expect would be equal time. Nicole would still be with them three or four nights a week, and it's not as if I had a lot of spare time for child rearing right now.

I drove back to Alison's house, noted the registration number on the car in the driveway and rang John Trobe.

"Mr Crow, it's been a while. How are you?"

"Good. I hear you're working for Mr Cooper now."

"Yes, indeed. How can I help?" I imagined a wry smile on his face.

"I need access to police records, prison records and anything else that the police use to track and identify people. I have people working on it, but we could use some inside knowledge. I was wondering if you could assist." Was that to the point enough?

"Sure Michael, but I'm not sure how much I can really contribute."

"Cooper is visiting my observatory this afternoon. I know it's short notice, but could you to join us there?"

"Let me clear it with the boss first."

That was almost too friendly. Was I mad? It was like a turkey inviting two wolves to supper. But, I needed their help, I needed Cooper's satellites and I needed Trobe's access to information. And, it would give me a chance to observe Trobe and Cooper together.

My phone rang.

"Michael, I've just received another email from the people who say they have James. This one reads, *James Roberts has been found guilty of crimes to humanity and has been sentenced to death.*" Mark sounded frantic.

I pictured James in some desert shit-hole, on his knees and with a gun to his head.

"What the hell do they mean by *crimes against humanity?*"

"Mark, I don't know. I'm trying to think of ways to help—"

"Do you think they're after money or a prisoner trade of some sort? Sometimes they cloak their real intent under the guise of religion or politics."

"I don't know. Does he have anything to do with the body part factory in Colombo?"

A silent pause.

"Michael, what the hell are you talking about?"

"Behind the Dutch cemetery, there's a field of body parts. I've seen it. You don't know about it?"

"God, no. Are you mad?"

"And behind that there's a tunnel that leads to a morgue..."

"Michael, I don't know what you think you saw. Perhaps the morphine had induced some sort of hallucination, but this is real and James is in serious trouble."

"OK, send me the emails."

I almost believed he knew nothing of what I saw. Perhaps only James was involved. Was that why they took him?

I stopped at a cafe and poured several caffeine drinks down my throat before arriving at the observatory just after noon. Alan pulled up the emails Mark had sent, and looked more excited than worried as he read. Perhaps he thought of himself as an international spy, or at least a virtual one.

"Can you trace them?" I asked.

"To a degree, but I may need to send in a Trojan to extract additional information about the origin of the email."

"Can that be detected?"

"It depends on how aggressive their virus scanning is. What would your reply be?"

I wrote down a response. *We would like to negotiate. Please specify an amount and an account number.*

I felt a rumble through the floor and ran down the stairs to the dome level. Once outside, I saw Cooper and Trobe emerge from a helicopter amidst the swirl of dust and rotor blades.

"I see you've found the place," I shouted to Cooper over the noise.

He strode forward without hunching over, as though the blades wouldn't dare touch him. "It's hard to miss," he said.

"John, good to see you again," my measured welcome met with a faint smile. I resisted the urge to ask him about the night he found me holding a limp micro-waved chicken on my front porch.

I showed them around, briefly explaining activities and equipment, as far as I felt appropriate. A half hour later, we sat in the meeting room on the terrace level, the glass wall providing an impressive view over the entire dome space.

Cooper started. "A satellite will be delivered here next week."

I guess that meant he approved of my facility.

"And the other satellites?" I asked.

"The schedule will be quick, weeks rather than months. Once the authorities approve the first, we'll confirm the rest. We hope to dispatch two a week."

"What's involved with the approvals process?"

"We need to meet strict guidelines on the size and composition, everything from electromagnetic emissions to function and instrumentation."

"I see, and has the prototype been approved?"

"Yes."

Cooper and I gauged each other. "I'm sure any slight modifications you may have in mind Michael would most likely go unnoticed, assuming appropriate measures are taken,"

Did he control everything and everyone?

"Who is manufacturing the SatFones for you?"

"We've subcontracted a Chinese firm."

"Could I have a few prototype handsets and a set of schematics?"

Cooper considered me for moment. He knew, and I knew, that he could swat me like a bug if I crossed him. He nodded in agreement.

"In regard to the Longbay cell tower. We had a slight issue with the local town planning authority. It's being built eight kilometers from Longbay Prison." Cooper stated blandly.

"Eight!"

"Is that a problem?"

"No, I guess we can work with that. John, how much do you know about law enforcement computer systems—database structures, access, encryption, that kind of thing?"

"I know how to access it, its limitations, but not the detail. There is an IT guy who left the force a few months ago. He knew the system inside out, and I think he's contracting privately now."

"Do you have his number?"

"As a matter of fact I do."

"Can we call him?"

"Sure," he hesitated. "Now?"

Cooper nodded and Trobe made the call.

"With all this," Cooper said, waving his hand. "You're going to need regular and sizable cash injections."

"Yes, I suppose so—"

"My friends and I have an interest in your work here. We would be pleased to assist in fund raising, if you are agreeable."

"I don't know what—"

"Michael, monitoring is the first step toward control. And controlling behavior, now that's the Holy Grail."

"Brendan, we're a long way from any kind of *control*..." I blushed.

"We are interested in upholding law and order, and my people merely see such donations as another tax. They don't expect free services," he continued

"Well, I'm not sure what you expect me to do about *law and order*. There is no magic wand, nor is there even a service for hire. In fact there is no corporation, no shares, no stakeholders, no accountants and no monthly reports."

"That's hardly the way of the world, Michael."

"Then consider this a *new* world."

"Aah, you mean a *brave new world*?" he smirked.

Trobe interjected, "Excuse me gentleman, David here would like to know what his consulting fee might be?"

"Two hundred an hour, but I would like our guy, Alan, to meet with him first."

We waited in silence while Trobe finished the call.

Cooper stood and we followed his lead. After a final round of hand shaking, we made our way back to the helicopter.

As the rotor started its whine, Cooper turned to me and said, "By the way, you'll never get the satellite through those doors." And with that he was gone in a hurricane of dust.

They say keep your friends close and your enemies closer, but I still wasn't sure which Cooper was.

CHAPTER 19

The morning view from my loft window showed a pristine ocean and clear sky, untainted it seemed, by the spoils of humanity. Unaffected by the evil I knew to be running rampant everywhere, and oblivious to the human trash that soiled every corner of the earth.

I calculated if one per cent of the seven billion living people living on this earth were prone to violent crime, then ten to seventy million murderers, rapists and child molesters were at large. If one per cent of them had the capacity to degenerate into war-mongering dictators, then that would be seven million people with the capacity to inflict enormous suffering upon every man, woman and child. Seven million rolls of the dice.

The phone rang and interrupted my daily nightmare.

"Mike, I've got some bad news. Mum's been assaulted and she's at South East Memorial hospital," Tom said with a trembling voice.

"How is she?"

"Some minor bruising to her head and a broken nose. Nothing life threatening so the Doc tells me, but she's sore and shaken. Someone broke into her house."

I tried to image the violation she would have felt. Although she remembered the bombs falling as a young child in Austria during World War 2, she'd started to believe there was hope, and that people were basically good and decent. Would that be shattered now?

A nurse led me to my mother's room and I found her sitting upright in bed. Tom was sitting on one side and her partner, Eric, on the other. Bandages covered her nose and forehead, but her spirit appeared undiminished.

"Michael, I hit him with my heaviest saucepan and he ran out the door like a scared rat."

"Good for you Mum. How do you feel?"

"Fine, but I'm not sure I want to go back to that house."

"I'm glad because it's time we found you a better place. We'll take Eric shopping and see what we can come up with."

She had lived in the same house for twenty years, but the neighborhood peaked long ago and was now rundown and overgrown. The sounds of discontented youth, police sirens, obscenities and junkies had replaced the carefree sound of young children playing.

So far, she had refused to move to a more pleasant area. To her the house was a symbol of her sixty-hour weeks for thirty years, paying the mortgage and sending Tom and me through school. While she sweated in an automotive parts factory, my father lost one job after another. The painkillers he took for his back and the stomach ulcers they generated depressed him to the point where one night he took too many, and ended his suffering, but not ours.

"What do you think about moving?" Eric asked her.

He was still in a state of shock. Their devotion to each other was unquestionable, but she usually led him and he was fine with that.

"Maybe it is time. But Michael, I worry more for you. You look terrible. Are you eating? Sleeping?"

"I'm fine."

"How is Helen? I pray for her every day."

"She's doing well. I'll take you to see her soon."

I motioned Tom outside, to the corridor.

"Take Eric, find a place on the North Shore and spend a couple million."

"Excuse me? You're *telling* me to do this and to *fund* it?"

"No, this one's on me."

He shook his head in disbelief, but nodded in agreement before walking back inside.

"Mr Crow, if you have a moment please?" a tall dark haired woman asked.

Once outside she continued, "I'm Dr Hails," we shook hands. "I have the blood tests on your mother and it indicates a degree of kidney failure, not from the assault, but from a degenerative condition. It's likely to become serious in a year or two."

"You mean incurable?"

"Yes, I'm afraid so."

I thought about the options, "I would like to have her transferred to St Georges."

"Mr Crow, as far as I know that is just a research centre."

"Yes, but it does have a small private ward where she can rest and recover. And the attending doctor there is a family friend."

I knew they had other spare beds, but wasn't sure whether Mark would accept her there in addition to Helen. Perhaps another donation would smooth things over just enough to get this one over the line too.

I said goodbye to the family and walked back to the car. I threw the cell phone on the passenger seat and dared it to ring with more bad news. It was only mid-morning, but I was already exhausted. I dialed a number.

"Alan, have you met with Trobe's friend yet?"

"Yes, David's right here tapping away on a keyboard."

"Good. I need you guys to crack into as many police, federal and other databases as possible. Anywhere and everywhere records are kept. Look for criminal and prison records, tax records, credit card transactions, DNA, personal histories, driver licenses, anything and everything. Also try the government system—political activists, known terrorists, enemies of the state, that sort of thing."

I half expected him to drop the phone and laugh, but, "OK, we're on it," was all he said.

Once at St Georges, I gave my mother's test results to Mark and quizzed him about her condition. I suggested the stem cell therapy might be a possible treatment and that it could be performed right here, and wasn't it a great opportunity...

Mark shook his head so many times I thought it might unscrew.

"Michael, we could lose our license if we get caught performing experimental procedures on human patients. That's why we have a facility in Colombo," he stressed, almost in a whisper, as though someone might be listening through the walls.

"Well, Colombo is off my travel list at the moment. Are the authorities here in the habit of conducting random audits?"

"Yes, they do audit us from time to time, as part of the accreditation process."

"But that's just paper shuffling, right?"

"Well—"

"They don't actually bust in during a surgical procedure armed with clipboards?"

"No, but that's not the point."

"Can she stay for at least a few days, until you've done some tests?" I pleaded.

"OK, but just don't bring in any more patients."

"It's not something I'm planning on."

"What about James?"

"Well there are a few things in motion. We've traced the emails and floated the possibility of making a payment..."

"We?"

"Mark, don't ask, it's complicated, but I should have something soon. Can you tell me more about your organization, internationally that is."

"Well, apart from here and Colombo, we operate a shared laboratory in Geneva."

"And the funding?"

"From people, much like you, who believe in the future of these technologies, and who can afford to help. I can't give you any names."

"All fine upstanding citizens?"

"Yes, I believe so. We do check them out, as you know."

"Do you think there's a possible connection with the Colombo lab and James's kidnapping? Any publicity there recently, good, bad or otherwise?" I asked, as it occurred to me that this might be my fault. Perhaps someone did follow me back from the hospital that night, and then saw me with James.

"Nothing bad as far as I know, at least not recently. We did have some negative press when we started up there, but that was four years ago— some religious objections. The Sri Lankan government have always been supportive."

"You mean you pay them well?"

He looked indignant, "Yes, we pay our taxes."

"Any other publicity?" I wasn't about to bring up the body parts factory again.

"We did advertise for a technical assistant some months ago. Several people were interviewed and two we hired."

"Do you have their files?"

"I'll send them to you," he looked worried.

"Mark, we'll find him."

"Alive, I hope."

I turned to the large white and silver monolith that sat square in centre of the room. The waveform analyzer measured two meters across and one meter high, with several monitors and test chambers packed into one end. The chambers made it look like a domestic oven, with a glass door and spotless metallic interior.

I started it up, the soft whoosh of cooling fans and the whiz of hard discs music to my ears. The screen came to life, with banners and icons scrolling and jumping about. I eagerly paged through the numerous menus while Mark watched.

"Tell me about your lab assistant." I asked.

"Warren Gibson, he's been with us for two years now. He's studying medicine at Sydney Uni and assists here part time. He is dependable and meticulous. Why do you ask?"

"I'd like him to help me with some of the more routine analyzer tests if that's possible?"

"Sure. He's in the back lab right now producing stem cell cultures for the next round of tests."

We entered this hidden domain, which hummed and buzzed like an elaborate beehive. Numerous fans and microscopes littered the confined space. Bunsen burners boiled glass flasks full of colored liquids and centrifuges spun at the speed of light, or so it seemed. In the midst, Warren moved around as if on roller skates, looking more like a thinking man's surfer than a lab rat.

"Warren, Michael would like your help with some tests, using the new waveform analyzer."

"You bet. I've been watching it, wondering if it might spring to life on its own," Warren said, exited.

The three of us returned to the main lab and wheeled up chairs in front of the analyzer.

"I'm not completely certain how all this works, so bear with me." I moved slowly through the menus. "The displays on each of these three monitors can be split into four parts. It allows us to observe multiple subjects over time and under different conditions. We can apply a range of electromagnetic radiation, from low frequency radio waves through to microwaves, visible light, ultraviolet and even low-end hard X-rays."

I scrolled, switched and tapped around some more. "The hard disc recorder can read and write data simultaneously, which means we can view changes in real time and then replay them in fast or slow motion. We can also add or subtract the images from each other to highlight differences and similarities.

Warren, can you pass over a fresh cell culture and place it in there."

He gently guided a dish of HSC stem cells into the first chamber, while I put my cell phone into the second chamber.

"The chambers are completely screened and isolated from each other, so there's no possibility of cross contamination." I pressed the auto detect icon for chamber two and within seconds the waveform analyzer had completed its job. The screen quickly filled with a complicated plot representing the electromagnetic radiation from the cell phone.

"This display shows a frequency spectrum graph."

"It looks like a DNA plot," Mark said.

"Yes, and that's why these graphs intrigue me so. They are like a window to the universe and can represent anything and everything. You can see the main waveform peak here, as well as some traces of harmonics, here and here."

I sensed straining minds behind me and was pleased to be moving them from their comfort zone, into mine.

"We can now set the waveform generator to simulate a specific part of the test waveform, or the entire waveform, and then reproduce it as an excitation signal to the cells in chamber one."

I tapped out the software routines and entered them as program macros.

"I'm now going to take the fundamental part of the waveform and increase the power in small steps, every few seconds."

Warren's eyes moved to within an inch of the screen.

"And this is where it gets really neat. It can digitally analyze the image of the cells and stop the experiment once any microscopic physical change is detected."

"But how does it know exactly what constitutes a change?" Mark asked.

"We put a sample of the result cells in chamber three, to represent our target image."

"Right, the nerve cells," Warren said, and almost ran to the storage chamber to retrieve a dish of those.

"And we'll need all the other cell types too, since we don't know for certain which way they'll be directed." I shouted after him.

Half an hour later, we had a variety of cell images digitized and stored to hard disk.

"I'll program the experiment to pause if more than ten percent of the subject image takes on any of the result image characteristics."

"Just imagine if Einstein had equipment like this," Mark whispered.

I clicked the start icon and the analyzer came to life. It displayed the excitation waveform as a plot on screen one, the subject cells in real time on screen two, and the digital images of the result template on screen three.

I turned to Mark, "Can we discuss Helen for a minute, while Warren stands watch here?"

We entered my sparsely furnished office.

"How is Helen's wound healing?"

I'd avoided being present at the changing of the dressing.

"We're keeping it clean and healthy, and will start the skin grafts as soon as we can. She'll require some sections of artificial bone and we may consider the use of stem cells to help repair tissue and muscle."

"Will the buttock reform naturally?"

"Hardly! We're nowhere near that level of science. I'm talking about implanting selected stem cells that may help the flesh wound recover, but not the regeneration of the entire macro structure."

"How will it look?" I said, more to myself.

"Depends on how far we can go. Let's just take one step at a time and hope for no rejection or infection."

"But, by increasing her own stem cell population, there'd be no rejection issue, right?"

"Well, that's right," he said, eyeing me suspiciously. "But you know we're not going to consider a procedure we don't yet understand."

"No, of course not."

We returned to the lab where Warren sat transfixed to the analyzer screens.

"No changes," he muttered as we approached.

I took a central position in front of the monitors and noticed the control screen indicating the experiment was almost complete.

"We've passed the level at which the phone nominally radiates, so either we need to add the harmonic parts of the waveform, or there's some other piece of the puzzle we're missing." I said.

"Perhaps the trigger has already started within the cells, but the external change is taking time to manifest, a molecular delay of some kind..." Mark suggested.

We stood silently and watched. A dialogue box popped up confirming the experiment had finished. More minutes trickled by, slowly and silently.

"I'd always wondered if cell phones would have a detrimental effect on people," Warren said. "But surely somebody would have noticed an effect like this before now."

"Assuming someone was looking, and on a cellular level," Mark answered. "But I think cell mutation through human skin is unlikely, as the signal strength would need to be ten-fold greater just to penetrate the skin."

We spent the next few hours with a mouse pinned next to a cell phone, but detected no additional or unusual cellular activity in the animal. Mark and Warren were looking to me for an answer, but I had less idea than they did.

"What's this mean?" Warren pointed to a dialogue box on screen two, *Chamber 2: Subject fingerprint changed. Recalibration required.*

I switched to spectrum analyzer mode and viewed the anomaly.

"This shows the cell phone has just emitted additional radiated peaks," which was puzzling. "Hang on, while I make a quick phone call."

I returned two minutes later with an ear-to-ear grin. "It's a quad band cell phone." I stated, as though that would answer all their questions. However, their blank expressions continued.

"The phone can operate on any one of four different frequencies for global compatibility. Whenever it loses a carrier, it just scans the other frequencies to find another compatible signal."

They slowly nodded their understanding.

"I'll program the same frequency pattern and repeat the experiments with the analyzer."

An hour later and we'd still made no progress.

"Why not put the phone next to the dish?" Warren suggested.

"Because we know that works," I said, a little too harshly. "I'll program a succession of frequencies, each with slightly different permutations and combinations."

After another hour, we sat around a table discussing more theories over stale coffee and hunched shoulders.

"In spite of the functionality of the analyzer, it's still missing something." I said, breaking the silence.

"And what's that?" Mark grunted without looking up.

"The Crow software," I said with a renewed grin. "Excuse me while I upload it."

I extracted the Vibrolert software from my home computer across the internet. Technically the code no longer belonged to me, but what the hell. After I modified large chunks of it, copyright would be arguable.

I completed the software graft just before 6 pm. Mark had gone upstairs to admit Helen, and Warren was in and out of the main lab every few minutes to see if I'd made any progress.

"Warren, let's give this a go. I've included some routines to perform a three-dimensional frequency analysis. Are you ready?"

"Sure."

"I'll start by performing a long, detailed scan of the phone output radiation again, to capture every nuance more precisely. It may take an hour or more and I need you to sit and watch the screen. If you see any error messages, call me. I'm going upstairs to see how Helen is settling in."

"OK... I'll be here."

Upstairs, I found Helen in bed watching TV. Two roast lamb dinners, complete with non-alcoholic wine arrived a few minutes later and we ate and talked more freely than we had in a while.

"How's your Mum doing?" Helen asked.

"She's had a shock and is a bit sore, but I expect she'll be fine."

"She's a tough old thing."

"That's for sure. And she'll be recovering in the room next to you, so you can chat at length."

"Great, some quality time with your mother is just what I need right now."

"Have you had any physiotherapy yet?"

"Tomorrow we're starting with simple bed exercises."

"How's the pain?"

"Not too bad, thanks to the drugs. So have you come up with any medical breakthroughs for me yet?"

"Maybe. I'd like to think the gene therapies we're working on might be useful sooner rather than later, but there's so much we don't yet understand."

She looked tired.

"I'll sleep in my lab office whenever I can, to give us more time together." I said.

"You mean to give you more time in the lab?"

"Try to believe it's for both reasons…"

"You don't think you're wasting your time there?"

"Time is all I have…" I said, kissing her on the cheek, slowly and gently. "I'll be back…"

"Sure, Doc."

I knew Helen was trying to understand, in her pain and the boredom of bed. Her natural humor and optimism constantly battled with anger and despair, neither far from the surface. She had become dependent and fragile, an unnatural state for her, but at least she was in good care. I thought about the scum that had stripped her of her independence and a white-hot anger surged through me—unfortunately an unwelcome but familiar feeling now.

"Warren, you'll go cross-eyed," I said, when I saw his nose almost touching the analyzer screen.

"The results of the scan are on display, but it looks like a drawing I once saw of a rough night on the high seas—with waves coming from all directions," he said.

"That's good, because it means we have a nice complex waveform to analyze."

"You can actually see something in all this mess?"

"Sure, there are a few nice patterns here. But, the first step is to apply a noise filter to eliminate everything that has no pattern. Then we'll apply another filter to eliminate anything that is just a shadow of other waveforms."

A few key strokes later and a new simplified image appeared on the screen.

"Now there's some interesting stuff," I pointed to familiar formations. "I'll get the software to process parts of the waveform progressively, adding more and more complexity until we get the desired response from these damn cells." I said.

"The analyzer will do that automatically?"

"Yes, it's a software macro. You're not familiar with them?"

"Not really."

"It's easy, I'll show you."

Ten minutes later, we had coded a new search routine for the analyzer.

"The process should take less than an hour and there's no need to apply any particular waveform for too long. I think we agree if something's going to happen, it'll happen quickly." I said.

From my lab office, I dialed Lou at the observatory.

"We've completed the first prototype of the new laser. It tested fine, but we need to be careful, it packs a punch. You think this will pass the required emission tests?" he asked.

"Don't worry about that right now. We need the maximum grunt we can get for these field trials. Can you calculate the power needed at distances of twenty to five hundred kilometers?"

"That's a hell of a range..."

"I know. I've organized for a satellite to be delivered to the observatory next week."

"I see."

I needed some innovative solutions and quickly. Increasing the input power wouldn't be practical, as it would most likely require a complicated and bulky chemical coolant for the waveguide.

Warren entered the office, "Just to let you know, the message on the screen reads, *Test Completed. Status, PASS.*"

"That was quick, too quick."

I hurried to view the result. Mark had also returned and we congregated in front of the analyzer.

"The cell culture seems to be in the process of changing," Mark murmured. "Can you magnify the image a little more?"

I increased the magnification tenfold but still found any change difficult to discern. He pointed out the cell duplication process to me.

"There's an abnormally high rate of replication of HSC cells. And here," he suddenly shouted excitedly, "a regeneration of HSCs to nerve cells."

He isolated some cells and viewed them under the electron microscope. "Yes, and there are other types of stem cells forming from the HSCs— Stromal cells."

My analyzer confirmed the same process with a software comparison to the target cell images.

"OK good. Now let's see if we can find that trigger." Mark pushed.

I selected the history tab and clicked on the *Event* icon.

"Here are several successive wave trains," I pointed to screen one.

"Can you bring up an image of the cells at the instant these waveforms were presented to the cells?" Mark asked.

I clicked on the icon *Diagnostics* and then *Replay*, to sequence through the recorded images in slow motion.

"Did you see that?" Mark almost jumped.

"What?"

"The first waveform, see what it does to the cell membrane. Can you magnify the image and concentrate on the cell membrane."

I used the digital zoom and enhancing software to bring the cell membrane into extra high magnification.

"There! It's incredible," Mark yelled. "The outer wall of the cell is vibrating, resonating. And there, when the second waveform comes along, the membrane is perfectly still and none of the cells are moving or dividing. It's as if they're receiving a signal and are in some kind of suspended receptor state. Then, when the power of the second waveform drops to zero, they start to regenerate. They're regenerating *now*!"

"Hey, look at this," I pointed to a message on screen 2. "The analyzer has detected a faint emission coming *from* the cells." I played around with the resolution and time base.

"I think I see something a few milliseconds *after* the excitation wave drops to zero." I scrolled through the time-stamped images. "There, did you see that? A burst of radiation is coming *from* the cells. At an extremely low power level."

"It's in the extreme ultraviolet frequency range." Mark noted.

"We'll send it through a UV trap and enhance it."

"All right!" Warren added.

"I'm going to instruct the analyzer to perform a match for the exact frequency of the UV fluorescence. Hopefully it will bear some resemblance to the original excitation frequency."

"Can we move forward to the second waveform?" Mark asked.

"OK, here is the image and there is the cell response. The response plot seems to be almost identical."

"Can the analyzer do a number crunch to work out the numerical correlation?"

"Sure, but we'll need to do more tests for any degree of certainly. Warren, now that you've seen how this all works, here's something that should keep you busy for a while."

I described a test routine involving multiple starts with HSC cells over a range of frequencies. The procedure would determine what waveforms predisposed the cells to open for regeneration, and what the codes were to direct that regeneration toward specific stem cell types.

"I'll arrange the tests sequences and the analyzer will prompt you when to insert new cells."

"If James was here now, we could celebrate with a drink or two," Mark's jubilation suddenly vanished.

"I should have some news soon." I offered, hoping David and Alan were making progress in the cyber world.

CHAPTER 20

I opened the window to let in the breeze and warm sunshine. The smell of freshly cut grass taking me back to my childhood, where I'd spent entire summers engulfed in the long green stuff. Perhaps I should spend some time now lying around in it, to help ease the pain in my chest and the drum beating constantly inside my head.

With a breakfast bowl in hand, I searched out the rabbit I knew to be residing somewhere in my back yard. He wasn't too hard to find as he came up to me and sniffed my hand. I offered him some wheat cereal, which he ate willingly. He was obviously finding life here agreeable, having put on weight after shredding many of my better plants.

I called Tom to let him know Mum was to be transferred to St Georges today.

"How did you go with the house hunt?" I asked him.

"We found a nice place with an indoor pool on the North Shore, two hours from the city."

"Sounds great."

After his initial reluctance, he seemed to be enjoying spending my money.

"I'll hire some guys to move the furniture before she gets home, speaking of which..." he prodded.

"I'm not sure when that will be."

"Hey, I came close to finding the scumbag that attacked her, but the police hauled him off before I had a chance to, you know, talk with him."

"Good, because that shit will get you killed."

"I might still get to *talk* to him, if they grant him bail."

"What's his name?"

"Arnold Fuller, street name, *The Ferret*."

"He sounds scary..."

While Tom rambled on, I checked my email, finding one from Cooper. There was no text, just a video attachment. I clicked on it and saw a man and a child in a sporting goods store. The child was smiling and pointing to a shiny new spear gun.

Obviously, Cooper was no stranger to mind games.

I arrived at the observatory just before noon and found Lou scratching his head.

"Any progress with the power to distance analysis we spoke about?" I asked.

"Good morning to you too," he said, a little irritated. "Here's a graph that shows power density at 500 kilometers..."

"But that's barely the level a mobile phone radiates at."

"I know, and the drop off is even worse than I expected. There was a fog around when we did the test, and water particles sucked up the energy like you wouldn't believe."

"Can we tighten the beam diameter?"

"We've got it down already, anymore would require a much longer waveguide."

"If we halve the diameter of the beam we could, in theory, quadruple the effective power over the same distance."

"Even if that were possible, we would still be operating at too low a power level. Michael, just tell me what you want and I'll work backwards from there."

After I detailed the requirement, Lou paused to consider the options.

"Off the top, I'd have to say impossible. If we boost the input power to that level we'd need a small power station in the basement to run it."

"Lou, I had an idea last night."

"You mean a dream?"

"A vision you could say." I felt his frustration and enjoyed it. "We could uplink the signal from here and use powered waveguides to redirect the signal from one satellite to another, and then to the earth station."

"But wouldn't the waveguides melt down?"

"You know how cold space is?"

"Yeah I've heard…OK, let me look into it."

I turned to Alan's nook, where I found him in a keyboard-tapping race with David. As Alan introduced us, I wondered how he had managed to clone himself so quickly.

"David, how was your time in the force?" I asked.

"Good. I spent several years in IT, working for the feds and a few other government agencies."

"So you were on the inside, so to speak?"

"Deep inside, as it turns out," Alan responded on David's behalf, pleased with his assistant.

"I worked on database design and implementation, here and overseas," David continued.

"Any private ventures?"

He smiled sheepishly, "Well, I've cracked into a few things here and there."

"OK, give these a try. I have a couple of names for you guys to research," and gave them the man with a penchant for spear guns, Alison's Neanderthal friend Bill, and Tom's nemesis, Arnold Fuller, aka The Ferret.

"Email me anything you can on these people. Also, what do you know about cracking into Middle East data?"

"Nothing, I've never had the need to try before. But I suspect it wouldn't be too hard."

"OK, give it a go, but you both know your work here is absolutely confidential."

They nodded and I got the feeling they enjoyed all this cyber-spooking a little too much.

Another wave of construction contractors arrived and for the next few hours, I discussed more alterations and additions. When someone asked if the massive concrete basement was in response to the North Korean nuke that landed in central Australia this morning, I had no idea what he was referring to.

I ascended to my loft, scanned the latest newscasts, and found that it was true—the rogue State had been firing dummy missiles again and one had landed in the Simpson Desert. In fact, six nukes had landed in different parts of the world. They had finally gone beyond words and troop build-ups, and crossed borders.

Other news told of human rights violations and economic breakdown in several African States. Oil-rich Nigeria—riddled with political instability, corruption and poor management. Somalia—instability. Bangladesh—poverty stricken and over populated. Congo—political instability and humanitarian crisis. Botswana—forty per cent unemployment and the highest AIDS rate in the world.

Disputes raged between Morocco and Western Sahara, while Ethiopia and Eritrea argued over land rights. In Eastern Europe, the Balkan states were fighting again, either with each other or with their former Russian dictator. Coups and counter coups, government brutality, insurgency, lawlessness—an epidemic across the globe. Stock markets were falling in most western countries, with a twenty percent drop across the board in the last three days alone—in response to global unrest and uncertainty, the commentators said.

Alan rang from downstairs.

"We have a response to the email we sent to James Robert's kidnappers. It's in your mail."

I pulled up the email on my computer. *'We thank you for your enquiry and encourage a generous donation to the People's National Liberation Force.'* It ended with a numbered account for a Nigerian Bank.

"Alan, can you track the email?"

"To a point, but it stops at an ISP somewhere in Madurai, India."

"India? Can you get more info on the ISP?"

"I've tried a few things, but let me work on it a little more."

"What about this Nigerian bank, can you get the account holder details?"

"I'll try."

I hung up from Alan and rang Trobe.

"The Nigerian bank account is most likely a slush fund and not useful," Trobe said. "Nevertheless they'll want to see a small deposit in good faith and then I suspect a serious demand will follow."

"What's a small deposit and what's a serious demand?"

"Small might be say, ten thousand dollars. The serious figure might come with a Swiss or Cayman numbered account. This amount could be anything from one hundred thousand to who knows what. It depends how much they think the guy is worth and who he is..."

"He's just a medical research scientist, a doctor, as far as I know."

"Either they think he's more important than he is, or they know what he's really doing. So what does he *really* do?"

"I don't know. I've only just met the guy, and he seems decent enough, one of the good guys involved in stem cell research. I think he just wants to rid humanity of ailments."

"I see..."

I could tell he wasn't convinced. Who could blame him, with all those years of seeing the worst in people, it would be hard to expect anything else. And, I was starting to feel the same way.

OK, send me what you have," he ended the call.

A call registered on my phone with Alison's number.

"Dad, hi, it's Nicole. Can I come and stay with you for a while?"

"Sure honey. What's wrong?"

"I don't like it here anymore."

"I'll talk to your Mum about you staying here more often. OK?"

I heard raised voices in the background.

"OK."

Alan was ringing on the other line.

"Hold on a sec Nic." I switched to Alan.

"I got a hit on some of the names you gave me. One guy has never had a traffic infringement, yet kills his wife and daughter. One's a career break-and-enter thug, and the other a wife basher. A nice lot, did you pick them personally?"

"They kind of picked me," my heart skipped. "Who's the wife basher?"

"Bill Turnbull."

"OK, keep digging."

I switched back to Nicole.

"Are you OK?"

"Yep."

"Look I have a feeling Bill won't be around forever, and I think your Mum will get better soon. OK?"

"OK."

In the basement, I checked over the van, which was as I'd left it. I put the battery rack on charge and tried not to think about what I needed to do next. However, one thing was for sure, I couldn't solve all the problems of the world with this van.

The evening light faded rapidly with the onset of winter. A sinking feeling came over me as I started the van and tested the eerily familiar systems.

I drove from the observatory onto the coast road unnoticed I hoped, and cursed the road trips that had now become a part of this strange new life.

Refueling the van at a gas station, I felt the cool crispness of the night air. In the shop, I picked up a bag of potato chips and scanned the newspaper. Under the main banner of sports news, a smaller headline read, *'Research Scientist Held Captive by Extremists'*. I flipped to page three and found a picture of the bruised face of James Roberts. A barrage of thoughts tore through me as I skimmed the text, *'Extremists demand the release of several political prisoners, including three of the Colombo hijackers.'*

Were these the same people who had caused Helen's injury? Had I exchanged emails with them? Would I have to talk to them, endure more of their guttural tones, and even hand over money to them? A lead weight descended on me, making breathing difficult.

I bought the paper, sat in the van and read. Several of the terrorists were known to authorities and were mentioned by name. I was tempted to call Alan to see if he could follow these up, but decided to keep my phone switched off, the tracking technology being what it is these days. And I didn't need anyone tracking me tonight.

It was pitch black when I arrived at Alison's house and I parked directly across the road. There were no other cars in the street or in her driveway. It looked quiet, too quiet. The infrared barely picked up a small figure through the wall, lying on an upstairs bed. I guessed that was Nicole.

I was about to exit the van and investigate but froze as a car pulled up behind me and turned into Alison's driveway. Car doors slammed, two figures got out and walked towards the house. I heard agitated, raised voices and scrambled to focus the laser sights. One person took off a hooded coat. It was Alison. The large man with her had to be Bill. He hovered over her, his face an inch away from hers. He was shouting and I heard the words all too clearly, *bitch*, *fuck-you*. Surely, Nicole would be hearing this. I resisted the urge to jump from the car and confront him—this guy was big enough to make a gorilla nervous.

Alison entered through the front door and the shouting continued inside. I had a partial view through an open front door. The Neanderthal was angry about having no money, and not wanting the responsibility of a child. I heard Alison screaming back at him, the venetian blinds accentuating the scene with kaleidoscopic impact.

Through an open upstairs window, I heard the sound of glass smashing against a wall—the directional microphone bringing it to my headphones with an ear-piercing stereophonic crash. I heard Alison screaming at him to get out, then Nicole in her room, crying.

A few minutes later, Bill emerged and stood framed in the front doorway. He sat down on the top step, lit a cigarette and took a long draw. As he expelled the grey smoke, I caught him in my sights and sent him a short pulse. His eyes flickered as the energy beam caressed his frontal lobe.

The telltale signs were immediate—a blank stare, a body slump and the cigarette now limply held. It was a look so completely vacant it appeared almost enticing, in a meditative kind of way.

Against my better judgment, I climbed from the van to have a closer look at the lobotomized Neanderthal. I'd sent the pulse through the van's closed window, so perhaps the effect had been lessened. I walked to within a few feet of the motionless figure, observing him closely and ready to scurry back to my mobile burrow. But he just continued to sit with his head bowed.

I moved closer, clicked my fingers under his nose and whispered, "Hey shit head!" but received no response. His breathing seemed normal but slow, his blinking quickened and the pupils darted about aimlessly, as if observing non-existent bugs crawling across the ground.

I guess I'd done the deed yet again, silently sucking out the mystical, persevering force that is life. A human, an individual, the very essence erased in the blink of an eye, leaving behind just an empty shell. I don't think I'd ever get used to this sight. It was truly fascinating, scientifically speaking.

I walked back to the van satisfied Nicole would now be safe and heard Alison comforting her upstairs. As I drove off, I looked back at the Neanderthal on the doorstep. He'd dropped his cigarette and left it lying smoldering on the ground next to him. I was pleased with myself for having removed such an oppressor, and felt only slightly uneasy. Perhaps this was getting easier each time.

I was glad to arrive back at the observatory, my bunker, just before midnight, and found Lou still working. However, his sullen look and hunched shoulders suggested progress was minimal.

My cell phone beeped with a text message from Tom, *'Michael, I'm in Kings Cross, I've been stabbed.'* The time stamp was an hour ago.

"Lou, I'll give you a hand tomorrow, I have an emergency to attend to."

I left him in mid-sentence and plunged down the stairs to the basement, making a mental note to install a bat pole.

Seconds later, I had the van tilting at extreme angles along the winding coast road, the sensitive equipment in the back rattling about wildly. I tried to think of what my brother had got himself into this time. I dialed his cell several times, but each time it rang out. This early in the morning the travel time to the city would be quick, and no more than forty minutes to Kings Cross.

I still had the locating device SatCOMM had lent me and turned it on with one hand, while negotiating hairpin turns with the other. I typed in his cell number and several seconds later, it had pinned down a street address that flashed on the screen.

Having caught a reasonable run of green lights through the outer suburbs, I was now on a freeway that led directly to the centre of town. I tried to calculate how long it might take for someone to bleed out from a knife wound, and suspected forty minutes was probably more than enough time.

I entered the city and veered off to the seedy inner-city rat's nest of Kings Cross. Here, the street bums stumbled in the shadows while the ultra trendy clubbers congregated next to them in long queues, which led to generic sub-woofer pits.

I noticed the locater no longer tracked Tom's phone—perhaps his battery had expired. I drove to the last address shown, through lanes and narrow streets hardly wide enough for a single vehicle, let alone this van. Hemmed in on all sides by the ass-end of buildings and industrial bins, I stopped at the street's dead end. There was no sign of Tom or his car.

I left the security of the van to search doorways, bins and lanes that oozed the pungent back-of-house odors, odors that seemed to smell the same all around the world.

I returned ten minutes later, without finding Tom, but noticing two men silhouetted against the streetlights at the top of the laneway. They had seen me. I pressed the van remote, opened the door, jumped in and engaged the central locking.

I started the engine, clumsily negotiated a five-point turn and drove slowly toward them. The two men stood defiantly in the centre of the road. I could see the shaved heads, the tattoos—street punks with the 'we-own-these-streets-so-fuck-off' look permanently etched into their faces. I could either stop or run them down. I stopped.

I set the targeting system to *'Acquire'* and heard the laser adjusting its aim behind me. The screen flashed *'Targets Locked'* and I stared at the shaved heads while they stared at me. This was all so ridiculous, so futile, so tribal.

I poised my finger on the fire button and hesitated. Surely, they deserved to be erased, but what had they really done? My heart hammered as one punk pulled a chain from his pocket and swung it around his head, a dumb-ass smile covering his face.

I put my finger on the touch screen and dragged the target icon from his head to his foot. I hit the *Enter* button and unleashed my invisible flame into his leg. He ceased swinging his chain, bent down and crawled over to the curb, dragging his incapacitated leg. I drove forward and past him.

Looking back, I saw the shaved head howling in the night like a crazed wolf. His friend stared at my van in utter confusion, as a dumb-ass smile now covered my face.

I found Tom in the emergency ward of The Mercy General Hospital. If nothing else, the last few weeks had been an interesting tour of Sydney's finest medical institutions.

I saw the left side of his chest covered in bandages.

"What the hell happened to you?" I asked.

"I'm OK. I'll tell you about it when you drive me home."

"Where's your car?"

"They took it."

"They?"

He signed the release forms, paid the bill and we left.

"What's this rig?" he asked.

"My work van."

"You're working for the power company now?" he noticed the logo.

"Not exactly. So, are you going to tell me what happened to you?"

"It's a bit embarrassing," he winced, seeking dramatic impact. And if he got any more dramatic, I'd let him walk home.

"I found *The Ferret*. I even got in a couple of good kicks before his mates got me," he grinned. "Then somehow, someone stabbed me. Just a lucky jab and I groaned and played dead. There was plenty of my blood around to satisfy them. They drove off in my car and I staggered around for a couple of blocks until I found a cop."

I shook my head in disbelief, "You're a fool."

"Why, because I won't take it from shitheads like that?"

"No, because you're not using your head and you'll get yourself killed."

"And what makes you such a damn expert?"

"I was born with more common sense than you."

"Yeah right, you're just chicken shit."

A stare, tempered by timeworn familiarity, lingered between us before I had to turn my eyes back to the road.

"I've been up and down the streets looking for you and had my own altercations." I said.

"What happened?" he sounded concerned.

"I survived."

"Well good for you."

"So what now?"

"I go and take my car back," he said, as though it was that simple and obvious.

"What if they stab you again? And you don't even know where it is. You see how pointless all this is?"

"No, it's not pointless. The story doesn't end with the meek surviving you know. These fuckers will inherit the place if we don't get them first."

"You don't know what you're talking about…"

"What's to know, it's kill or be killed. That's the way of the world, always has been."

"You think you can kill someone? You think even if you do, you'll be pleased with yourself?"

"So what if there's one less scumbag in the world. Hell, I'll be pleased. And I can't believe I'm having this discussion with *you?*"

"You know the hijack was political, it wasn't personal."

"I bet Helen feels it was personal. In the end, it's all fucking personal."

He was right. In the end, it was all personal.

"I remember the look in your eyes when I picked you up in Colombo. You would have killed them in a heartbeat given half a chance."

"And if I did, you would have flown me home in a coffin, so let it go."

"Shit no, the score isn't settled."

"And if he kills you, what do I tell Mum? Do I say, *well, it's the way of the world, the score wasn't settled.* Will that ease her pain? All those years of wiping your ass and blowing your nose, then you go and die in some gutter, with some brainless street punk standing over you, beating his chest."

Tom answered his cell and spoke with someone.

"The police found my car near the Navel Dock at Potts Point. Let's go get it,"

"You're sure you want to do this now?"

"Shit yes, it'll be trashed by morning."

I turned the car around and we drove to Potts Point in a screaming silence.

"Why are you so pissed off, anyway?" Tom asked, as if he hadn't heard a word I'd been saying.

"Because you're right. It is a dog-eat-dog world and civilization is nothing of the sort," I noticed his stupid grin reappear. "But your solution is flawed."

"Flawed?"

"Yes, he hurts you, you hurt him. Eventually someone gets killed and then relatives take on the task, then the village, then the whole damn country, and hey presto here we are in the twenty first century of war."

"Yeah well, shit happens. Look, there it is!"

His car was parked at one end of a large public car park, where a gang of youths huddled around it. The silver Mercedes coupe appeared undamaged.

I pulled up at the opposite end of the car park, a hundred meters away.

"So what now?" I asked.

"I go and get my damn car back."

"Sure, just like that? You might have to say *please*."

"Fuck that," he opened the door and jumped out.

"Maybe we should phone the police and let them handle it?"

"OK, you phone and I'll handle it."

Tom's fixation obliterated the tenuous hold he had on objectivity. He stepped out of the van and walked toward his car, and the youths. I couldn't believe my eyes—this was more than stupidity, it was just plain suicide.

I sprung into action and turned on the computer. The operating system asked me if I wanted an update to my virus scanning software, I declined and circled the entire gang as targets, then waited for the multiple lock icons to light up.

Tom was only twenty meters from the group, he was six-foot-four, a sporting man who worked out regularly, but I guessed his single-hand gang combat routine was a little rusty.

As the target locks confirmed, I noticed Tom with his hand in his back pocket. I zoomed in and saw he held something, a knife, a gun, or maybe he was going to throw his cell phone at them. The youths assumed the ritual pre-fight stance—the folding of arms, the flexing of muscles, the left and right neck jerks. It would all be so laughable if it weren't so serious.

I switched to infrared vision and confirmed the acquisition of all four targets, locking to the centre of each forehead. Tom was only a few meters from them and I saw no reason to wait. I initiated the pulse sequence and hoped it wouldn't mistakenly acquire him.

The laser hummed into action as the computer-controlled servomotors directed the energy beams with precision. I focused on their eyes, desperate to confirm the deterioration of brain matter before Tom sprang into his action hero routine and injured himself.

Two of the nearest youths immediately slumped to the ground, but the other two remained standing, and sported that familiar dazed look and rapid blinking. I looked at Tom and was stunned to see him pointing a small caliber handgun at them. He stood his ground, his ridiculously small weapon held tight with both hands. I wondered if it fired bullets or water as he pointed the weapon in rapid staccato at each of the youths.

I stepped out of the van and walked toward the circus.

"Hey Mike, search these fuckers for my car keys while I cover you." Tom shouted.

"Relax. The only thing you'll have to worry about from these guys is excessive dribble."

"What the fuck are you talking about?" he watched in disbelief as I casually strolled past him.

I studied each of the men in turn, the shaved heads, the tattoos of snakes and skulls painted over their street scarred bodies, the muscles that bulged and rippled, but were now strangely flaccid. As they say, the eyes have it, and in this case, the eyes had lost it. I grabbed one of the standing men by his shirt.

"Here you go. What do you want to do with him?" I shuffled the zombie to within inches of Tom.

"What the fuck...?" he took two steps back, still pointing his gun at the man.

"I just saved your life. Suggest you put that thing away, drive home and forget this ever happened."

"What did you—"

"The equipment in the back of the van—it's a microwave laser capable of frying brain matter at amazing distances."

Tom eyes became as wide as the moon now rising in the night sky behind him.

"And...*you* built it?"

"Yes."

He looked at me as if I had lost my mind, and that I might take his into Neverland with me.

"The girl thrown from the train a few weeks ago, you remember?"

"Yes."

"Well it's for her and the others..." I said, sounding melodramatic myself now.

"You can't be serious!"

I rubbed my brow, suddenly feeling tired. "Look, just go home and get some sleep."

"Oh yeah, easy for you to say! What are you planning to do with that thing anyway?"

"Disassemble it and use the servo motors in a go-kart for Nicole. Now help me move these guys to that industrial bin over there and let's get the hell out of Dodge."

A shuffling of bodies in the night followed as Tom kept eyeing me with a mixture of wonder and concern.

"So how does this not propagate the revenge cycle you were on about?" he asked with a smirk.

"Because this way it's all smoke and mirrors. There's no direct link to anyone or anything. The cycle never gets a chance to kick in."

"Yeah, right..."

I climbed into my van, he got in his car and we drove our separate ways.

At home, I parked the van in the driveway and sat there, deadbeat. The silence was total, except for the chirping of morning bird's eager to experience the new day.

I, on the other hand, had no such desire.

CHAPTER 21

I ate breakfast and watched the television news for stories on zombies, but found only the usual installments on sport and murder. I wasn't sure exactly what to do, which of the various fires needed stoking the most. I decided I couldn't face Mark without something concrete on James, so I rang Alan.

"How's the India-Pakistan connection going?" I asked.

"We're sniffing around a few things at the moment, but nothing just yet. We'll keep at it."

"Found much in the way of pictures, fingerprints or DNA?"

"Only small pockets of data here and there. Full scale DNA storage is coming along slowly in that part of the world."

I wasn't sure how capable Alan and David were at ventures like this, but hesitant to go searching for other talent.

Trobe rang as I drove to St Georges.

"I've heard more of the walking dead surfaced overnight," he prodded. Obviously, it was on the intelligence grapevine, if not yet the news. "There's even talk around that it could be a biological agent of some kind. Sounds like they might put a special task force on it..."

"Really?" I didn't ask him how he came to know all this or why I was suddenly at the top of his information-sharing list. "I appreciate the update John."

"No problem. How's David doing?"

"OK, I guess. But I think the serious intel is going to be hard to find. I hope David and Alan are up to it."

"If you're breaking into a house and the front door is locked up tight, where do you go to next?"

"Um…the back door?"

"Right, but remember someone's backdoor can be someone else's front door. It's all about perspective."

"OK," I think.

I rang Alan.

"Alan let's change tack and go straight for the big guys, the CIA and FBI. They'll have more on the mid-east than the mid-east has on itself."

"It might be difficult to get beyond the first security level there…"

"Maybe that's all we'll need. Give it a try."

I arrived at St Georges and called in on Helen. Her look tried to be welcoming but came out mixed.

"I'm sorry, but the last twenty-four hours have been full on. How have you been?" I started with an apology, aware I was failing her.

"Apart from missing you, I'm fine. But I think I'm getting too dependent on the pain medication."

"Have you told Mark?"

"No."

She seemed embarrassed to have let herself down.

"I'm sure he would have thought of that and have some plan to counteract it. I don't want you worrying about anything unnecessarily."

I studied her. She was still beautiful. A free spirit, but now caged.

"There's a restaurant just around the corner, nothing too fancy. Maybe we can grab a quick bite there this evening?" I suggested.

"With me in a wheelchair?"

"Yeah, I could wheel you there, you know, in a romantic kind of way." I wasn't sure whether she was about to laugh or cry. "It'll be good for you to get out for an hour or so."

"I don't know. Can I sit in a chair for that long?"

"I'll talk with Mark."

The nurse brought in soup and sandwiches for lunch.

"Can I steal one of your sandwiches? I forgot to eat last night."

"Late night?"

"Yeah…"

"What's her name?"

Even though it was said in jest, the words hung in the air. We both knew her sexuality was on hold, her feminine self-esteem as damaged as her body.

I whispered in her ear, "Her name is Helen and she's the most beautiful woman in the world. She even has her own team of doctors to put her back together again." I kissed her lips.

Mark looked up from his computer screen. "Any news on James?" he asked.

"No. We're still working on it, believe me. Do you have those files from Colombo, the job applicants?"

"Yes, check your inbox. The whole kidnapping thing is in the media now, it'll be a circus."

"Michael!" Warren broke the tension. "I was hoping to see you. I have a stack of test results to decipher. Do you have time now?"

"Sure."

Two hours later, we'd worked through pages of numbers, graphs and images that had been generated by the analyzer.

"So in summary," I began. "We can open a cell using a specific frequency within a tight band. Then we can apply a series of waveforms, using the key frequencies as well as several harmonics, to the cells. And the relative timing of these waveforms determines the direction for cell regeneration."

"Right," Warren nodded.

"Also the power of the waveform needs to be within a very tight band otherwise the cell either dies or just doesn't 'open' to receive the key."

"Right,"

"Not bad for a few days work," Mark acknowledged, but without much enthusiasm. "There's a problem however. I've found the cell DNA in some cases has been damaged."

"What do you mean?"

"Where do I start?"

He looked over-burdened, hopelessly lost at sea. I'd seen it before, when a researcher loses his nerve and succumbs to the vast unknown.

"Assume I know nothing, or at least very little," I said, watching Mark's annoyance build, and enjoying it.

"Deoxyribose Nucleic Acid, or DNA, contains the genetic instructions specifying the biological development of all cellular forms of life.

It's the molecule of heredity and responsible for the genetic propagation of inherited traits. During reproduction, DNA is replicated and transmitted to the offspring," Mark expounded robotically and without taking a breath.

"OK, and where in the cell exactly is the DNA?"

"In complex cells, cells that make up plants and animals, the DNA is located in the nucleus."

"Can you show me?"

We turned up the magnification on a specific cell image, but I saw nothing that resembled the DNA helix I had imprinted on my mind.

"So how do we test for DNA?" I asked.

"With a DNA analyzer," Mark answered, as though that explained everything.

"Of course, and I assume you have one of those here?"

"Yes. It's a TOR 9000 system, with dual channel detection to eliminate errors from fluorescence overlap. The fluorescence of the two IR dyes is separated by one hundred nanometers."

I guess he thought this technical verbiage would leave me intimidated.

"Great. IR is Infrared right?" I asked, with sarcasm he failed to catch.

"Yes. Two sets of optically tuned lasers and detectors measure fluorescence from the dyes independently."

"What causes the excitation?" I asked, but saw only a puzzled look in return. "What causes the fluorescence to occur?" I added.

"A laser."

"What sort of laser?"

"I'm not sure…"

I couldn't resist grinning as he stumbled into my world.

"Nevertheless, the question is—how do we stop the DNA corruption of the transitory cell," Mark continued.

"One step at a time, that's how. Specifically, I don't know. It's a vibe thing and it hasn't come to me yet."

His face showed an interesting combination of confusion and annoyance.

"I'll need the user manual for your DNA analyzer and two cups of strong, black coffee." I added.

Three hours later, Mark had gone home and even Warren was losing interest, but having read the manual from cover to cover, a few ideas had come to me.

If I understood this analyzer correctly, it excited the molecules using an infrared dye on DNA samples as they passed by a detector. The detector decoded the image as a sequence, a plot. So what if I just 'washed' the DNA sample with *light* of a specific frequency, to simulate the dye, and then pass this through another filter. I could identify the resulting bio-fluorescence without physically touching or disturbing the DNA material.

I decided not to discuss my idea with the others, as they might try to talk me out of it. That had happened to me before and these days I had the confidence to trust my instincts, no matter how primitive or ignorant they seemed at the time.

Warren left several DNA samples for me, complete with a chromatogram image for each. The images looked like my old friend—the frequency spectrum plot. I programmed the waveform analyzer with some test routines and set to work.

The results returned as I hoped, but the process required a very precise frequency to achieve the bio-fluorescence effect. And I was amazed at the ability of my analyzer to generate and detect wavelengths with such precision. Perhaps it was because of this that lesser analyzers persisted with cumbersome IR dyes. That, and the profit generated by perpetual ink sales at exorbitant prices.

The Vibrolert software helped with the frequency shifting and filtering, limiting the error to attain the required precision. I continued to play around with it until I had the same format used as the industry standard.

"Warren, I have a question. The DNA generated by your analyzer, what portion of total DNA does it actually decode?"

"Somewhat less than half, but it's all we need to differentiate one person from another."

"OK, but how did Mark determine that the stem cell DNA had been corrupted?"

"Well, I think the analyzer came back with *Sample Error*."

"Where's that sample now?"

"Here, in the conditioning chamber." He pulled out a dish and handed it to me.

I placed it in my waveform analyzer and performed a scan.

"What are you doing?" Warren asked.

"Just a hunch."

Ten seconds later, the analyzer displayed an elongated DNA plot across the screen.

"What's that?" he asked.

"A DNA sequence, I think."

"But it's looks too long."

"I'm operating at a higher resolution and bandwidth."

He looked at me, and the plot on the screen, but without understanding.

"Well, it may not be accurate anyway," I said, suddenly guarded. "Do you have the original stem cell batch these came from?"

He handed me another dish from the chamber and I repeated the scan.

"It seems we have different DNA from cells of the same batch. The DNA has *changed*. Maybe that's why your analyzer had a tantrum?"

"Mutating DNA? That's just not possible," Warren insisted.

"Look, no peaks in the spectrum here for the pre-irradiated sample, but peaks here after the irradiation."

"That's assuming your analyzer works correctly, and does really detect more genes."

"Could we have switched *on* a gene that was previously *off*?"

"That's unlikely..."

"How do we find out what a specific gene does?"

"Well, other than those we know of, we have to grow the cells, watch them, transplant them to a host, and watch some more."

"Sounds like a long process."

"That's why this kind of research is measured in years, not hours." Warren said with a hint of Mark in his voice. Even the assistants now attacked my methods.

"What's a *host*?" I asked.

"A mouse, for example."

"Ok, but let's try and trim this research to several days if we can," I suggested, as a frightened look shot across his face.

"Warren, can you run some more of these tests, same procedure as we've done before, but vary the triggers to confirm it's the same altered DNA response each time."

He held his hands up in dismay, "Sure, why not?"

"I'll set up a series of tests—just insert the samples as instructed. I'm off on a date with a babe."

"Half your luck," he shook his head but continued to watch with interest as I programmed the analyzer sequences.

I hoped Helen wasn't too worked up about dinner. Entering her room, I saw her seated in a wheel chair, dressed nicely and her face all made up. I guess my stare lingered on the chair a little too long, and her gaze dropped to her lap where her hands fidgeted with her handbag.

"Hey honey, you look great." I knelt beside her as the hijackers' balaclavas flashed through my mind, the evil in their eyes taunting me. I wiped the tears from her cheeks, and silently apologized for everything and everyone.

Mum walked in from her adjoining room, "Are you two going somewhere special?"

"Yes, she finally agreed to go out with me."

"Good for you. Have fun and don't stay out too late."

I wheeled Helen into the elevator, out through the lobby and along the street a hundred meters to a small Italian restaurant. There were a number of medical suites in the area and I guessed people around here wouldn't take much notice of a wheelchair.

I sat down at the table and recalled a similar scene only a few weeks ago, before the accident. I considered the word 'accident' and how it usually referred to nothing of the sort.

"I think I've been in hospital for too long, the smell of this place is amazing." Helen said, appearing more 'alive' than I had seen her recently.

"You're right, and I'd say there's no lack of garlic in the kitchen."

My phone vibrated and I glanced at the screen, "Sorry, I need to take this. Alan, what's up?"

"We just cracked it big time. I have a stack of information on scumbags all around the world flooding in, and it wasn't that hard to find once I found the keys. I've matched a picture of one of the hijackers in the newspaper to one of the job applicants in Colombo. I've got multiple hits with known associates, full histories and heaps more."

"Good work Alan."

"But I'd like to do some more cross referencing for verification before I release the data."

"Go ahead, but be careful."

"I'm routing through several ISPs in three different countries. I'm a cyber ghost."

I hung up, wondering if letting him progress from computer hacker to global spy was wise.

"Who's Alan?" Helen asked.

"He's one of our programmers."

"You're being a little mysterious about this new business of yours."

"It's early stage stuff at the moment, but we're progressing with a few interesting technologies."

"You're not getting involved in anything *illegal* are you?"

"No, of course not. Why do you ask?"

"Who is this *We*?"

"I've hired some research engineers and techs. You remember Lou from Vibrolert?"

"Yes, he's a nice enough guy. He left Vibrolert?"

"I made him an offer he couldn't refuse."

"I bet. And where are you all working from?"

"Well, you remember when we took a drive along the coast a few weeks back? We passed by an observatory, on the cliff overlooking the ocean?"

"You mean the one you couldn't keep your eyes off and nearly drove us off the road?"

"Yes, that one...Well, I kind of bought it."

"Kind of?"

"OK, I bought it and I'm renovating it into a high tech research facility." I might as well give her the full story. "There are dozens of people there right now, hard at work, day and night, pushing communications technology to new limits."

Her look was one of surprise and disappointment.

"Helen, I meant to tell you before now, but couldn't find the right time. Your health is more important, and I didn't want to sound self-absorbed." I added, but with little effect.

"No, but you've been acting self absorbed, so telling me why may not have been such a bad idea. What exactly are you working on?"

"Global satellite phone systems."

"So you just woke up one day and decided to do this?"

"Well, I was just in the wrong place at the wrong time."

"And where's all the money coming from?"

"I had some assistance from Cooper..."

"I see... your working for him now?"

"Well, he is a client."

"I thought you were going to distance yourself from him. I've told you, there's something about that man that's not quite right. You're on edge whenever his name is mentioned."

There was certainly nothing wrong with her intuition.

"Do you have any other *clients?*" she continued.

"No, not right now. I didn't want to bother you with all this. It's not that important anyway. What's important is making you better," I held her hand. "And we've had some progress with the stem cell research."

"There's that *we* again…"

"Yes, well that particular *we* is the research team at St Georges. We hope to help your body grow new cells, to reconstruct itself, a biological recovery, rather than an artificial one—"

"Michael, I do know something about medicine. And what you're talking about is at least a decade away, maybe more. Please don't fill me with false hope."

"Hey, you know progress is a funny thing, it tends to happen in steps, sometimes leaps. Tissue cells, blood cells, muscle cells, organs cells, even bone cells could one day be self-generated with these techniques. And, because there's no need to cultivate and implant foreign cells, any risk of immune system rejection is eliminated," I said in my best bio-engineer voice.

"And your contribution?"

"A sounding board, a wild card, you know, someone not constrained by too much knowledge but with research disciplines." But even my bio-engineer voice couldn't sway the questioning expression on her face.

She looked down at her glass. "Michael, let's talk about something else."

I opened my mouth, but no words came out.

"Your brother came in today," she said.

"How is he?"

"He seemed a little strange."

"Strange?"

"I asked him if he'd seen much of you, because I said I hadn't. He seemed uncomfortable when I mentioned you."

"He's just in awe, an issue he's always struggled with."

"Sure, anyway, he didn't stay for long. I told him you were downstairs in the lab. He mumbled something about Frankenstein and took off."

"Well you know he's a busy guy, suing and counter-suing. Don't worry about it."

"I have noticed something different about you too. You seem to be hiding something… and it worries me."

"Helen, I know we haven't really talked about what happened in Colombo. I'd be lying to say it hadn't affected me too."

"I'm worried you're going to get yourself into something…dangerous."

"Helen, what are you talking about? I'm just an engineer, what do you think *I* can do to any of these murderous pigs running rampant around the world?"

She studied me. I could tell she wasn't convinced, yet that left me strangely flattered.

"We should look at the menu, perhaps a non-alcoholic cocktail to start with?" I suggested.

An hour later, Helen was in good spirits, but I sensed a growing distance from her. The cancer of mistrust was growing. I wheeled her back to the room and tucked her into bed. I noticed Mum's TV playing just a little too loud and made a mental note to bring her a set of headphones.

With food and coffee surging through me, my energy levels were on a high. I found Warren and Mark in the lab, staring at a whiteboard full of DNA graffiti.

"Dinner went well?" Mark asked.

"Yes, we should do it again."

"You didn't give her any alcohol?"

"No, we both abstained. What's the hot topic?"

"Warren has replicated the experiments as you suggested and found the same gene anomaly turns up each time. We're just trying to figure out whether it's real or a measurement error of some sort. We've found the same irradiation sequence causes gene corruption in some cases but not in others, and we can't understand why the results differ for no apparent reason."

Mark looked exhausted. Was our lack of progress getting to him, or was it the situation with James? Perhaps it was both. Perhaps James' predicament should be distracting me more. Instead, I treated his disappearance as just another 'project' to timeshare with all the others.

"I have a list of results from the last batch of procedures you programmed." Warren handed me a computer print out two meters long. "But I don't know how to interpret them."

"OK, let me study it." I retreated to my office.

"I think I have the answer," I announced, emerging from my office an hour later, and waiting for an audience to gather.

"When the cell is unlocked and waiting for the direction signal, it's *this* period of time that seems to determine the cell redirection. If the second wave sequence comes in early, then only part of the regeneration code is received. This leaves a corrupt cell and corrupt DNA. But if the redirection signal is late, then nothing happens and the cell membrane is closed for business."

"And how do you know all this?" Mark asked.

"It's all in the numbers," I held up the printout.

"And how do you explain a cheap cell phone working within such exact parameters?"

"Good question and it wasn't that cheap. I figure it's just a combination of probability, coincidence and repetition. The cell phone signal strength is weak here in the lab and I've noticed the phone searching out a carrier signal for much of the time. It's this constant frequency shifting that eventually hits the mark and excites the cell."

"So we just stumbled upon the needle in the haystack?" Mark quipped, unconvinced.

"It happens every now and then. What about the cell replication rate and stem cell density?"

"Usually only 1 in 100,000 cells are stem cells. But at the division rate we're seeing here, the proportion could be a hundred times higher."

"Which would in turn lead to quicker cellular repair rates and therefore quicker organ re-growth?"

"Perhaps..."

"Why the concern?"

"Michael, the unknown is always a concern."

"You're right and the best way to find out is to move forward, knowing you might have to take a step back every now and then."

"That's not prudent research procedure."

"Pure research by definition cannot be prudent. The fact is, my approach works for me."

"Well, once we have collated *all* the results then we'll start on another series of culture samples, before rechecking and revalidating everything." Mark stated with his stubborn face, which was a red flag to me.

"Actually, I was thinking more of a host trial."

"What host?"

"A mouse, perhaps two—"

"That's much too premature."

"Hey, I'll even buy them."

We stood in silence while my colleagues gauged my mental state.

"Guys, either we do this here or I take my analyzer home to do it there." I said, resisting the urge to stamp my foot.

This raised a smile from Warren, but only more dark looks from Mark.

"Look, Mark, they're just mice." I said.

"We have a few sick mice at the end of their useful life, perhaps we can use them," Warren offered quietly.

Mark waited a full minute before nodding a reluctant approval, then left.

Apart from his need to maintain control, I sensed they were not just mice to him. They were treated and cared for like associates and their contribution to medical science never taken for granted. I thought about the rabbit now living contentedly in my backyard and the contribution he almost made.

CHAPTER 22

I sat bolt upright in my bed. Staring at the clock I realized I was already an hour late picking up Nicole for the weekend. I rang Alison and sensed something was wrong when she missed the opportunity to berate me.

But on this occasion, I had some idea what that might be.

I parked outside Alison's house and waited for Nicole to come out with her overnight bag. When she failed to appear after several minutes, I psyched myself up, walked to the door and rang the bell.

I heard the sound of footsteps approaching and then Alison opened the door, appearing withdrawn and sickly.

"Hi. Where's Nicole?" I asked.

"Cleaning her room, she'll be down in a minute."

"Should I wait in the car?"

"No, come in."

"What about um—"

"He's not here," she said, quickly dismissing the topic of 'him'.

"I'm sorry about what happened to Helen. It's all so...so senseless," she slurred through a veil of sedatives.

I felt uncomfortable and wished Nicole would hurry up.

"It's hard not to hate everything and everyone when something like that happens," she continued, as much to herself.

Nicole bounced down the stairs calling my name. It wasn't often I appreciated her high-pitched squeal, but this time it was music to my ears. She jumped into my arms and gave me a hug.

As we drove off, Nicole said matter-of-factly, "Mum's friend had a stroke and he's gone to the hospital."

"That's too bad. You know your Mum will need more help around the house, she'll be tired and sad while she looks after him."

"I guess."

"Shall we do breakfast?"

"Macdonald's," she answered quickly, as if the destination was obvious.

"Maybe not this time. We're going to visit Helen and Grandma in hospital."

"Have they got a MacDonald's there?"

"Not yet, but we can try some good old fashioned hospital food."

"Great…"

At St Georges, I left Nicole with Helen and Mum, and rang Lou.

"I'm still stuck on this damn power equation," he moaned.

"Listen, I had an idea last night."

"Let me guess, another dream?"

"Yes, you know how radio broadcasts go the distance without needing loads of power?"

"Modulation."

"Exactly, we can use a lower frequency carrier wave for the distance and then modulate a higher frequency waveform on top of that. We'll get the best of both."

"Let me look into it."

I sensed renewed enthusiasm as the cognitive wheels started turning again.

"Try the megahertz band for the carrier." I suggested.

"That will require some major changes to the hardware."

"Do whatever it takes."

I rang Alan to discuss his progress.

"We've been working through the night and found a few back doors, but progress is slow. We're cross referencing several databases at the moment to validate," he said.

"OK, push on."

I rang Trobe.

"John, sorry to bother you on a weekend..."

"No problem."

"The situation with James Roberts..."

"Yes. I've spoken with some people who know more about these things than I do. The official line is that the kidnappers belong to a group known as Al Assirat, translated *The Righteous*, a small organization based in Pakistan. Either this is the first time they've taken such extreme action, or they're being used as a smokescreen for someone or something else."

"The email accuses James of crimes against *humanity*? What's that about?"

"Could be anything or nothing. He might soon be handed over to the authorities, who then may let him return home."

"You don't sound confident."

"Well, other agendas might be in play."

"You mean trading him for the release of hijackers?"

"Maybe, or other political prisoners, or something else they want from the Government. This one's seems a little less cut and dry to the usual I'm told. There are several possibilities."

"Could it be as simple as Pakistan needs to be *seen* to be agonizing over this, and they'll let him go in due course?"

"Maybe. Did you know Al Assirat executed Samuel Edwards yesterday, the British diplomat who was in the hijacked plane with you?"

"Damn... look there's something else I saw in Colombo. I'm not sure what it has to do with James, but maybe there's a link." I told him about the field of limbs, the tunnel and the body parts.

He considered this for a while before responding, "There is someone else I'd like to talk to. I'll let you know if I find out anything. How's David doing?"

"Good, they seem to be having some success."

"Mr Cooper has contacts in the CIA—personal friends over the years I'm told. They're leaving the door ajar for us, a kind of informal blessing you could say."

I shuddered at the thought of Cooper having such friends, "Why would the CIA do that?"

"I don't know and I didn't ask. Perhaps it's for the common fight against terror and crime?"

"Right..." I wondered whether I was stepping too far out of my league being involved with him, and them, and whoever else was in this web I'd fallen into.

"I'd like to perform some tests, with a few more cell cultures if that's OK?" I suggested to Mark.

"What will you do with them?"

"I'd like to try a variety of irradiation patterns, with different power and frequency combinations, to get more of a feel for the lay of the land."

"How many cultures will you need?"

"A few dozen."

He looked shocked.

"Is that a problem?" I asked.

"I can prepare maybe five cultures a day."

"Can't we get more from outside sources?"

"Michael, it's not a mail order business."

"Then we'll use just the cells we've created, they're multiplying quickly enough."

"We could, but that's not good procedure, as you know."

"Maybe not, but I can work with it."

Mark left the lab only slightly irritated this time.

I started programming a sequence of tests with the waveform analyzer to determine which power density and frequency combinations would work best for Lou's new laser design. I wanted more impact at the target for less power input and I expected the answer to this lay somewhere along the power-frequency curve.

Four hours later, I'd finished programming the first test sequences and asked Warren to spend the rest of the day swapping new cultures into the test chambers and documenting the results.

It was late afternoon before I felt sufficiently guilty for not spending more time upstairs with the family. I entered Helen's room to find Nicole fast asleep beside her.

"She crashed an hour ago. She waited for you as long as she could." Helen said.

"I got caught up in the lab. Can I get you anything?"

"No thanks, not at the moment. Can you roll out the stretcher for Nicole?"

I prepared a bed for Nicole and placed her, still sleeping, into it. I stayed with Helen for a while before she too fell asleep and then returned to the lab.

Warren and Mark were glued to an internet newscast. The images pounded their tired eyes with scenes of devastation, filmed from a plane high above.

"A nuclear device has been detonated in Seoul." Mark explained.

Whilst the possibility of such an event had been there for some time, years in fact, the reality of it still shocked.

"Did it come from the North?" I asked.

"That's the consensus, but no one's game to make it official at the moment."

A man's voice, a reporter sitting in a Fox Studio somewhere, described the scene, but the vision was clear enough. It showed burnt corpses, piles of rubble, fire, smoke, with nothing living and no movement anywhere. No ambulances, no police, no fire brigade, nothing. I imagined this is what the end of the world might look like.

The report went on to speculate that the bomb was transported on the back of a truck and remotely detonated. It was a low-yield device, yet still managed to level several city blocks, killing many tens of thousands instantly.

Mark pounded the table with his fist, "Sheer madness, they were just innocent people, children, living their lives and bothering no one."

The televised images started at the epicenter—the city and moved outwards. We watched the coverage for almost an hour before the signs of life started reappearing. People were staggering about, crawling from broken buildings, from buried basements and from the rubble itself. They appeared confused and frightened. I saw a man carrying a young child in his arms, stumbling through the debris. My stare lingered too long before I understood, with sudden repulsion, the boy had no legs and appeared lifeless.

I searched the faces and saw no hope, and out of respect for the people of Seoul, we turned it off. The mood in the lab was subdued and any enthusiasm to continue working, extinguished.

"Here's a list of results from twenty tests completed so far. I'll finish the rest tomorrow." Warren left.

"Why is it like this?" Mark's voice croaked.

"You mean, why do people kill each other so consistently and with such vigor and imagination?"

"Yes, and will it ever stop?"

"Who knows? Perhaps it's not in our DNA to stop. Perhaps this *killing gene* protects us from extinction. But to me, it would seem to guarantee it."

"I'm not sure why I bother to do what I do. I mean someone somewhere will just use the science against us."

We sat in silence, consumed by thoughts of doom and gloom.

"I'm off to get some sleep," Mark said.

"I'll continue here for a while, and Mark..."

"Yes?"

"Mice? Um...I'll need a few to work with."

"Warren has reserved four candidates for you in cage eight over there."

He retreated to his office and came out holding a large bound book.

"These are the regulations governing the use of live mice in medical research. Read it and be gentle with them," he insisted.

"I will. And how will I identify them?"

"Use this marker, its non-toxic and won't wash off."

The book also contained a brief history of the four mice. They had served medical science for over a year and survived many tough battles. They were veterans, healthy mice with outstanding genes.

I selected the first mouse and marked an 'A' on his fur. I placed the mouse into the analyzer test chamber and subjected him to irradiation pulses for less than one tenth of a second. I did the same with the other three, varying the wave sequences slightly.

I should have used many more mice to cover the scenarios properly, but for now, four would have to do. I expected mouse A to die quickly, B to die over a period of days, C to live a long and prosperous life and D, well, he could go either way.

As I put A back in his cage, he already appeared a little sluggish. He continued to sniff, but struggled to move about. When I came back with mouse B, A had died. I took him out of his cage and placed him in a small plastic container and in the refrigerator. I would ask Warren to perform an autopsy when he returned. At least mouse A could now rest in peace, knowing his contribution to medical science was over.

I finished the tests and had the mice back in their cages. I noticed mouse B wasn't particularly interested in moving much—remembering a similar look in the eyes of humans from recent road trips. The other two seemed unaffected.

I left the lab just after 7 am, tired and with an overbearing sense of sorrow, both for the suffering of mice and the suffering of humanity, each stripped by others of their future.

I drank several cups of strong black coffee for breakfast hoping that would negate the lack of sleep. Tom was with Mum, and seeing him with a bunch of flowers made me spill my cup.

"Have you heard the news?" Tom asked.

I eyed him, hoping he'd have the sense not to—

"They've nuked Seoul."

"Oh no..." Mum breathed in deeply and held her breath.

Tom was ready to go on, but I cut him off, "It seems North Korea set off a bomb in Seoul. It was a small explosion." There was no need for the gory details.

Mum let out a long sigh, "I've read Nostradamus, it's all in there. He predicted the end of the world."

It was obvious where Tom got his tact. Finally, he came to his senses and changed the subject, "Mum, how's your treatment going?" he asked.

They looked to me, but I had nothing new to offer. "It's moving along," was all that came to mind.

I suggested Tom take Nicole to the playground for a while. It would be good for him to rest his brain for a while, and would give me a chance to catch up on some sleep.

I woke at midday in a vacant room, stiff from lying on a trolley bed, and smelling the aroma of lunch in the air. I entered the corridor and heard Mum playing a card game with Nicole. Helen was on the phone with a friend and all seemed well occupied without me. I made my way to the lab and found Warren working on the remaining cell cultures.

"I see you put in a few hours last night," Warren said.

"Yeah, I couldn't sleep. I subjected four mice to some tests."

"OK, let's see them."

We inspected the three mice in the cage and noted mouse B was more sluggish than the other two.

"Where's the fourth?"

"I'll get him."

Warren frowned when I presented him with a cold limp mouse.

"Can you do an autopsy?" I asked.

"What exactly am I looking for?"

"Exactly, I'm not sure. But you could start with cell anomalies, organ damage, that sort of thing."

He looked at me as though I was a direct descendant of Dr Frankenstein and any progress we'd made recently now somewhat lessened. The situation was obviously ridiculous. Nevertheless, here we stood, solemnly staring at a dead mouse.

"OK, and what do you think will happen to the others?" he asked.

"I think B will die soon, C should live and D, I'm not exactly sure. Can you just check him out and let me know if you find anything out of the ordinary?"

He shook his head and returned to the lab holding the dead mouse by the tail.

In the evening, I dropped Nicole back home and remained seated in the car while watching her enter the house. Through the lounge room window, I noticed Alison's gaunt form. The lights came on in Nicole's room and within minutes, they were off again. I guessed Nicole went straight to bed, without speaking much to her mother.

At the observatory, the place was a hive of activity.

"Michael, have a look at this," Lou said with more enthusiasm than I'd seen from him recently.

He gave me a rundown on the new laser design, with a barrel now reduced to half its original diameter. But at the other end, the waveform generator end, it was twice as large.

"Lou, it's shrunk *and* grown!"

"Yeah, I was hoping you'd overlook the grown part."

On a wall, he'd arranged an array of tiny receivers to covert the microwave energy to a voltage. He scanned the various parts of the laser with a thermal imaging device to confirm the starting temperature and programmed a five-second pulse. There was no noise while the computer received data from the microwave receivers on the wall and converted it into a plot on the screen. The result indicated a staggering 99 per cent efficiency rate. He had succeeded in significantly reducing the losses.

"How?" I asked.

"I thought you'd never ask. It was a combination of things. First, we used your idea with the carrier wave and then we modified the magnetic field generator to ensure maximum coherence of the laser beam. The magnetism seemed to have an ongoing effect on the wave spread. In fact, it held the wave tighter over much longer distances, therefore minimal beam spread and minimal losses," he salivated just before continuing. "We also created a vacuum chamber inside the laser barrel and phase shifted the waveform so a positive synergy formed with the magnetic field."

"You know what they say about something that sounds too good to be true..." I suggested.

He appeared bothered.

"What do you think you've missed?" I prodded.

"We haven't found a downside yet."

"OK, if a signal is sent from earth to a satellite, bounced through another satellite and then down to earth again, that could be a ten thousand kilometer round trip. Add in some cloud or worse, rain, and we could be back to extremely low power levels again."

"We'll set up a test for that scenario and let you know..."

"Lou, you've done a great job, but just recheck your design. And you'll need to prepare the laser for field trials in days not weeks."

He glared at me as I moved away to catch up with Alan, seated at his computer several feet away.

"It seems like no one sleeps much around here," I said.

"Looks like you haven't slept much either."

"Just another wild and crazy night..."

"Good for you."

"I even managed to kill something."

"Excuse me?"

"It was just a mouse. How are you doing?"

"Much better. We have access to an elevated security level on the CIA database. We've got more on Pakistan than Pakistan has on itself, and it's the same for most other Middle Eastern countries."

"Good. Where's David?"

"Upstairs asleep, we're alternating shifts."

"Any news on James?"

"Not much. Every corner of the internet is buzzing about Korea. Have a look at these web casts."

He scrolled through the web pages for CNN, FOX and several other networks, all covering the Seoul bombing. We watched a news flash scrolling across the bottom of the screen; *Saudi Arabia made history today by being the first country to buy another. Saudi will funnel a trillion dollars into the Sudan economy to improve living standards for the nation's 45 million people, and pay out their third world debt of 300 billion dollars, in full. The current Sudanese authoritarian regime, an alliance of the military and the National Congress Party, will hand over power to the Saudi's within seven days. It is believed Saudi have made similar offers to other neighboring countries, particularly those on the west coast of the Red Sea.*

"Can they do that?" Alan asked.

"Looks like they have."

"Why?"

"Perhaps it's the new age alternative to war—quicker, no bloodshed and probably cheaper too. What's the current cost of a medium size war?"

"Sure, but a trillion dollars?"

"Small change to them. Imagine how much they've squirreled away after a century of pumping oil."

"Yeah, that's scary shit."

"Alan, we need a direct microwave link to SatCOMM. Lou will help with the hardware."

"Isn't the SatCOMM building in the city more than a hundred kilometers away?"

"Ninety-eight as the crow flies."

"That's a serious microwave link."

"Get with the times, Alan. And keep on track with the database. I need access to as much intel as possible, and soon."

CHAPTER 23

Apersistent ringing in my ears finally ended the nightmare in which Satan and I joined forces to destroy the world. I wondered about the psychoanalysis of that as I dragged myself away from the fire and brimstone to answer the phone.

"Hey what's up?" Tom said. "You know if you need a hand with anything, I'm available..."

"I appreciate that, but what about your various businesses?"

"I can sell off some projects to make time. I'd like to help if I can."

A mid-life awakening?

"OK, there's construction work to manage at the observatory. The basement levels, the residential wing and a bunch of plant and equipment to install. You want to manage all that?"

"Sure."

The phone rang again, the caller id read *Cooper*.

"Michael, the satellite will be delivered to you shortly on four separate containers."

"Will we need a crane?"

"No, one will accompany it."

"I'm setting up a microwave link to SatCOMM, I assume you're OK with that?"

"Sure. I have a political analyst on staff. He helps us foresee problems we may encounter in overseas operations. If you could come by my office tomorrow at noon, I'd like you to hear his briefing."

"OK…" as if saying no was an option.

I got up, dressed and felt another headache brewing.

Lou and I met for breakfast in the village near the observatory and we discussed the satellite arrival. I was glad to hear the laser was ready for field-testing and asked him to join me for the installation.

As we loaded the laser into the back of the van, he was surprised to see the accumulated hardware from my previous experiments, especially the optical camera and servomotors, which would come in handy for the current trial. Lou expressed some concern at the idea of society observed from phone towers, but if it helped law enforcement he said, then so be it.

Arriving at the cell tower, I silently thanked SatCOMM for sparing no expense—this one had its own hydraulic lift and it was an easy ride to the top with all the gear. We installed the laser, the night vision filter and other hardware before taking a moment to view a spectacular sunset.

"What's that bright cluster of buildings way over there?" Lou asked.

"That's Longbay Prison."

"It's a lot bigger than I thought."

"Yeah, and I hear they're fully booked, with two more blocks planned for later this year."

"Privately owned and operated?"

"Yep."

"The more crime, the more criminals and the more profit these corporations make. Is that a social conflict?"

"Yep."

On the way back to the observatory, Lou and I stopped at a bar, chose a quiet corner and enjoyed a drink. Lou was a decent guy, who almost married a few years back. Shortly after, his fiancé was diagnosed with leukemia and he spent the next several months attending to her day and night, watching her die.

"I think I might have met someone," he confessed.

"Where would you find the time?"

"I know. Her name is Sue and she's a recruitment officer with an employment agency, the one I'm using to source technicians."

I smiled.

"She's thirty-two and widowed. Her husband was in the Middle East peacekeeping force. He was shot and killed two years ago. They never told her exactly where or how he died."

"How well do you know her?"

"We've been out a couple of times. She's taking the train to the village this evening to join me for dinner."

"Good for you, Lou. You know there will be some swish accommodation at the observatory soon, with a gym and pool. We'll need a few women around to help the place smell better."

"Michael, are we doing a good thing at the observatory?"

"Yes, absolutely. Global communications means the world comes together more, the differences are diminished and maybe it'll help us all get along better."

"Yeah, I'd like to believe that."

"Me too..."

I found Tom going over the plans for the observatory renovation in my loft.

"Not bad, but where's my penthouse?" he asked.

"Damn, I knew I left something out."

"And where's all the money coming from?"

"SatCOMM. We have a contract to supply communication systems to them."

"As in SatCOMM—the international conglomerate?"

"Yes, the same one that employs sixteen thousand people in ten countries."

"They chose you and this seaside retreat as their core technology supplier?"

"Pretty much. Now let's go over these plans."

It was a relaxing evening, spent in the most comfortable brotherly companionship we'd had for years. As well as bringing him up to speed on construction activities, I was glad to be handing over what he loved doing best—ordering people around.

We phoned for pizza, but a deepening headache started to steal away my appetite.

My head was still pounding the next morning when I ventured downstairs to find several technicians and Lou working on the Mark-Three laser design. The group resembled a surgical team operating on a patient, but this patient was mechanical. In another nook, Alan and David were tapping on their keyboards with a sense of purpose, their fingers reminding me of chickens pecking at grain. And outside, Tom was directing the contractors, completely happy in his natural state.

I disappeared into the basement and drove to St Georges to catch up with Helen before my noon meeting with Cooper.

Helen was just finishing breakfast when I entered her room, and quickly sensed her growing boredom and frustration.

"When do you think we can get into the treatment properly?" Helen asked.

"I don't know. Mark is being very conservative with the most promising procedures. It's all quite new, so it will take a little time."

She looked at me beseechingly.

"Michael, the pain is really bad at times."

I held her, but felt her now bony frame shrinking away from me.

In the lab, I found Mark hunched over his microscope.

"Michael, the mice—"

"I know, one of them died, I'm sorry."

"It's more than one, the one you marked B has also died."

"I'm hoping Warren will know more when he performs the autopsies."

"He's done them. Mouse A died from rapid organ failure, the blood simply stopped carrying oxygen, resulting in organ failure, and death. If I had to theorize I would say your irradiation interrupted the manufacture of the globin protein."

"Globin?"

"Yes, it's responsible for the binding and releasing of oxygen to cells. A few minutes without oxygen and the cells start to die, then soon after the critical organs cease working."

"I see," and all this from a split second pulse.

"Mouse B died after several hours, from leukemia. The most rapid progression I've ever seen."

"How does that work?"

"An excessive production of abnormal white blood cells overcrowds the bone marrow, spilling out into the blood. The result is decreased production and function of normal blood cells. It spreads to the lymph nodes, spleen, liver, central nervous system and other organs."

"OK, and mouse C?"

"Yes, well, C. He's a world first too, by dying of accelerated ageing. We estimate he's aged over a year in the last twelve hours."

He saw me struggling to comprehend.

"As we age our cells demonstrate a reducing ability to divide accurately. The accumulation of these mutations leads to a loss of key genes—ageing."

"I see," but not too clearly.

I sat down and tried to assimilate the information through a pounding head.

"Michael, you've somehow changed the core cell expression mechanism and altered the cell replication process..."

"OK, but what about mouse D?"

"We haven't completed a full run down on him yet, but he seems to have an unusually high proportion of stem cells. He appears super healthy in fact."

Mark looked at me as though I had an explanation for all these afflictions.

"Hey, I just programmed a variety of irradiation sequences. I wasn't sure exactly what to expect." I said.

"The famous Crow doctrine of research?"

"Yes, you've heard of it?"

"I assume you can replicate these sequences?"

"I think so, but can I suggest something else?"

"Sure, why not," his voice was thick with disdain.

"Do you have any sick mice?"

"Sick? Well, we have several with various forms of cancer and viruses, but they are in test."

"Can we include a couple of them in these tests as well?"

"I see where you're heading with this, but it's unwise to proceed in such an adhoc manner, not to mention cross contamination of tests."

I felt I should apologize, but looked at my watch and realized I had thirty minutes to get to SatCOMM.

"Just consider it, Mark. I'll be back later."

I left him pondering mouse ethics, and how far he was prepared to go along with my maverick ways.

I arrived at SatCOMM headquarters ten minutes late and took the elevator to the fortieth floor. I was still thinking about mouse ethics when the elevator door opened and Cooper lunged at me, hand extended. He ushered me into his office and closed the door.

"This is Andrew Wettril, my business advisor and expert on world affairs, as well as other things. And you know John Trobe of course," a vigorous round of hand shaking ensued.

"It's time to get you all up to date on certain sensitive information. What Andrew has to say will help us assess the degree of exposure for specific operations we are planning to undertake."

I didn't ask which specific operations he was referring to, or who the 'we' was. Andrew pressed a button on the desk and a world political map illuminated on the screen behind him.

He cleared his throat and began, "Of the many people who call themselves political analysts, only a few really understand how close we are to a global precipice right now. The recent events in South Korea and the intrusion of the Middle East into central Africa are public knowledge, but many more things are not," he took a deep breath to underline the seriousness of what was to follow.

"The unrest in Eastern Europe following the disintegration of the Soviet Union late last century has never been resolved. And the result of this has been a plethora of dissatisfied countries. Countries unlikely to ever operate at a profit. Countries who have only succeeded in plunging their citizens deeper into poverty. We've seen the same mismanagement in Africa and unfortunately history has shown us that the processes of fragmentation and consolidation are cyclic. And with each cycle comes enormous societal upheaval, pain, suffering, ethnic cleansing, coups and dictatorships. The UN, despite its professed mandate, has its own agenda and continues to do nothing to help these countries."

"What are the prime concerns?" Cooper asked.

"The entire African continent, the Middle East and parts of Asia."

That didn't leave much out.

"What are the specific and immediate threats?" Trobe added in seasoned monotone.

"Central Africa will retaliate against the Arab buy-out in the north east. Several African countries have acquired nuclear weapons. Nigeria is a target for acquisition, being a country with vast energy reserves, and with one hundred and thirty million people, it has the capacity to become *the* African superstate. Its income earning potential hasn't escaped the notice of Saudi and France either. Saudi is tired of the riff raff on their borders and wants to absorb these basket cases before they become a real threat, and France wants to re-colonize larges chucks of West Africa."

"Do the Saudi's have the military muscle for that?" Trobe asked.

"They'll throw more money instead of bombs. It's usually cleaner and more effective. If they control both sides of the Red Sea, they control what comes in and out of the entire region, not to mention the enormous methane seams lying under the Red Sea."

"What about North Korea?" Cooper asked.

"That's already a done deal. China and Japan are fed up with the constant conflict and have agreed between them to re-assimilate the Koreas. Japan gets the South and China the North. Korea will simply cease to exist. It's already been sanctioned by the NWO."

He mentioned the New World Order as though it really existed. The others said nothing, so neither did I. Silence hung in the air as the full implication of this registered.

"What else?" Trobe asked.

"The Russian federation will be reformed, a stated agenda of the newly elected Russian President. He already has the support of several disillusioned States."

"Why would they want that?" Trobe continued.

"Because some States have within them groups trying to fragment their countries further, and these States now realize they can't hold it together on their own. The new superpower will be a United States of Eastern Europe, of sorts."

"That doesn't sound too bad," I finally dared an opinion.

"Not on the face of it, but there are many different races and cultures in the transition zones around Eastern Europe, Asia and the Middle East, and they want their own sovereignty. I suspect many of these States will scorch the ground before they let a central group govern them, particularly a group of misfits like the Russian government," he paused. "And, more than one of these States has nuclear weapons, or at least knows where to source them should the need arise. Not the homemade variety either, these would be the real deal."

"What about Pakistan and India?" I asked about a subject closer to my heart.

"Most agree India wants Pakistan and Pakistan wants India, but our network can't come up with anything more specific at this time."

"After the upheaval, then what?" Cooper asked.

"Then consolidation will revert to fragmentation, and the cycle continues."

"Until we destroy the world completely," I ventured.

"It's possible, but unlikely. There's no profit in total destruction," the pontiff stated.

I sensed he enjoyed, with a sense of ownership, the prophecies he spun. He gathered his papers, the proclamation had finished.

"I'd like to thank Andrew for his time," Cooper said.

Trobe accompanied Andrew from the room for some private discussion. I was tempted to ask Cooper why he had brought me into this inner sanctum and what he imagined my role would be, but was afraid of the answer.

"Does that mean reduced SatFone sales in an unstable world?" I asked Cooper.

"On the contrary, Michael. We expect more sales into the third world than anywhere else, at least initially."

For what, coordination of troop movements, I almost ventured.

"How will these people pay for their phones? Most earn less than a dollar a day."

"There are ways to pay, other than hard currency."

"Such as?"

He appeared annoyed with my questions.

"They may have resources we want, but don't worry too much about that. How is progress at the observatory?"

"Good. How long can we have access to the satellite?"

"Three days, then it ships to China."

"OK."

I thought about making an exit.

"Michael, I'm sorry to hear about your mother. It would seem your entire family is a target. A feeling I unfortunately know too well."

"I don't think we are being targeted Brendan, but there's definitely some weird shit going on."

"If there's any way I can help...a new kidney perhaps?"

I suddenly lost the power of speech and my mouth hung open.

"Just let me know Michael," he said with a knowing smile, then turned and left.

Driving to the hospital, I wondered about the roller coaster I'd found myself on, and whether I could get off, even if I wanted to. I arrived at St Georges and entered the lab to find Mark and Warren looking at me suspiciously. How deep was the mistrust I wondered, and had the death of the mice been the turning point?

"Michael, I need to discuss something with you," Mark demanded.

I steadied my hand to pour a coffee.

"Warren and I have been postulating on how your irradiation techniques might be causing these cellular transitions. We think maybe it's not the cell DNA that is being directly affected, but rather the RNA. Have you heard of RNA?"

"Not really..."

"Ribonucleic acid or more specifically *messenger RNA*. Its function is to copy genetic information from DNA and translate it into proteins. mRNA is nature's way for living organisms to undergo evolutionary change faster, and with fewer generations than would otherwise be the case. By operating on the transmission process you've shortcut a way to induce the evolution of a new protein, without changing the original DNA of a gene."

"I see, you mean like a wormhole through the space-time continuum?"

Mark eyed me as a teacher would a disruptive student, and worse still, it seemed Hawking was not on his reading list.

"Michael, you have violated almost every principle of research and procedure," he blurted.

"Why, because the result hasn't come from *years* of painstaking trial and error?"

"No, because your approach is reckless and dangerous."

"Mark, you can call it reckless if you like, but in the end it always comes back to following hunches. Sure, they're not always right. In fact, more often they lead to dead ends."

Mark unlocked his stare but not his frown. I continued anyway, "You know that ninety nine percent of the time it's just sheer hard work and lots of it. Surely, you of all people should understand that. And I know the situation with James is distressing you, as it is me. Maybe we should all get more sleep."

"But something just doesn't add up."

"Well, I'd hate to have all the answers..."

"Usually the altered mRNA state persists for only as long as the stimulant does, the same way the new generation of painkillers operate. But in this case the stimulant, the irradiation, is present only for an instant, yet the miscoding continues indefinitely."

"We also don't know the exact mechanism by which the wave train acts as a catalyst," Warren said, finding it safe to rejoin the discussion now.

"You're right, we don't. How are the remaining mice today?" I asked.

"Well, I suspect C doesn't have long to live, but D is doing well." Warren offered.

"And the scan on D?"

"I'm still seeing an increasing proportion of stem cells."

"I'd like to investigate a few additional scenarios," I said, warily. "And, I can't rule out the possibility of more mice suffering." I waited for an indignant outburst from either of them before continuing, "I'd like to cause an injury to D and see what happens..."

"What sort of injury do you have in mind?" Mark asked, barely restraining himself.

"I'm thinking maybe the amputation of a limb, in the hope that it will grow back."

"And what makes you think it will just *grow* back?"

"A hunch."

Mark's face reddened in preparation of another onslaught, but I cut him off. "Mark, hundreds of mice suffer every day. I mean, hardware stores still sell mousetraps and rat poison by the truckload."

Warren cleared his throat. "There may be a basis for his hunch. I've noticed vigorous cell reproduction after irradiation and the cells seem to direct themselves as necessary, and with an accelerated division rate."

"OK, but we're talking about the *regrowth of entire limbs*." Mark said through clenched teeth.

"When I put D in his cage yesterday," Warren continued. "I caught his tail on the door catch. It was a deep prick in the thick end of the tail, but it stopped bleeding quickly and today there's not even a scratch to be seen."

Warren collected mouse D from his cage and placed him on the bench. We observed him as he sniffed Warren's hand.

Mark spoke, "OK, we can try some viral agents, perhaps even cancer agents to see if his immune system can fight those. But on the evidence so far, I can't see any mechanism for the likelihood of limb regrowth."

"If the stem cells have that kind of capability, why would they not respond to all threats and aberrations?" I persisted.

"Because the agents for limb or organ regrowth could be completely different from those to do with enhanced immune system response," Mark articulated each word slowly.

"But surely the mouse would rather have one less limb than cancer?"

Warren half smiled as Mark opened his mouth, but failed to speak, thinking perhaps there was no point.

I continued, "Hey, let's not lose our nerve here. We need to improve our understanding of what's going on in the quickest possible time. So why not irradiate several mice. We could sever a limb, inject a virus, induce cancer, and so on. We'll monitor and document everything, and who knows, after a few days we may even have some statistically relevant results to work with. Then we can apply the treatment to Helen and get the hell on with it."

There, I'd said it. I wanted to apply this treatment to Helen, in days rather than months or years. I braced myself for a reprimand or worse.

Mark started slowly in his *I'm-talking- to-a-loony* voice, "Michael, you're not thinking straight. We cannot apply this procedure to a human patient, even if we wanted too, without the approval of the authorities. We'd lose our licence, or go to jail for a very long time at worst. If the tests you suggest turn out to be successful, then we're only at the start of a possible procedure. And just because the stem cell proportion is high, doesn't mean the cell reproduction or repair mechanisms are stable. You could be inviting any kind of side effect. The possibilities for disaster are endless."

"The chances are, however, that if it's stable in the short term, it will be stable in the long term," I said slowly and calmly to mimic him.

"Perhaps, but the short term isn't twenty-four hours, it's more like twenty-four months."

Warren turned to Mark, "Those sick mice that were part of trial 1772, we could use them?"

Mark stroked the mouse nibbling at his fingers, "OK, Warren will gather and prepare three specimens. They'll have different ailments. Cure them all first and we'll talk more after that."

"Thank you." I said, accepting that he had to maintain at least the illusion of control.

I needed some fresh air and stepped outside. I made a call to transfer more money to the foundation, to maintain the illusion of my control.

After a quick visit to a local pet shop, I returned to the lab with a large white mouse hidden in my left pant pocket. The little guy was a determined escape artist and I had to keep pushing him down, hoping he wouldn't bite me in frustration. I placed the mouse in the top drawer of my desk to contain him while I located Warren.

He was in the back lab, standing in front of a sad group of mice in their separate cages. All suffered from a terminal illness of one kind or another—one had almost no fur, another oozed mucus from every orifice and another just sat still, lifeless except for an occasionally blinking. They all had a unique number imprinted inside their left ear.

"Usually we'd put them down at this stage," Warren whispered as though the mice could understand.

"OK, let's start by scanning them."

I started with DNA scans, before launching into the irradiation sequences. When we finished Warren returned the mice to their cages. I collected my white mouse and presented him to Warren.

"It would be best if you were to do it with a local anesthetic." I suggested.

"Do what exactly?"

"The tail…"

A look of disgust flashed across his face,

"Why am I not surprised? OK, but you can't keep him here. Mark would not approve of an external, unclean mouse."

"That's fine. I'll take him home with me and maybe, if he's in the mood, we can catch a movie. Perhaps *Stuart Little* and then we could hang out together while his tail re-grows."

I didn't want to stay around for the amputation, so I left Warren holding the mouse and convinced I really was a loony.

I found Helen watching the 6 o'clock news on her wall-mounted television. Images filled the screen of a five-storey building imploding somewhere in Uzbekistan, leaving mountains of rubble and hysterical people in its wake. Apparently, extremists of one sort or another had bombed an office block, which also housed a child minding facility on the second floor. Twenty-four children aged six months to six years were killed, and the same number again injured or crippled for life.

Helen shook her head, her eyes red with anger, "For God's sake, will it ever stop?"

I turned to another station, hoping to find *Seinfeld* or something similarly innocuous. Instead, another news story blared at us, showing a mass of skeleton remains in what looked like a large creator pit. The caption read, *'The new killing fields - Bangalore, Southern India'*. The reporter talked of tens of thousands of human bones found by chance last week when a cargo plane crashed in a remote part of India. Local authorities were at a loss to explain the finding or why no heads or torsos were found among the arms and legs. I turned the television off and we ate dinner.

We talked about friends we hadn't seen for a while, but I was more distracted than usual. Was there really a worldwide trade in body parts? Was that the resource of the impoverished Cooper had hinted at? But what had become of the human heads, the brains? The movie *Soylent Green* sprung to mind.

After dinner, I told Helen I needed to return to the observatory for a few days. She looked disappointed, abandoned and concerned. I gave her a kiss and slunk out of the room.

"How are the patients?" I asked Warren, with some trepidation.

"They're still alive, but I can't detect any real improvement, not even on a cellular level."

"What about—"

"Your mouse is in the last cage on the left. You can transport him in this box," he handed me a Chinese takeaway container.

"How is he?"

"Well, considering. I bandaged his tail, or what's left of it."

The mouse seemed a little sluggish, but I suspect he was pleased to be spared a terminal illness.

I left for home at midnight, with a Wong's Chinese takeaway box in hand.

CHAPTER 24

I named my mouse Zeus, the ruler of the heavens and father of Helen of Troy—a Greek mythology thing. I stopped at a pet shop to buy a home for Zeus and, noticing an attractive female mouse preening herself, I decided to make his day and bought her too. However, I had an ulterior motive—I needed to know whether the elevated stem cell activity might be hereditary.

I drove up the observatory driveway on a windy, rain-beaten Wednesday morning. Tom was standing at the edge of a muddy excavation amidst a sea of people and machinery, flinging his arms wildly at various contractors. The number and variety of vehicles scattered over the grounds made the place look like a used car lot, and the frenzied activity in the dome reminded me of the sales office. I failed to recognize most of the hundred or so people here, and smiled at the momentum I had set in action, feeling both a sense of control and loss of it.

Lou appeared busy with his many techs, so I turned to Alan and David, wondering how many computer keyboards these guys wore out each year.

"We've made good progress," Alan reported. "The CIA clearance is linking us to over sixty sites in various countries around the world, in a completely secure mode. You can forget back doors we beamed right in through the roof and we're accumulating data at a rate of a hundred giga-bytes a minute."

I followed his excited stare to a stack of hard disk storage units rack mounted in a large metal cabinet against the wall.

"What's the total capacity of those?"

"There are two hundred separate drives, each with a capacity of one hundred terabytes. We decided not to bother with backup..."

"Why download all this data in the first place? Couldn't we just leave it on the net and access it when we need it?"

"Sure, but if we lose our security clearances, or sites go down when we need the data, then we have nothing. And we can more efficiently cross-reference data from multiple sources if it's stored on local drives. Performing cross referencing searches on localized data takes seconds, rather than many minutes live across the net."

"And the cost?"

"We negotiated a good quantity discount... all up, just on 200k," he blinked nervously. "Um...Lou said you'd be fine with it."

I let him sweat on it for a few seconds, "Sure, that's fine. When can you run me through a demonstration?"

"Soon. At the rate we're accumulating data, in thirty days we'll have personal records logged for over a billion people."

"OK, let me get the feel of it before you go too far. I might want to change the structure or add to the type of data stored."

"Impressive database isn't it?" Lou commented from behind.

"Yeah, I'd always wondered what it would be like to actually *be* Big Brother."

"I was wondering about that too..."

"Who knows, maybe SatCOMM wants to know the credit status and buying habits of every living person in the world."

"Yeah, right." Lou was unconvinced and I knew he was itching for more insight into what seemed like a grand but secret plan. I admired his ability to refrain from asking too many questions.

"Speaking of SatCOMM," I turned to Alan. "What's the status on the microwave link?"

"We're all done at this end and just waiting for SatCOMM to connect. Michael, your lunch is making scratching sounds," Alan pointed to the Wong's Chinese box I'd placed on the desk.

"It's a mouse, and he probably wants food and water."

"A mouse?"

"Well, actually two of them. These guys have been genetically modified to write software at a staggering pace."

Alan looked pale as Lou and I left him and made our way to the kitchen.

I placed Zeus and Leda in their new house, perched up on a window ledge with a view of the ocean.

"How's the new laser progressing?" I asked while pouring coffees.

"We had to add a few things. Little things, like a special propagation controller for the higher energy waveforms."

"I see, and was it successful?"

"Yes, but the cost of the thing has skyrocketed. With all the specialized materials, it's almost ten times the cost of the initial design."

"How much per laser?"

"Just under half a million, including the peripheral gear, optical filters, servos—"

"OK, but we'll need two of them, pointing up through the observatory dome. You'll also need to work on those waveguides. We'll need two of them mounted inside each satellite."

"Two?"

"Yes, each satellite will have two independent waveguide systems for uplink and downlink to an earth station, as well as side linking to other satellites. And redundant servo motors, with everything to military spec."

"Before Monday?"

"Yes, and I've also sketched out a schematic for the electronic mods to the SatFone handsets. The handset samples are arriving with the satellite."

Lou was only slightly fazed and already processing the requirements for people and resources in his head.

"Did you know another bomb has been detonated?" Lou asked.

"No, what kind of bomb?"

"They called it an RDD, a radiological dispersal device. It still managed to flatten several city blocks."

"Where?"

"Kigali, capital of Rwanda, they say it's most likely related to the internal fighting between two tribes."

"Wasn't there some kind of a war there during the mid 1990s?"

"Michael, the fighting has been going on there for decades. Africa's always been a basket case."

"You know, two or three hundred years from now, people will look back on this time and consider it part of the dark ages."

Lou returned to work and I took the mice with me to the loft. I searched the internet and found out some recent history on Rwanda. I read about the Hutu extremists who were responsible for the genocide of several hundred thousand Tutsis in the mid 1990s. Hundreds of thousands of people slaughtered. How could I forget that? How could I have been so cut-off from the world and for so long?

I switched to a CNN webcast where images of the recent carnage inundated the screen. The debris covered more than a square kilometer of Kigali's city centre, but I had to admit, it wasn't easy discerning the blast zone from the usual city rubble.

The isolation of the camera made the images look surreal and impersonal, and I wondered where all the people were. I glanced behind me at the mice taking turns at running the wheel and wondered how they would judge us if they knew what we were doing to the planet, and to each other.

It was a grey and overcast afternoon. A black line on the horizon promised a classic storm assault on the coastline within the next hour or so. My head hammered, as it did most days, and I decided to take a walk to the village along the beach. It would take an hour or so each way and would clear my head, I hoped.

I crossed the coast road and climbed slowly down the fifty-meter craggy rock staircase carved haphazardly into the cliff face, then onto a broad expanse of yellow sand. The wind blasted me from all directions as waves crashed to the shore with a deafening roar. Mother Nature seemed to be reminding us that she was still a player, her energy most vivid where the sea met the land.

I walked along the rocky outcrops that separated long sandy stretches of beach. The tide was rising with a sense of purpose, which made me consider my purpose in all this. The confused waves barreled in, as the maelstrom of wind and rain obliterated any difference between sky and sea.

Looking to a cliff edge, I saw a dead seagull amongst clumps of weed and sea garbage. I climbed up several meters to find the gull's neck wrapped tight with fishing line and a metal lure stuck in its mouth. I knelt beside it and offered a silent apology on behalf of all humanity. Several gulls watched me from a sheltered ledge nearby, squawking wildly. I suspect their message to me was along the lines of 'go fuck yourself'.

Two hours later, I arrived back at the observatory cold and wet and with the hammering in my head only slightly dulled by hypothermia.

"You've been away for so long we thought you'd drowned yourself," Tom said.

"It was certainly wild out there."

"Did you see Lou at the village?"

"No, I didn't get that far."

"He got a call, something about Sue and drove off in a rush to the village."

I changed my clothes and inspected Zeus by removing his bandage carefully. Apart from a deep red color at the amputation point, his tail appeared to be healing well. I fed the pair and watched Zeus bounce off the cage mesh with excess energy. Leda seemed to be appealing to me, as if asking, 'why have you stuck me with this mad mouse?'

The loft computer networked to the others in the observatory and to the mass data storage units. From here, I could access whatever I wanted. As the storm raged outside, I patched through to SatCOMM and to the laser positioned high up on the Longbay cell phone tower.

I tested the targeting systems, which were responding well—the servomotor functions feeling smooth and accurate. I had a clear 360-degree view of the skyline, with the city to the east and the Pacific coast to the north and south. And there, eight kilometers to the west and spread out like a small village, was Longbay Prison.

I panned and zoomed with the visual optics as well as infrared, but the night vision test would have to wait until later. The servomotors were of the same type used to position a twenty-ton radio telescope to millimeter accuracy and they moved the laser array around like bunch of flowers. I spent some time fine-tuning the software to cater for all the scenarios I expected to encounter. I noticed a small bird sitting on the roof of one of the prison buildings and switched to infrared to lock the bird to the targeting system. I was encouraged to see the system tracking it without any delay, even once the bird started to fly.

I started to set up a short duration pulse when the phone rang.

"Michael, I'm at the Regional Hospital with Sue," Lou said, his voice distressed and hoarse. "She's badly hurt."

"What happened?"

"She was raped and bashed on the train coming from the city… four men. She's in a coma."

Déjà vu. My gut wrenched, my throat restricted. "Lou, I'm sorry, what can I do to help?"

"The doctors here say there's not much anyone can do… other than wait for the swelling to subside and hope there's no permanent damage," his words trailed off.

"Her family?"

"Both her parents are dead and she has no brothers or sisters. She hasn't talked much about anyone and I don't know of any family or friends here."

"Stay strong for her Lou, I'll be there shortly."

I drove into the storm, fighting to keep the car on the road. I couldn't help feeling someone or something was pushing me, taunting me.

I found Lou pacing outside the intensive care room.

"She's a mess Michael… her head, I barely recognize her."

I sat with him for a while as the doctor spoke. Shortly afterward, Lou insisted we get back to the observatory.

"Why would someone do that?" Lou asked as we drove through buckets of horizontal water.

"I don't know."

"I'll find them and I'll—"

"Lou, forget revenge. You'll be worse for it, believe me."

We arrived at the observatory and Lou went straight to work. He never wore his heart on his sleeve for too long.

I continued fine-tuning the targeting systems from my loft and integrated the various scan modes for the visual, infrared and night vision filters. I experimented further with the irradiation techniques, spreading them over an area rather than concentrating them in a tight beam as I had been.

The results were intriguing. I noticed through the night vision lens a slight bloom of light coming from a small field mouse I scanned. I scanned more of the wild life—birds, cats, dogs, whatever came my way in an attempt to detect any differences in the return waveform. I switched in an ultra high frequency digital filter, thinking that perhaps the return signal would be more noticeable in the higher bands. I captured the return waveform and performed a series of mathematical interpretations and pattern recognition routines on it. A tall order considering the light was as dim as a glow-worm from eight kilometers away, and lasted no longer than the blink of an eye.

I ran the raw data through the Vibrolert software to pick out components from the low to extremely high frequencies. I found, embedded deep within the white noise, an extremely weak signal in the highest microwave bands, which continued only microseconds after the outgoing scan ceased.

After a few more repetitions, it became clear that this return energy came *from* living things subjected to the outgoing waveform. It seems I had managed to reproduce the cellular bio-fluorescence I'd triggered with my waveform analyzer at St. Georges, but this time I'd achieved it over a distance.

I researched the online medical encyclopedias and read more about bio-phosphorescence and bio-fluorescence. The literature described how it could be initiated by infrared light—the approach I used in the waveform analyzer.

From the Longbay cell tower, I located several species of animals to study their unique energy signatures. The investigative power of the Vibrolert software, which had taken me several years and two hundred thousand lines of code to write, was now stretched to a limit it wasn't designed for.

Overlaying the waveform plots, I saw the bio-fluorescence components of the animals were ever so slightly different, yet for each individual animal, they were identical. I didn't expect to decode real DNA without some backdrop absorption to detect trace elements, but maybe there was something here similar to DNA.

I surveyed the prison yard, but found no activity. Looking to an adjacent park, I saw a young couple seated together on a bench. I was hesitant to scan them, without knowing the side effects of what was essentially low power irradiation. With the infrared scan on wide angle, I detected a distinct luminous image some fifty meters behind the couple. I zoomed in closer and confirmed it as a human form—a man crouched in the bushes behind the couple, observing them.

I didn't expect the remote DNA scan to have any harmful effects, but couldn't be sure until I tested it further. However, I decided this doubtful character was a worthy test subject anyway and sent him a short duration microwave pulse. I repeated the procedure several times and then superimposed each of the return signals on top of one another. Each plot lined up exactly, which meant the bio-fluorescence was relatively free of error. Now I needed a different subject to isolate the specific differences *between* the individuals.

Scanning the park further, I found what looked like a vagrant asleep next to a large industrial bin. I decided he or she would also like to contribute to medical science and scanned for bio-fluorescence. I repeated the procedure several times on the same individual and each time the return signature came back identical, but all slightly different from the first person. The task now was to decode and amplify this difference, and then to extract any useful information about the individuals.

I continued into the night, stopping only for stale donuts and a quick chat with a bright-eyed Zeus, who needed less sleep than his mate did. In fact, I couldn't remember the last time I saw him asleep.

The storm dissipated as the sun rose in the morning. I'd added almost a thousand lines of software and hoped this would help isolate the minute differences between the bio-fluorescence signatures. I stood up, stretched, and reheated a cup of stale black coffee while waiting for the Long Bay prison grounds to populate.

Minutes later, I jolted awake in the chair, covering myself in lukewarm coffee. I cleaned up the mess and returned to the screen to see an abundance of movement in the prison grounds.

A hundred or so people were walking, jogging, smoking and playing basketball. So ordered, it could have been staged. But behind the order were the group huddles, the covert glances and the deals. Even prison walls failed to stifle the universal equilibrium of supply and demand.

I performed a low-level scan of thirty or so people in the yard, starting with the meanest and most aggressive looking. I took pictures of their faces and emailed them to Alan, asking him to locate any information, particularly DNA data, for each.

I processed the bio-fluorescence signatures and started to encode them mathematically. I hoped that when compared with the official DNA plot for each person, I could come up with a translation routine to link both DNA 'languages'. As I tossed some stale toast into the Zeus' cage, I felt a low rumbling vibration shaking the observatory. I ran out from my loft and saw the hanger doors Tom had installed yesterday rolling open, bringing into view the first satellite.

I almost fell down the stairs in my haste to see four massive semi trailers lining up the driveway, and wondered what the neighbors might be thinking.

"Showtime," Tom shouted over the noise.

"Won't these trucks crack the driveway with their weight?" I shouted back.

"Who knows?"

"As a civil engineer, I thought you might have some idea—"

"Just don't bring in anything heavier."

I was pleased to see two SatCOMM engineers had come along to help put the satellite together. I didn't fancy reading the assembly manual and was pleased the IKEA logo didn't appear anywhere on it.

After several hours, and with the help of Lou's team of five engineers and eight technicians, the assembly was completed. The SatCOMM engineers were intrigued by our involvement in such a project and unable to contain their curiosity with endless questions. Our standard response was, 'We're just quality control consultants for SatCOMM'.

"So what do you think Lou?" I asked.

His face lit up, "Well it's no toy and I'm glad to see they left us some space under the hood. We could use that space as the waveguide compartment and change the solid outer casing here to a bi-fold door."

"Sounds good."

"We'll start working on it."

"How's Sue doing?" I asked.

"There's been no change in her condition, but the police tell me they have two suspects in custody."

"Did they give you any names?"

"No."

"Shit, have a look at this!" Alan shouted above the noise.

Lou and I rushed over to Alan's console, which displayed the CNN webcast.

The scenes were becoming familiar now—the desensitizing had started. Two separate mushroom clouds were rising from the debris that once was Pyongyang, capital of North Korea. The images were from high overhead and showed astounding detail of total destruction, body parts amongst rubble, and the walking dead stumbling through the destruction. A high definition violation beyond words. Raw, unedited and uncensored. A million people obliterated and another million who would succumb to the cellular deterioration that had been set in motion. Was this the re-assimilation of North Korea the Japanese were after?

The verbal stumbling of reporters and military experts became background noise as they espoused opinions on what, who and why. But it all fell short of reason, of humanity. Was it the South Koreans, the Chinese, the Japanese, or was it Islamic extremists seeking to pit their enemies against each other? One 'expert' even suggested the North Koreans nuked themselves, rather than be assimilated into another country. But no one knew for sure, which could make it the perfect crime.

"Michael ..." Alan said. "I've emailed you hits on some of the photos you sent. I had to dig deep for a few and there is a complete file on several individuals. You've got a few nasty customers there."

"Thanks."

I felt drained and retreated to my loft, to another webcast where The Association of Atomic Scientists set their doomsday clock to one minute before midnight, in a solemn and moving ceremony. I saw the new Pope, elected only weeks before, praying for all humanity—but I suspected he prayed just a little harder for the Catholics.

I rang Helen, to hear her voice. She said she missed me and I felt she was at her wits end, feeling caged and completely alone. I comforted her as much as I could over the phone.

I extracted the DNA plots from Alan's email and compared them against the bio-fluorescent spectrum I'd obtained from Longbay. I stared at the plots until my eyes ached and saw only rubble and blackened faces in the pixels.

I rang a friend from my university days. He had gone on to complete a doctorate in mathematics and now lectured at Sydney University. I hadn't spoken with him for almost a year.

"Barry, how are you?" I asked.

"You know how it is, one year the skirts are short and the next they're long again. It's hard to keep up with it all."

"University life is treating you well?"

"It's OK, there's always plenty of new talent coming through."

I assumed he referred more to the appearance of the girls than their intellectual abilities.

"Barry, I have a problem, a mathematical one."

"Do tell."

"I have a DNA analysis and a frequency spectrum plot. I think they both contain similar information, but I can't find a formula to link them."

"Sounds interesting, same information but sourced differently?"

"Yes, the frequency plot is packed tight with data and I've identified numerous component waveforms. I've played around with it a bit to find a way of characterizing each plot. I thought it would be neat to reduce the whole plot to a single number, but I know when I'm in over my head. So I saw the light and called you."

"Wise move. I've just started on two weeks leave, so I'll have some time to play with this. How many separate sets of data have you got?"

"About thirty."

"That's a smallish sample size, but I should be able to come up with something. Email me everything you have and I'll take a look at it."

"You're a legend."

"It's been said before. You should come and visit—I've just installed this great new telescope in my office."

"You're into astrology now?"

"Not exactly …"

I fell into bed and eventually slept amidst the incessant sound of Zeus treading his wheel to destruction.

CHAPTER 25

Friday marked the end of another week. Not that weekends and weekdays were that different these days, weekends just seemed slightly less chaotic. I turned on the television and searched through the channels, finding only images of mushroom clouds and military pontiffs, who were fast becoming the new reality TV stars.

Aid agencies were beseeching the world to donate funds and goods, and the televised violence fed emotions, while the real violence killed them.

A call from Cooper disrupted my morning fix of global turmoil.

"Michael, we need to reappraise the satellite program in light of recent world events. I would like to send the satellites directly to China, without prepping them here. This will accelerate the launch schedule. You'll need to send a team to China to do your final modifications there."

"I see." I disliked the idea, but there was no point objecting, "When do you want us to go there?"

"We're going to ship one unit every two days, starting tomorrow. I want your technicians to be at the launch site in China by Monday."

I rang Lou and told him the news, aware of the implications for him. How prepared was he? I couldn't ask him to leave Sue, but if he didn't go, I'd have to.

"Lou, the research I'm involved with at St Georges shows promise. It's to do with stem cell manipulation and genetic engineering."

He looked at me in disbelief, as though I'd just told him I was leading a secret life as a woman.

"Helen is being treated there and we hope to trial some new procedures on her shortly. It may be an option for Sue as well..." I continued, without adding *what's she got to lose...*

"I don't know..."

"You can say you're her next of kin and sign her over. Not exactly legal but..."

"Michael, this is a lot to take in. Let me think about it."

"OK."

"We'll push forward the laser and other component deliveries and reroute them to China."

"Lou, you're under no obligation to go."

"I know. I'll ask the techs for any volunteers to come with me."

"You've brought me a present, how sweet," Helen opened the box I presented.

"This is Zeus." I said.

"A mouse?" she shrank back into her pillow.

"I thought it would make a nice change from flowers."

"It's a change all right ... but a *mouse*? What do you want me to do with it?"

"Just thank *him*."

"Thank him?"

"He's tested a new treatment. One that looks promising for you and he's passed with flying colors."

She peeked into the box to have a closer look, "You're right, his ass looks just fine."

"No, we amputated his tail several days ago."

She inspected the tail a little closer, "Perhaps it's a little short, but it looks normal."

"That's right, it does. We cut his tail off here..." I pointed as she grimaced in pain for the little guy. "Then we performed some bio-engineering stuff and his stem cell count shot through the roof. His tail has been reforming for the past few days."

"How?"

"Well, the same way it does in the womb, by stem cell direction and duplication."

She looked at me with suspicion while stroking him gently, considering seriously the possibility for the first time.

"I need to take him to the lab for some checks. I'll see you for lunch, OK?"

"OK..."

I met Warren in the lab and showed him Zeus.

"This is the same mouse?" his voice sounded shrill.

"You can confirm that too when you run the tests."

"Unbelievable!"

"Where's Mark?"

"I'm not sure, I didn't see him yesterday and he hasn't been answering his cell today."

"Did you try his other numbers?"

"Yes, his house, but no answer there either."

"He's not married is he?" I said, realizing how little I knew about him.

"No."

Warren started the test routines on Zeus, which included a CT scan and full blood and DNA workup. He anesthetized the poor guy and pinned him under the microscope to get a closer look. I was proud of Zeus, he was proving to be a worthy lab mouse, and I understood why they really were the true heroes of medical research.

I entered my office and read a yellow post-it note stuck on the keyboard. It was a memo from Mark.

"Mark's gone to Colombo." I called out to Warren, who quickly appeared holding Zeus by the tail.

"Colombo? Why?"

"I don't know. He's probably gone in search of James, but all he'll end up doing is getting killed."

"I'll ring the research centre to see if they've heard from him."

While Warren rang Colombo, I rang the observatory.

"Alan, do we have anything new on James' kidnappers?"

"Nothing since the last email, and we came up blank in Sri Lanka and India. We back-grounded hundreds of suspects, but found nothing. No solid leads, no links through known associates, nothing. It's all so basic over there, sparse on detail and what there is, is usually wrong or out of date."

"What about the CIA database?"

"We're still loading a ton of raw data onto hard disk from that and other sources. When it's complete we can start a more comprehensive search and match routine."

"Make it a priority and let me know as soon as you get any hits. Also search the name *Moctas*, I think it's a company name. I need to know who they are, shareholders, the whole bit."

"Nothing from Colombo," Warren said. "They had no idea he was coming and they haven't seen him yet. I've asked them to check the airport and hotels, and to keep us informed."

An hour later, Warren had finished subjecting Zeus to numerous tests and scans. He passed them all, as did the other irradiated mice with their ailments. I had a feeling this was all proceeding too well.

A call from building security let me know the MRI machine I'd ordered had arrived. I told Warren, who eyed me with disbelief, although secretly I'm sure he was a believer.

Two of the supplier's technicians had come to help commission it and we all gathered around a device that resembled a Hollywood time machine. Serious hardware never failed to entice and we spent the next few hours totally enthralled.

I took a break to phone Lou, Alan and Tom. I asked Tom to source sixteen large high definition plasma screens and mount them on the observatory wall in a four by four matrix, for a visual experience spanning several square meters.

I drove home in the early hours of the morning and viewed the city lights behind me in the mirror. Suddenly engulfed by stardust I started to sink into a soft silky marshmallow. I couldn't breathe and began to suffocate. Gaining strength as the fear kicked in, I pushed myself free. The marshmallow dissipated and I gulped air before coughing in a fit.

As the shock subsided, I realized what had happened. I'd crashed my car into a roadside tree and the airbag had activated. I shoved the bag loosely back into its pocket in the steering wheel and opened the door, the cold night air bringing me back to reality. Luckily, I'd travelled slowly before nodding off, so there was only minor damage to the car, and to me.

I sat on the car bonnet and rested for several minutes, before driving home with all the windows open, fully awake and ice cold.

I managed only intermittent sleep, waking often to push away a never-ending barrage of marshmallows. A constant scratching sound outside my window finally annoyed me to the point where I couldn't sleep any longer.

Obviously, there was a SWAT team staking out my backyard and I'd have to deal with it sooner or later.

I climbed out of bed and slowly parted the curtain. Looking down, I saw a large white rabbit scratching at the side of the house. Seems he'd tired of eating the plants and was now looking to me for more interesting handouts. I opened the window and offered him some stale toast from a few days ago, which I still had festering on my bedside table. He limped as he came toward me. When I picked him up he squealed and I felt dried blood matted on his fur. His leg was broken and hanging on by skin.

I found a cardboard box and gently placed him in it.

I arrived at St Georges and put the cardboard box in front of Warren.

"What's this?" he asked.

"It's a rabbit with a broken leg."

"And what's it doing here?"

"I'd like to fix him."

"Are you serious?"

"Yes."

"Maybe we should just open a veterinary clinic?"

"I think we should start with an MRI scan."

"Why, what have you done to this poor animal?"

"Nothing, I just need a baseline."

Begrudgingly, Warren injected the rabbit with a light anesthetic and placed him in the MRI machine. The rabbit looked dwarfed by the internal cavern that was tightly covered in pristine white surgical leather.

The phone rang.

"Michael, I'm worried about your financial situation," Lewis blurted without preamble. In addition to his law practice, he was also a qualified accountant, but I used that service more out of convenience.

"There's a problem with the MRI transaction?" I asked.

"No, that's gone through, but I just thought I'd let you know, you're down to your last two million. Which is not a problem for most people, but you're going through it quicker than most."

"It's OK, I have it under control. Thanks."

"You haven't told me about your new business in any detail, perhaps we should schedule a meeting?"

"Sure Lewis, let me get back to you on that."

I'd hoped ten million would go further and thought about ringing Cooper, but then decided to let my desperation build a little more.

An email from a Barry Sullivan confused me, until I remembered the conversation with him about mathematical relationships between bio-fluorescent spectrum and DNA plots. *Mike, enter the raw data for your frequency plot through the attached formula. It will translate a standard DNA plot. It will look a little different to the standard if you use all your data, as you seem to have a much longer DNA. Is this for real? Whether this extra stuff means anything is up to you to decipher. Have fun. BS.*

The formulae he provided were long and convoluted and how he came up with this stuff was beyond me. But now I could remotely scan for DNA, produce extended DNA plots and encode an entire genome into a single number—unique for each individual on the planet.

For the first time in a while, I craved a cold beer, but settled instead for the flat warm Coke I had on my desk.

I sat in front of the computer and recalled data on the prisoners I'd scanned at Longbay. I had pictures, names and criminal history, as well as DNA from the various databases we'd managed to access. The files showed these were truly evil men with murder, rape and grievous assaults in their repertoires—all except for a handful. One of these non-violent types was inside for twelve months on tax evasion and another for two years on unlawful kidnapping—of his own child.

I superimposed the DNA plots for thirty prisoners over each other as transparencies. Twenty-eight of the scans showed the same peaks in the same part of the extended DNA plot. However, the plots for the two 'non-violent' types showed no such peaks. I was certain this portion of the DNA represented the undiscovered area of the human genome—an area I suspected was responsible for aberrant behavior. In other words, rogue genes for a rogue human. However, I wanted just a little more data, since this conclusion was rash even for me.

I linked through to the Longbay cell tower and found the system response times reasonable enough via the remote connection. The area I scanned at 11.15 am on Saturday morning was buzzing with activity. People moved about freely in the park and with more seriousness in the prison grounds. I decided to scan people at random and uploaded twenty

DNA plots from people in the park and a dozen more from inmates at Longbay.

While I waited for the system to process the information, I watched the webcasts of current news. One local headline jumped from the screen. *Park Rapist Strikes Again: Two people were assaulted in Matraville Park, near Longbay Prison. A twenty-four year old man later died of stab wounds, and a twenty-one year old woman remains in intensive care. This latest attack follows three similar incidents over the last four weeks. The additional police presence has so far failed to identify any suspects.*

I searched the observatory database over the remote link and found the scans I'd uploaded from the cell tower a few nights ago. I pulled up one saved as *man_behind_park_bench* and uploaded his DNA. I discovered the same rogue gene peaks I'd identified for the other violent prisoners at Longbay.

I initiated a DNA search through the entire database, which I guessed would take anywhere from one hour to one week. This is where encoding the entire store of DNA data through Barry's formulae would come in handy and reduce searches to a matter of seconds.

Suddenly, too quickly, *Match Found* flashed up on screen. The time stamp on the scan was today, and only a few minutes ago. Still trying to comprehend this, I jolted upright when a picture of a man appeared on the screen, the same man who had walked through the park only minutes earlier. I switched to a live feed and panned around, searching for a man in a grey-coat.

I scanned through trees, bushes, toilet blocks and fences, the ultra high frequencies travelling easily through clothes and timber.

Soon enough I found grey-coat lying on the grass surrounded by families with children, reading a book, or feigning to. I zoomed in and noticed his eyes darting about—another fox in the hen house. I waited, hoping the database would discover something more about him and pondered my options.

"I've performed an MRI scan on your rabbit. You should see the resolution of these images, they're amazing. The different layers of soft tissue as clear as day," Warren pronounced from the door of my office, startling me.

"Great. Warren, but I'm still working on my mods. I'll be with you soon."

I pretended to dial a phone number while looking back at the screen to see grey-coat had moved. I panned around, engaging the infrared filter and noticed a cluster of heat images behind some dense brush, off to the side of a grassy patch.

Upon closer inspection, I identified two images, a larger one on top of a smaller one. I sent out a low power scan for DNA and quickly received back two separate bio-fluorescent returns. The resulting DNA indicated one was definitely grey-coat and the other was female, and not a rogue.

"Why can't you just place the rabbit in your waveform machine for irradiation?" Warren said, sending my heart into my throat.

"Because we want to test the operation of the *modified* MRI scanner, and I can only do that once I get the emitters mounted and connected. And none of that will happen if you keep interrupting me."

I wondered which pulse sequence to send to grey-coat—cancer, immune deficiency or accelerated aging. A tough choice, but none of those would help the girl in the next few seconds. Unfortunately, the new laser design no longer gave me the option of instantly frying his brain. So I tried the next best thing—a twist on the oxygen depletion scenario using a few additional frequencies. Hopefully, this energy cocktail would do the trick.

With the laser locked onto grey-coat's head, I pressed the enter key and watched the two figures intently. Seconds later, the figure on top slumped forward and lay limp. I saw the smaller figure crawling out from underneath and switched to visual mode in time to see a partially naked girl run out from behind the bushes. I couldn't hear her scream, but her actions said it all.

I called out, "Warren, I need a mouse to test a theory. It would be best to have one that's already ill, as I think it might result in a quick death..."

"This will advance our knowledge of medical science somehow?" he said, arms folded and standing at my door.

"I think so."

He eyed me with contempt, "We have an older mouse. She's outside the age range we normally use for testing."

"Great, she'll do."

I programmed the test procedure on the waveform machine, exactly as I had moments earlier for the cell tower laser.

"Her name is Camille and she's been with us for a couple of years now," Warren said.

"Yes, a long tour of duty. She must be tired."

He held the old, trusting mouse carefully in his hand, stroking her.

"Shit Warren, don't make this harder than it needs to be. Just put the mouse in the damn analyzer."

He responded slowly, drawing out the moment in a ritual.

With the mouse in the chamber, I sent the identical pulse sequence as I had to grey-coat, but scaled down in power to match the reduced body mass of the mouse. Immediately after the pulse, the mouse flopped down and ceased breathing.

"Um... you can now conduct an autopsy for cause of death..."

Warren gently picked her up and withdrew to the back lab, without comment or glance in my direction.

I returned to my screen and to the image of grey-coat. He lay completely still, lifeless. Police had arrived to search the bush and the usual crime scene procedures began playing out. Ambulance, detectives, forensic experts arrived and congregated around the body. A growing crowd of spectators were kept behind the yellow tape. This was certainly a decent crowd for a grey-coat.

I read an email just received from Lou, *Michael, I'm ready to sign the release for Sue's transfer to St Georges.*

I replied, *OK, I'll arrange things and let you know when we can move her,* and hoped Mark wouldn't burst a blood vessel when he found out.

"Instant brain death, as if she'd just been turned off." Warren announced, as an accusation.

"I see."

"The irradiation must have impacted on brain stem signals to vital organs—a severe electrical interruption."

"OK. Thanks."

"That's it?"

"Yes." I resisted the temptation to ask if she'd suffered.

I watched grey-coat's body carried away on a stretcher and dumped into the back of a coroner van. I guessed Warren would afford Camille the mouse more care and ceremony, and rightfully so.

In the prison grounds, afternoon exercises were now in full swing. I programmed an automatic routine to scan them all for DNA and to reference any rogue matches we had in our database. The system would look for key words like 'murder' and 'rape' in their files. Various colored halos would act as an identifier for each, as an active tag following them as they moved about the prison yard. A green halo would indicate non-violent types and those with violence listed in their files would have a yellow halo.

Any who scanned positive for rogue genes would have a bright red halo fixed over their heads.

I poured myself a coffee and made a few phone calls while watching the screen. The halos buzzed about like multicolored fireflies and after a few minutes, most had turned to red, several were yellow and only two remained green.

I pulled up the file for one of the yellow halos and found Jason Sharp, convicted of killing his elderly mother, claimed it was euthanasia—his mother was dying of cancer. He was now into the fourth year of a ten-year sentence. If he really were innocent of a violent crime, then the absence of the rogue gene was a positive result for my theory.

I focused on the red halos and scanned their files. They all seemed to be violent career criminals. A familiar face caught my attention and I remembered this mousy man holding the hand of a young girl in a sporting goods store. Over his head, a red halo glowed brightly.

I rang Trobe.

"John, I've got a few names I'd like to run past you, if you have a minute?"

"Sure."

I was relieved he didn't ask why and read him the names. He remembered some and others he looked up in his records. I gave him the name of the man who kidnapped his own child, and of Jason Sharp, accused of killing his terminally ill mother. Trobe described what I suspected—they were marginal cases and in his view, non-violent.

"Michael, before you go. I've managed to get some information on James Roberts. My sources believe his kidnappers may hand him over within the next few days."

I wanted to ask him how he knew this, but was more concerned that he didn't sound overly pleased.

"That's good news isn't it?"

"Well, I didn't say he would be handed over alive."

"How would killing him help their cause?"

"A bunch of theories, but all a little too convoluted for this hometown detective."

"James' business partner, Mark Woodcock, left for Colombo a few days ago. We can't seem to get a hold of him either. He may have gone to search for James."

"Look, I'm off to China on Monday for SatCOMM business. I could stop over in Colombo and see what I can find out."

"That would be much appreciated."

"I'll have a word with the boss about it."

I noticed increasing activity in the Longbay Prison grounds, with a wave of inmates flooding the yards. This was as good a time as any to perform some long overdue 'weeding'. I tapped away on the keyboard and programmed several irradiation sequences for random use by the automatic firing routine. The ailments would result in either slow or rapid deterioration, depending on the energy cocktail they received. The system would log the wave sequence used on each prisoner for later analysis.

Targeting only the red halos, I clicked on the start key and watched in morbid fascination as an assortment of energy pulses were unleashed upon the unsuspecting riff raff. Some inmates immediately started to stagger, with several dropping quickly to the ground. Less than a minute later, the laser routine had concluded and a large portion of the prison's population had been 'processed'.

Guards tentatively approached the fallen and tended to them. Soon there was shouting, prodding and then real panic as more guards swarmed into the yard. The commotion reached fever pitch as too few guards were overburdened with too many of the incapacitated.

I watched the guards at the sentry towers scouring the nearby parklands and skies with binoculars, presumably for an external perpetrator. But they would find none.

CHAPTER 26

The evening news on television led with a story on the possible reunification of the Soviet Union. Several commentators agreed that most States would defend their hard won independence to the death. Another story saw images of refugees flooding the screen, as the mass exodus from Sudan continued in the wake of the Saudi buyout. Across the border in Ethiopia, we saw a Sudanese resistance force preparing for battle, and on the West African coast, a reporter told of how France's offer of cash and infrastructure had succeeded in enticing more than one country to join a renewed French Empire. Troops were already heading to Cote d'Ivoire at the request of the government there to maintain law and order in anticipation of a transition of power.

"A French Empire! Are we going back in time? This is insane." Helen said.

"Who knows, perhaps independence hasn't worked for some."

With the barrage of international news, I was hopeful there would be no mention of the recent incident at Longbay Prison.

"I'm no political analyst, but this looks like blatant opportunism." Helen said.

"Let's just get you all fixed up first, then we can fix the world."

"Yeah I wish. What are you up to now?"

"I have some equipment to prepare in the lab. I think we're close to finalizing a procedure for you."

For this I needed to reuse selected parts from the Longbay laser in the modified MRI machine, and unfortunately that meant another field trip to SatCOMM's cell tower under the cloak of darkness.

It was pitch black when I parked the van beneath the tower, high up on a desolate hilltop. I unlocked the control pad to the hydraulic lift, keyed in the code and watched the lift descend. I was on edge, feeling that someone was watching me. I sensed rather than heard movement in a bush behind me and turned to light up the area with my pitifully small flashlight. I found nothing, other than my own paranoia.

I loaded my tools into the lift and despite the cold, started to sweat during the three-minute ascent to the top. The only sound was that of barking dogs and distant cars moving along a freeway. The view was captivating, with the glow of Sydney on the eastern horizon and Longbay Prison to the west, lit by powerful sodium lamps that gave an eerie yellow glow to the large cluster of buildings.

As I dissembled the laser, a cold breeze stiffened my hands, forcing me to work slowly. Forty minutes later and somewhat frozen, I descended. Stepping off the platform I jumped as a bright light illuminated me. I felt like road kill about to happen.

"Sir, can I ask you what you're doing here?" a man's voice resonated from behind an intense light.

I squinted and saw the outline of a police uniform. My breathing stopped and I hoped my heart wouldn't with it.

"Just breakdown maintenance, Officer."

"What's the problem?"

"Some faulty gear on the cell tower, they need it repaired ASAP."

"Sure, can I see some ID sir?"

I searched my pockets.

"I'm sorry, I left in a rush and I don't have it with me."

"You work for the power company?" he saw the logo on the side of the van.

"Yes, we have a maintenance contract with SatCOMM."

"SatCOMM? I think one of our guys now heads up security for them."

"John Trobe?" I hoped.

"Yes, that's right. What's your name?"

"Michael Crow."

"I still need to see some ID Mr Crow, otherwise you'll have to come with me," he said, sternly.

"Can I call Mr Trobe for verification?"

"It's almost midnight and a bit late to be bothering people…"

I dialed Trobe's number hoping he was still in the country and handed the officer my phone. Trobe answered after several rings and they spoke about life after the force. He hung up and handed me back the phone.

"Carry on, but make sure you don't fall off that thing. You guys should be working in pairs. You know work safety and all that."

"I know. My partner has taken the night off—the wife giving him grief."

He smiled knowingly, returned to his car and crunched gravel into the night.

I placed the laser components and tools into the van, jumped in and sat shivering for a few minutes, as much from the chill in my bones as from another altercation with the law.

Back in the cocoon of St Georges, I grafted the various laser components into the MRI machine. The microwave emitters fitted neatly into the various cavities of the MRI shell. In this case, I wanted an even spread of energy rather than a concentrated beam, to initiate the stem cell propagation uniformly across the patient. These cells would then knowingly seek out the body parts requiring repair, or so I hoped. The subdued lighting of the instrument displays and their constant soothing hum made it easy to work through the early morning.

A blaze of light from the overhead fluorescents woke me from a deep slumber in my office chair. I stumbled from my office to the kitchen and poured a cupful of black tar.

Back in the lab, I found Warren examining the modified MRI.

"Nice work, have you finished?" he asked.

"Almost, I just need to test it. Something I avoid doing when I'm tired, as it usually ends up in an electric shock. Although right now that doesn't sound too bad."

"I think your rabbit is still in pain. You want me to keep him dosed up?"

"Yes, thanks."

We surveyed the animal cages and saw Zeus had worn out a second wheel. He stood up on his hind legs sniffing expectantly for another replacement.

"A mouse on a mission," Warren observed.

"How are the others doing?"

"Good... well not so good in some cases, but certainly no worse."

"I was hoping for better than that."

"Some were a long way gone, frankly I'm surprised they're still alive at all."

It took two more hours and five cups of coffee to graft the remaining parts of the laser into the MRI. Once complete, I hooked up the computer, fine-tuned the drivers and tested the automation routines.

"I think I'm ready," I announced.

When no response came, I found Warren glued to his computer screen, watching a news web cast. The images showed a long line of men, women and children with no more than the clothes on their backs and a few bundles of belongings, shuffling along a well-worn dirt track somewhere in desolate Africa.

"What's going on?" I asked.

"They're Sudanese refugees. They say the entire non-Arab population is on the move."

"Expelled?"

"I think they used the term *relocated*."

Of the fifty million Sudanese, the majority were not Muslim, and they were on the move. Unfortunately, they would find closed borders at Ethiopia and other neighboring countries, countries with their own problems and incapable of absorbing so many so quickly.

The vision panned to two young boys, seven or eight years old. The one standing was trying to pull the fallen one back on his feet, but neither had the will or strength. No one seemed to take any notice, all too involved in their own suffering to care for others.

I went to the bathroom and sat on floor holding my head, wondering why technology progressed while human nature did not. Jealousy and greed—the same lethal mix over and over, since the beginning of time. We still considered life too cheaply, detached from suffering too easily and feared those who were different, too much.

I'd pulled myself together, slapped some water on my face and returned to the lab where Warren had prepared the rabbit for an MRI scan.

"He's weak but ready. A mild sedative was all I could risk."

"OK, let's give it a whirl."

I started with a series of soft tissue scans, before programming the microwave emitters and bio-fluorescent receivers. I pressed *activate* and performed a long-sequence DNA scan. The scan on the rabbit returned without rogue genes, at least he would not go on to rape and pillage in my backyard.

Next, I initiated a low power succession of frequency-shifted pulses that corresponded to the pattern I'd applied to Zeus. The whole procedure was finished in less than a minute. We stared at the rabbit, willing him to stand up. When he didn't move, Warren picked him up and gently laid him in his cage.

"When will you do a stem cell count?" I asked.

"I'll draw blood every hour."

In a neighboring cage, Zeus was busy working on another wheel. Through the blurred multicolored spokes, I studied his tail and saw it had regained all of its initial length. I opened the cage and held him by the tail, half expecting it to detach from him. His legs kept moving as though the wheel were irrelevant to the whole exercise—a true gym junkie.

"Warren, have a look at this. The wound has healed and his tail regrowth is complete."

"Yes, all fifty-eight millimeters to be precise."

"And his condition, his fur, his muscle tone, the clarity of his eyes…"

"Yes, I agree, it's a good result."

"Good? It's fantastic!" I stressed.

"Sure, but let's not forget this mouse could drop dead anytime and for whatever reason."

"What about his cell count?"

"Still highly elevated."

I checked the time, "I'm going upstairs—there's a new patient checking in this morning."

Like a zealous puppy, he followed me upstairs.

"Michael, what do you mean *a new patient*?"

"Her name is Sue."

"Human! Are you serious? Does Mark know?"

"Yes, we talked about it before he left," I lied.

"Why is she here?"

"She's had a head injury and is in need of some remedial therapy," I said, watching his face redden.

"But we can't handle that here." he insisted.

"Warren, you're starting to stress and sound like Mark."

Sue's face looked swollen and bruised, and Warren, whose gleaming new nametag read Dr W Parker, stood behind me as if scared to get too close. He grabbed at the chart from the bed end and avoided eye contact with me.

"We'll need to call in a specialist neurosurgeon," he pronounced.

"Warren, could we delay calling someone else for the moment?"

"Your mouse is one thing, but this is another. We're not set up for intensive care."

"But we could treat her in the MRI this afternoon—"

"What!"

"You've seen her chart?"

"Yeah I agree, a recovery is problematic, but this is way out of our league."

"Her brain swell has subsided and she's doesn't seem to be in any immediate danger."

"Really, Dr Crow. Apart from our lack of facility, *I'm* really not equipped to deal with this."

"Warren, take a deep breath. What if these cellular propagations can repair the damaged cells? Then there may be a chance at a complete recovery. It's worked in the mice, so why wouldn't it work in humans?"

"I don't want to talk about this. Does she have family?"

"Yes, and they've agreed to the treatment." I lied again.

We stood in silence and considered each other for a moment.

"I don't want anything to do with this," he said

He was really just a kid, and now deserted by his minders. I felt sorry for him.

I left St Georges and drove to the observatory. The coast road was bathed in perfect sunshine this afternoon, yet within just days, the winter storms would lash these cliffs relentlessly for months.

I found Lou in the main dome hovering around a satellite that was spread-eagle across the floor, like a dissected black and silver crab. I wondered if it were about to jump up and hang from the ceiling.

"Michael, how's Sue doing?"

"She's all bedded down and we hope to start some initial procedures soon—you're OK with that?"

"Yes, if you're sure."

"I'm sure. How's the waveguide fitting in?"

"Very snugly. The servo motors are rock solid and we've fitted the mod you wanted for the variable beam diameter control."

"Good work. What about the outer bay doors?"

"Titanium. They fold out to allow the waveguides a full 270-degree rotational movement. They close together so well you wouldn't know there was a door there."

"And the waveguide itself?"

"The last job to be done and being fitted now. As you can see, the two lasers for the dome are mounted and the techs staying here with you will have them operational in a few days."

"How much power will we lose through the dome's glass ceiling?"

"We've decided not to use glass. We're testing a plastic material, which is microwave safe," he smiled. "It's made of compounds with negligible absorption to microwaves."

"Sounds great. Anything else I should know about? Any problems?"

"Not unless you're going to spring more changes on us in the eleventh hour."

"No, my only concern is the visual optics. After the signal bounces through two waveguides and back to earth, I'm a little worried about the final resolution."

"I've spent a bit of time on just that. We're doing a frequency split and digitizing each component separately to simulate the transmission through the waveguide. The tests show we can achieve high definition television resolution at ground level and at two hundred frames per second."

"Fantastic. What about the SatFone handsets?"

"Ah yes, the handsets. Your design?"

"Only the minor additions are mine."

"OK, they're all done and the prototypes are ready for shipping. I've also finalized the high speed microwave link to SatCOMM."

"Looks like you've covered everything. Are you and the team ready to leave for China tomorrow?"

"Yes," he hesitated. "Michael, I get the feeling there might be more to all this than just global communications. And whatever it is, I just want to let you know that it's been great working with you again."

"I appreciate that Lou. I feel the same."

The mutual admiration was a little uneasy, and I felt guilty for not giving him the full picture.

"So where is this place we're launching the satellites from?" Lou asked.

"A desert site in the north of China, near a town called Lanzhou. It's nice and secluded and I hear the weather is wonderful this time of year."

"Yeah, I bet…"

At the other side of the dome floor, an increasing army of clones flanked Alan.

"Alan, I've had a look at your database and it's good to go."

"Thanks, we've run the DNA encoding routine through the whole system. Every two hours there's an automatic search for new DNA plots to transcribe and the search-and-match routine is lightening fast."

"Good, but I'd prefer to perform the DNA cleanups every few minutes, rather than hours."

"Sounds like you're planning to acquire a lot of data very quickly. We'll have to increase the processing power—"

"And, the database needs to have a capacity for two trillion DNA records."

"Damn, we'll need to double the hard drive stacks and upscale the processing power again."

"OK, but we won't need all that capacity right now. It can come progressively, say over a week."

"A whole week!" he said, as his fellow geeks turned toward me in unison.

I retreated to my loft to read the waiting emails and found one from Nicole. It contained a drawing of a fish she'd scanned. I rang and was pleased when she answered the phone instead of Alison.

"Hey Nic, I just got your email. Nice fish."

"Thanks, it's called a jpeg."

"I haven't heard of that species before."

"No silly, that's the file format."

"How is everything?" I asked.

"Bill died in hospital a few days ago."

I heard Alison in the background scolding her for mentioning it.

"That's too bad. What else have you been up to?"

While Nicole chatted, I opened an email from Cooper and read.

Apparently, some unfortunate incidents occurred at

"Mainly drawing, I want to take art classes."

Longbay Prison the other day.

"Great." I said,

I say it couldn't happen to a nicer bunch of people.

"I'll see you next weekend, Dad."

The investors are pleased.

"OK. Bye honey"

Investors!

"Bye Dad."

Keep up the good work. BC.

I arrived at St Georges late in the afternoon and met Tom in the car park just as he was about to depart. I noticed the absence of Warren's car.

"How's Mum?" I asked.

"She's not in any discomfort and seems to be doing well, but she's bored."

"Has Eric been in?"

"Yeah, every day as far as I know. Haven't you seen him?"

"Well, I'm usually down in the lab."

"Yeah, Dr Frankenstein I bet."

"What are you up to now?" I asked.

"Now? I thought I'd go home and relax. Why?"

"I might need a hand with a few things..."

"Like what?"

"A procedure."

"What kind of procedure?"

"It's just a simple thing and shouldn't take too long."

I lead him to the lab, where the retina scans and whooshing security doors gave me a sense of ownership, and I suspect impressed Tom just a little.

I checked on the animals and noticed Warren had applied a splint to the rabbit's leg. The mice were all quite active and looking well. They eagerly devoured the food I fed them and, with my vast medical experience, I'd found hunger to be a reasonable guide to state of health.

"So what's the deal, you're a vet now?" Tom asked.

"No, I'm just checking on some test results."

"What *exactly* are we, am I, doing here?"

"Well, that's an MRI machine, complete with some turbo charging I added recently."

"Great, so what?"

"It provides structural and bio-chemical information about tissue matter."

"Nice… you need me to help you move it around?"

"No, I need you to help me put Helen in there."

"Helen! What! Now? Aren't there doctors around here to do that sort of thing?"

"All you need to do is wear this white coat, look calm and help me lift the patient."

He hesitated, but followed me upstairs to Helen's room anyway.

"Hi. I thought you'd gone home Tom?" Helen sat upright.

"He pushed me into this," Tom said, pointing at me.

"Into what?"

"We're going to take you to the lab for a scan. Is that OK?" I cajoled.

"What? Now? The both of you?"

"Yes."

"What kind of scan?"

"Just a preliminary MRI. It'll give us some helpful data prior to your upcoming procedure."

"You know how to work an MRI?"

"Sure, it's part of my research."

"Where's Warren?"

"He's taken the evening off, but we're lucky to have Tom to assist."

They smiled nervously at each other.

"It'll all be over in a few minutes, so let's get the show on the road." I smiled.

The nurse on duty paid little attention as we wheeled Helen to the lab—maybe they thought I ran the place now in the absence of Mark and James. Once in the lab, we positioned Helen in front of the MRI machine.

"*In there?*" she almost shrieked.

"Yes," I said brightly, hoping her agitation wasn't a sign of claustrophobia.

We maneuvered her from the trolley and onto her stomach and then onto the MRI platform. The elaborate dressing on her buttock was visible and I was aware of Tom looking to me for reassurance.

"Don't worry. I've done a few of these," I said, ignoring the tension in the room. "I'll do an initial pass and you'll hear a slight hum. You may even feel a warming sensation, but it's nothing to worry about. OK?" My face was sore from trying to smile too much.

"OK..." she said.

After we settled her into position, I pressed a switch to activate the conveyor, which hummed as it slowly sucked her into its bowel. I checked the programming of the MRI three times before starting the scan phase and was aware of Tom giving me the *I-hope-you-know-what-the-hell-you're-doing* look.

"First, I'll do a standard pass and then a long-form DNA scan." I said.

I drew my next breath only after I saw the absence of rogue gene indicators on the DNA plot.

"OK, we're nearly done. Just one more scan."

I loaded the irradiation sequences and watched the monitor closely. My hands shook in spite of holding onto to the bench. The MRI buzzed once more for a few seconds.

"OK, we're all finished." I announced.

I put the conveyor into reverse and extracted Helen.

"That's it?" Tom said, visibly relieved.

"Good, because I'm feeling a bit of pain," Helen winced.

"Where?" my voice cracking.

"Buttock."

"More or less than usual?"

"It's hard to be sure. It depends on the painkillers. Maybe I just need to plug back into my IV."

"Sounds like a good idea," Tom quipped.

Back in her room, we reconnected Helen to her machines.

"There, just rest." I sat with her for a few minutes until she closed her eyes and drifted off.

Tom cast me a suspicious look as we left the room.

"Now let's get Mum down there." I said.

"What? No fucking way."

We locked stares.

"This will help her kidney condition somehow?" he moaned.

"Yes."

Mum was reading a magazine, appearing comfortable and relaxed. Forty minutes later, we'd completed her scan and had her back in her room.

"What are you boys up to now?" she asked.

"Probably grab a bite to eat," I said.

"That's nice, and you make sure he eats," she ordered Tom while pointing at me.

Once we were in the corridor, I turned to Tom, "One more thing…"

"Hey no way, I didn't sign up for the whole night."

I heard him groan as he reluctantly followed to Sue's room.

"Hell, what happened to her?" he asked.

"This is Lou's girlfriend, Sue. She was raped and bashed in the village the other night."

"Damn, she's a mess."

"She's in a coma. We'll need to unplug some of this gear and take the ventilator unit with us."

Tom's face was white, yet he no longer protested or even questioned. Maneuvering her onto the trolley proved a ghastly exercise as she flopped from side to side. We were both glad when the procedure was over and Sue was back in her room.

"The Italian place around the corner?" I suggested to Tom, as I plugged Sue into her support systems.

"Anywhere but here would be fine."

Over dinner, Tom occasionally prodded me about my work at St Georges, but I didn't feel much like talking. I felt an overwhelming guilt about the procedures I'd just performed, and it flushed through me in hot waves.

CHAPTER 27

I staggered like a hunched form from a silent laboratory, straining to straighten my back before entering Helen's room. I found her sitting upright and eating breakfast with newfound gusto, in complete contrast to my mood.

"How are you feeling?" I asked nervously.

"I feel good, in fact better than you look," she said as she shoveled scrambled egg into her mouth.

"Glad to hear it."

She looked behind me, "Warren, I feel much better today. Seems yesterday's MRI had some therapeutic value as well."

"MRI?" he shot a questioning look straight at me.

"Yes, an MRI scan," I said. "To help us better identify the healing pattern, as we discussed." I watched as his angry face returned.

"I think Warren will want take a blood sample from you this morning." I continued, avoiding Warren's stare, "And most likely for Sue and Mum too."

I escaped to Sue's room while he picked his jaw up off the floor. Sue lay peacefully asleep and I noticed her swelling had subsided, the bruises now a more healthy shade of brown.

Warren entered the room behind me. I could tell he thought she had improved as well, but he wasn't about to admit it. I left the room and disappeared to the elevator before he regained his power of speech.

At the observatory, various web casts ran continuously on several screens. One showed a long line of tanks rolling along a well-worn jungle track.

"Whose are they?" I asked Lou.

"French military, they've just *secured* several mining interests in Cote D'Ivoire and Ghana and are expelling local tribes from many parts of the country."

"Why?"

"Who knows? They say the tribes are on some kind of spoiled land. They're offering them a better life in other provinces."

"And they believe that?"

"I guess they don't have a lot of choice."

A mountain of invoices lay strewn across my loft desk and a quick summation revealed I was in a million dollars of debt. I logged into my bank account, hoping I'd be able to cover it and stared at the balance. Twenty million dollars, in credit.

I counted several more SatCOMM payments over the past two days. Was this the Longbay payoff? I ignored the thought and quickly transferred payments to the various contractors.

Tom entered the loft.

"How's Mum?" he asked.

"Improving. In fact, they all look better this morning."

"You do know what you're doing?"

"Sure."

"Playing with lives?"

"I'm not *playing* with anything."

"No?"

"How's the construction going?"

"The building security systems are complete and general services will be fully operational tomorrow. The residential wing, or resort I should say, should be ready for occupancy within two weeks."

"Pay them more and see if you can get it completed by the end of the week."

"Excuse me? Even if that were possible, it would mean a hell of a surcharge."

"Pay it. I want everything finished, including the perimeter wall."

"Yes sir!" He clicked his heels and threw me a salute, his smartarse grin annoying me more than usual.

Beneath us, the floor rumbled. I took to the window and saw four big transporters pounding down the driveway. The satellite, disassembled and crated up, was on the move to China.

"Alan, how's the additional storage and processing capacity coming along?"

"It will all be online today."

"What about the security and firewalls?"

"Already online."

The CNN screen caught my attention, with the anchor announcing the number of displaced persons was doubling each day, as refugees poured out from several African states. Closed borders met them wherever they turned and the camps quickly turned into places of unbearable suffering. Experts gave grim reports of unprecedented levels of famine and crime, and the doomsday prophecies playing repeatedly after each ad break. One commentator proposed that the spoils of natural resources were the prime motivation for the French re-occupation of western Africa, as though that were a breakthrough in thinking. Another suggested the Chinese troop movements into Mongolia were supposedly at the request of the ruling MPRP party for 'assistance', and nothing to do with the huge oil reserves recently discovered there.

The backseat taken by the USA and Great Britain hadn't gone unnoticed either, with some commentators suggesting they were becoming introspective and hoping to ride out the winds of war this time. A 'self-preservation' strategy they called it. But there was no mention of the New World Order, which Cooper took as fact.

Share prices of resource companies shot through the roof as the popularity of the home bunker devoured concrete and steel in huge volumes. Most other stocks were now less than half the value they were only a few weeks ago. I saw a world I no longer recognized or understood and drove to St Georges in a state of depression.

I found Warren glued to his microscope.

"What have you found?" I asked.

"Ah, you." His voice, if not overly welcoming, was calm.

"How are the patients?"

"I assume your referring to the human ones?"

"Yes."

"Well, there appears to be heightened levels of stem cell activity in Helen's blood. I took a biopsy of the wound area and found signs of muscle and tissue regrowth. Whether that's due to the irradiation or would have occurred anyway—it's hard to be certain at this stage."

"She's still feeling energetic?"

"Yes, despite a constant body temperature of two degrees above normal, she seems alert and well."

"What about my mother?"

"Similar elevated temperature and increased stem cell count."

"Any improvement in kidney function?"

"It's too early to tell. I'll perform some tests tomorrow specifically for that."

"And Sue?"

"Similar numbers, but no obvious sign of improvement in her condition. She's still in a coma."

I peered into the rabbit's cage and saw him standing on his hind legs, reaching for the celery stick Warren had placed in the top rung.

"He's still tentative on it, but an X-ray shows the equivalent of several weeks of healing," Warren offered.

"In a few days?"

"Yes. And the mice seem to be recovering well also."

"Recovering from cancer?"

"It appears so, but I have detected a decrease in Zeus' stem cell levels."

"Back to normal?"

"Not yet, but maybe that's where it will end up. We still don't understand the mechanisms and we're flying blind, as you know."

"Let's just keep flying then. You know there's no progress without uncertainty."

"Michael," Warren waited for my full attention. "I need to know in advance about anything else you intend to do here."

"Sure Warren, I understand." It was sweet how he undertook the caretaker role for his MIA colleagues.

"Do you know when Mark will return?" Helen asked.

"He has some business in Colombo and should be back soon. Why?"

"I'd like to talk to him about my treatment. When it will start..."

I thought about lying, but decided to tell the truth this time. "Well, it already started with your MRI scan..."

"The scan you performed last night?"

"Yes. I'm sorry, I should have told you. I just didn't want you to get too worked up."

"You're saying it was more than just a scan?"

"Yes. I added some high frequency energy pulses, specifically designed to induce an elevated level of stem cell activity. And to cause said stem cells to regenerate into specific types, in order to repair damaged tissue, organs, muscle and bone."

"You're shitting me?"

"No."

"And, apart from your mouse, who else has had this *treatment*?"

"Well, there is Mum, Sue next door, and a large white rabbit."

She shook her head in disbelief. "Have you gone mad and taken over completely?"

Where are the real doctors in this place? "Well, Warren is a doctor, almost."

"So, who *exactly* knows what you're doing?"

"Just Warren, kind of—"

"Kind of? Has it occurred to you that you're playing with lives here? My life!"

"Yes it has, and that's why I've spent hundreds of hours in the lab, building prototypes and testing. We have made some good progress and I sure as hell don't consider any of this as *playing*."

"God only knows what else you have going on."

"Helen, I'm on the right course."

"How can you be so sure?" Helen asked, wanting to believe but feeling used.

I drove home and slept in a bed I now hardly recognized, only to wake an hour later to the reverberating sounds of sirens. I shuffled to the front door and saw police, ambulance and a crowd of people gathering in the street.

With relief, I realized it was not my house that was the centre of all this attention, but the house directly opposite. I stepped onto the sidewalk as a neighbor approached for the traditional kerbside conference at such times of tragedy.

According to him, the father had just killed his wife and two children, before shooting himself. To me, they had seemed an ordinary, decent family. I remembered the twelve-year-old girl and recently finding a leaflet she'd left in my mailbox. She was advertising her baby-sitting services and she sounded sweet, caring.

But why did it come to this? What was the trigger? Did the father suffer a sudden bout of insanity? And what exactly did that mean anyway? Was *insanity* the poor cousin to evil? It was a ridiculously circular argument—the more heinous the crime, the less we understood why and the quicker we labeled it as *insane*. And having labeling it, that somehow this diminished the act itself and therefore the punishment. Yes, we the jury find him not guilty by reason of *insanity,* said *insanity* brought about because his mother molested him as a child, or had just locked him in a cupboard for too long when he was young and impressionable. So now, we exempt him from any further responsibility, as it's only the *insane* part of him that's the problem and not really *him*.

I quickly tired of gazing at the misery of others and went back to bed, this time with earplugs in.

I woke at 8.15 am, which seemed only minutes later. After a shower and breakfast, I felt I might be able to get through the day.

I drove out of the driveway, carefully avoiding the yellow tape surrounding the neighbors' house and watching the passing cars and pedestrians pausing in morbid curiosity. Perhaps I should erect a sign so there would be no confusion. *Here, some mid-life affected loser extinguished three innocent lives last night.* I would have liked a sample of the father's DNA, to probe around for some clues, in anticipation of some possible pre-emptive bioengineering.

Tom had not been idle. I was greeted at the observatory by a two-meter high brick wall and the removal of all scaffolding from the main dome and surrounding structures. Fewer contractors now parked in the grounds and in the basement, I found a vacant spot stenciled with the words *Crow*.

A retina scan opened the security door with a hiss and an X-ray scanning airlock searched me electronically for any suspect materials. I took the lift to ground level where a steel door opened, allowing me entry to the dome space.

The final testing of the various systems was underway, as well the dismantling of the temporary computer bays the techs had used until now. Tom was in the switch room with the electrical contractor and I saw them both peering down at the main transformers and back-up generator, through the glass observation panel in the floor.

I retreated to the privacy of my loft and spent the next twelve hours completing the additional software upgrades I'd need to bring on line soon. Around midnight, I broke out in a cold sweat and felt nauseated, perhaps from the smell of stale pizza that reached a crescendo at the same time each night. I made it to the toilet just before throwing up a foul green liquid.

I rang Lou in Lanzhou via SatFone to ask about his progress.

"We doing great and have everything we need. Our team and the Chinese techs are getting on well. They've provided a translator, but we seem to have reasonable communication through body language."

"The satellite?"

"The first one is on the launch pad now undergoing some final checks."

Lou sounded confidant and the line was clear. They had prepped the second satellite in only two days and now had the confirmed schedules and destinations for all. The first would be the 'hub' unit over Australia, followed by one over India and then China, all in low-level geostationary orbits. Seven others would follow them over Africa, India, Europe and the Americas.

After only three hours of broken sleep, I woke with an insistent coughing and sneezing. I decided to start the new day, satellite launch day, early. I had a few hours before the first launch and drove to St Georges to check on Helen, feeling too unsettled to bother with breakfast.

Helen was asleep. Next to her, a computer displayed her vital statistics—dissolved oxygen, blood pressure, heart rate and most importantly, her stem cell count per one thousand cells. In the room next door, Sue was breathing without a ventilator and any facial swelling seemed to be reduced. She looked alive again.

I ventured down to the lab.

"How are the patients today?" I asked Warren.

"Fine," he gestured to the cages, where Zeus was busy running yet another wheel into the ground— this one was stainless steel. "They're eating twice as much as normal and tests show no residual trace of any illnesses. I would almost be prepared to call it a miracle."

"Let's just call it science." I denied the quickening of my heartbeat as the rabbit hopped toward me on two perfectly good hind legs.

"What about stem cell activity?" I asked.

"The count is still higher than normal in all of them, but reducing slowly in most. Zeus' levels have stabilized just above normal."

"You think the elevated cell count is a transient condition?"

"Possibly. When RNA manipulation is applied during drug therapy it's never a permanent or self perpetuating condition, as far as we know."

"Well there's only one way to find out..."

He thought about it for a few seconds, before a look of complete disgust crossed his face. "You can't be serious!"

"Warren, it's in the interests of science. If we cut off his tail again and the stem cell count increases on its own, without any additional irradiation, then we know it's a continuing response. Worst case, we'll just irradiate him again and fix him."

While Warren reluctantly prepped Zeus, I rang Lou, who confirmed the first launch had occurred without a hitch, twenty minutes ago.

I sat in my car in the observatory basement for several minutes as the incessant pounding in my head rendered me incapable of movement. I threw down a couple more painkillers and exceeded the daily allowance, entering the dark world of excess. Normally this kind of deterioration in my health would see me at the doctor, but I didn't really care anymore. Perhaps I was daring fate too much these days.

The techs were having trouble with the data stream from SatCOMM, trying to break through rigid firewalls and elaborate comms protocols. An hour later, the blockage was removed and the high-speed link lived up to expectation.

Once the second satellite was online, it would open up communications from the Red Sea in the west to China in the east, servicing billions of people. Dataflow was restricted at first to satellite control and response telemetry, as well as digital streams for internet and cable services, but soon enough SatCOMM would flood the world markets with their high def audiovisual handsets.

I retreated to my loft computer and initialized the test procedures, starting with the waveguide servo motor operation. I fed the satellite coordinates into the computer to activate the infrared position locking. This would ensure the incoming ends of the waveguides aligned perfectly at all times, as even a slight miss-alignment could permanently damage them. When the satellite detected the locking beam, the bay doors would open and the waveguides would deploy. The SatCOMM direct link acted as a backup, should the satellite link fail or need recalibration, or to confirm a successful deployment.

My SatFone buzzed.

"Michael, I've made a couple of adjustments to the servo mechanisms, which should provide a really..." a burst of noise cut Lou off.

I hit the *re-establish* button, but heard only a continuous tone in my ear. I hurtled down the stairs from the loft two steps at a time and landed at the dome level with a thud.

I logged onto the main console, where the response was quicker, but still the cause of the communications breakdown evaded me. I heard only static and the occasional broken words.

"Lou, can you hear me?" I asked.

A minute later, the intermittent communication gave way to a continuous, but lower quality one. "Michael, there's a commotion going on here. The Chinese techs are really worried about something."

"Lou, we've lost bandwidth on the satellite for some reason."

"I'm hearing something about a problem in Shenyang. I think it's somehow related to the comms failure we just had."

"Where's Shenyang?"

"It's about two thousand kilometers to the north-east, and not far from the North Korean border. But none of this is making much sense at the moment." I heard agitated, foreign voices in the background. "Wait ... I'm hearing the word 'bomb' mentioned."

I keyed in the waveguide initiation sequence and a dialogue box flashed up on screen fifteen, large and clear. The infrared laser guide system had locked with the satellite waveguide right on cue. I waited for confirmation of a direct link to the satellite over India.

Seconds later, *Full Link Established* appeared on screen and, with breath taking clarity, the entire horizon view of the Indian subcontinent unfolded before me. I saw the Nepalese mountains descending into the urban sprawl of New Delhi. To the east, I saw Pakistan and the terracotta concrete of Islamabad and Karachi cradled between desert and snow capped mountain. Along the coast of the Arabian Sea lay Mumbai, and the Indian subcontinent unfolding to the south and east. Further south, the small island of

Sri Lanka raised the hairs on the back of my neck, and northeast, the flooded delta plains of Bangladesh washed into the Indian Ocean.

It felt like a video game, completely surreal, the digital filtering and reconstruction algorithms creating a mind numbing 3D effect. I had pan-and-zoom control that gave me a serious bout of vertigo as I balanced on the edge of my seat.

"Michael, do you know what's happening?" Lou's voice sounded urgent in my ear.

"Wait a minute Lou. I'm connecting with the satellite over India."

I quickly entered the coordinates of Shenyang into the waveguide tracking system, and saw it sweep eastward, coming to rest at a horizontal view over thousands of kilometers of mountains and desert.

"I can only get a horizon view of Shenyang." I told Lou.

The city itself was too low on the horizon to see it clearly, but there appeared to be a strange ghostly haze in the sky directly above the city. I switched in different filters to look at the various components of radiation forming the cloud. Then, in the low gamma ray band, the cloud turned from transparent to solid, indicating the presence of sub-atomic particles.

"Lou, I can't get any detail from this satellite. I'm just too far away, but I think it's detecting radiation of some kind," my mouth was dry. "Perhaps you should come home."

"Michael, I've got a job to do. Call me when you're sure of something."

As soon as the phone disconnected it rang again. It was Cooper, his voice uncharacteristically tense.

"I've told our people in China to launch a satellite every six hours. Trobe is currently in Shanghai and can assist with locating your colleagues in Colombo when his business there is complete." He hung up, obviously in no mood for small talk.

I brought up the news channels at a touch, but none reported anything unusual in China, focusing instead on soaring world energy prices and the problems on the Korean peninsula.

Tom entered the dome. "Hey, the screens are up! Nice."

I reset them to test pattern mode.

"What's up with you, you're as white as a ghost," he said.

"Lou needs more techs in China for an accelerated launch schedule and I need to get Trobe from Shanghai to Colombo to help extract Mark and James."

"Look, with all the construction winding down, let me do the courier work for you."

"I don't know...it might be dangerous in Colombo."

"Hey, danger is my middle name. What's the big deal anyway, it's easier to dodge a nuke than a bullet."

Did he know the meaning of danger or was it just an act?

I left the dome space for the seclusion of my loft and entered the GPS coordinates of the Colombo research facility into the tracking system. I watched the image move from the horizon to almost straight down onto a city of a million people. I zoomed in on the main entrance of the research facility on Lotus Road and observed life on the other side of the world through the leafy canopies of tropical palms.

I dialed Warren.

"Have you heard from Mark?" I asked.

"No, nothing."

"Can you ask someone in Colombo if they've heard from him?"

"I'll call our administrator there and let you know."

I needed to check Madurai, India, the place the kidnapper's email had originated, and entered the GPS coordinates.

"Alan, have you got an address on that Madurai ISP?"

"Just a minute..."

Madurai appeared on screen as a large city, typically adhoc and cut in half by a river. Two bridges connected the old city to the new city.

"Michael, it's just listed as The Government Polytechnic Institute, that's it."

"Can you overlay a city map on the satellite image I have?"

"Yes. And the database should be ready to go live in a few minutes."

Alan's street map transposed over the satellite image, making it easier to find my way around. I found the point where the railway branched from one to three lines and found the Institute between the east and south lines.

"Alan, can we access a list of people who have access to email at the Institute without alerting anyone?"

"Now?"

"Yes. And did you find anything on the Colombo hijackers or any other political activists in the Madurai region?"

"I got no hits the last time I tried, but I'll give it another go now."

Names scrolled across the screen, as a search through the City of Madurai law enforcement database yielded 27,443 hits. From those we selected any with a history of violent crime and political activism. Ten seconds later, 1332 names with last-known addresses for most and DNA for some streamed from top to bottom of the screen. Of those, three names glowed in red.

"Michael, we have three men who fit the profile and were using the Institute computer at the time the email was sent. I'll send you their files."

I typed these names into the database and performed a global search, visualizing a cyber arrow travelling at the speed of light through a mass of hard drives on the level below me.

I watched the streets of Madurai while I waited. The local time correlated with the thin light and long shadows, it was early morning. The computer beeped with a positive hit. One of the men was found in a *Pakistani* database was Achmed Mata. He was suspected of involvement in the 1985 hijack of an American airliner in Karachi. At the time, he was just sixteen years old and had now several aliases and a long list of crimes to his credit.

Using these aliases, I referenced the CIA database and found a pile of additional information on him. He referred to himself these days as a *human rights warrior*, which was a little different to the standard terrorist line.

"Alan, we have a hit on one of the men and there's DNA on file with the CIA. Can I download this without ringing any alarm bells?"

"Look at the top right corner of your screen, does it say *internal?*"

"Yes."

"OK, you can do whatever you want. *Internal* means you're not actually live on the website, your just accessing a copy stored on our local drives. If it's *external*, then you'd be entering the host website in real time and I wouldn't recommend that. To go under the radar we use a nice stealthy worm to slink around and extract information. It's undetectable."

"What if I want to refresh the information?"

"Then you can check the box marked 'refresh' and the worm is sent into the field. You'll need to be patient as it could take several minutes or longer if the worm thinks there's a potential for detection."

I loaded the suspect's DNA into the laser tracking system and set it to watch for him at the institute entrance. The system would scan people coming in and out. If it detected a match, the system would alert me and automatically start tracking the target. The only risk was if the target entered a concrete building or subway, where the scan would have diffi-cultly penetrating.

I called Warren. "Do we have DNA on file for James and Mark?"

"We have for Mark, but I'm not sure about James. Why, have you—?"

"No, it's just a precaution. Send me the file on Mark."

I watched the sunset over the Pacific Ocean from my loft window, before deciding to risk eating some cold pizza. It wasn't so much to quell the hunger, but to allow my stomach to cope with additional headache pills.

CHAPTER 28

M ichael, I've heard from Colombo. Mark was just in the office authorizing a release of funds." Warren said.

"Funds?"

"He's withdrawn two hundred and fifty thousand dollars."

"For what?"

"He didn't say. Maybe to pay a ransom?"

"How long ago?"

"He's just left the building."

My SatFone beeped with a message, *Target: Mark W. Acquired: Colombo, Sri Lanka.*

I turned to my computer screen and found vision of a man walking along a Colombo street. A green halo over his head indicated his DNA was without rogue genes and that he had no criminal history on file. The text box over him identified the subject as *Dr Mark Woodcock.*

He entered a city building with a briefcase in hand, reappearing several minutes later and climbing onto a bus. The system started to track the bus and from the course it took, it appeared to be heading toward Colombo International airport.

Another message flashed on screen, *Target: Achmed Mata, Acquired: Madurai, India.* This vision showed a dark skinned man emerging from the Polytechnic Institute and hailing a taxi. I watched the taxi meander through the narrow streets and noticed it too appeared to be heading to an airport. In his case, it was Madurai airport.

I called Alan. "Any chance of getting into the airline databases?"

"Maybe, but which city and which airline?"

"Colombo. I'm not sure of the airline. Try them all. I need to know if Mark Woodcock is listed on any outbound flight and where he's going. Also try to get a fix on Achmed Mata or any of his aliases, outbound from Madurai."

"Dates and times?"

"Sometime in the next twenty-four hours."

"OK."

I searched the news websites for updates on the various wars in progress. It appeared journalists were struggling to get news on Shenyang, but there was a local story gathering some attention. Apparently, a mystery illness had struck down most of the inmate population at Longbay Prison.

The sky over the observatory was black, as the first of the winter storms started to roll in from the Pacific. From my loft, I heard slow and heavy drops of rain tapping the roof. I looked through the internal window to the terrace level and below to the dome level. I studied this once humble 'hobservatory', now transformed into a technological masterpiece, the high arching dome with its twin black lasers pointed at the heavens, invisible arms reaching across an entire globe. The matrix of plasma-screens mounted above the command console, controlled by several supercomputers and displaying every square inch of the world, in high definition and three dimensions. Soon the contractors and technicians would finish their work and leave me as the sole keeper of this new age lighthouse.

My SatFone buzzed with a message from Lou, *China satellite just launched and Tom arrived at the airport with the techs.* I collected my notebook computer and SatFone for the drive to Alison's place to pick up Nicole for the weekend.

I locked the notebook into the custom-made dashboard console and connected it to the SatFone. An image from the other side of the world soon filled on screen, showing Mark standing at the entrance of Colombo International airport. The briefcase in his hand most likely containing the two hundred thousand dollars he had withdrawn.

In Madurai, I saw the terrorist's taxi pulling into the airport terminal building. Whenever I wasn't navigating a hairpin bend along the coast road, I stared too long at the images. Mother Nature too was busy unleashing her full fury in the black of the night, slapping me repeatedly from one side of the road to the other. I sensed she had taken issue with me, and like every action, this was her reaction.

I arrived at Alison's house where Nicole answered the door and immediately hugged my legs.

"You're late again," Alison said from behind the door.

"Have you seen the weather—?"

"Child raising isn't weather dependant."

She was obviously in old form again. Perhaps the psycho-babblers might call it a *withdrawal mood*.

"You're all set to go?" I asked Nicole.

"Yep."

"Look after her," Alison said, suddenly sincere, but strangely so. "Promise me you'll look after her."

"Sure."

I drew Nicole under the umbrella and we ran together to the car. Over the noise of the storm outside, Nicole yelled, "Dad, what's that picture on the screen?"

"It's just a town somewhere."

The SatFone buzzed with a message from Lou, *Satellite 4 Launched: AFRICA*, then a call from Alan on my cell phone, which had Nicole laughing as I juggled multiple handsets.

"Michael, we've confirmed Mark Woodcock is booked on a flight to Karachi, Pakistan. It's scheduled to depart in one hour, but we have no hits yet on Achmed Mata."

"Can you find if James Roberts was listed on a flight from Colombo to Karachi, sometime in the last week?"

"I'll check."

"And Alan, I suggest you and David vacate the observatory and patch into the main computer from home."

"Um… OK. When?

"Today."

I needed to perform the next phase of my work in private.

"Are we going to the hospital again?" Nicole asked.

"No, I've got a new place in the country, down on the coast."

"A holiday house?"

"Sort of."

"Has it got horses?"

"Not yet."

We arrived at the observatory amidst sixty-knot blasts of wind bolting inland from the sea cliffs.

"Wow, this place is awesome!" Nicole squealed.

"We can move into one of the apartments on Monday, but for now you'll need to stay in my loft upstairs. But be careful this place is dangerous, there's still unfinished work around, OK?"

"OK."

We emerged from the elevator and took the stairs to the terrace level. Nicole pounced into the loft and immediately found Leda, sleepy in her cage.

"You can have her beside your bed, but give her some food and water before you go to sleep. I need to finish some work downstairs."

"But I'm not tired yet."

"OK, you can read a book, but stay here."

At the main console, I pressed a key that dispersed the test images from all sixteen screens. The images quickly swirled into familiar program icons. I designated one of the observatory lasers as the download unit and the other for upload. I could send radiation pulses to satellite waveguides for rerouting to earthbound targets, while simultaneously uploading data in the form of visual images from the other waveguide.

Images from the China satellite displayed on screen 11, directly above screen 15. I checked the time, 12.15 am local and 10.15 pm in Lanzhou. I dialed Lou.

"When is the Middle East satellite launching?" I asked.

"In thirty minutes and we're ahead of schedule. Michael, the guys here are a little nervous about Shenyang. There has been a lot of rumor around and the Chinese techs think we might be a target. No one wants to stay longer than necessary..."

"I don't blame them. Just do what you need to stay safe Lou."

I heard a shuffling behind me.

"Dad, what are you doing?" Nicole asked, shielding her eyes from the bright screens.

I terminated the call, "Just testing a few things..."

"Are you watching all these TVs at once?"

"Yes, and you should be asleep."

"I was, but the storm woke me. Is that Mum's house on that TV?" she pointed at screen 7.

"It's just a picture of your house, to remind me of you."

"Can you come and read to me?"

"Sure, did you bring a book with you?"

"Yep. It's called *Watership Down*. It's a story about rabbits."

"Yeah, I know the one."

I watched my daughter standing there, fragile and vulnerable, then she fell from a moving train, then she held the hand of a man in sports goods store, and then shuffled along a dirt track somewhere in Africa. I shook my head and walked her upstairs.

"But only a couple of chapters, OK?" I said.

"OK."

An hour later, I returned to the console to find images streaming in from the Africa satellite and a glorious sun—large, luminous red and low on the horizon. A glistening Red Sea lay in the centre, bounded by the raw sands of Saudi Arabia, which faded off in the western horizon. To the south, the dark blue of the Arabian Sea and to the east, Egypt and the river Nile, a lone streak of green dissecting the emptiness. Further to the east, the dunes of the Sahara formed a stationary sea of waves and in the far north, the vast Mediterranean Sea separated Europe from the anarchy, or did it?

I studied the thick haze that blanketed the central African land mass and by applying digital filtering to the incoming signal I began to see through the haze and located several black patches. Some patches still spewed a thick black smoke high into the stratosphere, while the fire beneath burned bright and hot. I superimposed a geographic map over the visual to help with the identification of borders and cities. The names of rivers, lakes and other landmarks quickly appeared on the screen in their right position.

I zoomed in on one of the fires near Nimule, a small border village between Sudan and Uganda, and found a bonfire measuring two hundred meters in diameter and fifty meters high. I watched a crane collecting debris from an adjacent pit and heaving it onto the fire, sending successive explosions of embers into the sky.

With the sun moving lower on the horizon, the dark shadows made it difficult to pick out much detail. Switching to infrared didn't help either, with the fire effectively pluming the entire screen. I decided to record the live feed, whilst modifying the visual filtering software a little more.

With an enhanced light filter, I was able to adjust the individual wavelengths sufficiently to tame the offending components. I watched the first few seconds of the clear-vision replay, my eyes daring not to blink as a crane bucket cut through a mass of people standing tightly packed in a pit. Living, breathing people—men, women and children. The bucket lifted the bodies high overhead before depositing them on top of the fire stack. The entire stack seemed to move as flesh struggled, popped and burned.

On the ground, two lines of army troops drove the victims forward, the infrared mode highlighting the short, sharp plumes that were bullets streaking from their guns. The military men fired repeatedly into the crowd to keep them moving forward, toward the pit. Once at the end of the line, the refugees simply stumbled into the pit, almost willingly at that stage.

As I watched, I was surprised I didn't feel sick or squeamish, my head no longer ached and my stomach felt untroubled. The fire illuminated several square kilometers of a darkening African sky and I traced the line of people from the pit as it snaked tens of kilometers into Sudan. Along the unbroken line, thousands of troops with guns prodded the emancipated forms toward their execution, with a hundred thousand people or more in this one line.

I zoomed in on an army man dressed in khaki military gear and brandishing a weapon. A logo on the arm of his shirt looked vaguely familiar, but even at the highest resolution I could just make out a snakelike pattern and the letters M and T. The night vision lens couldn't discern his nationality or skin color. I ran a DNA scan on the man and displayed it on screen 10, but was disappointed to see it void of any rogue gene. I scanned several other armed men and they too returned without rogue DNA.

After a few minutes, I'd manually tagged a hundred army men along the line and curiously found only eight with rogue genes. I cross-referenced as many of the individuals as I could through the various DNA databases we had accessed, but found no hits on any of them.

In any case, nothing excused the atrocities I was witnessing and my anger took over. It was time for action, and with two waveguides on each satellite to send pulses and receive visual recon simultaneously, I programmed the rapid death scenarios and set the laser humming into action.

Several seconds later, I'd delivered over a hundred invisible arrows to the troops on the other side of the world. Some of the men crumpled where they stood, while others stumbled before sitting or lying down. A few kept prodding at the line of refugees with their guns, some for a full minute before they went down.

I gave the same treatment to the troops around the bonfire and now it was they who were pushed into the pit, by the refugees. I also made sure the crane driver sat silently within his tomb.

The death march slowed and dispersed as more refugees sensed freedom, slowly at first and then with a sense of purpose. It reminded me of when, as a child, I would break the line of an ant progression with my finger and wonder at how quickly order turned to chaos.

Armed men were running toward the dispersing line of refugees from various trucks parked along the route, like drones from beehives. Flashes of machine gun fire intensified and the mayhem made any further manual tagging of troops impossible.

I decided to freeze the image on screen and circled three of the armed men. I engaged a software routine that would break down the image and identify each form, much like a visual fingerprint analysis. However, the problem I had at night was the lack of the color and detail, with everything just a shade of green. Automatically determining killers from victims would be difficult, but I continued to refine the routine.

Several minutes later, I switched to live feed and set the new recognition software loose on the madness that instantly filled the screen. It scanned individuals, performed analysis and generated halo markers. I had disabled the live firing to be sure I wouldn't hit the refugees by mistake. It took less than five seconds for the system to tag and analyze one hundred people. When it finished, I froze the screen and replayed the vision of the tagging process in slow motion.

I found to my dismay that almost half of the people tagged were not military, but refugees. The routine had failed. I considered the alternatives, my mind racing and finding it difficult to concentrate with people dying right in front of me.

I focused on the refugees. What was specific to them? What was specific to the troops, other than what they wore? Perhaps, if I traced the gunfire back to its point of origin, I would find a deserving military target to neutralize.

I made the software changes in four minutes flat and decided to bypass the test sequence and engage live firing immediately—since if I did nothing they would just die anyway. Screen 11 came up live and I pressed *Execute*. I heard the hum of the laser as it acquired and processed targets, fifty in the first ten seconds. Slower this time as gunfire needed tracing back to its origin, before it confirmed a legitimate target.

I studied the tagged targets as they flashed by and was pleased to see that only two appeared to be the almost naked, emancipated refugees. Unfortunately, those two had somehow acquired guns and were shooting at the troops. I guess one hundred percent success was unrealistic anyway.

I watched the military uniforms dropping to the ground in a geometric pattern the system utilized for its search and response. I punched the air in exhilaration as the neutralization count passed two hundred and set the search area to a one hundred square kilometer area around the fire. When the acquisition rate in the grid dropped to zero, the system would move on to the next grid and so on. It was unfortunate I couldn't work in multiple areas simultaneously, as this would require more waveguides. At this rate, it would take several days to work through the enormity of central Africa. But at least machines didn't suffer exhaustion, hunger or conscience.

With that part of the world under control, I sent images from the Australian hub satellite to screen 7 and was pleased to see the digital filter experienced no difficulty in seeing straight through the local storm here, revealing towns and motorways to the north and south of Sydney.

I pointed the cursor at the centre of the area I wanted magnified and progressively clicked my way to Alison's house. I saw two people walking up the steps to her apartment and the system quickly acquired and performed DNA scans on each.

One, a male, scanned clean, and the other, a female, scanned positive as a rogue.

CHAPTER 29

I jumped up from my seat and looked around, trying to orientate myself. It was 8 am and I'd been asleep for four hours. In front of me was a matrix of screens displaying bizarre and unfamiliar images of people and places. I rubbed my eyes and tried to remember. Yes, the observatory, the systems are online, Nicole is here somewhere, and last night I had a front row seat to mass genocide in Africa.

There was an eerie silence in the dome space, with just the sub-woofer drone of the lasers as they satisfied their insatiable desire for energy.

I staggered to the kitchen and found Nicole spreading jam on toast.

"Good morning Dad, you look terrible."

"Thanks."

I refilled the coffee machine and looked outside to see a strange sight—sunlight and no wind—the eye of the storm?

"Can we play outside after breakfast?" Nicole asked.

"OK, but not for long."

Back at the console, I tuned into the global situation. The neutralization count stood at 3,634 and a fast motion replay of the last few hours showed the acquired targets all wore military uniforms. The last area scanned was the outer perimeter of another fire, close to the town of Gonder in northern Ethiopia, two hundred kilometers south of the Sudanese border.

With the China satellite now online, I typed in the coordinates of Shenyang and zoomed there. The city appeared intact, but deserted. Cars and bikes lay about haphazardly, abandoned. I viewed the streets, rooftops and parks, but found no people, no life. The entire city looked frozen in time.

I pulled up several news channels, but found little that came close to what I had seen. It seemed the flow of news was slowing and it stank of government control gone mad. Did the New World Order now control everything?

Alan rang, the caller ID informing me he was at his home.

"Michael, we got a hit from an airline database on Mark Woodcock. It confirms he arrived in Karachi, Pakistan, an hour ago. We also found James Roberts arrived in Karachi ten days ago and I've got a hit on an alias of Achmed Mata, currently inbound to Karachi from Madurai."

I keyed in the GPS coordinates for Karachi International and from high overhead watched as few people moved around the airport building in the dark early hours of the morning. The scan identified Mark as he entered a taxi, with the system tracking him to the Marriott Hotel, where he got out.

I rang Tom on his SatFone.

"Where are you?" I asked.

"We just landed in Shanghai to a wonderful sunrise. We're waiting for someone to come and pick up these SatFone prototypes. Hey, you should have seen the ride we had on approach. We dropped two thousand meters in free fall, with lightning and thunder all around us like you wouldn't believe."

"That sounds great. Listen, after you hand over the SatFone samples, John Trobe will join you for the Karachi mission."

"The Karachi mission?" he chuckled.

"Yes, Mark is at the Karachi Marriott Hotel. That's where you're heading next."

"Sure, OK chief."

Warren rang.

"Helen and your mum are ready to leave..."

"Oh."

"You're not pleased?"

"Yeah sure, I'll come over and pick them up now."

Helen was sitting in front of her bathroom mirror, brushing her hair and dressed in loose fitting pants and black t-shirt. Several bags were neatly packed and placed on her bed.

"Do you feel up to taking a ride?" I asked.

"I can't wait. Shall we go to a tropical island or a snow covered mountain?"

"I was thinking more of a barren cliff face, lashed with gale force winds and torrential rain."

"Sounds delightful. Let me just take a bathroom break and I'll be with you."

She rose from the chair, slowly and steadily, and reached out to hug me. I held her and looked behind her to a mirror, noticing the flatness where her other buttock should have been.

"Can I see you for a few minutes?" Warren asked me as he entered the room.

I left Nicole with Helen and followed him into the corridor.

"Sue's awake, you need to see her," he said without expression

She was sitting upright in bed, her injuries no longer visible and looking completely healed.

"Hi, I'm Michael Crow, Lou's friend." I said, wondering if she could understand words.

"Hi, how's Lou? I haven't heard from him in a while."

"He's in China, commissioning some satellite communications gear for us. He asks about you every day."

"When is he coming back?"

"I'm not sure exactly, but soon."

Warren spoke to her about her condition and she seemed stunned at the severity of her injuries, yet pleased to be recovering. She said she had no memory of the attack that almost killed her.

We were back in the corridor before Warren spoke to me, "I will ask a specialist neurosurgeon to check on her. And we may still need to transfer her to another hospital."

"She might surprise you and discharge herself."

"That would certainly raise fewer questions."

"What about our four-legged patients?"

"They're all progressing well."

"Would you say the procedure is a success?"

"That's still a little premature. And I think it might be best for you to remove your MRI," he said as though he now considered it an instrument of the devil.

"Sure, I'll have it picked up in a few days."

"Any news on Mark or James?"

"We've found them both in Karachi."

"Pakistan? Why?"

"I'm not really sure. We have someone heading over there now to pick them up and bring them home."

"That's great news."

We dropped Mum off at her new home. It was a timeless regal mansion that she would become accustomed to in time, despite her protests that it was big and flashy. I gave her a hug and promised to visit her in a few days.

The next wave of storm clouds dropped their load of torrential rain upon us just as Helen, Nicole and I arrived at the wrought iron gates of the observatory.

"This place is huge," Helen shouted over the noise of the downpour.

"And there's even an indoor pool and spa," Nicole explained, "As well as a gym, a sauna and lots of rooms. There's even a playground!"

I could feel Helen watching me with growing suspicion, as we drove down the ramp into the basement car park and the noise of the rain abruptly ceased. I unfolded the wheelchair but Helen insisted on walking. I put the bags on the chair and we took the lift to the apartments, stepping out into the central atrium.

All the apartments faced each other across a swimming pool. At one end of the pool was a spa and at the other, a wet bar. Palm trees stood perfectly still under an enormous glass canopy, as the wind roared outside. Through the glass, we could see the dark evening sky. It gave a feeling of being in a biosphere. I watched Helen, with her noticeable limp, following Nicole to the cascading waterfall.

"You two have a look around," I suggested. "Our apartment will be the larger one over there. If you're hungry, just press the button marked R on the intercom and you're through to the village restaurant. They'll deliver whatever you want. I need to finish some work in the main dome, OK?" I assumed they heard me, but neither turned around.

I needed to see the screens so urgently I almost ran to the dome and the command console.

Screen 15 showed the Karachi Marriott Hotel with the tracking icon indicating Mark was inside. I searched through the recording and found Mark entering a taxi outside the hotel. I watched as the taxi wound through progressively tighter streets before stopping at a large mosque on the outskirts of the city. Mark entered the mosque, briefcase in hand.

Ten minutes later he emerged empty handed. I noted the mosque's GPS coordinates and watched the taxi take him back to the Marriot. I set an active scan at Karachi International for Achmed Mata. It was currently 1 pm there.

Further to the west, in Africa, the morning sun glowed on the eastern horizon where the targeting system had suspended operations in the town of Kumasi, Ghana. The neutralization count stood at 16,233. Here, a large number of locals dressed in rags moved freely around the village, as uniformed bodies lay in the streets and fields, hacked to pieces. Villagers dragged body parts to the fire and heaved them in. I noticed the uniformed bodies had white skin and upon closer inspection recognized the round hats and insignia as French soldiers.

I reviewed the recording through the night vision lens and saw the targeting process had performed efficiently. As the gunmen shot into the crowds, the laser acquired and dropped them to the ground a second later. It appeared the intent of the French had been an indiscriminate slaughter of the locals—an ethnic cleansing of Ghana. Was this the so-called annexing of the country by 'mutual agreement' the commentators spoke of? Was the French intent to add this 'colony' to Cote D'Ivoire and continue acquiring more countries along the West African coast?

I rewound the recording to earlier last night, to a previous bonfire, where the location indicator read, Ati, Chad. In comparison, here the fire was smaller, measuring only twenty meters across and several meters high. The human remains that had fuelled this fire were still visible. But the uniformed men who lay dead here were not French—these soldiers wore turbans on their heads and some had a shoulder insignia, with an M and T on either side of a snakelike figure.

In live mode, I scanned to the west, along a line of scattered bodies on a track from Chad to Sudan. All along this track, the emancipated locals were collecting the bodies of their fallen neighbors, ignoring those in uniform and leaving them to bloat in the sun.

"What's going on here?" Helen's voice tore through me like a knife in the back.

I turned to see Nicole and Helen standing directly behind me, their eyes darting from screen to screen.

"See, there's my Mum's house!" Nicole pointed.

I sent the screens to test patterns. "I'm just testing some new systems," I offered as an automatic apology.

"Where are those pictures coming from?" Helen asked.

"They're from various cell phone towers around the country. They assist with local law enforcement—some deal SatCOMM has done with the police department."

"Who are all those dead people...?" She pointed to the screen with wide-eyed fury, as though I'd just killed them.

"That's an internet news feed—it's the war and famine in Africa."

"It doesn't look like any news feed I've ever seen."

"I've tapped into the raw signal from the networks...through Cooper's satellites."

She looked to me, then back at the screen, unsure of what she was seeing, but sure of her mistrust for me.

"Has dinner arrived?" I tried to break the tension.

"That's why we came here. You've been gone for a while."

"OK, let's eat."

We did, but largely in silence, except for one exchange.

"Helen," I heard Nicole whisper. "What's wrong with Dad? He's not much fun anymore."

"I agree honey," Helen replied. "But I'm not sure I want to know why."

After dinner, Helen read to Nicole while I returned to my console.

Walking under the glass canopy to the dome, I heard the wind and rain battling in their own private war.

A message flashed onto the screen confirming the detection of Achmed Mata at Karachi International. I switched to the live feed and found the taxi he'd entered moving through the streets of Karachi. On screen 15, the stationary image of a mosque suggested Mark had returned there. I replayed the recorded images and saw he had taken with him another briefcase, and he'd now been in the mosque for over an hour. The time there was now 2.30 pm and I scanned people as they moved about in the open courtyard within the mosque. I found no rogues or people matching anything we had on the database.

I turned my attention to the streets of Shenyang and manipulated the Vibrolert algorithms to investigate the strange cloud blanketing the city. If this were high-energy subatomic particles, it would destroy anything living, leaving only buildings and infrastructure intact. The perfect weapon of mass destruction, assuming the radiation dissipated sometime in the current millennium.

With the gamma-ray filter overlay, I discovered the density of these particles was decreasing, with a decay pattern too rapid to have resulted from nuclear fission. The extrapolated decay curve indicated a half-life of weeks rather than centuries. This really was the perfect weapon of mass destruction and very hi-tech, but who was responsible for it?

I panned back for a wide-angle view of the African continent and found more mist in central Africa, opaque in the gamma-ray band. This one was several kilometers across and centered over the city of Abuja, capital of Nigeria.

Scanning east, I found another mist along the Gulf of Guinea coast, over Lagos. Both cities looked empty, lifeless and with the same radiation decay pattern as Shenyang. Was this the same weapon and therefore the same perpetrator?

I watched military people and hardware move from Sudan, Chad and Cote D'Ivore toward a common intersection in Nigeria. I searched the internet for articles on recent discoveries in the Gulf of Guinea, finding several reports on sizable reserves of natural gas and oil just off the Nigerian coast. I wondered what was happening to the 'free' press and who could be behind this cloak of silence.

Screen 12 caught my attention with thousands of people congregating near the Korean-Chinese border. Most wore uniforms and were surrounded by serious military hardware. The assortment of tanks, helicopters and missile racks moved slowly toward the border zone. In the midst of all the military muscle, civilians went about their daily business, making for an incongruous scene.

Movement on screen 7 caught my attention—Alison's apartment. A figure emerged from the apartment wearing a hood and dragging a large garbage bag. The figure struggled to deposit the bag into the boot of Alison's car before returning to the apartment. Shortly after the figure returned and dragged several more garbage bags from the house and into the car boot. I scanned the figure for DNA and confirmed it was Alison, rogue genes and all.

She drove off into the night, alone. I set the system to track her and wondered what she was up to, and if her rogue gene was hereditary.

CHAPTER 30

The time was 8pm in Sydney and 2pm in Karachi. The SatPhone rang.

"Michael, we've just arrived in Karachi. We're at the airport but there's some issue with customs."

"OK, call me when you get through."

"Sure chief."

I watched the mosque and saw people moving about freely in the relative cool of the night. The system confirmed Mark was still inside the west building, as was Achmed Mata.

It was 12 noon in Africa and the eastern sun clearly illuminated a line of troops that had closed to within a few hundred kilometers of the Nigerian border. At the North Korean-Chinese border, it was 6 pm and there too the military lined the border for a hundred kilometers.

I contemplated the options one last time before deciding to just take out the rogues and hope for the best. Anyone firing weapons would be neutralized, with or without rogue DNA. Collateral damage they called it. Perhaps not a plan Eisenhower would have come up with, but he had more experience in matters of global warfare.

I set the pulse sequences to patterns I hoped would result in quick disablement or death and was now ready to unleash my invisible strike upon the scourge of war. I defined a theatre of operation for both regions and set the system to full automatic.

The first laser quickly hummed into action and within seconds, the status indicator was showing accumulated neutralizations.

I turned to the Karachi mosque, to the west building, where the thatched low-density roof would offer minimal resistance to my scans. With laser two, I opened the beam spread as wide as possible, a meter in diameter and initiated a succession of scans across the roof of the building.

As the beam tracked across the roof, it paused periodically to detect any bio-fluorescence returns. Even if the return signal was too faint to decode DNA, I hoped to get at least an indication of life within.

To my relief, the system confirmed five people within the mosque building, all of them male. A few seconds later, DNA data for each scrolled across the screen. One was a match to Mark, and another, a rogue, was a match to Achmed Mata. One of the other three males also returned rogue DNA, but without DNA for James I couldn't be sure he was not a rogue.

I rang Tom. "You need to get out of the airport and into a taxi."

"What I need is a five course lunch at the finest restaurant in this shithole."

"I have a fix on Mark and maybe James as well. There in a mosque on the north-eastern edge of the city and they could be in trouble."

"OK chief, I'll call when we're mobile."

The 'chief' stuff had progressed from mildly amusing to irritating now.

Alan rang. "Michael, I've found out a little more about MocTas, the name you asked me to investigate?"

"OK, what did you find?"

"Well it wasn't easy. It's a registered company and for some reason the owners want to remain well hidden. And they are, under a barrage of shelf companies in three different countries."

"OK, so who owns them?"

"Well, the trail stops at SatCOMM."

I felt the blood drain from my face.

"Michael, are you there?"

"Are you sure?"

"Yes, and it was starring us in the face the whole time."

"What do you mean?"

"MocTas spelt backwards is SatCOMM..."

I wrote out the words on a piece of paper, and noticed the M and T. Was this the same M and T insignia on the jackets of soldiers I saw in Africa?

"OK. Alan, don't mention this to anyone and make sure you've left no trace of yourself behind, anywhere."

I turned to screen 7 and saw Alison pulling her car onto a dirt track, stopping a few minutes later near a dry lake bed. There was no need to tune in the night filter as the full moon and her headlights lit up the area like daylight.

She stepped out of the car, opened the boot and heaved the various garbage bags onto the ground. One bag split open and a large round object fell out, rolling slowly across the gently sloping ground. I zoomed in and saw it was a human head. A man's head, with eyes bulging and an open mouth, and a face I didn't recognize.

Alison took a shovel from the trunk and started to dig at the soft edge of the dry lake. I watched for several minutes before deciding to ring her.

The phone must have rung from somewhere inside her car, as she stopped and looked back to the car. She ignored the ringing and continued digging. I dialled again and this time she walked to the car and picked up the phone.

"What are you doing?" I asked.

"Why is that your concern?"

"Because it doesn't look good."

She dropped the shovel and snapped her head from side to side, searching out the landscape around her.

"What the hell are you talking about?" she screamed.

"Who does the head belong to?"

"Where are you? Are you here somewhere?" She ran up a nearby mound of dirt to peer about in deranged confusion, her breathing frantic.

"Did *you* kill him?"

She stood still as I zoomed in on her face, which slowly drained of emotion.

"Why?" I prodded.

"Because he was a pig," she sat on the ground, "because you're all pigs."

"Who?"

"Men. They control, they hate, they manipulate and they eventually destroy everything."

It was hard to argue that, but I had never wanted to destroy her. I didn't know what to say or do.

"I know Nicole hates me," she whispered. "I can see it in her eyes, but I have to beat her—"

"You beat her?"

"Girls need to be beaten," she spoke like a child now, with her body rocking from side to side. "My father knew that."

I didn't know much about her father, except that she hated him. She never talked about him and cut off all contact with her family when she moved out of home. Her mother died the year after she moved out, from an accident of some kind, so relatives told her. She never spoke about that either.

Alison got up and walked to the car. "Do something for me?" she asked softly, in yet another voice I barely recognized. "Tell Nicole I love her."

I saw her put the phone down on the roof of the car, then reach in and pull out a handgun. She raised it to her head. I stood and yelled into the phone, to the screen in front of me and then closed my eyes as the sound of a gunshot punched my ears.

When I opened my eyes, I saw her laying face up on the ground, near the severed head and with a dark pool of blood slowly silhouetting her head. I thought about rewinding the recording, hoping this time I could talk her out of it. But I only managed to slump down onto the floor and stare at the screen.

Nicole ran into the dome calling, 'Daddy!' I pounded on the hotkey to blank the screens and a swirl of screensavers transformed the bleak into a rainbow of colors.

"Dad, what are doing on the floor?"

"Just looking for something, what's up?"

"I feel sad. Are you are going to be happy again?"

"Of course honey. Don't worry, it'll all be OK." I could tell she was unsure about many things, about her mother, about me. Had she sensed the death of her mother just now? I held her in my arms, her face resting on my shoulder so she couldn't see my eyes, which were red and wet.

Just as suddenly, she pulled herself away. "Are you coming in the pool?" she asked, bright and happy again.

"You should be getting ready for bed."

"Please...just a quick splash?"

"OK, I'll be there in a minute."

I watched her run off and contemplated the various forms of energy not yet understood and perhaps would never be.

I summoned the strength to move my legs and walked to the residential wing. I splashed water on my face at the pool edge and looked up at the glass canopy. Outside, I saw the rain whipping across the glass in squalls and imagined the trees doubled over. Yet here within my cocoon, I felt detached from the madness. Or was I really in the dead centre of it?

Helen was lying back in a deck chair and looking more relaxed than I'd seen her of late.

"Michael, come and relax for a while, you look tired," she said.

"Sure, but just for a few minutes, I've still got some work to finish."

"But it's almost 9 o'clock? You are obsessed with this work of yours and it's unhealthy. I thought you were going to take it easy for a while. Remember what Vibrolert did to you. What happened to the new carefree Michael Crow?"

"Yeah, I don't know, he kind of slipped away before I had a chance to get to know him."

I played with Nicole for a while, but it wasn't long before I was back at my console. The African situation caught my attention as troops headed toward Nigeria. The soldiers coming from the east through Chad appeared to be Arab and those from the west through Ghana, were dressed in French uniforms. The neutralization count in Africa was 4742, of which only 712 were rogues. I wondered if this ratio were higher for the military than for the general population and filed this away as an interesting exercise to pursue, should I get some time between wars.

At the North Korean border, a fire burned where the Chinese had penetrated the line at a bridge just south of Dandon. They now marched towards the North Korean village of Sinuiju beneath jet trails that littered the sky in all directions. The neutralization count here stood at 3332.

Tom rang, "Hey chief, we're on the streets of Karachi and mobile."

"OK. There's a mosque an hour or so to the north-east. I've sent you the GPS coordinates on your phone. Once you get there, go to the southern entrance and keep at a safe distance. And one other thing…Alison is dead."

"What! How?"

"She killed herself."

"Fuck."

"I need you make an anonymous phone call to the police in Sydney."

"Why?"

"To tell them where her body is. I've sent you those coordinates as well. You should use a local phone somewhere and don't use your credit card."

I panned across Pakistan and found a line of troops in the east, along the Indian border. A message from Lou flashed up, *Two satellites just deployed over Europe. One over Ukraine, one over France.* I wasn't looking forward to Eastern Europe, particularly around the former Russian states, for fear of what armies might be lurking there.

I turned to the sun-baked mosque on the outskirts of Karachi, with its four solid red sandstone minarets standing proud at each corner. In the larger building to the west of the central courtyard, I saw five people—Mark, a non-rogue in the left corner and three others in the centre. I couldn't tell if they were standing or sitting, but one seemed to walk over to Mark every few minutes and back again.

The SatFone rang.

"We're having coffee in a market place south-east of the target mosque. We have the southern entrance in view and confirm the coffee is black and strong," Tom reported.

"Mark and I assume James, are in the west building, with two, possibly three hostiles."

"Roger that, you want us to raid the place and throw coffee beans at them?"

"No smartass, just keep a taxi on standby and watch the mosque."

"Will do, chief."

"If you see Mark and James come out, grab them, head to the airport and get the hell out of there."

"Sounds like a plan..."

I observed a taxi driver pulling over in response to Tom's arm movements as I focused the laser on the first of the rogues inside the mosque. Without warning, the screen exploded in a blaze of white hash, leaving me staring at black and white dots in complete confusion. Seconds later, a message flashed up, *System rebooting, please wait.*

The diagnostic confirmed both waveguides from the Indian satellite had gone offline. With the direct link through SatCOMM, I activated the remote satellite reboot sequence. Beads of sweat trickled down my neck as my fingers fumbled over the keyboard. I refocused a waveguide from the China satellite into the western horizon and long seconds passed as servo-motors realigned and images started to stream through. I searched the area but found the distance from this satellite just too great and the resolution insufficient to determine a cause for the blackout.

A few minutes later, the Indian satellite returned images to screen 16 and showed the street activity around the mosque as it had been before the blackout. Pulling back the zoom and switching in the gamma filter revealed a familiar mist rising from the foothills of northern Pakistan. The position locator estimated ground zero as the city of Islamabad.

I saw Tom and Trobe sitting back, drinking coffee, relaxed and oblivious to whatever else was happening around them. And what else was happening? Who was this other player in the mix? I needed to make a move and get these people out of there.

I fired a pulse at the two rogues in the mosque and, with a low power scan of the interior, saw a man tending them before he ran from the building and crossed the courtyard to the eastern side. Seconds later, he was running back to the building with three others in tow, a rogue among them. A DNA scan confirmed this rogue was Achmed Mata.

Mata was the first inside the west building, gone before I had the chance to gather myself and frame him in the sights. The other two weren't so lucky and I dropped them to the stone floor of the courtyard in mid-stride.

I opened a link between Trobe's and Tom's SatFones and spoke to them, "Mark and James are in the centre room of the west building and they could be injured. There are two hostiles with them. One is Achmed Mata, a known terrorist and extremely dangerous."

"OK, let's roll," Tom, quipped.

"No not you. Let John go in first, he's the pro."

Without any obvious haste, Trobe walked through the mosque gates and into the courtyard. With several men crumpled on the stone paving, the beehive had been disturbed. People were moving hurriedly in all directions, except for a group of five men who crossed the courtyard on a direct route to the larger building.

I targeted all five and fired, dropping three to the ground with two managing to evade and escape through the door. Trobe was inside the building, but the frenzied motion made it difficult to identify any individual by scanning through the roof.

"John, what's happening?" I shouted, but hearing only the sound of scuffling and shouting.

"What should I do?" Tom asked.

"Nothing,"

"Yeah, fuck that."

I saw Tom, almost at a run, entering the mosque and then a voice I didn't recognize, guttural, from Trobe's SatFone. Was this Achmed Mata, the man who crippled Helen? I heard several gunshots and people appearing as confused blurs of motion. I shouted into the SatFone, yet heard only screaming and shouting in return. Two shots from a gun punched the airwaves and I entered a special instruction to Trobe's SatFone handset and waited.

The handset performed a DNA test on the person holding it and at once confirmed it was Achmed Mata, I pressed the enter key to initiate a burst of ultra high frequency microwave energy from the handset, directly into the ear of the holder.

I scanned the building again, this time finding return signals only from Tom and Mark. No one else scanned as alive inside the building.

Almost a minute passed before I saw Tom emerge from the building, supporting Mark draped over his shoulder. The area was already thick with onlookers, official vehicles and authorities. Through his handset, I heard Tom arguing with the taxi driver, who wanted more money now that suspect activity was involved.

"Here take it all, now drive shithead." I heard Tom yelling.

The Karachi screen turned to hash again and my fingers moved quickly over the keyboard to find a horizon view from the China satellite. I found more atomic mist, this time over New Delhi. Had World War 3 formally commenced?

"Come on Dad, stop playing computer games." I jumped from the seat and turned around to find Nicole standing there, straight from the pool, looking like a wet rat and stamping water in all directions. I turned the screens off.

"Am I staying here tonight or going back to Mum's house?" she demanded, sending another spray of water into the air. I felt invisible, neither situation entirely real.

"Go back to the pool before you get electrocuted. I'll ring your Mum."

When she left, I turned on the screens and found Alison's body lying where it had been earlier. Police and medics were photographing and searching the area, and a pounding rain tried desperately to cleanse the scene.

"It's all fucked up," Tom's voice shouted through the SatFone. "James and Trobe are dead."

"How?"

"When I got inside I saw James' body strapped to a chair, tortured and mutilated. Trobe was on the ground, with a bullet hole in his forehead."

I waited for more.

"It was a butcher shop, there was blood everywhere." Tom was stressing.

"How's Mark?"

"He's beaten up pretty bad, but not enough to kill him as far as I can tell."

"You should head to the airport and get out of the country as quickly as you can."

"No shit Sherlock."

I didn't tell him about the atomic mist a few hundred kilometers to his east as I tracked his taxi through the crowded streets. With the traffic slowing at times to a frustrating standstill, I tried to direct them to less congested routes. Tom seemed to have lost interest in how I could in fact 'know' all this.

My SatFone rang.

"Michael, is there a situation that you need to tell me about?"

"Which situation is that Brendan?" my heart raced even faster.

"John Trobe has been killed."

How did he know so quickly?

"Yes, and so has James Roberts. My brother is trying to get Mark Woodcock out of the country at the moment."

"I see. I'm concerned at a few other things that have been happening recently, some business interests of mine that are being disrupted."

"Brendan, what are you talking about?"

"In fact, I'd like you to shut down your observatory immediately."

My breathing stopped as I tried to piece all the bits together.

"I can't do that Brendan."

"You're placing your life and the lives of the people closest to you in danger."

Now that the threats started, I felt I had the control and not him. Otherwise, why would he call me? Why wouldn't he just shut me down if he could?

"It seems danger is now a part of my life, it's something I'm coming to terms with."

"If you don't shut down Michael, I'll do it for you," and with that the screens in front of me turned to white hash. I checked the satellite feeds and they were offline.

"Do you need to be reminded who's really got the power?" he said.

"Brendan, tell me about the body part factories in Colombo and Africa."

"Factories? I think you mean our processing plants." He paused. "Michael, the world is overpopulated by people who take and do not give.

It simply can't be sustained and there are many who have just themselves to give."

"But they don't just give themselves do they? You kill them and take them."

"Yes, but they live to the ripe old age of thirty-five and they are well looked after. We will even provide a free SatFone from the age of ten."

"I guess no one could complain about that…"

"Have you seen how these people have been living without our help? My alternative is much better and that's why *they* sign up, we don't need to coerce anyone."

"I'm sure I saw some coercion in Africa last night."

"We'll unfortunately there are still elements of chaos here and there. This is after-all, a transition phase, a new beginning. But the detail is not my concern, I'm just a business man and not an enlightened world leader. The New World Order will soon clean it up."

"You really have lost your mind…"

"Michael, you have no idea. Do you really think the world's greatest democracies are sitting this out? No, they are the instigators and *we* are the pawns. You and I, we do their dirty work. *We* have been working for them for some time now and being well paid, if I need to remind you."

"So the New Order will determine who lives and who dies, who prospers and who fails?"

"Yes, leaving it to the masses hasn't worked. You've seen that first hand."

Part of me wanted to believe this ideal, but the reality was flawed because it involved the suffering of innocents and I had seen that first hand too.

"You are either with us or against us Michael. I'm on my way to Washington and don't have a lot of time to chat."

"Is the SatFone selling well in the US?"

"Yes, we have the only license to operate such a service and with the new satellites the quality is astounding, isn't it?"

The screen on my SatFone came alive and I found myself staring into his eyes.

"See, no framing at all. We can deliver high definition visual images to any point on the globe at 200 frames per second," he said.

I pulled up his SatFone handset status on screen 1 and the position indicator confirmed he was over Hawaii in the Pacific Ocean.

"Michael, I should say," he said quietly, moving the phone closer to his face, "Just between you and me… I don't see myself as being a pawn forever. My time will come. Work with me and we can rid the world of whomever and whatever displeases us. We need each other."

"Brendan, I think I know what you need." I said, as his expression change from supreme arrogance to something only slightly less.

I hit the 'enter' key, activated his SatFone's modified circuitry and watched as his eyes glazed over and the frequency of his blinking increase.

"Brendan, can you hear me?" I asked.

He looked at the phone blankly and said nothing. I saw his fingers tapping at the screen and then scratching at his head. I watched him for a while, as he played with the phone and then put it down. When only the cabin ceiling was visible, I disconnected the call.

I was pleased Cooper had used one of my modified SatFones and that it only required a short duration burst to retard the cerebral synapse function, permanently. I surmised that the pulse hardened the synaptic membranes sufficiently to impede neurotransmissions. A subtle skill that left no marks or other indications, yet simply reduced the intelligence and speed of the brain. It also left the target alive and therefore raised fewer questions.

I activated the security override I'd implanted into the SatCOMM computers some time ago and took back control of all their satellites. The screens came up live showing Karachi International Airport and a steady stream of military aircraft taking off toward the Indian border.

I hunted for news updates, yet found only limited reporting on border incursions in Korea, Africa and Pakistan.

"Michael, we're entering the airport perimeter and there's a bunch of military vehicles and troops here. I think we're fucked." Tom groaned into his SatFone, in complete resignation of torture and death in a foreign country.

"Just don't panic and proceed to customs. Has Mark got his passport?"

"Let me check."

"Can he walk?"

"I think so, but I'll need to clean him up in a toilet somewhere. He's got blood all over him."

"OK, but try to at least appear calm."

"Yeah, easy for you to say. OK, I found his passport."

"Good. When you get out of the cab, find a space somewhere out in the open, sit down and wait until I tell you to get up."

"What!"

"Just do it."

I heard footsteps behind me. Helen and Nicole. I turned the screens off.

"Who are you shouting at?" Helen asked.

"Just Tom."

"How about forgetting Tom for a minute and consider your daughter. Nic's concerned about her Mum, have you called her yet?"

"Yes, Nicole will stay here tonight. Just give me a few more minutes and I'll be with you."

"Come on Michael, it's after ten o'clock, what's so damned important here?"

Tom was shouting in my earpiece, telling me he and Mark were sitting on the kerb outside the airport, 'like ducks in the open season'.

"Tom has a problem in Pakistan and I need to make sure he can catch a flight out."

"Who the hell are you talking to?" Tom yelled in my left ear.

"You're a travel agent now?" Helen said.

"Give me a few more minutes,"

"No, *now*, people are staring at us," from Tom

Nicole put on her best pout and wrapped a towel around herself.

"Fuck, we're going to die in this shithole..." Tom groaned.

"I'm hungry again." Nicole said.

"Hey, why don't you ring for your favorite pizza?" I suggested to Nicole.

"Sure, we'll have one with the lot and hold the anchovies," Tom quipped.

"Michael, we need to talk. I mean *really* talk, and soon. Come on honey, Daddy's being selfish, let's leave him alone." And with that they left, hand in hand, women against men.

"Hello, anyone there?" Tom yelled.

"Wait a few more seconds."

I programmed the pulse sequence for stem cell proliferation and fired it squarely at Mark's hunched form.

"OK, you can get up now." I said.

Tom jumped up and helped Mark to his feet.

"We need to talk when I get back," Tom said, scanning the skies above him.

I noticed a freshening wind pushing them towards the airport entrance, as the screens turned to hash again. The Karachi satellite went down for a third time and five seconds seemed like an eternity before it came back.

I scanned for damage and mist, the system confirming the epicenter of another gamma particle burst—in the old city of Karachi, to the east of their location. The toxic mist would spread westward on the wind, directly toward the airport in a matter of minutes.

I scanned the old city and found people staggering about, seeking refuge in buildings and cars stopped haphazardly, abandoned.

"Tom, a bomb has gone off near you. You need to hurry."

"I didn't feel it."

"You will soon enough. Move it, *now*."

"It's been a while since you said please."

A trail of black smoke was rising from a building outside the perimeter of the airport. Zooming in, I saw the tail of a commercial airliner stuck in a mound of building rubble, engulfed by flames and thick black smoke.

Two more long minutes passed before the Lear Jet started taxiing toward the runway, the atomic cloud having already closed half the distance to the airport.

"You've only got a couple of minutes before the fallout hits you from the east. I suggest you fly out to the west and then south over the Arabian Sea," I said.

"Pity we didn't hire the model with after-burners."

"Maybe next time..."

"No way, this courier just retired."

I could hear Tom talking to the pilot while I examined the skies around Karachi.

"The airspace around you is clear. *Go now.*" I shouted.

Seconds later, the Lear Jet surged forward and left the ground as the cloud engulfed the airport buildings. They were safe and climbing high over a deep blue Arabian sea.

Tom's voice screamed in my ears, "A military jet just buzzed us and it's turning around to come back!"

I adjusted the vision and found it hard to pinpoint the rapidly moving object. Finally, I found a dull grey jet closing in behind them. I considered what happened to aluminum foil in a microwave oven and quickly programmed a long duration high-energy pulse. I aimed it squarely at the cockpit of the military jet and saw a flash of lightning streaked along its length from the front to back. Seconds later, it was spiraling downward into the sea, disintegrating in a burst of black and yellow on impact.

Deafening alarms sounded around me and a warning flashed up on screen, *Overload*. The dome plunged into darkness as I ran to the electrical switchboard. I tripped over a chair and sprawled across the floor. I hit my head on a metal equipment trolley sending instruments and tools crashing to the floor around me. I felt a warm liquid covering my head and hands. Dizzy, I hobbled the last few meters to the power meter, switched off the alarm and reset the circuit breakers.

The power recorder showed a surge had just spiked through the system, the result of frying the military jet I suspected. Thankfully, there was no smell of burning electrical wiring.

I wrapped my bloody head in a towel, limped back to the console and watched the Lear Jet and its passengers escaping from death, one more time.

"Mike, you should've seen what just happened. The fucker dropped from the sky like a brick!" Tom hooted. "Did you do that?"

"Don't be stupid, it was probably a surface to air missile from the war going on behind you. Just keep to the south-east as fast and high as you can."

CHAPTER 31

I needed coffee and lots of it. The dome machine was empty and I found Helen in the apartment kitchen.

"You should be asleep." I said, pouring coffee for us both.

"And so should you. What happened to your head?"

"It's nothing. I tripped and hit my head on a trolley."

"You look like you've been in a war zone".

"Yeah, it sure does feel like it. Is Nicole asleep?"

"Yes, finally."

I hesitated. "Helen, I couldn't tell you in front of Nicole, but... Alison killed herself earlier tonight."

"Killed herself! How? Why?"

"She shot herself. I don't know why exactly, but I guess she was troubled. The police rang me an hour ago."

"Why was she so troubled?"

"I think it might have something to do with drugs. I had suspected it for a while."

"Oh, God! Poor Nicole. When are you going to tell her?"

"In the morning, I won't wake her tonight. I've still got some work to finish."

"Michael let it go. What the hell are you doing in there anyway," she pointed to the devil's lair.

"I'm trying to get some communications systems on line before the morning..."

"And that's it? You expect me to believe that?"

"Yes. What the hell else do you think I'm doing?"

"I think you and Cooper are into something...sinister."

"Sinister?" I tried to mask the truth with a half laugh.

"Helen, there's nothing sinister going on in there or anywhere else, at least not by me."

She stared at me and I felt her probing around inside my head.

"Michael, I'm not sure I can stay here... I'm thinking about going back home, tomorrow."

"But you need care..."

"I'm doing fine," she swayed slightly and leaned against the kitchen bench for support.

"Are you OK?"

"Yes. I'm tired and I'm going to bed." She looked sad and annoyed, but otherwise healthier each time. Perhaps I should send myself through the MRI.

"I think they poked something in Mark's eye, it was bleeding and two of his fingers are missing. He might have a few broken ribs by the noise he was making. I used some painkillers and bandages from the planes medi-kit and he's finally asleep now," Tom said.

"You're OK?"

"I've got everything I came here with, except my sanity."

I checked their position.

"You're making good progress across the Indian Ocean and should be touching down in eight hours."

"That's eight hours too long."

"How's the pilot?"

"He's stopped shaking."

"Fuel?"

"He says we'll make it."

At the China-Korea border, the automated routine had clocked up 25,321 neutralizations. In Africa, the mid afternoon sun baked the military convoys that crawled slowly across Chad. On closer inspection, they appeared a little less organized and somewhat slower than before. In Ghana, a tent city had sprung up along the convoy lines, stopping just short of the

Toga border. I could make out the Red Cross flags flying over several white tents scattered across the countryside.

I turned to the satellite over Eastern Europe and brought up images of the states bordering Russia, the entire sixteen-screen matrix now showing the full extent of the global crisis. I imagined myself at an international news desk, but not those strangled, censored and bought off. This news desk had information first hand and in real time, and this desk came with the power to *create* news.

In Eastern Europe, a darkening evening sky reduced the detail on the ground. I searched the Ukraine before moving southeast along the coast of the Black Sea, towards Georgia. Scanning the lowlands and over the mountains to the town of Vladikavkaz in southern Chechnya, I counted two hundred tanks and support vehicles. Most had the old Soviet symbol painted on the side and some even flew the soviet flag.

I programmed a systematic search of the lands that bordered Russia, from the Balkans to Kazakhstan. The system quickly identified eight convoy lines, all with the same black tanks and all heading outward from Russia. It seemed more aggression would be unleashed upon the ordinary people of the world, people who wanted nothing other than to be left alone and to live in peace.

I programmed a search routine whilst watching a line of tanks snake through the countryside. I couldn't penetrate their steel, but I could monitor the convoy to catch soldiers as they moved in and out of the vehicles. I set both lasers to full automatic and heard for the first time their combined harmonic hum.

The sound of the brave new world resonated through the floor and into my bones. I marveled at the array of screens, the quick and clinical manner in which the targeting systems scanned and processed targets. Methodically gathering data on every man, woman and child. Storing, processing and neutralizing threats, every second of every day. This was indeed the dawn of a new age, my age.

I looked behind, to the electrical switchboard, to make sure the power supply was coping and saw Helen standing behind me, watching. I froze.

"You need to be honest with me Michael. Don't bullshit me anymore. What is all this about?"

I gathered my thoughts and took a deep breath.

"These are images from satellites orbiting the earth," I pointed to the screens. "There is a world war in progress right now, but you won't find the usual media outlets caring too much about it. Apart from the Korean destruction that you know about, radiation bombs have gone off across Africa and China. And from one end of Africa to the other, tens of thousands of refugees are being burned alive in human fire pits fifty meters high, disposed of as quickly as they can be expelled from their homelands. Others have their internal organs harvested, to enable others with more money to live longer, and then what's left of them is thrown into mass graves.

I pointed to screen 9, "These tanks are moving to reclaim the Soviet Union, where many thousands more will die. That screen shows military convoys from at least two different countries converging on Nigeria, a country of a 100 million people, in an all-out grab for resources."

I saw Helen struggling to comprehend and switched to a bonfire still smoldering in Africa. I zoomed in on the blackened grotesque forms lying at the base of the fire. It took a little imagination, but the mutilated bodies of men, women and children were unmistakable. I panned around the litany of body parts, the bloodied machetes lying on the street and around the empty villages where thousands once lived.

Helen moved closer to the console and starred at the breakdown of humanity in front of her.

"Is this for real?" her face contorted.

"Yes."

"So why doesn't anyone stop it?"

"I don't know, perhaps it's the beginning of some new world order, globally sanctioned genocide, scorch the earth and start again, who knows. But what I do know is that I might be making a difference."

"Making a difference. *You? From here?*"

"These lasers," I pointed to the black cylinders in the centre of the dome. "They're sending radiation in the form of high frequency microwave energy to orbiting satellites, which in turn redirect it to other satellites and then to ground targets around the world. These ground targets are," I wondered how to say it without sounding silly, "well, they're the bad people."

"The *bad people?*" she laughed nervously, "Are you for real? And how do you know they are *bad?*"

"Well, apart from those who I actually see slaughtering people, I've discovered how to scan and read DNA remotely. In fact, I can decode more than twice the gene sequence than a standard DNA. And I've identified a rogue gene that predisposes people to violence. The slaughters of the innocent and these rogues are the targets, the bad people, whom I neutralize."

"*Neutralize?* Michael, what the fuck are you talking about? Have you lost your mind?"

"I send to these targets, these bad people, a series of radiation sequences which can cause a variety of effects. I can inhibit the immune system, induce cancers or deplete oxygen in vital organs. And if I'm feeling less malevolent, I just detune their brains and make then otherwise inert, much like a lobotomy. But most will die—either slowly or quickly."

"You're *killing* people!"

She took a step backwards, rebalancing on her good leg, as if to distance herself from the devil.

"Helen, I know it's a lot to take in—"

"You're *insane*. You're playing *God.*"

"Not really, but *I am* making a difference. See all the dead soldiers there, just minutes earlier they were slaughtering refugees."

I saw her study the numerous screens and then pause at one that displayed a crime scene, and Alison's body.

"Who is that!" she asked, her hand reaching behind to steady herself at the desk.

"That's Alison."

"You killed her too?"

"No of course not. I was tracking her because she was acting weird and I was concerned for Nicole. Look, I'll show you."

Helen started to sway uneasily.

"Why don't you sit down?" I pulled a chair up next to mine but she remained standing.

I replayed the last moments of Alison's life and Helen closed her eyes when Alison put the gun to her head. I stopped the replay.

"Oh my God," she said slowly.

I stood up to hold her, but she moved away from me, her expression one of disgust,

"Helen, look it's basically the same process you were subjected to in the MRI, but instead of repairing cells, I can also destroy them too. Each in its own way is for the good of mankind."

"No Michael, killing is killing and it's always *wrong*, no matter what" she was adamant. *"This* is wrong," she waved her hand at the screens and then pointed at me, *"You* are wrong."

nt to know what *wrong* really is." I raised my voice and moved

. "*Wrong* is when a three-year old girl is thrown from a moving train, for a thrill. Wrong is when people beat the elderly, because they can. *Wrong* is when women are raped and bashed. *Wrong* is when innocent people are rounded up and slaughtered like cattle for their body parts. *Wrong* is when tens of thousands of men, women and children are hacked to pieces and burned alive because they were born in the wrong place at the wrong time. *Wrong* is when *millions* of people are displaced and murdered because governments are greedy, because greed and jealously are what rule this world, and human nature will *never* rise above it."

Helen looked at the carnage on the screens, expressionless.

"Helen, who really knows why it's come to this. Differences breed fear and jealousy. Throw in greed, ego and a few rogue genes and there's your doomsday cocktail. There are over seven billion people in the world and I've calculated that's ten to twenty million or so evil creatures. Creatures who I'm going to find, each and every one, and send them straight back to hell." I let my words hang in the air and wondered if I was going a little far.

I lowered my voice, "And apart from you, no one else knows the real purpose of this place and that's the other reason this will work."

She simply gazed at me, probing deep into my soul. Was she searching for evidence of demonic possession? Would that make it easier to dismiss me?

She studied the main screen, where three sets of numbers incremented in the top right hand corner. I answered her unspoken question.

"The top number represents people scanned for DNA. The one beneath are those identified with rogue genes and the bottom one represents the accumulated neutralizations."

"Thirty thousand?"

"Yes."

"People?"

"Yes.

"Killed?"

"Well, neutralized." I corrected.

"*Killed.*"

"Yes, ultimately."

"From when?"

"Today."

"You're killing thirty thousand people a day?"

"Yes and I expect that rate will increase."

"Mass murder is your new career? That's what you want to do with your life?"

"Helen, it's not what I want, it's what I have to do. Anyway, there's no need to make it a big deal. The global population is growing at around sixty million a year, if we take out several million rogues each year, there'll still be plenty of people around. It's not like the shopping malls will be empty—"

"Michael, take some responsibility for what you're saying. Use the *I* word, don't hide behind some non-existent cowardly *we*. I don't see anyone else here," she waved her arm around the room.

"Maybe they are not here, but there are many who have had enough of being victims. It's as if you weren't in that plane with me!"

I could feel her revulsion toward all this and toward me growing, if that were possible.

"Helen, it's only a matter of time before someone with enough money, enough resources and enough *will* takes the initiative."

"Michael, you should grow a moustache and we can all salute you with an extended right arm."

"The aim is to get rid of oppressors and aggressors, killers of the weak, killers of the innocent, killers of the children. It's not obvious to you what it will take to save the world?"

"Save the world! And who makes that call? Who decides who lives and dies? You?"

"Then whose call should it be? The USA, the UN, some peacekeeping force? They all become corrupt sooner or later. You know, absolute power corrupts absolutely and all that. Look at what happened to Cooper."

"Brendan Cooper?"

"Yes, he needed to be dealt with..."

"*You killed him?*"

"No, but he had to be 'defused'. And what about the USA and other so called 'world leaders'? It's all strangely silent on those fronts. I guess they have their own agenda, one which I'm still trying to understand. But if we wait long enough maybe God himself may intervene? But which God? Mohammad? Buddha? Jesus Christ? Maybe they could all get together and form a panel. Better still perhaps the job should go to a consultant—a big accounting or legal firm, who could be independently audited every year, which in turn could be audited by another big accounting firm, and so on."

"I can't believe I'm standing her listening to the ranting of a lunatic."

"And you know uranium stocks are at an all-time high."

"*This* is insane. *You* are insane," she turned and walked toward the door, with only a slight limp.

"I could try to heal people from the effects of those radiation bombs," I said, more to myself.

"Michael, you're fooling yourself if think you're on the side of good. You are as evil as the people committing those atrocities," she pointed at the screens, "Maybe more so."

She closed the door behind her and silence returned to the dome.

I leaned back in my console chair, inside my cocoon, the centre of the world and surveyed every corner of the globe through my sixteen eyes. A note on the central command screen confirmed two more satellites, over North and South America, had come online.

On screen 5, several unread emails waited. One was from Cooper, time stamped several hours ago, before his meltdown. He let me know donations had started pouring in from around the world—from individuals, companies and government departments. Financial offerings for our privatized law and order project, as he called it. He referred to a communiqué from an unnamed party in Washington, which read simply, '*Congratulations on your efforts in fighting crime and terror,*' and attached were the GPS coordinates of every prison facility in North America, as well as access codes to all law enforcement databases.

I activated the North American satellite and filled screen 16 with the vision of the White House in Washington D.C. I scanned the skies over North America and found numerous jet trails high in the stratosphere. I followed them from their origin above the Arizona desert all the way to China and Africa. I guess I'd found the smoking gun, the 'other' player.

The observatory cameras registered movement in the basement and displayed the image on Screen 1. I watched Helen bundle Nicole into the car and drive out toward the road. The car shuddered as the windstorm broadsided them. She turned left, toward the city and away from the devils lair.

I dialed up an internet music station and closed my eyes. The classic rock ballad failed to hide the constant low drone emanating from the lasers. I put my feet on the desk and felt the pulsing of raw energy as it set off to distant places around the world, electrons the perfect warriors for this new age.

I listened to the words of the song that played from the many speakers in the dome, and which echoed around me in a circle of chant. Then the memories flooded back, as did the tears, but they were dry tears now, from a dry soul.

I remembered the young girl in the train carriage, Cooper's child, who searched me out as death tapped her on the shoulder. I saw clearly in my mind the words she mouthed to me, that day so long ago now. 'Save us', she had said. *Us.*

And the voice that echoed through this room, on this black storm-ridden night, on this desolate cliff and within this God-forsaken place belonged to Bob Dylan. And like a prophet of the ages, he cries out, to me...

Oh, who did you meet, my blue-eyed son?
Who did you meet, my darling young one?
I met a young child beside a dead pony,
I met a white man, who walked a black dog,
I met a young woman, whose body was burning,
I met a young girl, she gave me a rainbow,
I met one man, who was wounded in love,
I met another man, who was wounded with hatred,
And it's a hard, it's a hard, it's a hard, it's a hard,
It's a hard rain's a-gonna fall.

.